T0332307

Acclaim for
LIGHTRAIDER ACADEMY

"... full of action and adventure ... it captures the hearts, doubts, and questions of believers at all stages of their faiths ..."

— KIRKUS REVIEWS

"Simple prose and candid heroes enjoin biblical truth, highlighting Scripture-like verses and faith as means of vanquishing external enemies."

— LOREHAVEN

"James R. Hannibal's final installment in the Lightraider Academy series does not disappoint. *Lion Warrior* is packed to the brim with rich world-building, lively characters, and Hannibal's deft wordsmithing. I highly recommend this series for teens (and adults!) searching for a faith-affirming tale full of adventure, humor, and heart."

— LINDSAY A. FRANKLIN, award-winning author of *The Story Peddler*

LION
WARRIOR

LION WARRIOR

LIGHTRAIDER ACADEMY | BOOK THREE

JAMES R. HANNIBAL

For Cindy, John, James, David, Kerry, Josh, Brannon,
and all the Lightraiders teens.

I could not ask for a better raid party
as we set out on this incredible quest.

Orvyn's Vow

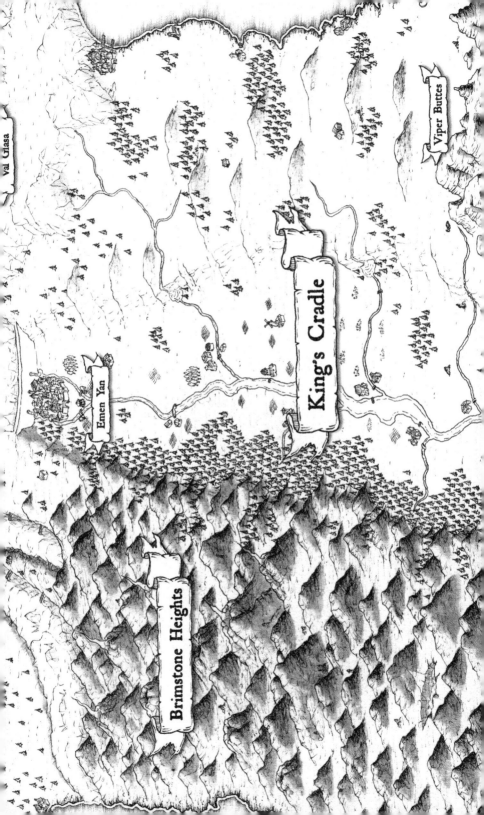

PART ONE

FLAMES

"We are afflicted in every way but not crushed; we are perplexed but not in despair; we are persecuted but not abandoned; we are struck down but not destroyed."

2 Corinthians 4:8-9

1

CONNOR ENARIAN
KELEDEV
CELESTIAL PEAKS

DUST KICKED UP BY A RIDER'S HASTE DREW
Connor's gaze southwest—the Airguard herald he'd been waiting
for. An airship's blast, echoing across the high scree slopes of
the Celestial Peaks, had called his squadron to the plateau under
Hope's Spire. Connor and his lightraiders and watchmen had
reached the plateau first.

The herald waved a frantic arm, shouting something about the
Western Vale and ore creatures. Not until his horse had carried
him nearer to the waiting squadron did his message take full form.

"Orcs! Marching for Mount Challenge. Ride, Sentinels!
Make haste!"

Haste is an enemy all its own—or so Swordmaster Quinton had
taught them.

Connor lifted a hand to calm the herald. "How many?"

"The spotters saw a great number marching as one unit.
Perhaps three platoons in total."

"Four or more times our number," Connor said, reaching to
his belt for the horn that had long ago replaced the shepherd's
whistle he once carried. "Not the best odds." He turned and blew
a hard note to send the call farther eastward, sped on its way by a
prayer. He nodded to his troops. "To the Western Vale!"

Teegan launched the falcon from her arm and circled their small force of cadets and watchmen. "You heard him. Form up!" She ensured all were ready before galloping to the column's head to join Connor. "I wish the Airguard spotters could sail closer to the peaks and give us more time."

"The winds are too powerful. We let evil cross the mountains. Now our fliers must suffer the same hardships that barrier imposed on our dragon enemies."

The column rode hard, light, and fast as befitted a sentinel squadron—the name Master Quinton had given the twelve small units he'd created to guard the upper range. Too small for Connor's taste. Their numbers were few and their recruits inexperienced.

"How many do you think?" Teegan asked, as if reading his thoughts.

"Sixty, if the herald got the spotter's message right. Perhaps less. More than our fourteen either way. If only we had Dag."

The big miner was worth three or more in a close fight. He'd taken to the Sphere of the Vanguard as if born and reared in their tower. But Dag had his own squadron.

Teegan lifted her chin. "I'm your Dag today. I'll take your share of the fighting if you're not up to it."

Her jest changed the grim press of his lips to a grin. "Don't be foolish. I'll take yours."

Connor gauged the countenances of their troops. Seven of the twelve had yet to see battle—six young men and a young woman, all new cadet stalwarts from the Eastern Hills. He returned his eyes to the trail and lowered his voice. "Or perhaps it's best that we both take theirs. I fear for every one of them. How many lives will we lose while we allow evil to march on these slopes?"

"While *we* allow it?" Teegan's eyes flared. "Don't the Scrolls tell us the Rescuer is sovereign?"

"They also say he lets us deal with the consequences of our actions."

Boulders narrowed the trail as they left the tree line for the last time, forcing Teegan back in her gallop. When she came alongside him again, disquiet creased her brow. "You believe someone in Keledev caused the breach."

"What I believe doesn't matter." He stood in his saddle to speed the gelding. "What matters is our homeland will never be safe again until we end this war once and for all."

The retort he expected never came. Teegan pointed skyward. "Aethia's found them. Over the next rise."

Connor signaled the column to slow. Up there, near the highest of the Passage Lakes, there were no pines to catch the horses' dust. A telltale plume might cost them the advantage. Aethia might also give them away. He nodded to Teegan. "Call your bird back. Orcs can smell a falcon."

"No need. She knows her business. She'll stay east to keep her scent clear."

The three watchmen archers riding with their squadron joined Connor and Teegan at the front. With small numbers, a sentinel squadron's attack hinged on the opening volley.

"Our falcon scout has them over the next rise," Connor told them. "The moment we crest the top, choose your targets and shoot at will. Two arrows cach, then follow us in with sword and hammer."

"If they are too much for us," one of them asked, "to where will we retreat?"

"There is no retreat. Beyond this rise is the last stretch of the road to Mount Challenge Lake. We hold them there, or we die in the attempt. Are you all ready?"

They answered with nods and grunts of bravado, though the pallor of the younger ones' faces spoke otherwise. Even so, shields glowed to life on their arms. Breastplates appeared on their chests and helms on their heads—gifts credited to them by the Rescuer.

"Good." Connor's own silver shield appeared at his forearm yet did not hinder him as he set a stone in his sling and drew the dragonslayer Revornosh from its scabbard. He raised the sword high, so the purple starlot in its hilt caught the sun, and spurred his horse. "Onward!"

2

THE SQUADRON CHARGED OVER THE RISE IN TWO
lines with the archers at the rear. These halted at the crest and
raised their bows while the others gained speed on the downward
slope. Teegan, whose gelding bore a lighter burden, spurred her
horse out in front. Connor loosed the stone from his sling to fly
before her.

An orc archer turned to face the incoming threat, bellowing
at its companions. It fell to Connor's stone, and the orc beside it
dropped its bow when a gray arrow sailed over Teegan and lodged
itself in the fiery joint at the creature's shoulder. Two heartbeats
later, Teegan rode that one down. The orc behind it died to her
trident, spilling molten innards from three holes in its chest plate.

Her courage opened a wedge, and Connor took advantage.
He let go of his reins and steered the gelding with his knees, as
Teegan had taught him long ago, and swung Revornosh at any
exposed orc flesh he could see.

"Connor! On your left!"

An archer's call turned Connor's head in time to see a black
pyranium scimitar stabbing at his flank. His shield flashed. The
blade snapped in two.

The orc howled in rage.

Connor answered with "For the Rescuer!" and tensed his shield arm to bash it in the face. Only by the force of the blow did he hold his mount. Connor swung the gelding around to bury Revornosh in the reeling orc's chest.

He might have thought this a success, except for the score—seven orcs down for him and Teegan with an archer's assist, but barely more than an orc each for the rest, leaving eight times as many still standing. And still advancing.

A watchmen archer had lost her mount. The horse lay dead beside her. Three orcs closed in. Connor traded his sling for his Aropha crook—a tool and weapon forged by the Elder Folk—and pointed with its spiked steel foot. "Stalwarts! To the right flank! Defend her!"

The new cadets rode in, wildly swinging hammer, axe, and sword. Five formed a line against the orcs while the other two helped the archer up onto one of their horses.

Fighting side by side on horseback took training these stalwarts had not yet gained, and it showed. The orc line pressed against them, forcing a slow retreat. If the rest of the squadron failed to close around them, they'd surely die.

"Teegan, fall back! Protect the young ones!"

Fall back. Hadn't he told them there'd be no retreat?

The geldings backed away with admirable control, giving their riders a chance to fend off blows and drop more orcs from the enemy's numbers—many more—but Connor counted at least thirty remaining. He stole a glance at the road behind his force where the glistening waters of Mount Challenge Lake waited, perhaps a hundred yards away. He had those hundred yards to change the tide or give himself and his squadron to the eternal rest of Elamhavar.

Rocks and steep terrain on either side of the road kept the orc flanks from curving around to hem the sentinels in. That blessing would not last all the way to the lake, and his sword and Teegan's trident could not bring the numbers into balance fast enough.

They needed help.

Connor raised his eyes to the swirling ice among the Impossible Peaks, catching the midday sun, and began a lightraider battle prayer. *"Yi rusa kazelatesh elevana. Men taya veni zoweresh?"* *I lift my eyes to the mountains. Whence comes my help?* The second portion of the prayer rolled down from the heights as if in answer. *Men ke'Premor, bi keshema po kezavol ke'Krafor.* *From the King, the Maker of the heavens and the earth.*

The tenor song of a sentinel's horn overcame the clamor of orc roars and clashing blades, followed by a falcon's cry. Aethia flew on the rising dust of a second sentinel squadron galloping to their aid with Dagram Kaivos storming forth at the head of its spear formation, twin axes held high. The horse that carried the miner stood many hands above the rest—one of the Gladion line, bred for battle in the days before the rising of the peaks and set to haul the Keledan plows in the days after.

Behind him flashed the pale red tunic of the very herald who'd brought Connor the news—an Airguard volunteer, neither spotter nor fighter, who had no business joining the battle. What was Dag thinking? No sooner had the thought come to Connor than a black arrow pierced the young man's neck. His horse veered, and from there his fate fell out of Connor's sight.

The orcs' rear guard, shrieking with rage, had turned toward the reinforcements, easing the pressure on Connor's forces. His squadron's retreat slowed, but it did not stop.

"Hold!" he shouted, spurring his gelding to halt its fade. "Hold this line!"

Too late. The terrain flattened as the rocks gave way to the long, sandy expanse before the lakeshore. The orcs had eaten up too much ground, and now their flanks spread wide to envelop their foes.

Connor pushed his troops left and right to counter. "Don't let them pass! Don't—" His cry caught in his throat. Four black creatures rose from the orcs' northern flank, taking to the air—

birds with wingspans as long as a horse and thick, gangly necks. From the talons of the center bird hung a black leather satchel chained to an iron ball. The creature bobbled with the weight while the others hung close, protecting this strange cargo and its carrier.

Teegan saw them too. "What are those?"

"Buzzards of some kind. Worry more about what they carry." Connor pressed his current opponent back with his crook and waved Revornosh. "Archers, look north! Stop those birds!"

An easy command to give. Not so easy to follow. The watchmen archers were busy battling enemies of their own. Only one had hands to spare—the young woman who'd lost her mount, riding behind her comrade. She brought her bow to bear.

One, then another black buzzard fell from the sky. The others veered, and the archer's third and fourth shots missed wide.

While Connor watched, the air changed. A great shadow darkened the lakeshore.

A dragon? It can't be.

Looking up, he saw he should have had more faith.

Not a dragon. An airship. Some mad stormrider risked the terrible winds close to the high slopes to join the fight. At first, the three great silk envelopes of the airship held their course, straight toward the buzzards, but then they shuddered and turned, taking the wicker ship with them. The craft swung into unnatural flight—sideways and falling fast toward the white scree hill beside the lake.

The watchmen archer set her aim on the bird with the satchel, but its last escort swooped in and took the missile. It plummeted to the ground while the other pressed on and dove toward the lake.

"No!" Connor screamed.

As if hit by his voice, the buzzard jerked, then jerked again, knocked backward in the air by mighty blows. The creature slammed down in the sand and sent the sickening *crack* of a hollow spine breaking to Connor's ears, dying barely a yard short of the water with its burden still clutched in its talons.

North of the lake, the airship crashed between the scree hill and the mountain slope behind. The silk envelopes, visible above the hill, caught fire. What brave pilot had given his life this time? Still, the tide had turned. The two sentinel squadrons crushed the orc platoon, and while Teegan thanked Dag, Connor rushed to the buzzard near the lakeshore. He found a pair of Airguard harpoons lodged in the creature's eye and throat. Before he could inspect the bird's satchel, crunching sounded from beyond the scree hill. Connor leveled his sword, ready for a new fight.

A young blond man about his own age stumbled out onto the shore, face scratched up and tunic torn and blackened at the chest and sleeves.

Connor's mouth fell open. "Aaron?"

Aaron Ilmari, Sireth Yar's former watchmen companion, staggered left and right, still finding his bearings, then saw the dead bird at Connor's feet. He hefted a big Airguard harpoon bow to his shoulder, with a piece of charred wicker railing still caught in its mounting clamps, and offered a woozy salute. "Looks like I got him. You're welcome."

3

"BALANCE! HOLD YOUR BALANCE!"

Kara glanced down between the blue talanium planks of the chain bridge where she trained her latest pack of novices, wondering how Sireth Yar, the outpost watchmaster, might react if her efforts caused one or two of them to fall. She'd hate for him to return from his patrol to such news.

That, of course, assumed he might ever return. Sireth and his son Tiran—Kara's fellow lightraider cadet—had been gone for days.

Nearly a league beneath Kara's feet, the smooth fjord waters and the low clouds passing over them gave her the feeling of looking up into a deep blue sky, made more striking by the two airships idly floating on sealed wicker hulls.

Her own balance began to drift.

Kara snapped her eyes up to meet the gaze of the lead novice. More and more Airguard pilots and spotters had been added to her training cohorts of late, sent to Orvyn's Vow by Councilor Zayn Boreas for combat training. In this group, the lead novice was an Airguard pilot's mate, fully trained as a pilot. With brown eyes half-hidden by a mop of black hair, he stared back, shoulders steady and unperturbed by the shifting chain bridge. "How long must we do this, Miss Orso?"

"Until you get it right, Mister Ray."

Samar Ray—certainly the most gifted combat novice she'd trained. Too gifted. His natural skill made him overconfident.

The young man held his sword out over the chain rail and flipped it so the blade twisted in the air. The bridge wobbled, but his head and torso did not move in the slightest. He shrugged.

Kara frowned. "You and your party are one." She nodded past Samar to the other eight novices, lined up two by two behind him and wearing a mix of terrified and frustrated expressions. Most were losing the battle to hold a simple guard position on the unsteady bridge. The air didn't help, so much thinner up here than what the flatlanders and hill-country herdsmen were used to. One looked as if he might soon expel his breakfast into the wind. "None of you have it right until all of you have it right. Understood?"

Samar pursed his lips but held his tongue.

"Eyes on me!" Kara tried to regain control before she lost one over the side. "Focus. Breathe. In . . ." She inhaled deeply, tracing a small circle with her sword tip. "And out . . . In . . . Out."

The wobbling ceased.

"Good." She paused to let them enjoy the calm. "Hold . . ."

Samar lifted his chin toward the main lodge of Orvyn's Vow, built on the outpost's highest cliff, on one of the many thick fingers stretching out into the Sea of Vows. A large, blue-gray bear watched their training from a timber extension of the courtyard. "Perhaps your talking bear might join us. Or is she afraid of heights?"

"Ioanu is not *my* bear. Nor is she afraid. The bears of her clan fear nothing."

"Then why isn't she out here?"

"She needs no training."

"Nor do I."

"I beg to differ." Kara lifted her sword a little higher and addressed the group. "Keep holding . . . breathe . . . and now . . . raise one leg."

"You can't be serious." Samar looked back at his companions, all grasping for the chains as each raised a foot to the front, back, or side. "They should be sparring, learning to fight. Not this. They look absurd."

"They look like one unit. Your unit. Join them, Mister Ray. Now."

"You don't want me to do that."

Kara darkened her eyes. "Oh, I most certainly do."

"Fine."

Samar complied in the worst way Kara could have imagined. He leapt to the chain rail and balanced there despite the shaking caused by his comrades, then lifted a boot and planted the sole on the inner bend of his knee. Holding Kara's shocked gaze, he stretched out his sword and free arm. "Happy?"

"Stop that, Samar," Kara said, forgetting protocol and using his given name. She carefully lowered her foot and waved at the others to do the same. "Stop that this instant!"

"Why? Am I doing it wrong, great lightraider mistress? My apologies. I shall adjust." Samar leapt to pivot in the air. He landed on the other foot, facing away from her. "Better?"

"You know what I meant. Come down before you cast yourself into the fjord."

He obeyed with sudden humility. "Right. Of course. As you say."

Samar's meekness surprised her, until Kara followed his gaze to the next ridge over, on the far side of the bridge. Smoke and flames rose from the trees. Samar glanced back with an expectant look.

Kara shook her head. "Don't even think about it. You're not ready. Lead the rest back to the main lodge and alert the watchmaster."

"What about you?"

"I've a job to do."

She raised an arm, but Ioanu was already on the move, lumbering down a switchback to a timber-and-steel platform nestled in the bridge supports. The bear leapt onto a wooden cart, sending it sailing down a set of four talanium cables running under the bridge—a cargo system joining the fjord's cliffs.

Kara ran, but the bear and the accelerating cart would soon outpace her stride. She'd hate for Ioanu to beat her to the fight. Best to join her. Kara would have to judge this right in two planes. The increasing speed of the cart might cause her to miss on the north-south plane, and the wind could cost her a safe landing in the east-west plane. Without a safe landing, she'd have only the fjord a good twenty furlongs below to catch her.

She closed her eyes and prayed. *"Podovu motah se natholiond. Shalorovu se sumiond."*

He will not allow your foot to slip. Your protector will not slumber.

Eyes open once more, she took a last breath and swung over the rail on the upwind side.

The wind carried her under the bridge as expected, but the drop took longer than she'd planned. With Ioanu's weight, the cables dipped much lower than usual. The cart looked sure to fly by, until the balls of Kara's feet touched down inches from the rear edge. She reached to keep from falling off the back. "Ioanu!"

A hand, not a paw, caught Kara's. Samar pulled her in next to the bear and gave her one of his prideful smirks. "What was that about not being ready?"

"How did you get here?"

"Same way you did, but with far more grace."

The cart still had plenty of speed to finish its run, thanks to the lower height where it met the far cliff. Kara pushed Samar out of the way and pulled a hand brake. Sparks flew. The cart jolted to a stop.

The three raced up a switchback and along a smoky trail until they came to a clearing. Kara and Samar raised their arms to deflect the blazing heat from a burning way station.

The first Keledan to venture to these high, sheer fingers stretching east from the Celestial Peaks had built the Orvyn's Vow outpost in pieces—many structures separated by the fjords and joined by bridges, cart runs, and boat launches. The four highest and longest fingers of land held watchtowers with commanding views of the eastern boundary of the Celestial Peaks and the wall of Storm Mists out in the Sea of Vows. Shorter, lower fingers like this one held way stations for storage and rest. They were rarely manned.

The station across the next fjord burned as well.

"This is no accident," Samar said.

Kara, with sword poised, snapped open a whirlknife in her shield hand, spreading its two blades into the flying position, and gave him a sharp look that said, *Yes, we know.*

Ioanu lowered her nose to the trail. Dark blue armor glowed to life all around her. "Goblins. Still near."

As if called by her announcement, two creatures materialized out of the smoke and ran at Samar. Kara pushed him out of the way.

He scowled. "What are you doing?"

"Saving your life."

Goblins in small numbers posed little threat to a lightraider cadet scout. In a dual sweep of sword and whirlknife she dispatched them both.

Two more attacked from the other flank, but Ioanu gladly ended them with her claws. The forest cliffs went quiet again, with no sound but the wind and the crackle of the burning way stations.

Samar crossed his arms. "You could have let me fight. Is that not what we're training for?"

"I'll say it again. You aren't ready, and I've no time to carry a wounded fop right now."

Ioanu lifted her snout toward the fire. "The flames are deep in their meal. We may yet protect the trees around the clearings, but the stations are lost."

"Then rebuild them," Samar said with a shrug.

Kara snorted. "I doubt Sireth will waste the ticks or the men, not with the enemy spreading in Keledev." She walked past Samar to Ioanu. "But that is his concern, not ours. I received a raven this morning. I must ride to Ras Telesar for a council. I'll leave the novices in your care."

Samar leaned to place his face in her view once again. "No need to ride, Miss Orso." He lifted the collar of his tunic, showing her the symbol embroidered there. "You have a pilot at your disposal."

"Pilot's *mate*, if I understand your order's new ranks correctly."

He flattened his smile. "You want to fly or not?"

4

CONNOR
KELEDEV
RAS TELESAR

CONNOR WATCHED THE AIRSHIPS FROM THE EIGHTH-level ramparts. The green glade outside the academy gates had turned brown from the many takeoffs and landings, one of the few places on the slopes with winds calm enough for the Airguard pilots to safely touch down. Great silk triple and quadruple envelopes in deep blue, green, and scarlet cast shadows over the ruined grass. At the glade's edge sat the wreckage of Aaron Ilmari's ship, which Connor's squadron had hauled down from Mount Challenge Lake.

The ship with scarlet silks touched down, and Kara climbed out, followed by her pilot—dark haired and olive skinned. Strong jaw. An unexpected tinge of angst churned in Connor's chest at the sight of him. He had the urge to call out to Kara, despite the great distance, but a voice at his shoulder stopped him.

"You'll see her soon enough, Mister Enarian." Master Belen laid an aged black hand on Connor's forearm. "She'll be waiting for you in the Hall of Manna."

Connor's eyes did not leave the pair. The pilot said something to make Kara laugh and smile, a feat Connor had yet to master. "Will she?"

"Have faith, my boy, as she has faith in you. For now, follow me. We must exchange counsel."

The guardian—the head of the Tinkers' Sphere—brought Connor to his tower workshop. Aaron's wreckage had not been the only thing Connor's sentinels hauled back to Ras Telesar. They'd also carried the bird creature that flew toward Mount Challenge Lake and its satchel.

When Belen opened his workshop door, Connor expected a horrendous stink from the carcass, but he smelled naught besides salts and vapors, and he saw no bird. The scarred, blocky top of Belen's worktable held only a bundle and a journal, open to empty pages.

Belen sat on a stool behind the table and gestured with a charcoal pencil. "Describe your encounter. Tell me everything you recall about these buzzards."

"I dragged one home with us so that you might study it yourself. Where has it gone?"

"Burned, as we burn all dark creature husks after battles on this side of the barrier."

"But sir, if—"

Belen held up a hand. "You believe we may study a dragon's evil corruption to learn how to fight it? Discover its weaknesses?"

Connor nodded.

The guardian shrugged. "I'd say your friend Aaron discovered the only weakness we'll need when he shot the creatures out of the sky." He peered over a set of spectacles he'd taken to wearing during the last year—a much lighter variation of the invention he'd made for Lee, nothing but lenses set in a thin metal frame. "How many ticks should we devote to carving into the dragon's corruptions, bloodying our hands with their innards and spilling their infections and poisons onto the furnishings?"

"Very little, when you put it in those terms."

"Exactly. We must recognize evil when it approaches. I make my notes as Master Rayn Hayabuck made his before me, and we use this knowledge to prepare our cadets. But we do not make a meal of darkness. We do not immerse ourselves in it." He raised his pencil again. "Now, tell me what you saw of the creature in flight."

The description took a full quarter tick, as Connor recalled the ungainly bird's flight—the long, lurching neck and the spread of its oily wings. "To my eye, it seemed something between a buzzard and a vulture, but larger than both. More a carrion-feeder than a bird of prey."

Belen grunted and nodded, taking his time with his notes. Once finished, he set the journal on a shelf behind him and laid a hand on the bundle. "Now to this. You say the birds tried to drop it into Mount Challenge Lake."

"So I assumed from the path of their flight." Connor frowned at the satchel. "But, if caution demanded we destroy the dark creature, Master Belen, why risk bringing its cargo inside?"

"Ah. An excellent question, and one I asked before taking such a risk. With helpers and great care, I opened the bundle on the rocks east of the glade and found its contents to be more a matter of natural philosophy than dragon sorcery. Think of it as a sword rather than its wielder, neither good nor evil until put to its purpose. Do you see?"

Connor gave him a hesitant nod.

"You'll understand better once I show you." Belen unwrapped the bundle to reveal a mass of silver powder.

"Shairosite. Banishing powder."

"Just so. Untainted."

"Banishing powder carries enough danger on its own. We used it to close Valshadox's portal on the northern slopes, and the reaction destroyed his entire stronghold. With Zel Boreas, we used it to excite storm clouds and transit the barrier. In both efforts, we used far less than I see here. What might so much shairosite have done to one of the Passage Lakes?"

"I don't know, and I've no intention of making an experiment. The dragons may have intended to disrupt or destroy the lake, hindering our travel into Tanelethar. Or they may have intended another purpose so disturbing I won't mention it until I know more. Either way, we must guard against further attacks at the Passage Lakes. Those vales will need their own squadron."

Connor chuckled. "Manned by whom? We've no one to spare."

"A hard truth." Belen wrapped the bundle up and slid it aside. "On that topic, there was more in the satchel—something I hope may aid our defenses."

The tinker set a covered glass dish on the wooden table between them. Inside were several diamond-shaped stones of coppery, iridescent metal, covered in olive oil. Briefly removing the cover, he picked one up with tongs and set it on the wood. "Do you know what this is?"

"Not the slightest notion."

"Brimstone metal, near as soft as clay, mined only from the obsidian under the burning mountains in the Brimstone Heights of Tanelethar. The wealthiest blacksmiths buy it to enhance their fires, for it burns white-hot. But it seems this metal has another property of which I was not aware. Observe."

The tinker cut a sliver and dropped it into a stone dish of water. The metal sparked and sizzled, then glowed white-hot and exploded.

Connor jerked back, shielding his face. "It works like diver's folly."

"Except the opposite. Diver's folly ignites as soon as it leaves salt water. It seems brimstone metal ignites on contact with any water." He tamped the piece with a wool cloth, taking several attempts to put it out. "Very hard to extinguish. And there's more."

Belen cut a few more slivers and laid them on the table, spaced a finger apart. Then he dipped his tongs in the water and allowed a single drop to fall on the nearest sliver. The first sliver exploded as before, but then each sliver, untouched by the water, exploded in rapid sequence.

"The metal is sympathetic to its own kind," Connor said, remembering a term for chain reactions from Belen's natural philosophy class.

This seemed to please the guardian. "Yes, yes," he said, again fighting to put the fire out. "Very good. You were always a top-notch student, my boy. Top notch."

"So what was its purpose?"

"Hmm?" Belen appeared to have lost track of the conversation, as was often his habit. Lee said this was because of his cleverness. Tiran usually countered that this was because of his age. Connor pressed him back to the topic at hand. "In the bundle, Master Belen. What was the brimstone metal's purpose?"

"Ah. Yes. To act as an incendiary, I think—a fire to burn with the force of a blast under water. I'd say the dragons intended for water to seep into the shairosite, causing the brimstone metal to explode as you saw here, thus spreading the powder through the lake."

"Destroying one of the Rescuer's portals."

"Perhaps, and that is the least sinister of the possibilities. Let us hope we never feel their full intent, yes?" Belen put the brimstone away, continuing as he worked. "Now. All of that is a matter of speculation over application. In truth, I brought you up here for a different reason—one of much greater import." He reached into an inner pocket of his cloak. "You see—"

The deep bell of the Hall of Manna rang below, and Belen drew his hand out, empty. "Our intrigues must wait, my boy. The headmaster calls. Go on ahead. I'll follow in a moment."

5

HEATED WORDS DRIFTED UP TO GREET CONNOR AS
he descended the central staircase to the sixth-level ramparts. He
slowed and peered around the corner from the steps.

Councilor Stradok, the Assembly's liaison to the academy, had
barred Aaron Ilmari's path, waggling a finger. "Do you understand
the cost of each of those airships? The Assembly's investment of
time and treasure?"

Connor could not see the upturned corner of Aaron's mouth—
his trace of irony and wit—but the tenor of the Airguard lieutenant's
answer left little doubt. "I was not aware, Councilor Stradok, that
the Assembly concerned itself with treasure."

"Then you are a foolish child. Keledev is small, its resources
finite. That ship you crashed represents a prince's portion."
Stradok's balding head grew as crimson as his assemblyman's
robes. "And another thing—"

"Councilor!" Connor jogged down the ramparts, waving.
"I'm so glad to catch you and Lieutenant Ilmari here, outside the
hall. I suppose I'm not as late as I thought." He draped an arm
over Aaron's shoulders, feigning a lack of breath, and guided him
around Stradok to head for the oversize doors to Salar Peroth—
the Hall of Manna. "Thank you both for waiting. I do so hate to

enter an important gathering alone. Always feels like every eye turns upon me."

Stradok followed a few paces behind, grumbling, "An illusion of your pride, Cadet. A trait too many of you young people share."

Connor felt Aaron tense as if to reply and pinched his friend's upper arm to stop him, then whispered in his ear, "A touch of prudence might serve us both about now. Keep silent if you wish to retain your rank. And keep walking."

All eyes did indeed turn upon them as the three entered the great, wedge-shaped hall. Master Jairun sat on a stool on the raised platform opposite the doors, his long staff resting against his shoulder. The rest had gathered at the tall stone table closest to him—one of many ancient tables built for the Aropha, or Elder Folk, huge compared to the Keledan and formed with incomprehensible skill as if grown like hedges from the floor.

Even Swordmaster Quinton, largest of the guardians, looked small when seated on the benches. He thrust a grizzled chin toward the newcomers. "Glad the three o' ya could fin'ly grace us with yer presence."

Connor made no reply. He didn't need to.

Stradok seemed to think he did. "I answer to the Assembly, Master Quinton." The councilor breezed past him to take an empty place near the head of the closest table to Master Jairun. "I do not run at the peal of a lightraider bell. I arrive at my own pleasure."

A quiet laugh escaped Master Jairun's nose. "Then we're grateful it pleases you to join us, for the Assembly must have a say in these proceedings."

Dag sat apart at a nearby table, chin resting in his hands.

Connor walked carefully up behind him. He knew the hurt that ailed his friend but knew not which words to offer in comfort. He merely placed a hand upon Dag's broad back. "They're starting. You should join us."

"And offer what? Thoughts that get men killed?"

The herald who'd warned them of the orcs' coming to Mount Challenge—the one who'd joined Dag's charge—had perished from his wounds.

"We had only one loss in a battle where the orcs outnumbered both our squadrons together. Some might call it a triumph."

"Not I. He died before he reached their line and served only as an obstacle to my horsemen. Had I not bowed to his request to join the fight, we might have found victory all the sooner. He died for nothing—in a place well removed from his calling."

"His calling was to defend his homeland," Connor countered.

"With his voice and horn, not his sword."

Time was needed for Dag's heart to heal, time they did not have.

Pedrig, the Havarra wolf who'd walked with Connor's patehpa Faelin Enarian, rested on the platform near Master Jairun with his paws crossed—his usual place and posture at such meetings. His golden gaze fell on the two young men, and a low growl escaped his throat, an order as clear as if Master Jairun himself had spoken it. *Take your seats.*

Connor wasted no more words compounding his friend's grief. "Come," he said, lifting Dag's heavy arm. "Whatever your mood, your wisdom and knowledge are a boon to me and to the guardians."

The two took their places on either side of Kara, across from Swordmaster Quinton of the Vanguard and Dame Silvana, the head of the Rangers' Sphere. Connor squeezed Kara's hand as he sat down. "It's good to see you."

"You as well, though I wish I were here with better news."

"You and me, both."

Stradok shot them a glare for this interruption of whatever argument he'd already started, then returned his gaze to Master Jairun to propel it onward. "What do you mean by a change of strategy, Headmaster?"

"Just that. A new course, not merely for the Lightraider Order or for the watchmen, but for Keledev as a whole. The war has entered a new phase. The dragon strategy is shifting. We can all feel it. And in doing so, they're gaining ground. We must shift our own strategy to counter."

"Have encounters and skirmishes not been common for almost a year now?" Stradok asked. "I, for one, feel no shift."

Dag grunted and gazed down at his big hands. "Then you should leave the safety of this fortress once in a while."

There were a few pointed coughs at the table. Connor reached around Kara to flick Dag's side and whispered through clenched teeth. "That is not the wisdom I spoke of."

Stradok directed his ire Dag's way. "We all have our callings, a topic I'm told you learned much about in your recent skirmish. Since, thankfully, you did not pull me into the battle as you did the poor herald, perhaps you might describe it to me."

Teegan, seated one place down from Dag, stood before the miner could answer and bury himself for good. "I will describe it," she said, giving Stradok a dark gaze, "if Master Jairun so pleases."

Gaining a nod from the headmaster, she went on. "A platoon of orcs charged one of the sacred Passage Lakes. That alone is a dark change in their former course. It showed purpose beyond harassment and killing—a purpose we have not fully discerned." She gave an account of their battle, including the bird creatures. "It cost us an airship and a life to stop them."

"I'm well aware of the cost," Stradok countered, addressing the headmaster instead of Teegan, as if she had merely projected Master Jairun's words like a carnival puppet. "And I'll grant that a new form of dark creature holds a modicum of interest even for those outside your small order. But orcs have made many charges on these mountains in the past two seasons. How can you say this charge bore a greater purpose?"

"I'll answer that." Connor gave Teegan a nod and waited for her to sit before speaking. He'd rather Master Belen take this part, but the tinker had not appeared, having likely become waylaid by his own experiments, as usual. "These bird creatures—"

"Gall buzzards," Aaron said, nudging him. "That's what I've been calling them, after the sound they make."

Connor shot him a sidelong glance to stop him from mimicking the birds' call. "Yes. Thank you, Lieutenant. These . . . gall buzzards were more than a new type of dark creature in this battle. They carried a satchel of shairosite."

He waited for the gasps and mumbles from this revelation to cease before going on. The link between the silver powder and Taneletharian portals had become well established in the last two years, along with the fact that one such portal had sent dark creatures into Keledev.

"How much shairosite?" Master Jairun asked.

"More than I've ever seen in one place outside the Crystal Meadow in Tanelethar, more than we used to collapse the fortress of the dragon lord Vorax, along with a mechanism designed to spread the powder through the lake. Master Belen and I think the dragons may hope to destroy the Passage Lakes. They may be trying to cut off our entry into Tanelethar."

This sent new and heavier murmurs up and down the table.

Master Jairun raised his hands for order, aided by a low bark from Pedrig. "These tidings are but one symptom of the renewed strength in the enemy's onslaught. You need only look around this table for another. Don't you see the empty places? They represent gaps in our defense—cracks in a dam holding back the flood."

Connor had yet to notice the small number. How had he missed it? Sireth Yar, Teegan's tehpa, had become the head of the watchmen company at Orvyn's Vow, yet he was not there for such an important council. Nor was his sehna, Tiran, or Zel Boreas, the captain representative of the Airguard, or Connor's closest friend, Lee Trang.

He looked to Teegan. "Where are your tehpa and brehna? Where are Lee and Zel?"

She answered with a gaze that seemed on the edge of tears. "No one knows."

6

LEE TRANG
TANELETHAR
MINER'S FOLLY

LEE TIED HIS ROPE TAUT TO A HOOK IN THE CAVE WALL
and flipped the varied lenses of his spectacles up and down,
examining the finished curtain. "You think she'll hold?"

"Now that we've installed it right side up?" Zel asked, tying off
her rope on the other side of the cave. "Yes."

The curtain had been the hardest piece of this new outpost to
bring through the hollow tree in Darkling Shade—a heavy blend of
silk and canvas wrought by the Sky Harbor silk spinners, meant to
mimic the surrounding rock. When Lee and Zel had returned in
their ship—weeks after he and Connor had brought the canvas here
on foot and set it in place—they'd realized the two had installed it
with the rock colors facing down instead of up.

"You jest," Lee said, "but the upside-down curtain and the cave
remained untouched in our absence, a testament to our chosen
place for this sanctuary."

Zel took a seat on an overturned mine cart and shook out her
arms after the hard work of hauling up the canvas. "If you'd told me
a year ago the Airguard and the Lightraider Order would build an
airship post in the Dragon Lands, I'd have called you mad."

Lee smiled. "I believe I told you exactly that a year ago. And you
did call me mad."

"Oh right." She winked, as if to let him know he'd walked into a trap.

"I never said you were wrong. This whole endeavor is indeed mad, and I'm content to say so. As you might recall, none of this was my idea."

Connor had been the first to suggest a sanctuary capable of concealing and launching a stormrider airship, inspired by the underground Aropha sanctuary they'd discovered in the Fading Mountains. Tiran and Dag—even Kara—had laughed, but Lee took his friend seriously. In quiet but earnest discussions through many meals in the Hall of Manna, the two worked out the practical aspects. They'd started with identifying the right location in the Dragon Lands.

The hollowed-out hills of Miner's Folly, east of the Upland Wilds, seemed the perfect place. Their sister hills, Miner's Glory, to the west of the Wilds, still yielded copper, gold, and other riches after ages of mining, but the tunnels of Miner's Folly had run dry in their first season. That hadn't stopped hopeful Aladoth from digging for more than a century afterward. Thus, the hills were pocked and scarred with pits and furrows, some hiding great caverns of bare rock and pure emptiness.

Connor and Lee had devised a plan to claim one such cavern and give it new purpose.

To their utter shock, Master Jairun consented and pled their case with Councilor Zayn Boreas, the leader of the Airguard. From there, they'd only needed to find the right chamber. The councilor had insisted his daughter Zel accompany the lightraiders on the quest to find one. She'd been part of most quests to build the post ever since.

Zel let out a sigh, leaning against the wall. "We have all we need here. A spring runs through the rear of the cave where our supplies and map table are well sheltered. When we drop the curtain to launch, it falls vertically to hide the antechamber, transforming what appears from above as an empty, shallow hole into nothing more than an empty, deep hole. I have only one concern."

"And that is?"

"Goats. I've seen many in these hills. What if one falls in and spoils the effect?"

"Goats are surefooted. Rest at ease." Lee joined her, sitting down to rest next to the mine cart, and surveyed their work. Roughhewn walls. Timber supports. A table and a few crates and lanterns.

This place was no great Aropha sanctuary like the one in the Fading Mountains, but it would serve—the work of Keledan hands built deep in the enemy's territory and a forward post for the gift of flight the Rescuer had given them. "So. What will we call it? The Mine?"

She wrinkled her nose. "Don't be absurd. My father chose the name the night your headmaster proposed this venture. And since we're supplying the ships and pilots, he says naming this place is his right."

Lee shrugged. "I won't argue."

"Like anyone can argue with Zayn Boreas."

"You can." Lee had seen it. He'd watched Zel, the councilor's one and only daughter, change his mind or bring the gifted orator to utter silence on several occasions. "What's the name?"

"He wants to call this sanctuary after the other posts we've built in Keledev—the cloudlofts. This one will be Cloudloft Stratus."

The red light of dusk seeping in at the edges of the curtain above caught Lee's eye. "Time is fleeting," he said. "If we wish to complete the second part of our mission tonight, we need to get moving."

She nodded, and both stood. Lee saw his own soreness in the slowness of her rising. All time to rest had been stolen at the first moment of their entry into Tanelethar in the new airship. Their stormride—the fourth ever attempted and only the second used to cross the barrier—had brought them to the wrong place, far to the south to the Highland Forest in Berothor Province. At least, Lee saw it as the wrong place. Zel had a different notion. Either way, it had set them back several days in coming here.

Preparations for the next flight took half a tick, so that by the time they dropped the curtain to expose the sky, night had come.

The new airship's single large lamp burned with a dim fire,

darkened by minerals the Apothecarists' Guild had added to their fuel concoction. Once Lee had doused the lights and secured the ropes behind the curtain, he hopped the gray-painted rail. Zel added a second vial of fuel, and the ship rose.

Gray silk snapped, a sign of a stiff breeze dipping into the mine to catch the envelope—one envelope instead of the usual three. Lee heard the sound, but looking up, he hardly saw any movement. "The new silk catches no light."

"Yes. The spinners did well." With skilled hands at the pulleys and the rudder, Zel kept the ship centered. "They made the envelopes of the first airships with the whimsy of the winds in mind, in rich colors, never intending for their work to see this side of the barrier. This ship has a different purpose. The dye makes us one with the clouds. *The Merlin* is a true leap forward in our fight."

The Merlin. Smallest and darkest of the falcons. An apt name. The Airguard had built many new ships—some larger, with stronger silks and pitch in their hulls for water landings, and some with devices that spat fire to make them run against the wind. *The Merlin* and sister ships of the same size looked tiny in comparison. But a small falcon could fly where great owls and eagles could not.

"We're clear," Zel said.

Just in time. The wind picked up and carried them near broadside over the hilltop. Below, the hidden cloudloft showed no sign they'd ever been there—no hint of the curtain, though it rested in plain sight. "Excellent. Our plan came together nicely."

"Right. Sure. But also"—Zel gestured down at the sage and rocks surrounding the hole—"no goats."

He gave her a flat look, then turned his gaze to the sky ahead. "Are you sure we'll blend with the clouds?"

"So the spinners and the shipwrights say."

"Let's hope they're right. The last airship to enter Tanelethar was spotted, and you, Kara, and Connor found yourselves on the hot, pointy end of a dragon, and tonight, we're flying even closer to that very dragon's stronghold."

7

THE FLIGHT FROM CLOUDLOFT STRATUS IN MINER'S Folly to Sil Shadath took less than two ticks.

Zel lowered *The Merlin* out of the high, southerly winds into the relative calm much closer to the expanse of black pines known to the locals as the Forest of Horrors.

To the Aladoth in the surrounding villages, those horrors were wanderers, shades, and ghosts—the false dead cobbled together from mist and soil, animated by the dragons. To Lee the horror of this forest ran much deeper. This place and its dragon lord had shown him his lost brother still lived and then had stolen him away again.

"You won't see Shan on this mission," Zel said, easing Lee back from the rail. "He's not down there."

"You don't know that. This is where I saw him last, fooled by the dragon lord of this forest into taking the mantle of a sorcerer."

"He betrayed you. He betrayed all of us."

"He was weak, as we are all weak without the Rescuer." Lee shook his shoulder free of her grasp and returned to the rail. "But if I can find him, I can still reach him."

"Is that why you came—the reason you've been badgering me since our stormride brought us to the Highland Forest, leagues from here? Is that the reason you pressed my father to risk a flight straight into the Storm Mists?"

Lee didn't answer and kept scanning the trees.

He, Connor, and Zel had first discovered stormriding under the guidance of the Rescuer, pushed by his hand into the Storm Mists, which carried them like a hollow tree portal into the Dragon Lands. They'd also learned that casting shairosite powder into the lamps allowed a ship to turn a heavy-laden cloud into a similar portal, and such storms sent the ship north to the Fading Mountains and then home again to Keledev.

This time, it was not the same.

Despite Lee's urging, Zayn Boreas had waited for a sign before sending a ship willy-nilly, as he called it, into the Storm Mists for another attempt. No sign came for many months, and in the waiting, Lee made himself a liaison of the Lightraider Order to the Airguard so that he might be near when the time was right. Then, finally, the sign emerged—an incredible sign even an assemblyman like Boreas could not ignore.

Excited to seek his brother Shan from the air, Lee had joined Zel in this twofold quest. They were to test *The Merlin*'s ability to launch from the new outpost. Once finished, they were to scout Sil Shadath and determine the disposition of the Aladoth army Valshadox had been building.

The stormride—the first purposeful journey of an Airguard ship from Keledev to Tanelethar—brought them through swirling clouds and streaks of purple light into the Highland Forest, hundreds of leagues south of Miner's Folly. But a second stormride attempt took them nowhere and nearly ripped the ship in half. They'd spent a day making repairs and six more working their way north to the outpost.

According to Zel, they should have stayed in Highland Forest and searched out the reason the Rescuer brought them there. Lee had argued instead for a rush north. He'd waited long enough.

"I pressed your father because I understand the importance

of this mission," Lee said. "We need to know how big these camps have grown—how close the Aladoth army is to marching." He lifted his eyes from the trees to give her a sharp look. "And yes, I do hope the Rescuer will lead us to my brother."

It seemed a hollow hope. Lee saw nothing among the pines except the mist and the ghostly green-and-yellow flashes common to this strange place. His spectacles, as much as they enhanced his vision, were not sufficient to break out one man in Tanelethar's largest forest.

Lee nodded at a contraption lying between the ship's two wicker benches. "It's time. Help me get Baldomar's device properly mounted."

The two heaved a mass of blue talanium and polished glass up to the rail and cinched down its clamps. Master Baldomar had conceived of it, building from Master Belen's spyglass design. Short but near as thick as an oak trunk, the shipglass, as he'd dubbed the contraption, allowed stormrider spotters to see greater distances.

Zel was the first to look through the eyepiece, working the knobs. "Why must we look through the side of the thing to see out its front?"

"The inner workings are an intricate contrivance of mirrors and lenses. You wouldn't understand." Lee only said this because with all his knowledge and ability to remember words and figures, he didn't fully understand the workings himself. His foot tapped the wicker hull. "Are you done fussing with it? I'd like to have a go."

"Sure." She frowned and backed away. "All yours."

Belen had fashioned a special lens for Lee's spectacles that fitted close to Baldomar's eyepiece. He blinked and waited.

A circle of drifting pines came into focus, but no camps—not even a tent, let alone barracks and fences. "Are you certain you've brought us to the right place?"

"We charted the camps' positions as best we could. Kara's brother Keir and his former captor Priam are the only Keledan who've ever set foot in them. One was a tortured prisoner, and the other was not in his right mind, infected by a mocktree. I'd say their descriptions were imperfect."

Lee glanced up from the eyepiece. "So . . . no, you're not certain."

She scrunched her nose at him.

He returned his eye to the lens. "This may take longer than we'd hoped."

Not as long as he thought. Soon, the mists parted, and he found a rise among the trees with a sculpture of flaming hands forming a man out of clay. "Zel, I—"

The hands vanished. The forest went dark as a heavy bank of clouds passed over the moons.

He straightened. "Hold this position. We're close."

"I can't hover. The breeze is too strong. The best I can do is drop lower and turn her into the wind, but that'll put us closer to whatever creatures are hiding down there."

Lee drew a breath, then nodded. "Do it."

The ship hissed as Zel pulled her levers to release vapors through the envelope's forward vents. *The Merlin* nosed down and turned, like a galley listing on the back slope of a wave.

Lee moved to the bow. A patch of deeper black seemed to grow in the darkness. He lowered a pale yellow lens into place. The black took the shape of a winged monster.

"Look out!"

The Merlin lurched up again at Zel's command, tilting to port at the same time. The creature soared beneath the starboard skid—a huge bird with greasy black feathers reflecting the scant light of the stars.

"What was that thing?" Zel asked.

"A buzzard of some kind." Lee kept it in sight with the aid of his spectacles, barely a shadow against the trees. The shadow banked. "Watch yourself. I think it's coming back."

The Merlin turned, far nimbler than the larger craft Lee had flown in, but much less nimble than a real bird. The birds of

Keledev, according to the pilots, always fled before these manmade intruders in the sky. Not this one.

Lee watched it wheel around and aim straight for the silk envelope. He drew a double-bladed sikari throwing knife from the sheath at his thigh, took a half beat to aim, and let it fly. The creature shrieked and veered, falling. On its fading scream, Lee thought he heard an angry phrase. *How dare you!*

He and Zel exchanged a glance. Both let out a long breath. Their relief lasted only a moment. Zel widened her eyes. "Other creatures will have heard that cry. We must leave. Now."

"Not yet." The clouds were passing, letting the moons shine again. "One more look. We were closer before. I know it."

He hurried to the shipglass and pressed his special lens to the eyepiece. At first, he saw nothing but forest. Then a broken fence line appeared. Then another fence and a long building that could only be a barracks. "I see a camp."

Not a soul or even a soulless apparition moved. Lee gave Zel direction, and she steered the ship so that he could trace the glass along the circle Keir had described. Keir's memory proved accurate, and Lee saw more fences and barracks, but they were all the same.

Empty.

8

CONNOR
KELEDEV
RAS TELESAR

ARGUMENTS BETWEEN THE GUARDIANS AND
Stradok carried on for more than a tick, growing louder. Under
the clamor, Connor leaned closer to Teegan. "What did you
mean by what you said a while ago, that no one knows where our
friends are?"

The answer clearly pained her. She cared deeply for Lee,
Connor knew. And Sireth and Tiran were all that remained of her
family. "Lee and Zel have not returned from their mission," she
said, "putting them several days past their expected homecoming.
And my brehna joined my tehpa as a lightraider advisor to the
watchmen. The two left Ravencrest four days ago with a small
troop and have yet to report in."

Kara touched her hand. "And I thought my news was bad."

Pedrig's sharp ears heard her. His wolf's voice carried over the
many in the room, settling the din. "Speak your news, daughter of
winter. I fear it bears deeply on the decisions made here."

The tale she told brought Connor back to the first goblin
he'd ever encountered, thought to be the first to have breached
the barrier through the dragon Vorax's portal. That creature had
slaughtered sheep in his family's barn and threatened his parents.
The goblins Kara encountered at Orvyn's Vow had burned two of

the fjord way stations to the ground.

"Goblin mischief," Stradok said. "A small fire. The villages on the Central Plain suffer far greater injury from lightning strikes each fall." He glanced at Connor. "Children in the five vales do more damage with clumsy feet and overfilled lanterns."

Dame Silvana had watched the exchange with pursed lips. She shook her head. "I rarely agree with the councilor, but in this, I must echo his sentiment. To burn, torture, and destroy is a goblin's nature. Now that they roam our land, such must be expected."

Pedrig laid his ears flat. "Forgive me, but you're wrong. I see more purpose than mischief here."

Connor had to wonder how long it had been since anyone beyond Stradok had told Silvana she was wrong. She pulled her chin back. "Excuse me, Master Wolf, but—"

Master Jairun rose to his full height—a considerable height bolstered by his long legs and the raised platform—and tamped his staff on the stone floor. "All your points are well made, but whether the goblin fire is mischief or worse, the greater picture is clear. The enemy action is increasing, and our forces are split and fractured"—he cast a somber glance at Teegan—"with some beyond the reach of horn or raven. Such fractures will only widen if we fail to adapt."

Quinton shifted in his seat, brow furrowed. "What're ya sayin', Headmaster?"

"I'm saying we, the watchmen, the Lightraider Order, and the Airguard are a dam on the verge of breaking. And when we do, the flood will wash all Keledev into the sea."

His claim sent the table into a flurry of arguments, all separate and all intertwined. Baldomar argued for more forges. Stradok spoke of new campaigns to call up the able-bodied in Keledev or to cease the volunteer efforts and force men into service. Silvana proposed a new regimen of training to teach stealth and hunting tactics to the outpost companies.

All sounded to Connor like variations on past notions, ways

to harry the dragons but not stop them. For a long while, his mind had been set on another option, one with the potential to finish the war for good. He'd kept this hidden in his heart, sharing it only with Lee and Kara. Now was the time to speak it aloud.

"I know what to do."

Only Kara looked his way, and her blue, almost indigo eyes told him the words at his lips would break her heart. He saw no other option.

Connor stood and shouted, "I know how to end the war!"

The hall went silent, except for Stradok, who crossed his arms. "Oh, do you, Cadet? Well, go on, then. Let's hear your brilliant plan."

Stradok had a way of stuffing hay in Connor's throat. This time was no different. Connor coughed to clear it. "We can use . . ." He coughed again, seeing that he was losing them. "Lef Amunrel. The Red Dagger. We can use it to kill Heleyor himself."

Master Jairun's gaze held a warning. So did Pedrig's. Connor refused to let either deter him.

Stradok interrupted again. "A worse answer than any I might have expected, boy, even from you." He snorted. "Lef Amunrel is gone. Your own grandfather let it fall into mystery."

"Not true," Connor said. "Before he gave his life to destroy Vorax, Faelin discovered the dagger's resting place." He lifted a hesitant hand toward the headmaster and the wolf. "And he shared it with Master Jairun and Pedrig long ago."

9

"MISTER ENARIAN!" DAME SILVANA STRUCK CONNOR with a glare that sat him down again.

Master Jairun waved off her rebuke. "Let the cadet speak. If there was ever a time to out secrets, it's now." He nodded to Connor, gaze inscrutable. "Continue."

"Master Jairun placed me in the Navigators' Sphere under the urging of the Helper. We, the navigators, steer the course and discern paths in the dark. That's our calling. A darkness lies before us now, and I feel the Helper telling me the Red Dagger is our course. Lef Amunrel is within our grasp. Let's use it."

"What of the other young navigator?" Silvana asked, raising her voice above the resulting clamor—equal parts support and objection. "What does she say?"

In the year since the quest to recover the Rapha Key and bring home Kara's brehna Keir—the year since Kara and Connor had been named navigators at the Turning of the Spheres—the two had discussed what he'd learned about Lef Amunrel many times. They'd been opposed and in agreement, often swapping sides, tossed to and fro on the experiences of the day or season. Connor had never fully decided on the best path for a weapon rumored to have the power to destroy Heleyor—not until that moment. But what had Kara decided?

He tried and failed to read the grim press of her lips as she stood.

"I agree with my fellow navigator," Kara said to Connor's relief. "We must reclaim the dagger and use it if we can."

Stradok crossed his arms. "Appropriate phrasing. *If we can.* And to be clear, we—or you, the Lightraider Order—most certainly can't. Only one of the Aropha can enter Ras Pyras uninvited."

"Don't be so certain, Councilor!" A new voice had entered the argument. Belen strode into the hall, raising an object wrapped in a blue velvet cloth with silver knotwork embroidery.

The group parted, making room for Belen to lay his burden on the table and unwrap it.

Stradok bent closer. "Is that . . ."

"The Rapha Key," Belen said with a nod, "thought to open the Bread Gate at Ras Pyras."

The revelation turned the assemblyman's hard gaze on Connor. "You found it, then. Why was I never told?"

Master Jairun shrugged. "You were present when I gave him the assignment. What did you expect?"

"I expected him to fail, like his grandfather."

"Then you've only your prejudices to blame for your lack of knowledge." The headmaster ignored Stradok's scowl and spread his hands. "Mister Enarian spoke true. I know the location of the Red Dagger. Whether or not the Rapha Key will allow a raid party entrance to Ras Pyras"—he turned his gaze on Belen—"*undetected* is another question, as is whether or not the Rescuer intends for a mortal lightraider to destroy Heleyor." He bowed his head. "We must pray for guidance."

Master Jairun let every noise in the hall settle before continuing. He prayed for help in finding the right course of action, ending by reciting the High One's words from the Sacred Scrolls back to him. *"Kidef yi kethon do ya kethez panov, ker decton thimiov. Ker kevy, po alerol shurniov."*

Your ears will hear a voice. This is the way. Walk in it.

Stradok, not Master Jairun, was the first to speak after the prayer, and though the mere sound of Stradok's voice often perturbed

Connor, this time he felt sure the man's words were true and correct. "This is a decision for all Keledan," Stradok said. "We must end secrecy and lay the choice of using Lef Amunrel, the last celestium weapon, in the hands of the Assembly."

Master Jairun grunted his agreement—a near match to the grunt that came from the wolf beside him—and turned his gaze on Connor. "This is your course, Navigator. So you must be the one to present it to the Second Hall." He tamped his staff one last time, signaling the end of the meeting. "The Rescuer is with us."

The rest of the gathering, except for Connor, stood and answered as one. "Always and forever."

Stunned by Master Jairun's final pronouncement, ears suddenly ringing, Connor rose a beat behind the others. He spoke the litany with only half a voice. "Always and forever."

———◆———

BY THE TIME THE RINGING IN CONNOR'S EARS SUBSIDED, the table had emptied around him. Still, he felt eyes upon him. The guardians and Stradok, Pedrig and Aaron, all had broken off into small clusters, yet from within their conversations, they still watched him.

Silvana had waylaid Kara on her way to the hall's overlarge doors, making big gestures with her diminutive arms. Connor started their way with a quick step to give Kara his support but made it only two paces.

Belen blocked his path and steered him to the far end of the hall and the warmth of the large Elder Folk hearth. "Miss Orso must fend for herself, my boy. Trust me, she's quite capable. And I'm afraid you'll both have a battle just to get out of this room."

The tinker used his own gaze to direct Connor's to the various corners of the hall. Quinton and Stradok hung together among the stone tables in halfhearted conversation, each trying hard not to let the other see his glances in Connor's direction. Pedrig paced on the raised platform, making no secret of his hard wolf stare.

Belen chuckled. "Before you head south, most who attended this gathering will hope to bend your ear."

Connor flattened his lips. "As you are now, sir?"

"Most definitely. Can I help it if I'm a step ahead of my peers?" The guardian positioned himself between Connor and the rest of the hall, making his cloak as good as a curtain. From within it, he drew the Rapha Key in its embroidered wrappings. "You must carry this with you."

"You want me to carry the key?"

"Not so loud, my boy." The tinker widened his eyes behind his spectacles. "Do you want them all to hear?"

So much for an end to secrecy.

Belen seemed to read this thought in Connor's face. "There are dark creatures in the land now, and their master wants this key returned. The Assembly must be told of its existence, but perhaps it's best if its location remains unspoken."

Wise reasoning, Connor supposed. But why should he be the one to carry it? "Am I to hide it in Sky Harbor when I go?"

"No, my boy. Carry the key with you always so that the next time the Rescuer chooses to send you into Tanelethar, you can leave it there."

The silver embroidery of the key's wrappings captured the flicker of the hearth to become living bands of fire on the blue cloth. Had Connor and the other cadet scouts not risked all to find this relic and bring it here, to Keledev? "Why would I return this to Tanelethar? Does that not increase the danger that it will return to Heleyor?"

"The danger of keeping it here is greater." Belen frowned and sighed. "I've been studying the key ever since you returned from the Fading Mountains. And I've found the Aropha understanding of keys is not the same as ours. Do you see?"

Not remotely.

Connor tempered his answer. "I might need a little more explanation, sir."

"Right." After a glance over his shoulder, Belen pressed the key into Connor's hands and signaled him to tuck it away, out of sight. They sat on a pair of round stone stools rising from the floor. "To us, a key opens a door or a gate. To the Elder Folk, a key gave access to a path that crosses a great distance, sometimes to a specific place and sometimes to other paths."

A path that crosses a great distance. "You mean a portal," Connor said.

This earned him a subtle nod. "The Rescuer chose to let us come and go to Tanelethar with hollow trees, the Passage Lakes, and the Storm Mists—new portals for his new creation. The Aropha paths are part of the old creation, along with the hollow hills. I'm not sure the Rescuer intended us to keep a key to those paths on this side of the barrier."

"Are you saying that by bringing the key here, Lee and I may have created a connection between Tanelethar and the academy? One the dragons might use?"

"I'm saying we should return things to the way they were as best we can until we know for certain. Place the key in the relative safety of a sanctuary and leave it in the Rescuer's care." A shade hung for a moment over Belen's features, then fled as he unhooked a satchel from his belt. "Now, on to other business. Since you *are* headed to Sky Harbor, I want you to deliver this."

When Connor asked to whom he should take it, Belen smiled. "Councilor Zayn Boreas, head of the Airguard and master of the Apothecarists' Guild. Inside you'll find the vial of oil holding the brimstone metal. I hear his people are creating concoctions that explode with flame, much more powerful than festival sparkles."

Connor lifted the strap over his shoulder, feeling a weight too great for just the vial. He could guess at the remaining contents. "And the rest is the shairosite?"

"For his pilots, with the compliments of the Lightraider Order. The Rescuer has revealed stormriding to the Airguard. They'll need as much shairosite as they can find if they hope to learn how to harness that gift."

10

LEE
TANELETHAR
SIL SHADATH

LEE SAT ON THE AFT BENCH WITH HIS HEAD IN HIS
hands while Zel steered *The Merlin* north toward Miner's Folly.
"He's gone, Zel."

"Who. Shan?"

The scribe looked up. "No. I mean yes, but . . . I'm sorry.
They're gone. Shan, the Aladoth prisoners, the orcs, the barkhides.
They're all gone. The army Heleyor built to destroy Keledev is on
the move."

Zel turned and dumped a vial of fuel into the lamp, sending
The Merlin into a sharp rise.

The pitch of the bow nearly threw Lee from the bench. "What
are you doing?"

"Storm ahead." Zel nodded toward the bow. "Building
between us and the cloudloft. We'll have to climb over it."

The cloudloft. The mention of the new outpost shook Lee
from his grief, clearing his head. "Don't climb. Turn southeast,
toward the Celestial Peaks."

"What? Why?"

"We can't take *The Merlin* back now, Zel. We need to find that
army. And I'll wager they're headed south."

She held her rudder steady and frowned at him. "You mean

we need to find your brother."

"I mean the Aladoth army. That was our mission, right? We haven't finished it."

Ahead, the clouds billowed—silver tops spreading toward the moons, pressed up by a dozen shades of blue, gray, and black.

Zel turned a dial, increasing their lamp flame to send more vapors into the silk. "The Lightraiders and the Airguard tasked us with putting the final touches on Cloudloft Stratus and then learning the disposition of the Aladoth army. We've done that."

"Have we?" Lee gestured behind them to the black forest. "The dragon's army is gone. That's no disposition."

"I'd say it's a clear disposition. The army is on the move. Time is short. We must report back and get new orders."

He gritted his teeth. Like always, arguing with Zel was as fruitful as arguing with an oak tree. "If time is short, aren't we of more use hunting the army to learn how much their numbers have grown or how they plan to enter Keledev?"

"Not our call."

"But if we just—"

Zel stomped her foot. "You're not going to find him, Lee!"

A flash and a crack of thunder gave strength to her rebuke. The dark, bulging masses ahead threatened to outpace their climb. She gritted her teeth at Lee, then turned her lamp dial to its highest degree.

When Lee lowered his head, she let out a sigh. "I'm sorry. You'll find Shan, I'm sure, just not tonight." She followed this comfort with a quiet chuckle. "What was your plan, hmm? To leap over the rail and face him down, along with whatever wraiths or golmogs march with him? Are you prepared to face the dragon Valshadox himself?"

Lightning crackled again, and Lee lifted his eyes. "I'll leave that in the Rescuer's hands." He stood, pushing between her and the lamp.

"What are you doing?"

Lee ignored the challenge and dumped a purse of shairosite from his manykit into the flame. With the quickness of his movements, Zel had no chance to stop him. And once he pulled the vent cords, she had no chance to stop *The Merlin* either.

The ship plummeted toward the billowing clouds. Blue smoke spread from the lamps to surround them. Matching blue vapors spiraled up like a grasping hand from the storm.

"We're going in!" Lee shouted over the wind. "Pray with me! Pray he'll take us to the army!"

He lifted his face and closed his eyes, hoping Zel had done the same.

A sense of falling surrounded him, and with it, the cool wetness of the clouds. Tingles of static danced across his skin, invigorating him. "You'll see! The Rescuer will show you I'm right!"

11

THE SHIP JOLTED TO A STOP IN THE SKY, THROWING
Lee and Zel to the deck between the benches. She landed on top
of him with an "Oompf!"

Zel rolled away, then rolled back over and punched him full
force in the arm. "What were you thinking?"

"Shh!" Lee put a finger to his lips. "We don't know how close
we are."

"Close to what?" She planted a palm in his chest to push
herself up.

"Ow! The army, Zel. The Aladoth army. Aren't you paying
attention?"

Zel looked down on him with scorn. "If the army is below us
now, we've wasted half our night." She offered him a hand. "Get
up here and look."

Lee accepted her help and leaned over the rail, adjusting his
spectacles. The blue smoke from the lamp wafted away on the
breeze along with wisps of storm cloud they'd brought with them,
revealing a clear night.

No Aladoth army marched below them—no orcs and no
dragon. No Shan. Lee saw only steep hills of rock and grass and a
great big hole in the earth. Slowly, he lifted his gaze to meet Zel's

burning glare. "We've returned to the cloudloft."

"I know." Zel stomped up to him and punched him again, this time in the chest.

"Ow. Stop that!"

"I can't believe you!" She hit him once more. "This is my ship. I'm her captain!"

Zel hauled back her fist for yet another punch, and Lee raised his hands in defense. "I'm sorry. I'm sorry!" He glanced over the side. "I just thought . . ." His hands fell. "Never mind."

She let her fist fall to her side. "Help me get her stowed."

Neither spoke again until Zel had brought the ship down into the cloudloft and the two had raised the canvas into place and secured the ropes.

Zel struck a lantern, surrounding herself with a wavering sphere of yellow-orange light. "Did you hear yourself? 'The Rescuer will show you I'm right.' Did you hear the foolishness?"

Her words—his own words thrown into his face—struck Lee harder than any of her punches. "I hear it now."

"Good. Because not only did your pride endanger our friendship, it endangered *The Merlin*." She touched a finger to a patch embroidered on the sleeve of her tunic—a stone tower in the clouds. "Do you wear one of these?"

He lowered his eyes. "No."

"Why not?"

"That is the emblem of the Airguard stormwatchers, not the Lightraider Order."

Her finger moved down to a second patch depicting a horse galloping on a storm. "And this? Do you have one?"

He didn't answer. He didn't need to. No one in all Dastan, the whole world, except for Zel wore such an emblem. She alone had captained an airship to ride a storm.

"Well?"

"I mean. Perhaps I could wear one now, because—"

"Lee!"

"No." He lifted his gaze and held up his hands again, fearful of another punch. "You're right. I'm no ship captain and no stormrider."

"You might have destroyed the ship and killed us both. Remember what happened in the Highland Forest."

At the start of their quest, when Lee had convinced her the Rescuer wanted them to simply fly into a storm and see where he took them, it had not gone well. The wind had blown the shairosite vapors clear of the lamp, and the buffeting had tossed them about so hard they both feared the trusses would break. From that moment until this night, they hadn't tried another storm.

Lee looked up at the silk envelope. "She looks sound. No tears in the silk. No cracks in the trusses. She's fine."

"By the Rescuer's grace alone." Zel stroked the gray wicker like a rider stroking a beloved mare. "If you hadn't pulled the vents open—if you'd wanted to climb instead of descend—you might have easily ripped our envelope in two. Remember what happened in the Fading Mountains?"

He did. Their first stormride in Tanelethar had damaged *The Starling*, their ship at the time. Lee himself had argued this had happened due to lack of full understanding of stormriding. "You learned the cause of the tear?"

She nodded, leaning an arm on *The Merlin*'s rail. "Back then, I argued my father's design was flawless. When I returned home, he showed me I was wrong. Not one of us is flawless, even in our daily work." Zel looked up at the silk. "Together, Father and I searched for the cause and learned a stormride may carry a ship instantly to high, thin air, leaving thick air inside the envelope. This change may burst the silk. We have to pull the vents each stormride to prevent this."

Lee let out a long breath. "You might have told me."

She pressed her nose close to his. "I didn't think I had to, since *I'm the captain, not you.*"

He backed away. "A point well made. Truly." He waited for

the tension in her jaw to ease, then shrugged. "I'm sorry for the mutiny, but we're left with an unanswered question. Why did the storm bring us here?"

Zel traced a gloved hand down one of the trusses and rubbed her thumb and forefinger together. "I've an idea about that."

"Which is?"

She brushed her hand on her side. "That there's more to stormriding than dumping shairosite into a lamp. The Rescuer might have shown us how to steer a course just now by the unity of his creation—by the very dust and rocks of Talania. I'll tell you when I know more. I wanted to seek my father's advice before another stormride, but since you forced us . . ." Her expression darkened.

Lee frowned. "I said I'm sorry."

"I know. And I forgive you. For now, consider that the Rescuer may want us to grow in our use of this gift of stormriding—to take the reins of the steed, if you will."

To Lee's ear, it sounded like she wanted to wrest control from their sovereign. That didn't sound right. "Are you saying we shouldn't pray and let him send us where he may?"

"Partly." Zel carried the lantern into the cloudloft's antechamber and sat on a stool by the map table. "We should pray, certainly, but we should also try to discern his will from his Scrolls and listening for his voice, and then choose our path and go." She set the lantern down and fixed Lee with her gaze. "The Rescuer is not a magic wishing well like those gifted to men by the dragons in the early days of their deception."

Lee knew that. "Praying is not wishing on a well."

"It is if you expect him to spin up a storm and pop you out at the right place with no thought at all. To do so takes no effort to seek him, no relationship."

He wasn't sure he fully understood where Zel's thoughts were leading her in terms of stormriding, but she refused to explain more.

Instead, she called him over to the map table. "Where shall we go next?"

Lee furrowed his brow. "I thought you wanted to report back to Keledev."

"I did. But now we're here on the ground, where I can set my whole mind on the question, I've come to a different conclusion. You were wrong to take the ship, but you were right about seeking the Aladoth army."

"Time is short," Lee said, repeating his argument from before.

She nodded. "And getting shorter by the tick. I agree with your reasoning, if not your full purpose. We must find that army before it crosses into Keledev. And when we find it, we must be ready for a fight."

12

CONNOR
KELEDEV
RAS TELESAR

CONNOR WOKE WITH THE DAWN ON THE DAY OF HIS journey south. He thought the rest of those in the cadet scout barracks were sleeping, until an absence of sound took hold of his ear. A glance at Dag's bed told him what was missing. Snores.

The rhythmic snorts and huffs of Dag's slumber, which had come to be the lullaby that rocked Connor and his friends to sleep most nights, were not there. Nor was the miner.

Connor found him on the barracks balcony. "Couldn't sleep?"

Dag shook his head.

"The herald?"

"Gair was his name. From Lamb's Glen. He came north to do his part and found a place as a herald for the Airguard spotters because of his skill with horses—or so the pilots tell me."

Gair. A name for the muster roll of those laying down their lives for Keledev and the Rescuer. Gair, in his zeal, had joined Faelin Enarian and Barnabas Botloff and many others in this fate. Connor feared their number would grow all the faster unless someone wrought a change.

He pressed his shoulder against Dag's and breathed deep. "You are a cadet scout of the Vanguard. Death is no deterrent—no barricade to stop your charge."

"My own death," Dag said. "Not another's. I can't lead a sentinel squadron. Not anymore."

This was not good news. Connor forced back a frown, leaning on compassion rather than rebuke. "You can't step away. We need you. Keledev needs you."

"They need me to fight, not lead. I'll name a younger cadet in my place."

The set of Dag's big shoulders told Connor he would not be swayed. Connor swallowed and nodded. "All right. I don't envy you the fight when you tell Master Quinton."

Connor left Dag to consider this and dressed. His day was off to a hard start, with many hard ticks to go, and like Dag, his own sleep that night had been fleeting.

Belen's prediction that all the guardians and Stradok would want Connor's and Kara's ears after the gathering proved accurate. Three ticks had passed before he managed to escape them all. By then, the night was getting on, and he'd still had packing to do and an important arrangement that needed tending.

Neglecting Kara during those ticks was never his plan, but that's how the night turned out. They hadn't seen each other for weeks before Master Jairun's council, and the two hadn't had a moment to speak since. The arrangement he'd made took longer and more negotiating than he'd expected, but it had seemed of the utmost importance at the time.

Now he wasn't so sure.

He found her in the glade, loading her kit into the airship designated to carry them south to Sky Harbor. Connor hurried to her side and bent over the rail to place his folded cloak beside hers. "I looked for you," he said, attempting to head off a rebuke, "in the Vanquish chamber, where I usually find you playing on nights such as last."

"Then you must not have looked hard." Kara flung her manykit harness with its sheathed blue-green whirlknives down on top of their cloaks. "Or perhaps you came late." She turned to glare at him. "Very late. I waited more than a tick."

A tick. Truly? How long had his other business kept him?

"Kara, I–"

"Ho, there!" Samar Ray, that oh-so-striking Airguard pilot who'd brought Kara in from Orvyn's Vow, sauntered across the glade toward their ship–Samar's ship, as it happened, which was why Connor had been forced to do some maneuvering the night before.

He gave her a fleeting smile. "One moment. Can we come back to this?"

She didn't answer, and he didn't have time to wait. Leaving her side, Connor hurried to intercept the approaching pilot. "Good morning! I'm surprised to see you up so early."

This earned him a confused stare. "I don't see why. This is my ship, and it's my honor to fly you and Miss Orso to Sky Harbor on your very important mission."

Connor took the risk of wrapping an arm over Samar's shoulders and turning him about, back toward the fortress gate. "Actually, the ship belongs to the Airguard, not a fairly green pilot's mate, correct?" He pointed at Aaron Ilmari, emerging from between the academy's huge, Aropha-carved towers at a jog. "And flying that ship today will be *his* honor."

Connor shot Aaron a *You're late* frown. For which he received an *I'm sorry* wince.

"You must be mistaken," Samar said. "Lieutenant Ilmari has no ship, because he crashed his into a mountainside."

"Possibly saving all Keledev. For which he must be rewarded–a message I wish to convey to Councilor Boreas with the lieutenant at my shoulder." Connor released Samar as Aaron reached them, giving the pilot's mate a light push toward the incoming lieutenant.

At the same time Aaron swept a hand down to snatch an elongated leather case from Samar's grasp. "Is this our fuel? Thank you so much for preparing it for me, young sir. You saved me a great deal of time."

"Young sir?" The push and the stolen fuel seemed to have carried Samar past the point of civility or rank. "We're the same age. And you've no right, Ilmari. My ship. My charges."

"*My* mission," Connor interjected. "And as an uneasy flier, I'm afraid I prefer a more experienced pilot. How long have you been with the Airguard? Half a season?"

Samar crossed his arms. "A full."

"Lieutenant Ilmari has been with them four, almost since the beginning."

Out of the corner of his eye, Connor saw Aaron raise four fingers and wiggle them.

"Fine," Samar said. "Enjoy your journey, and pray your favored friend makes this flight better than his last."

When the two returned to the ship, they found Kara sitting on the bench with arms crossed. It may have been a trick of the morning light, but the blue-gray swirls of freckles on her cheeks and forehead appeared to pulse. She narrowed her eyes at Connor. "What was that all about?"

He shrugged. "You know how I feel about flying. I trust the weight of Aaron's experience."

She huffed and pushed open a wicker door—known as the rail hatch. "Whatever you say. Let's get going."

The crimson silk of the four huge envelopes snapped taut as Aaron brought the ship's lamps to a full, rushing flame, and the wicker hull left the grass.

Connor kept his gaze inside the rails. He hated this part. And the landing part. And every part in between. Samar may have mentioned a prayer in spite, but Connor closed his eyes and spoke one anyway. *Rescuer, keep us safe and speed us on this journey as we do your work.*

When he opened his eyes again, he looked to Aaron, who worked the vents to keep the bow pointed south. "What is she called?"

The lieutenant's lips parted. "I . . . uh . . ."

Kara rolled her eyes. "She's *The Kingfisher*, which her real pilot would have known."

"I am her real pilot," Aaron said, shifting his gaze to the horizon, then added in a lower voice, "at least for now."

The mass of winds rolling against the Celestial Peaks—the great wheel, as the Airguard called them—churned in such a way that the low winds held still after sunrise, and the high winds pushed out across Keledev toward the sea. But this close to the mountains, they were unpredictable. The last few seasons had taught the pilots that a night launch from the mountains could be treacherous. A morning launch was safer but required help.

A long rope clipped to a ring in the bow hung down to a matching ring in a gelding's saddle. The horse and rider would race down one of the long gravel roads recently added to the academy's ancient glade, towing the ship to give it speed, until the threat of the cliff at the road's end forced the rider to rein up. Pushing the limits of this short race had become a game among the volunteers who made the runs.

Aaron made a final adjustment to his vents, then advanced between his passengers to call over the bow. "Ready!"

Connor watched from the port rail, waiting for the rider to spur his mount, but the man seemed distracted, looking back toward the academy gates. Connor followed his gaze and groaned. "Samar. What is he doing now?"

"Something brave and foolish, I expect," Kara said, looking back with him, but with less disdain and more admiration than Connor would have liked. "It's in his nature."

Samar waved to the rider, and with an exchange of words, the two came to some kind of agreement. The rider hopped down, and Samar took his place.

Kara joined Aaron at the bow to watch.

Connor, unwilling to be shown a coward by sitting hunched on the bench, got up to stand with them.

"You know Samar from your order, Aaron," Kara said. "Has

he ever ridden for a launch before?"

"I doubt he's ever had the chance. Pilots have other work, and there are only a couple of tow runs like this along the whole of the Celestial range."

Fighting his distaste for heights, Connor leaned over the bow and shouted down, "You'll get yourself killed! The horse, too!"

A jovial salute and wave from Samar left little doubt that he hadn't understood a word of it.

Connor snorted and waved back, but Aaron leaned close to his ear. "I don't think he was waving at you. Or me, for that matter."

Both looked to Kara, who was also waving—and smiling. Then she patted Connor's arm. "Hang on," she said, gripping the rail. "Samar doesn't do anything halfway, and I know you hate flying to start with."

He let go of the rail and crossed his arms. "I'll be fine. He's the one who should be worried."

With a hard kick from his rider, the gelding took off, and the slack in the rope quickly vanished. *The Kingfisher* lurched, sending Connor flailing back onto the bow bench. He was sure he heard Kara laugh as he fought his way to his feet again. "He knows there's a cliff at the end, right?"

At Master Jairun's insistence, the road builders had added a stretch of upturned earth at the end of each tow road as a last hope to stop a horse from going over. The riders called it the pit, and none launching an airship had ever come close to testing its worth.

"He's going for the pit," Connor said. "Or well past it."

"Of all the prideful—" Aaron shook his head and growled. "If he goes over the cliff, he'll take us into the forest. The bow can't take the weight of a horse." He drew a knife from his belt. "Pray this blade is sharp enough to cut quickly."

Kara cupped a hand to her mouth. "Samar, stop!"

Whether by her call, or by his own plan, Samar jerked the reins, and the gelding planted its hooves. Horse and rider slid past the edge of the gravel in a cloud of dust.

Aaron slashed the line. The rope fell free.

The Kingfisher sailed out over the forest valley.

Kara ran to the stern rail with Connor close on her heels. When he caught up, he saw the rope falling into the spruce below— but no horse or rider. Samar must have released his clip at the same time Aaron cut the line.

Eyes tracking up the cliff, Connor saw the young pilot's mate waving from the pit, still seated atop the gelding. Behind him, the watchmen, airmen, and cadets in the glade all cheered. Connor noticed a touch of blush in Kara's cheeks. She knew Samar had done it for her, not them.

Aaron worked his rudder and vents. "It cost us a rope, but I'll give him this. That must be the fastest launch ever made from Ras Telesar. He's brave. And skilled."

"I don't care," Connor said, sinking onto the stern bench next to the pilot, keeping his voice low so Kara wouldn't hear. "I don't like him."

13

SWORDMASTER QUINTON WAS NOT PLEASED.

He'd made this clear in no uncertain terms to Dag and Teegan before they left the academy, not long after Connor and Kara departed.

Kara, dispatched with Connor on the critical mission to convince the Assembly that the Lightraider Order must retrieve Lef Amunrel, had left Teegan with the responsibility to train the novices at Orvyn's Vow. This meant Teegan had to pass leadership of her and Connor's sentinel squadron to one of the younger cadets.

When she went to tell Quinton, the author and commander of the sentinel squadrons, she'd found Dag already in the swordmaster's chambers, sharing precisely the same news for an entirely different reason.

"Thank you for being there yesterday," Dag said as the two rode east together on their second day of travel. "Having a friend beside me eased the sting of Quinton's ire—and perhaps its force."

She crossed her arms over her saddle's pommel. "What are classmates for?" Teegan glanced up at him. Dag rode head and shoulders above her mare on his Gladion stallion. She allowed herself a laugh. "I felt like we were back on our first full day of training, with him shouting at us to lug boulders up and down the lists."

The miner's soft smile faded. "Would that we were."

They heard a groan behind them. "I still can't believe he took my ship."

Both Teegan and Dag turned to look at their unhappy companion. Samar rode with them, heading back to Orvyn's Vow in a manner he'd perhaps never expected.

"Just marched up and took the lamp fuel right out of my hand."

"Oh, give it a rest," Teegan said, returning her gaze to the trail ahead. "Your lost ship is the least of anyone's problems." She swallowed back the rest—the fallen herald, her missing friends Zel and Lee, her missing tehpa and brehna. Neither she nor Dag had breathed a word of complaint since they'd left Ras Telesar that morning, but Samar did not have such control. He'd whined about it the whole of their first day's ride, and if she heard *He took my ship* once more today, she might shove him off his horse.

The three rode the high eastward trail toward the Sea of Vows, staying north of the tree line for a better watch against marauding dark creatures. Teegan trusted Dag to keep his eyes roving, but despite all the skill Samar had shown with the tow horse, she found his scouting talents lacking.

"Instead of complaining so much," she said, "you might take to heart that the Rescuer has you on this path for a purpose."

"Which is?"

"I don't know. Keep silent for a time and listen for his voice."

It almost worked. Samar did keep silent—for all of three or four beats before the trail widened and he rode up beside her.

"You weren't there." He drew his boots out of his stirrups and turned about in the saddle, trusting her horse to guide his. "You didn't see the way that larcenous Ilmari robbed me of the fuel case after his friend Enarian pushed me."

The young pilot seemed to give no thought to balancing against the sway of his mare. Teegan, who'd ridden her whole life, could not imagine sitting that way without falling.

Show-off.

She shook her head. "Don't bring Connor into this."

"Why not? I'm certain he was the mastermind."

"If Connor commandeered your ship on Aaron's behalf, he had a good reason."

Samar dropped his chin into his hand. "Oh, I know the reason, and she's—"

Aethia swept down from the sky and flew across his face, ruining his perfect balance. Samar grabbed his saddle and swung himself back around to slide his boots into his stirrups. "What's wrong with your bird?"

"Nothing." Teegan held out an arm, allowing Aethia to land, and gave her a sliver of meat. "She's doing the job you can't seem to master—scouting. Hush and draw your sword."

"I left my sword in the armory at Orvyn's Vow, where it belongs." Samar lifted a long knife from a sheath at his belt and waggled it at her. "I'm a pilot. This is all I carry, a knife for cutting ropes and wicker. What use have I for a sword in the air?"

"You might crash during a battle," Dag offered with utter sincerity.

One corner of Samar's mouth turned upward. "Crashing is Ilmari's tactic, not mine."

Teegan sent Aethia skyward again, then spurred her mare and pushed ahead. "Keep up and try not to get us killed."

She held her lead, as much to keep Samar out of her way as to protect him, and rode to follow Aethia while Dag brought up the rear. The falcon hung low over the trail in her racing back and forth from Teegan to their quarry, hard to break out from the rocks for any but her mistress. The turn of her wheeling told Teegan the dark creatures were northeast of them. But how far?

As Aethia's wheels grew shorter, a soft scuffing reached Teegan's ear, out of rhythm with their horses. She raised a fist for a halt at the edge of a tall rock formation. Samar almost rode past her anyway. Teegan caught his reins and eased his mare back next to her, whispering, "Don't you know what a raised fist means?"

He shook his head.

"How long had you been under Kara's instruction at Orvyn's Vow?"

"Three weeks." He bobbled his head. "More like two and a half."

Her expression stayed flat. "Perfect. Stay here with Dag and be ready to act."

Teegan dismounted and pressed herself close to the rocks. She crept to the edge with her trident at the ready.

Heavy breaths reached her ear. Something waited, just around the corner.

She pounced, leaping out with her trident leveled. "Ha!"

The trident's tines clanked against the steel head of a war hammer, inches from a familiar bearded face. She lowered her weapon. "Tehpa?"

"Shh." Sireth Yar motioned for his behlna to lower her voice. "I saw your bird. Let's pray no one else did the same." He inclined his head to the north. "Orcs are near. Follow me."

"Wait." She stopped him with a hand before he could turn. "Dag is with me, and another—a pilot named Samar who has no weapon or training. He's not prepared for a fight."

Sireth leaned past the rock to regard the pilot for a moment and grunted. "Then he walks these mountains in folly. For now, if he can manage the test of sneaking about with a horse, it won't be a problem."

For the next quarter tick their party made no sound beyond the soft *scrape* and *crunch* of hooves on rock and gravel. Sireth brought them to a winding and rising corridor between rock formations. The horses, even Dag's Gladion, gave no sign of worry in the tight space.

"How far off our path is he taking us?" Samar whispered to Dag, loud enough to make Teegan cringe.

Her tehpa cast a stern look over his shoulder. "No farther than this. We're here."

The corridor leveled and opened to a half-moon patch of gray dirt and gravel hemmed in by jagged pinnacles. Four watchmen crouched within, three men and a woman. Tiran had laid himself out upon a shelf in the highest pinnacle, eyes north.

Overjoyed as she was to see her brehna whole and healthy, Teegan made no move to disturb his watch.

The young woman in the party asked Sireth a question with a mere widening of her eyes.

"Two lightraider cadets and an Airguard pilot," he said in answer. "This is the owner of the falcon we saw." Sireth nodded toward Teegan and the bird as Aethia came to light on her arm. "She's my behlna."

With a few gestures, he bid Teegan leave Aethia with her mare and follow him alone up one of the northern pinnacles. Together they looked out between the spires.

The terrain beyond their little enclave dropped sharply into a scree valley. Teegan saw nothing but bare rock, until her tehpa nudged her and pointed. One flat boulder leaning against another in the northwestern corner formed a shallow cave. Shadows moved beneath. Focusing her gaze, she caught sight of a leathery foot and black armor.

A second prompt from her tehpa brought Teegan's eyes upslope and slightly east to a ledge. Three gall buzzards lay flat with wings spread—a posture she'd never seen in any living bird. Grit and dust from the valley had turned their greasy black feathers drab and gray.

Teegan risked a whisper. "Are they dead?"

"Once, perhaps. Or perhaps the veins and tendons of whatever rotted creatures the dragons made them from remember death in some way."

Together, they returned to the patch of dirt to rejoin his party. Orcs were to be killed on sight, a long-standing directive of the Order, now affirmed in a unanimous vote by the Assembly for all Keledan combatants. Why was her tehpa defying them? "Are you preparing your attack or waiting for reinforcements?"

One of Sireth's men had taken charge of their horses, now lined up with the watchmen's mounts. He scratched the ears of Teegan's mare, keeping well clear of the falcon perched on the saddle, and answered for his commander. "Neither. Killin' 'em won't do no good—not yet anyhow."

"What Daron means," Sireth said, "is that we've been killing these things for nigh on a year, and their numbers are only growing. There's more going on here than border incursions. We want to try a different tactic."

"Which is?" Samar asked.

"We've been following this small orc platoon for days. And we'll keep following until they lead us to their masters."

14

TEEGAN WATCHED SIRETH DRAW CURVING LINES IN
the dirt, then a small circle to represent their little enclave behind
the pinnacles. "We're here," he said, "on the southern edge of
this scree valley." He kept his deep voice lower than a whisper.
"The orcs and their birds are over here, where they've remained
for days."

"Doing what?" Dag asked.

"Waiting. Once in a while, a runner comes in. Another goes out."

Tiran had traded with one of the men and joined his tehpa in
the huddle. "We think this is a messenger relay post. We tracked
what we thought was a scout, and he led us here. When a runner
went out, we waited until he ran beyond his comrades' sight, and
we killed him."

"We did the same with the next," Sireth said, "harrying their
communications, but to what end? Soon enough we'd be discovered
and have to kill them all."

Teegan met her tehpa's gaze. "But if one of those runners
should lead you to the commander . . ."

Her brehna nodded. "We achieve a far more valuable goal."

Sireth returned his attention to his sketch, drawing paths from
each end with his stick. "We have two choices. East or west. One

of those will lead us to the source of the orders passing through this relay. We tried west two days ago, and the runner we followed met up with a small platoon heading farther northwest."

"Did you allow the thing to return?" Dag asked, and Teegan could hear disquiet in the question. His sphere, the Vanguard, above all, did not suffer dark creatures to live. "Or did you kill it?"

"Neither. The creature stayed with the platoon. A missed chance."

Dag's grim expression darkened. "For certain."

Samar, who'd remained quiet thus far, let out a chuckle. "Or not. Don't you see? The platoon heading northwest may well have been the same unit your two sentinel squadrons destroyed at the Passage Lakes. For all you know, the runner fell to your trident and your axes. Am I right?"

Dag lolled his head over to narrow his eyes at the pilot. "And for all you know, the runner loosed the arrow that killed Gair. This is why we kill orcs on sight."

"Oh." Samar sat cross-legged on the dirt. "Never mind."

A quiet *humph* escaped Sireth's throat. "Alive or dead, the orc runner's western path yielded nothing of value, which leaves us waiting."

The watchman on the pinnacle shelf leapt down and landed with a quiet *thump* next to the huddle. "Watchmaster, we have movement."

Sireth straightened. "An eastern runner?"

"A bird. One flew in from the south with a parcel in its clutches. Now an orc looks to be preparing the parcel for another. If the fresh bird flies east, do we follow?"

"No man can track a bird overland," Samar said. "Neither on foot nor horseback—nor even in an airship."

Teegan leveled her forearm, calling her falcon. "Aethia can."

Sireth nodded for his man to return to the shelf, then lifted his chin toward Teegan. "I know Aethia's skills well. If the creature flies east, set her to the hunt." He turned to Samar. "The horses must stay here so we can move with stealth. You will stay with them."

Samar scowled. "I can fight."

"Can you?" Sireth set out an open palm, and the young woman in his troop quickly filled it with the hilt of a sword. He passed it to Samar.

The pilot wove a series of graceful strikes through the air and finished with a thrust. He held the blade in that pose, with his other arm arced over his head and his right foot balanced against his left knee.

The watchmen just looked at him.

Sireth crossed his arms and raised an eyebrow at Teegan and Dag.

Teegan shrugged. "Something Kara teaches them."

The watchmaster dropped his arms and shook his head. "Fine. He can come. We'll have to ride, though. I won't leave the horses here alone."

"Sir!" A harsh whisper came from above. The lookout waved and pointed. "The creature flies east."

Teegan brought her lips close to Aethia's smooth head and whispered, *"Asarol amorgol."* She showed the falcon a flat hand held low, then lifted her arm and sent her flying. "She'll stay close to the rocks, circling back once in a while to keep us on the trail."

Sireth rallied his watchmen with a twirl of his finger. "Then let's get to it."

Samar had spoken true when he said no man could track a bird overland. Without Aethia, they'd have lost the gall buzzard, especially with the day quickly fading. But had he not insisted on coming, and thus forced them to ride instead of walk, they might have fallen too far behind. The creature moved far more swiftly than Teegan had expected.

Night was coming, and with it that space between the sun and the moons where only the stars gave faint light. The falcon kept both the party and their quarry in sight, coming back to Teegan low, a hand's breadth above the rocks, and waiting for her sign before returning to the hunt.

Teegan laid eyes on the buzzard only twice during their

pursuit. In each case, the creature had landed, likely from the exhausting speed of its flight. On the second sighting, the party had gained ground, thanks to the horses and level terrain, and Teegan was sure she saw the creature give a despairing, frustrated shake of its head before leaping into the air again. Did it despise itself or its masters? Or both?

When the creature stopped for good, none in the party saw it—except Aethia. The falcon hovered, then returned to Teegan's arm, her signal that the quarry had not moved for some time. But when they crept up a rise to look, they saw nothing.

"Your bird is defective," Samar said.

Dag frowned at him, an imposing frown raining down from the great height of his saddle. "Quiet, you. Keep looking." In that moment, Teegan decided he'd be a great asset as a swordmaster at Orvyn's Vow. Either that, or he'd send the novices running scared back to their villages.

Aethia had brought them to a flat gravel plain broken by a single large rock feature—a long bulging cylinder like a fat worm the size of a cathedral.

"Where's the creature, girl?" Teegan stroked the falcon's head. "Where'd that nasty bird thing go?"

Aethia chuffed and clucked, black eyes burning into the giant rock worm.

Samar snorted. "Defective. As I said."

Aethia had first belonged to Teegan's mehma, her tehpa's first and only love. He'd joined her, and later Teegan, on many hunts and had often spoken of the falcon's worth and the surety of her eyes. Teegan spurred her horse to come alongside his and bent near him. "She's telling me the creature's inside that stone worm. And I believe her."

"As do I," Sireth said, dismounting. "Keep low and follow me. I know what this is."

Leaving the horses, they ran along the darkening rise to the shelter of another rock formation. From there, Teegan could just see the eastern mouth of the worm. The roof sloped low over the gravel plain, but the mouth was still broad enough to march a platoon of orcs inside.

Samar shook his head. "It's an aboveground cave. No wonder the Airguard spotters never saw any dark creatures here."

Dag knelt beside Teegan and her tehpa. "I've seen this before."

"As have I—on the road from Ravencrest to Mer Nimbar, and other places in these mountains. When the Rescuer brought the peaks up from the hill country, whole caverns and tunnels rose into the light. I'll wager this worm, as Teegan called it, was part of an ancient underground river passage, now isolated and exposed on the surface."

"Which makes it an excellent hideout," Teegan said. "Large enough for a company. We must take care. There may be hundreds inside."

The flat plain made a stealthy assault impossible. Sireth gathered his party close. "We must discover what that worm conceals, but there is no safe approach. Elamhavar waits for us. Today is as good a day as any to enter."

"So . . ." Samar said. "By that, you mean—"

Dag thumped him on the back. "You should stay here."

"I will not. Why must you all count me out at every turn?"

The miner's hard features turned angry. "*Stay. Here.*"

The watchmen muttered their agreement, and Sireth thrust his chin at Samar. "Do as he says. If we don't return, ride hard to the nearest ravenpost and get word of this hideout to Ras Telesar." After a grudging nod from the pilot, Sireth turned to Teegan and Tiran. "I would say the same to you, beloved children. Not only for your sakes, but for my people. When you fight as lightraiders, I leave you in the Rescuer's hands. When you fight beside me, I'm tempted to guard you with my own—an insult to his sovereignty and a danger to my watchmen."

"But you know," Tiran said, lowering his chin, "that it's folly not to use such lightraiders in this assault."

"Just so."

Teegan nodded. "Then be at peace. We're honored to fight beside you."

With no other words, Sireth hefted his war hammer and charged across the gravel plain. The rest followed.

Even Samar.

Hearing more crunching footfalls than she should have, Teegan glanced left and saw him. "What are you doing?"

"Oh," he said, looking surprised. "You wanted me to stay behind? I guess I didn't understand." He shrugged. "Must be my lack of experience."

Neither she nor Dag had time to argue. A roar from ahead demanded all their attention.

A winged creature with a reptilian face—like a cross between a dragon and a man—flew out from the worm's mouth. Jeweled rings glowed upon his fingers, as did the runes etched into his talons and the horns jutting out from the cape at his shoulders.

"Granog!" Dag shouted, pushing out ahead of even Sireth. "Keep back!"

The creature landed on the plain in a ring of deep red fire and answered him. "Lightraider. It will be a pleasure to make you my first kill in this twice-cursed land."

15

FOUR GOBLINS RAN OUT FROM THE MOUTH OF THE worm-shaped cave, rushing the party—cave goblins, gray-skinned with bulbous warts.

The young woman from Sireth's party loosed an arrow at the incoming creatures. The missile passed too close to the granog, and he slashed it from the air with a flick of his long, curved sword. The pieces burst into flame.

At the same time, another watchman shot a crossbow bolt. This made it past the granog and sank into a goblin's chest. The creature pitched forward into the gravel and skidded to a stop on its face, unmoving. The granog growled.

Dag growled back. "Soulless corruption. These are your last breaths. Use them well, for naught but the empty void awaits you."

Before his words had settled, the goblins reached him. One lost its head to his axe. A second ducked the swing of Dag's other axe, but Teegan struck out with her net, and her weights pierced its mushroom flesh with many wounds. The goblin dropped to its knees, and Dag finished it off.

The last flung itself at Teegan's tehpa, whose ghostly Keledan shield glowed with the rose color of a sunset, flashing against rabid blows from the goblin's knife. He stepped into the attack with an underhand swing of his hammer and bashed the creature back into its master's fire, senseless.

"Trespassers!" Sireth shouted at the granog. "What is your purpose here?"

The granog lifted the charred goblin by its neck, until its webbed feet dangled. "To reclaim that which belongs to Heleyor." He tossed the goblin with such power that it sailed over their heads, and he grinned at the sickening *crunch* as it landed behind them. "We've come to take back what is ours."

Smoke gathered around the granog's rings. With a pass of its hand, it sent a dark cloud rolling toward the party.

"Shields!" Teegan cried. "Don't breathe!"

All obeyed, so it seemed. The colors of their shields lit the plain. A watchman coughed. The cloud pressed in upon him. The granog spewed black slime his way.

The watchman's shield flickered, burning much of the slime into white vapor. Some, however, got through and clung to the watchman's cheek and neck. He howled and turned away. "No! I can't die here. What good would it serve?"

The watchman's sudden retreat exposed his back. A dart flew from the granog's hand.

With armor blazing gold, another from Sireth's party threw himself into the dart's path. His shield held and sent it spinning off into the dirt.

Dag and Tiran shouted a cheer.

Teegan smiled to see such skill and self-sacrifice until, through the shimmering gold Keledan helmet, she saw the fighter's face.

"Samar?"

"Don't gawk. Kill it!"

"No!" Sireth bellowed. "I want it alive!"

Dag either did not hear or did not obey. He charged into the ring of fire. Sireth watched him for a beat, then charged after him. Axe and hammer swung so close together they almost met, but the creature dodged both, taking to the air. He cast a black gem that burst into fire upon Dag's shield while simultaneously fending off a stab of Tiran's sword.

Likely, the lightraiders alone among the fighters knew anything of granogs—their dangers and weaknesses. Granogs hated to fly but would not hesitate to take to the air if needed in battle. Still, because they rarely used their wings, they were not skilled in the air.

Samar had shown agility in saving the watchman. Now he stood apart, guarding the wounded man, twirling the borrowed sword as if waiting for his chance.

With a glance skyward, Teegan uttered a sacred verse, a directive from the High One known to wound self-serving corruptions and the dragons that animated them. *"Men soqafel do ga'ol pal sehnol, dar bi tevremat kuran kashah someh precor ka'ov."*

Do nothing out of selfish ambition, but consider others more important than yourselves.

The granog jerked and dipped in his flight. She narrowed her focus to a thick, fleshy bulge where his right wing met his back and let her trident fly.

The tines found their target. The granog roared and fell toward Dag and Sireth. Both landed hard blows that flashed against his pyranium armor and knocked him away toward Samar.

The creature tumbled in a chaotic bid to regain his flight, spewing black slime in all directions.

"Samar, now!" Teegan shouted.

The pilot was already moving. He launched himself off a small boulder and brought his sword over his head in a high arc. The blade cut deep into the granog's neck. The creature slammed into the rocks.

By the time the granog landed, Dag was there. He shouldered Samar away, earning a frown from the pilot, and set his axes to work. Tiran and the remaining watchmen arrived a beat later to add strikes of their own, but perhaps without need.

Sireth barked at them all to cease, but by the time the fighters pulled back, little that was recognizable as a creature remained of the head and torso. "Did you not hear me?" he asked Dag, pounding his hammer into the gravel. "I wanted the thing alive so we might question it."

"Better that you didn't." Teegan recovered her trident, still embedded in its wing. "Granogs are dangerous in close. Their claws are deadly and poisoned, and they employ all manner of dragon sorcery. A wounded granog is perhaps the most dangerous of all." She shifted her gaze to Samar, who was using the creature's cape to wipe the black blood from his sword. "Don't use that, Samar. But . . . well done."

He let the cape go and acknowledged her praise with a nod.

Sireth shook his head. "The last few days were all for naught. How are we to know the granog's purpose here?" As if to answer his own question, he turned his gaze to the aboveground cave.

Before inspecting the cave, the party saw to their wounded comrade. Their archer cleaned the man's cheek and neck, removing the slime, which left behind an ugly rash. Teegan applied a balm from her manykit, and together, she, Tiran, and Dag asked the Rescuer for healing.

"Stay with him," Sireth told Samar.

The pilot didn't question the order this time. "I will, sir."

"And I will too," Dag added, looking around. "It wouldn't do for a stray creature to ambush just two."

Sireth seemed to consider this. They didn't know what they might find inside the cave, and Teegan could see he thought of Dag as a great asset in battle. But after a moment, he relented. "All right. The three of you, then. Stay here."

The rest hurried across the plain to the mouth of the rock worm, wary of more dark creatures. Only the gall buzzard came at them, shrieking its *Gall! Gall!* cry. An arrow from the archer brought it low, and Teegan's trident took it down. Tiran removed its head with his sword.

Inside they found a large, winding cavern littered with animal bones and scattered firepits.

Sireth struck a torch he found near the entrance, where curtain walls, a mattress, and a chest of clothes marked the granog's lodgings. Within the curtained room, they also found a makeshift table formed by boulders and a large, flat rock. Ashes and charred parchment scraps were strewn about its top. Teegan poked at them with her dagger. "This was a map. Still warm. The granog burned it before coming out to challenge us."

Her tehpa lifted a silk tunic from the chest. "I did not know any dark creatures dressed this well. What purpose do granogs serve north of the barrier?"

"They manage the other dark creatures," she told him.

Tiran nodded. "They keep the Aladoth constables and town leaders in line. In Tanelethar, they are dragon administrators."

"Here, I'd say they may function as generals." Sireth rubbed the silk between his fingers. "But where are this general's troops?"

Fire lit the cave deeper in. The watchmen had found stands with larger torches and set them ablaze, exposing row after row of dust and straw gathered into what might have been goblin-size beds. "They're gone," the watchmen archer said. "There were a hundred here, perhaps more. They're all gone, and the earth under the cooking fires is stone cold."

Sireth let the granog's silk tunic fall and wiped his hand on his trousers. "We've come too late."

16

THE KINGFISHER STOPPED ONLY FOR PROVISIONS, landing on larger timber platforms in Silknest and Elamnest, both towns that had sprung up around new Airguard cloudlofts. Connor was grateful for these stations—for the chance to touch solid ground for a bit—but also because they were positioned deeply inland. The last time he'd made an air journey between Sky Harbor and the academy, Zel had flown them up the coast, and the Rescuer had thrust them into the Storm Mists for an unexpected mission.

Aaron and his passengers all slept on board, taking shifts at the rudder so they might travel all the faster. He showed Connor and Kara how to keep the bow straight and use the vents to fly with the changing height of the wind. And he made them promise to wake him at the slightest hint of trouble.

"Don't worry," Connor had told him as Aaron laid his head down on the stern bench for his first rest. "You'll feel the toe of my boot the moment I spot so much as an overlarge hawk or a darkened cloud."

They neared the southern peaks of the White Ridge Mountains in the midmorning of the second day, around the time the high winds flowing south were gaining speed. Aaron brought

The Kingfisher lower to slow her down, aiming for Skynest, the Airguard's main cloudloft on Crescent Ridge, which hooked out around the city harbor.

The blue dome of the Second Hall shone from the harbor plaza, the chief jewel in a dazzling mosaic of a thousand smaller gems— the many-colored rooftops pressed together along the arched stone roads leading down in step after step from the foothills to the sea.

"You never told me of the city's beauty," Kara said, taking Connor's arm and resting her head against his shoulder. "I might've made the trip sooner."

Did she know this was the first time she'd leaned against him since they'd left Ras Telesar? He didn't ask but savored the kindness and warmth of her touch and hoped he might not say something to put her off.

"I . . . um . . ." he began. "I never saw it from this height, to tell the truth. Last time, Lee and I arrived by water and left under the cover of darkness." A tinge in Connor's chest warned him to let the statement end there, but he ignored it. "Perhaps I'm glad you didn't want to see Sky Harbor. As busy as the Order keeps us, you'd have had to come without me, likely carried by your friend Samar."

She dropped his arm.

Connor closed his eyes for a beat. Right. Why hadn't he just kept silent?

She looked up at him. "Why do you dislike him so?"

"I'm sorry. I've behaved poorly toward him since the moment you two arrived together. It's just that he's so . . ."

"Striking? Agile? Confident?"

Connor looked down and saw her smirking. He frowned. "He made you laugh."

Her smirk faded. "Oh. Well . . . you make me laugh too."

"Not with such ease."

Behind them, Aaron coughed. "I hate to interrupt, but would you two mind moving apart so the pilot might see where he's going?"

They obeyed, but Kara patted the wicker as she took a seat on the bow bench. "Sit with me, Connor." Again, she took his arm, much to his relief. "Does returning to the capital feel strange? You must get the sense all this has happened before—a bit of bloviating by Stradok sends you rushing south to stand before the Assembly in the fabled Sky Chamber."

"I do get such a sense," Connor said, half-distracted by the lavender scent of her platinum hair. He cleared his throat. "That part . . . um . . . worries me a bit."

Kara glanced up at him with a crease in her brow.

He met her gaze and shrugged. "Last time, I never made it to the Sky Chamber."

17

"LEWAKERS."

Connor heard the grumbled judgment as he passed the guards at the entry to the Second Hall. The word was an insult to lightraiders, common enough in the capital, implying they carried imaginary burdens of service to the Aladoth.

Zayn Boreas caught his upper arm before he could turn and answer. "Leave it, Cadet. I'll deal with him later. Right now, keep your mind on the task at hand. Too much rides on you and your friends in this moment."

Too much rides on you. Oh, how Connor felt this.

Before the councilor's caution, he'd wanted to snap at the guard. Now he wanted to flee. From the tension in Kara's hand, clutched in his, she wanted the same.

Not possible.

Flanked by Boreas and three younger assemblymen, they had no choice but to continue up the steps and into the colorful light of the Sky Chamber's high stained glass windows.

A wall of voices met them—a curtain of sound Connor had to push through to keep walking. On scouting missions in Tanelethar, he'd seen palestran in the villages—round timber or stone structures with thatched roofs and stepped benches along the wall. Fighting rings. The Aladoth used them for wagers and beating one another to a pulp.

The Sky Chamber had its beautiful windows, the glade-green marble floor, and the starry-sky mural above, but to Connor it looked and sounded much the same. And he and Kara were the fighters.

The loud murmur from the circular gallery changed as his party entered, not louder or quieter but different—more directed. What wagers were these assemblymen placing? Did they expect the lightraiders to leave this day with a prize or with swollen and bloodied faces?

Boreas bid them stay with his followers on the marble floor and climbed a round podium, raising his hands. "Good councilors!"

The noise continued.

"Good councilors! Let us have quiet, please!"

A few others around the chamber repeated his call, and the clamor settled.

Boreas gave them a grateful nod. "Shall we pray?"

The Airguard and Apothecarists' Guild chief lifted his eyes to the crystal skylight at the center of the dome and praised the High One. He offered thanks for the provision of sustenance and life to all Keledan and asked forgiveness for all in the name of the High One's son, the Rescuer. He implored the High One to banish the dragons and restore all Talania under his care. Then, finally, he asked for wisdom.

Connor knew Boreas well enough to understand his sincerity in prayer. But what of these others in the palestra gallery? Were they praying the same in their hearts, or were they seeking their own understanding?

Which was Connor seeking?

Kara leaned close. "Connor. Wake up."

Boreas had finished the prayer and posed some kind of question. The chamber waited on the lightraiders' response.

Boreas coughed, casting Connor a sidelong glance. "I shall

repeat myself to be sure *all* in the chamber heard. Cadets Enarian and Orso, I understand the Lightraider Order believes the Taneletharian incursions are worsening. Is this correct?"

Connor did not manage a response until one of the councilor's followers subtly poked him in the ribs. He straightened "Yes. It's not a belief. It's truth."

A few groans and chuckles from the gallery told Connor he was botching this. So did one of Boreas's men. The councilor's follower whispered in Connor's ear. "Some here in Sky Harbor have made a rule of not saying *truth* except in reference to the Scrolls, and they draw offense from those who do. Take care with your words."

Connor took his meaning. *Stick to the script we rehearsed at Skynest.*

"Please," Boreas said, gesturing to Connor and Kara, "come up to the podium and elaborate."

Keeping to the plan, Connor and Kara walked up the short steps together. He raised his voice to start again, beginning with the opening phrase Boreas had taught him. "Good councilors—hearts and tongues of Keledev . . ." What was that last part? Oh, yes. "Thank you for granting us your ears. We—"

A call from the gallery interrupted him. "Stop shouting, boy, or these ears of ours may all go deaf."

Some frowned. Others laughed.

Boreas had warned him. The dome served a purpose beyond beauty. All those beneath it could hear the speaker, no matter how softly they spoke. That was why the chamber had seemed to grow so loud the moment he stepped onto the marble floor.

Connor gave his detractor a fleeting smile and softened his voice. "We come with news from the Celestial Peaks. The dark creature presence grows stronger."

No one showed much surprise. Rumors had traveled south. His declaration only gave them credence. Together, he and Kara told the Assembly of the recent events—a near doubling of skirmishes with orcs and goblins, the missing watchmen led by Sireth Yar, the missing lightraider and Airguard scouts, and the gall buzzards' attempted strike at Mount Challenge. They did not mention Zel Boreas's name in this report, at her father's request. Neither did they mention Lef Amunrel—not yet. Boreas had warned them against this too.

An argument depends not on your words alone, he'd said, drinking hot cider with the cadets on the highest platform of Cloudloft Skynest while Aaron tended to their ship. *Success hangs upon the way you present those words. You must play your part in the drama well and lead your opponents in playing theirs.*

Kara had not seemed to like this. *It sounds as if you're describing deceit.*

Boreas had answered with a soft grunt, the kind a parent gives a child. *Not deceit, Cadet. Strategy, as sure as any strategy your swordmaster teaches you for the battlefield. And you must learn it well if we hope to take your plan forward.*

Following his own script, Boreas looked to the gallery and spread his arms beneath his crimson robes. "Good councilors, what remedies do you propose? How can we meet these new threats?"

The noise began. How any one of them understood the others, Connor could not say. Amid the melee, he heard solutions and counters like those proposed at Master Jairun's gathering.

"We need more weapons."

"And who will wield them?"

"A new wave of fighters. The outpost companies must send recruiters to the towns."

"Not my town, thank you. Ours is emptied of its young and able. We've no one left to tend the flocks or fields."

After a time, one voice rose above the others—another of Boreas's followers, standing near the top of the stepped gallery. "What of the Red Dagger?" Again, part of the script.

This bought a moment's respite from the clamor, and Boreas took full advantage. "Do you mean Lef Amunrel, the last celestium weapon?"

"Yes, good councilor. Could it not end this war and solve much? Can it not destroy Heleyor? If only we knew where to find it."

"If only!" The same assemblyman that had rebuked Connor for his shouting now shouted as well. He pushed his way down to the green marble floor and lowered his tone, though it carried the same scorn. "But that is a dream, since a lightraider lost the dagger years ago."

This was Connor's cue, an expected argument from the very man Boreas had told him would make it. Connor gave the planned response, sticking to the formal tongue of Sky Harbor. "Good councilors, Lef Amunrel is not lost. That lightraider, my grandfather"—the formal word for patehpa felt strange on his lips—"found the dagger years later. With your permission, a lightraider party might set out to retrieve it this very night."

Connor's announcement rekindled the uproar in earnest—a cycle he was beginning to understand.

Boreas nodded. They were winning. What had seemed a festival drama when the councilor proposed it was, indeed, a battle plan—as good as any blend of advances, feints, and flanking Quinton had taught them.

All went well until the next quiet, when Connor, at a subtle wave from Boreas's follower, proposed a daring raid into Ras Pyras to destroy Heleyor while he lounged on his flaming throne.

"That is not your place, Cadet," the man who'd pushed his way down to the floor said. "Not yours or any lightraider's. Heleyor's destruction belongs to the Rescuer."

This, also, Boreas had anticipated. A Keledan's right—or lack of right—to strike out at the heart of evil stood at the very core of the argument against the Order's existence. These were the voices who'd shuttered Ras Telesar, dispersing the lightraiders. Despite all that had happened in the last two years, their influence remained strong.

Boreas had given Kara the next act of the drama, as one who'd been rescued from a life under dragon oppression. He thought she'd be the Order's best advocate.

But Kara never got the chance to play her part.

"You fools!" Aaron Ilmari shouted from the gallery. "You mindless, doddering fools, squandering precious beats and ticks in your grand palace!"

"Where'd he come from?" Connor whispered to Kara. "We left him at Skynest."

The councilor opposing their cause had the same question. "How did you get in here?"

Aaron ignored him and walked down the benches to the floor, lecturing them all as he went. "You sip your spiced teas on this sun-kissed harbor, far from the dangers of the barrier, while the Airguard and the watchmen spend their blood on icy slopes to protect you. And you think you have a say in how we—"

A guard—the same guard who'd called Connor a lewaker—ended the pilot's speech by wrapping an arm around his neck. He and others dragged Aaron stumbling and shouting from the floor. The guards hauled him out of the room, voice fading to nothing outside the circle of the dome.

The opposing councilor shook his finger in Aaron's direction and addressed the Assembly. "This is what such radical ideas breed. Contempt for order. Disregard for tradition. Disrespect for the leaders appointed by the Rescuer and his Keledan!"

Boreas tried to respond.

The man shouted him down. "Was that not one of your own Airguard pilots? I saw the cloud symbol on his tunic sleeve." He let out a hard laugh. "Ah. Now I see it. That young man was part of one of your famous dramas, concocted to steer us. We'll have no more of it, Boreas. This discussion is ended. Time for a vote." He turned to glare at Connor and Kara. "All those who are not elected assemblymen must *leave*."

The remaining guards helped Connor and Kara down from the podium, if *helped* meant tugging and shoving. The chamber's massive bronze doors clanged shut behind them.

The two walked out into the cool breeze blowing off the harbor. Connor plopped down the plaza steps, between the columns of the Second Hall's portico, not far from Aaron. The pilot sat with his head in his hands.

"So"—Kara sat between them—"that went well."

18

"WE NEED TO GET WORD SOUTH," TEEGAN SAID. "WE need to warn them of what's coming."

She unrolled a map from her manykit on the flat rock, under the light of Sireth's torch, and traced a finger along the original route she and Dag took from the academy. "Aethia found you north of our road, watching the orc messenger post, and then tracked the gall buzzard here." She tapped the flat plain where they'd found the aboveground cave. "The nearest ravenpost is the new one, two ticks south."

"One tick, if we ride fast." Her tehpa glanced over his shoulder at his wounded fighter, whom Samar and Dag had brought into the cave. "We'll need to split up." He thrust his chin at Tiran. "You and Cadet Kaivos take my watchmen and ride to Orvyn's Vow, the nearest outpost. They'll need you if the goblins are headed there. Teegan and I will race to the ravenpost and send warnings in all directions."

When they reached the horses and mounted up, Samar steered his mare to ride next to Dag's Gladion stallion.

The miner shook his head. "No. Go with Teegan."

"But," Samar said, "Orvyn's Vow is my posting. It's where I belong."

"It's dangerous. If the goblins are there, I won't be burdened with protecting you."

The pilot looked to Teegan. "Do you hear this? I think he's forgotten the whole of this evening."

"Dag . . ." Teegan said.

But Dag shook his head. "Take him with you. A ravenpost is far safer than an outpost under attack."

Teegan didn't want to argue, and Sireth only rolled his eyes. She sighed. "Come on, Samar. Ride with us. And you'd better not slow us down."

"My," the pilot said. "What a harshness you all carry in your hearts."

Sireth spurred his gelding to a trot. "This is a harsh world. Much more so than only two years ago."

They made good time on the way to the ravenpost, leaving the paths and trails and racing overland when necessary to keep the straightest line. Teegan was first to spot the tower under the rising moons. "A light burns in the upper room. The ravenmaster is still awake."

Not true.

They found the ravenmaster on the tower steps, with all his life poured out through many cuts and stab wounds.

Samar turned aside, ill.

Sireth closed the man's eyes. "He's been tortured. But to what purpose, I can't imagine."

"To the purpose of suffering," Teegan said. "The goblins thrive on it. Such was the Evil One's design when he twisted fungus to make them. In Heleyor's cruel mind, torturing the High One's beloved creations also tortures the High One himself."

They spoke a prayer over the old man's body, then continued up the steps with weapons drawn. They moved slowly at first, until Teegan drew a breath. She looked to her tehpa. "The ravens."

All three ran.

Birds lay strewn about the upper room and in the bottom of

their cages, dead and bleeding. A few still lived, suffering from severed wings. Teegan and her tehpa did for them what mercy demanded. Every stroke of her dagger broke her heart. "Wicked monsters," she said through her tears.

Samar held back at the edge of the room. "Are there none left to carry the warning south?"

Sireth shook his head.

"But you have a bird, Teegan. Could we not tie a scroll to Aethia's leg and—"

"No." She glanced at the window and the pines outside. Aethia had taken up a perch there to watch. She seemed sad as well. Ravens were not among the creatures she saw as prey. "She's a huntress, not a messenger. She needs a quarry. Even if I could convince her to fly south, she'd circle back when I failed to follow."

"Then we must take it ourselves." In three long strides, Samar crossed the room to the ravenmaster's desk, at the end of the cages. He brushed dead birds aside, causing a ripple of thumps as their bodies hit the wood plank floor.

Teegan drew a sharp breath.

Sireth scowled.

Samar glanced over his shoulder and grimaced. "Sorry." Then he lifted the lamp and raised the desktop to show them a carving of the tower and the surrounding terrain on its underside. "The Airguard and the ravenmasters worked together when we built these new ravenposts." He panned the lamp over the carving. "Each has a map of the station like this one. Also, there may still be a . . . Yes!" Samar dropped the desktop and started for the stairwell. "This way. Pray the goblins didn't find it."

"Find what?" Sireth asked, following with Teegan.

A hatch in the ground floor revealed a second set of stairs— outside on the south face of the slope below the tower. Samar led Sireth and Teegan down these to a platform hidden by a half dome of timber and woven pine boughs. Under the dome, with its one silk envelope hanging loose upon its frame, stood a small airship.

Samar patted its wicker rail. "Since we've no birds left to do the job, we must make the flight ourselves."

"How fast can you make her ready?" Sireth asked.

"Give me one tick. If they've gone deeper into Keledev, we may yet outpace this goblin company. The air is rough at night, but it moves fast and low on these mountains."

Teegan was not so certain. She remembered her first encounter with goblins, farther south in Dayspring Forest, on the road to Ravencrest. That night, though she, Connor, and Tiran rode on horseback, the goblins had passed them by in total silence, gaining ample time to prepare an ambush. "You haven't seen these creatures as I have. They are far faster than humans and near tireless on the march."

"So are these airships," Samar countered. "This is a newer one, lighter and faster." He paused, lowering his hands. "But it will only carry two of us. One must stay behind to aid the launch." Samar turned and gave them a half grin. "And you can't set me aside this time. I have to fly it."

Sireth walked to the ship, inspecting its wicker hull and the bags of sand around it. "Just tell me what to do, Pilot. I must take the horses on to Orvyn's Vow, anyway, and rejoin my watchmen."

With the other two helping, the pilot had her ready to fly in half the time he proposed. With the single lamp burning and the envelope full of vapor, the skids hovered a hand's breadth above the platform.

"The slope leaves no place to run a horse for the launch," Teegan said, climbing aboard.

Samar worked the dial on the lamp, and the ship rose a step higher. "Your father is the horse." He lifted a rope attached to the bow ring and guided Sireth in the work of tracing it to a sandbag. "When I give the signal, toss the bag over the platform's edge. I'll do the rest."

Once they were at treetop height, Samar gave Sireth a sharp salute, and the watchmaster heaved the sandbag off the platform.

The rope ran through a pulley on a tall post and another pulley a good half furlong away, towing the ship into motion.

"The Rescuer is with you!" Teegan called to her father as Samar slapped a lever to release the rope. They sailed out into the night with Sireth waving behind them.

Samar managed the rough air well, heading downslope along the tips of the pines. *The Jackdaw*—the name burned into the ship's bow rail—bucked and shook.

"She wants to fly higher!" Teegan shouted, gripping the wicker bench. She had yet to ride in one of these things and quickly decided they were even worse than Connor claimed.

Samar never took his eyes off the dark line ahead between the trees and the night sky. "Of course she does. That's her nature. But the lower air is faster until we pass Red Willow Hill."

By the time Teegan saw the famed willow off the starboard bow, her stomach had turned inside out. Only the desire to be strong in front of the prideful airman kept her from casting what little food she'd eaten that day over the rail.

Finally, Samar added flame to the lanterns and released *The Jackdaw* into the smoother air she desired. They climbed high enough to see far out over the Central Plain. The light there held Teegan's gaze. She rose from the bench and walked on uneasy legs to the bow. "Are you certain you've pointed us south, not east?"

He gave her a flat look. "Yes."

"I only ask because of the light on the horizon. It looks like the dawn."

"We've barely broken the second watch of the night. Dawn is many ticks away."

He was right, but also as mystified as Teegan. They both stared hard. From what Teegan could tell, the orange light stretched from the bank of the Anamturas to the Eastern Hills. Indeed, as she'd first thought, it lit the clouds above it like a sunrise.

Samar spoke aloud the thought on both their minds. "This is a dire sign."

19

WAKE, SLAVE. WAKE AND MEET YOUR QUEEN.

Shan's eyes fluttered open to meet a dark no different from when they were shut. He sat up in his bed and pushed the silk coverings to his knees.

A year before, when he first met Lord Valshadox, the dragon's thoughts in his mind had been as a powerful will vying with his own. A painful and fruitless battle. Once he'd bent to that will, joined his to its flow, the pain vanished. Since then, he'd become accustomed to the voice. Always there. Always instructing. Always protecting him.

He rose and lit his lantern, keeping the fire dim. The embrace of night gave him comfort so that he hardly remembered ever wanting to walk in daylight.

Dress. Wear your armor. Pack for a journey.

The time had come, then. The army, driven by the wood troll Moach and his barkhides, had left days ago to begin its final march. Lord Valshadox had bid him stay behind. *You'll join them later,* the dragon had told him. *You have other tasks that need attending. Enjoyable tasks.*

Shan hoped tonight might bring one of those. He lifted a knife from his stone sorcerer's table—a lightraider sikari knife with two blades extending from a central hilt—and hefted it in his hand before tucking it into his belt. Usually a sikari was part of a set, called sikaria. The owner must feel the loss of this one. "Oh, Trang, my brother. I suppose you were close. Let's hope you may still find me."

The army had carried most of what he required when it left so that when he joined them his tent would be waiting. When Shan walked the steps down from his tower in the southeast corner of the dragon's stronghold, he wore only a small pack over his hooded cloak and black armor.

A pair of wanderers, with their wan, deathly faces and lanterns forever outstretched, met him at the stronghold gates.

"So," he asked, smirking, "where are we going?"

The creatures only turned and floated ahead, leading him down the trail. Shan had expected no response. He doubted they could speak.

Sil Shadath's gray-green mist gathered at his knees, and Shan waded through, enjoying the cool kiss of the wisps rising to his cheeks. Passing a low branch, he allowed one of the spiders with its bulbous, pulsating abdomen to walk upon his finger. The foolish insect crawled across the jeweled knuckles of his armored glove and then attempted to jab its fangs into the pyranium steel.

Shan snorted and touched a finger to the insect. It burst into dark orange flame.

The wanderers slowed, and one turned to stare at him with empty, hollow eyes.

Shan frowned. "For its insolence. Lead on."

They brought him to a nearby hill, but rather than follow the trail to the top, the creatures led him around its base to a cave opening and stopped.

"Inside, then?"

Neither answered with word or motion.

"Inside, it is."

The cave's walls and its low ceiling boasted crystals of many colors, catching the flicker of his lantern. And at the far end, he found an arch filled with black smoke. Streaks of purple flashed from the edges. This was one of the infamous hollow hill portals, lost to men. And no wonder. The dragons must have built their strongholds near most of the hollow hills—on paths no Aladoth dared to walk without invitation.

He took a step toward the smoke.

Wait.

The dragon voice in his mind stopped him, taking charge of his limbs as well, so that Shan could not have moved if he'd wanted to.

This one changes. You must enter at the proper time . . . now.

Limbs freed, Shan stumbled into the portal and stumbled out again a beat later into far different surroundings. He had the sense of a great cave, walls dripping and stinking of mud, but he couldn't move his gaze from the woman standing before him.

A lady in gray-and-scarlet robes regarded him with amber eyes. A crescent moon was etched into the flesh under her right one.

"Maldora." The name escaped his lips, though he had not known it a moment before.

She took his armored hands and walked backward, leading him down short steps to the chamber floor, then bent close and kissed his lips.

A rush of cold flashed through him. Exhilarating.

Shan smiled when she pulled her lips back again and spoke the name a little louder. "Maldora."

The woman released his hands and walked away. "He'll do."

"I'll *do?*"

Quiet, slave!

Shan's limbs locked in place, a harder, more painful lock than he'd experienced before entering the portal. The voice in his head was not Lord Valshadox. Another name came to him. Lord Zonox.

Arms and legs still frozen, Shan gained control of his neck. He lifted his gaze to the far end of the chamber and found a dragon curled up in a pool of black-and-gray mud. The creature lifted its long snout and unfurled narrow, ribbed wings with a broad span. Mud fell from yellowed spikes of bone protruding from the wing points.

She is your queen, favored one. Be grateful for that blessing, for Maldora is far above your station. You could train for a human lifetime and never meet her skill. She is of the Scarlet Moon.

A Scarlet Moon sorceress. Shan had never met one of their kind, taken as children born on the night Molunos showed its color and taught the craft almost from their first breath.

"Beautiful," he said, regaining his power of speech.

The woman glanced back with a wry smile. "I know."

He felt life in his arms and legs again but held his place. "Why am I here?"

"Don't you know?" Her back remained turned. She worked at a stone table at the center of a circular floor etched with runes. Something gurgled beneath her touch. "You and I are to be wed. We will rule."

Finally. "My kin, yes?"

The dragon's head rolled to one side, and a yellow eye fell upon him.

You and Maldora will be the true king and queen while two others sit on the thrones. Such arrangements have often been of service to us in centuries past.

"So we are to be advisors."

"In title, we'll be the duke and duchess." Maldora raised a dagger above her head, allowing the dragon to blow a curl of deep green smoke around it, then plunged it down. The thing on the table twitched. "Until such time as the king and queen fall prey to tragedy. Then we will take our place."

Shan eased a step forward. Then another. Feathers. He saw black feathers on the table, covered in slime. Blood trickled from grooves cut in the table's round top. "And our army . . . my love?"

She looked back with a dark stare. "There's no need for that."

My army, the dragon said in his mind, *not yours. It waits at the crossing. Your master will serve me by holding this end open while I lead them through. But there have been delays.*

After this, the dragon seemed to focus on Maldora. She continued her work, unperturbed by its malice, and lifted a bundle from the floor. "The orcs gave the last bird away. Their march drew too much attention. This one will fly unseen to a new target I've divined."

It is not what we planned.

"It is better, my lord." She looked up at the dragon. "I assure you."

What a powerful woman indeed to speak to a dragon lord this way. Shan took another two steps and saw her stuff the bundle inside the twitching thing on the table. Had he not heard her discussion with the dragon, he would not have recognized it as a bird, but a bird it was—broken and ungainly with huge wings and a crooked neck.

Maldora touched the dagger to a ring on her finger, and the blade grew white-hot. This she applied to the bird and closed the wound she'd made, sealing the bundle within. "Stand."

The creature obeyed, buzzard head bowed. It squawked, and under those terrible noises, Shan heard words. *Why must you hurt me? Why do you hate me?*

"Silence," Maldora said. "This is your purpose." She held a dark gray stone to its beak. "Swallow this. It will lead you to your goal once you pass the breach. Go."

Without another sound, the creature spread its ugly wings and flew up through a hole in the chamber ceiling.

Maldora held up the still red-hot dagger with a hand covered in blood and slime. "Now, my husband. Come near and let us sanctify our union."

"Heh . . ." Shan said with a quick and nervous grin—without drawing near. Not yet. He held some value in this union. Else, Valshadox would not have chosen him. "My kin. The Keledan. They will suffer, yes?"

Maldora touched her finger to her dagger's tip, as if to test its sharpness. "Yes."

"When? For I desire retribution. How long must I wait?"

"Oh, husband." Maldora closed the gap between them and traced the dagger along his breastplate. "Fret not." She lifted her eyes to his. "Their suffering has already begun."

PART TWO

WINDFIGHTER

"But when he saw the strength of the wind, he was afraid, and beginning to sink he cried out, 'Lord, save me!' Immediately Jesus reached out his hand, caught hold of him, and said to him, 'You of little faith, why did you doubt?' When they got into the boat, the wind ceased. Then those in the boat worshiped him and said, 'Truly you are the Son of God.'"

Matthew 14:30-33

20

"DRAGON! A DRAGON IN KELEDEV!"

Bells rang all over the city, shaking Connor from his sleep. A terrible cry he'd heard in his dreaming came to his ears in wakefulness.

"Dragon! A dragon in Keledev!"

The scent of smoke added credence to the claim.

Kara appeared at his door, fumbling with the straps of her manykit. "Do you hear that?"

"How could I not?" Connor threw on his own manykit and sheathed his ebony crook at his back. His sword, Revornosh, he kept ready in his fist. "Can it be true? Would the Rescuer allow a dragon to enter Keledev?"

The look Kara gave him told him she had no answer. But they'd both discussed their suspicions. Goblins had come. Then orcs and trolls. Why not a dragon next?

She stepped back from the threshold to give him room as he entered the hall. "We must find Boreas."

They didn't need to look far. A middle-aged man wearing a blue-gray Airguard cloak flagged them down as the two stepped out from the small residence where the Assembly had put them. He towed a pair of mares behind him. "Lightraiders, Councilor Boreas requests your presence at Skynest. Your skills are needed."

"Yes, they are." Connor sheathed his sword and swung himself into the saddle. "We must reach the fighting as soon as possible. Your commander should've sent a ship."

The airman glanced over his shoulder toward the cloudloft. "There were none to spare."

The bells never ceased their clanging as the three rode downslope to the main road. Citizens shouted. Boots and hooves pounded stone and gravel. Archers appeared at the battlements of the capital's new watchtowers, gazing skyward. City guards in rich livery, well armed with halberds and swords, ran past at every crossing street.

"Where are they going?" Kara asked.

"Some to their posts," the airman replied. "Some, I imagine, don't know. Confusion reigns."

"And the dragon?"

"I've not seen one yet, nor any other dark creature."

"Typical of the Keledan," Connor said. "Battle is upon us, yet we can't find the front."

The airman lifted his chin to the north. "It's there, I think. The sky glows hot on the far side of the White Ridge Mountains, leagues away. Based on the heading, and the way very clouds look to be on fire, I'd say Val Pera burns."

Val Pera. The Sea of Grain. What was it the wheat and barley farmers often said? *Without Val Pera, all Keledan would starve.*

Had Heleyor sought to prove them right?

As the airman turned their party from the main road, upslope again toward the crescent ridge, Connor saw dozens of orange dots brightening and dimming—the flames of airship lamps. He caught the occasional glimpse of rippling moonlight on silk. It seemed the whole of the Airguard had taken to the sky. "They're leaving us behind."

"They're doing their duty, Lightraider." For the first time, Connor heard a touch of anger in the airman's voice. He, too, was being left, unable to join the fight for which he'd trained. "As am I so that I might come running to wake you."

They found Boreas in Skynest's long stone-and-timber hall at the edge of the cloudloft launch platform, poring over a painted map of Keledev sculpted from wood.

"I can hear your thoughts, Cadet Enarian," the councilor said without looking up. "This is a poor imitation of the Aropha map table at Ras Telesar, but we can't all share the privileges of the Order."

Connor wished he could deny thinking as much, but he couldn't. And he had no interest in trading barbs for the sake of rivalry—not while the kingdom's breadbasket burned. "Where is the dragon?"

Boreas came around the table and snapped his fingers toward the shadows in the corner of the hall. "Here comes your dragon now." A pair of airmen dragged a corpse into the lamplight and tossed it at Connor's and Kara's feet.

A cave goblin. Its armor and chest were pierced with a familiar pattern of wounds. Connor looked up at his host. "Did a trident do that?"

"Winnowing fork."

When Boreas said no more, Kara prompted him. "A farmer killed this creature?"

"And many more, before his life was spent, fighting with his wife beside him." Boreas met Connor's eyes. "Don, they called him. Dandy Don and Catherine. I'd have named him Don the Valiant. He'd have made a great warrior."

Connor nodded. "He did make a great warrior, by the sound of it. Catherine too. But what do you mean by saying this creature is our dragon?"

The councilor used the toe of his boot to roll the goblin over, exposing a strange addition to its armor. Two cylinders were bolted to the back. They looked much like the holders for a standard-bearer's pole, except smaller, and both the armor and the creature's fungal flesh were charred above them.

"Some kind of torch," Kara said.

"Correct. But using the tricks of an apothecarist." Boreas gave his men a nod, and they dragged the corpse away. "They used the same brimstone metal Connor brought me, in a cylinder of water. A host of goblins ran through the fields of Val Pera with these mounted to their backs, spouting unquenchable fire in all directions."

Connor watched the airmen disappear with their prize. He wondered what purpose the thing might serve for Boreas now that he'd gleaned from it what information he could. Belen had warned against keeping dark creatures around, even dead, but Connor kept this thought to himself. This was Skynest, not Ras Telesar.

"How do you know of this host?"

"Catherine escaped and reached Cloudloft Barleynest alive to bring us that vital word. A party of airmen returned with her to fight any stragglers. Two small cloudrunners launched for Sky Harbor, each carrying a dead goblin as evidence. One burned and crashed attempting to fly over the fields, taken by the rising embers. The other landed here moments ago."

Connor walked to a tall window looking out across the launch platform. Only one ship remained, with a single envelope—presumably the cloudrunner that had arrived from Val Pera with its rotting cargo. Already, a new crew was making her ready to fly, fixing small crossbows to the rail. "Where are you sending them all?"

"To form a line across the mountains. To engage any foe they find, whether in the scrub or the skies. Val Pera is a great loss. We may not survive another fire attack so close on its heels."

"And us?" Kara asked. "Why didn't you let us fly with your airmen? The man you sent for us said you needed our skills."

"Not your fighting skills. Not tonight, anyway." Boreas shifted his gaze to Connor. "Tonight, I need your statesmanship."

Was he serious? "That is a skill I don't possess."

"Wrong, Cadet. You are untrained"—he raised his brows—"very untrained, but not unskilled. There is a difference. You only need guidance."

"From you?"

"Well, certainly not from Stradok." He joined Connor at the window. "I know you want to be out there, boy. But there are guards in this city. Archers in our towers. My airmen have formed a wall of armed spotters across the mountains. We are defended by those able enough to serve that purpose. They may give their lives this night. Your lives, however, we cannot afford to spend. You and Cadet Orso must be the leaders the Order proclaimed you to be when they placed you in the Navigators' Sphere."

Connor began to catch the assemblyman's intent.

Before he could fully form the thought, Kara gave it voice. "You mean to use this tragedy to change the Assembly's mind. You need us to convince them to reclaim the Red Dagger."

21

SKY HARBOR FAILED TO GLEAM IN THE EVENING THE
way Connor remembered. A haze hung low over the White Ridge
Mountains on the day after the attack, and the sun struggled to
shine through it, leaving the many houses dull and gray. Rain had
come in the morning—a blessed answer to prayer—but it had left
a wet cold clinging to the city.

He found Kara outside on the landing platform, cloak
wrapped tight about her shoulders against a southward breeze
that still smelled of cinders and loss. "Still angry?" he asked.

"Aren't you?" Before he could answer, she shook her head.
"No. Why would you be? You got what you wanted."

"I wanted none of this."

Boreas and his followers in the Assembly had been swift in
their response. *We must reassure the people,* he'd told them. *Once
unleashed, a dragon is hard to contain—even harder, the rumor
of a dragon.*

Connor and Kara had taken this to heart. Not so, the rest of the
Assembly. Those few that gathered at Boreas's call—those willing
to leave the safety of their hearth rooms while the bells still rang
and guards still ran in the streets—insisted on more deliberation.

Ravens were dispatched. New meetings were called for, some

held in the Sky Chamber and others in secret places where lightraider cadets weren't welcome.

"Precious time squandered," Connor said. "For the result is the same."

"How can you say that?" Kara turned to glare at him, her blue-gray flourishes burning on cheeks flecked with dew by the lingering mist. "Had we launched immediately on this quest to seek Lef Amunrel, you and I would be doing it together." She set her gaze on the city again. "Instead I must stay here, a captive of the all-powerful Councilor Boreas, sold to him by our own Order."

Sold seemed a harsh manner of looking at it, but how could Connor argue? "I'm not pleased either. You know that."

When the answering raven had come from Master Jairun, Connor had been stunned. The Order, as expected, accepted the Assembly's change of heart and their decision to send a raid party after the Red Dagger. However, Kara was not to join the quest.

Teegan's own report had been included in the raven sent from the Assembly to the Order, since she and that preening pilot Samar had landed during their deliberations—far too late—with the news that a goblin company had marched from the mountains. Master Jairun counted her presence in Sky Harbor a gift from the Rescuer and bid Teegan go to Tanelethar in Kara's stead.

"Why must I stay here?"

He laid his hand over hers on the cloudloft rail. "Must I really answer?"

"No." She let out a short growl. "The ramblings of that infernal bear are to blame."

"Your good friend."

"Yes. She is." Kara glanced up at him. "But just because a talking Havarra bear says Heleyor wants to capture us both and turn us for some evil purpose doesn't make it true."

He held his expression flat.

Kara sighed. "Perhaps it does."

Much that Connor had witnessed in the last two years bore

up Ioanu's concern, especially the whisperings under the song sorcery of the dark creatures and the invasive thoughts of the dragons Vorax and Valshadox. *Prince. Liege. A royal pair.* In his mind's eye, he saw Valshadox pursuing them both on the wind. *We can be allies.*

He shuddered.

Connor did his best to hold true to Master Jairun's orders in word as well as deed. "We must find the wisdom in the headmaster's choice, no matter how much we wish to have our own way. If we know the enemy's purpose, why place ourselves in his talons?"

"You're going."

"But not both of us. And that's the key, I think."

Kara leaned against him. "When are you leaving?"

"On the morrow. We're waiting for a ship. The whole fleet has gone far afield in their search for the goblins." He let his fingers intertwine with hers. "And you?"

"This very tick, so I'm told. But I'm still unsure of my purpose in the Airguard's care."

A deeper voice joined them from behind, unmistakably Boreas. "I can help with that."

Connor pulled his hand away and turned, and his heart sank. Boreas was not alone. He stood with a pilot, dressed from his neck to his boots in some odd leather and silk kit.

Connor darkened his eyes. "Samar."

The young man grinned. "Ah. Mister Enarian. I'm so glad you remember my name—a tiny gesture of respect after your little ambush at Ras Telesar." He gave a tilt of his head toward the largest airship Connor had yet seen, with five silk envelopes in black with gold scrollwork. "As you can see, I have a new ship to pilot. A better ship. And it is I who must commandeer—"

Boreas coughed.

Samar shot him an apologetic glance. "*We* must . . . borrow your friend Miss Orso." His smile became a smirk. "For the foreseeable future."

"Come, Cadet Orso," Boreas said, gesturing to the ship. "It's time."

Kara cast a long look at Connor as she went. And he gave her a confident nod. But as she turned away, Samar shifted his steps to walk next to her, and Connor could swear he saw the pilot wink at him.

He scowled, muttering under his breath. "I truly do *not* like him."

22

BOREAS HAD INVITED HER FOR A SUNSET SAIL IN HIS
flagship *The Barn Owl*. That was all Kara knew before coming
out to the cloudloft launching platform. She cast a sidelong
glance at Connor, now trudging back to the lodge as if the goblins
had burned his home village as well as Val Pera. Perhaps he was
taking their parting as hard as she was.

"Are you certain I'm needed this evening, Councilor?"

"You need the distraction, Cadet. As do I. Your master's
raven informed me my daughter and Cadet Lee Trang still have
not reported in. My heart is heavy with the news. The high sea air
and the shifting colors of dusk will do us both good. Please"—he
opened the rail hatch for her and acknowledged an airman at the
lodge door vying for his attention—"make yourself comfortable. I'll
return momentarily."

Samar had been fussing with the moorings. Neither he
nor Boreas had yet explained the pilot's strange garb—a leather
overshirt and leggings with folds of blue-and-gray silk hanging
everywhere. A pair of sword hilts stuck up from sheaths at his
back, half-hidden by a large, flat pouch.

"Samar," Kara said, no longer able to quell her curiosity and
wishing to take advantage of the councilman's absence. "What are

these clothes you wear? Are you dressed for war or a wedding?"

"Neither."

Samar said nothing more—loyal to his commander, it seemed. He continued preparing the ship, and within a quarter tick, they were flying southeast from the harbor, low, keeping the great crescent ridge between themselves and the city.

Not until Samar flared the five lamps to begin a climb, far away from Sky Harbor and the gray haze, did Boreas speak the truth about their journey. "Thank you for your patience, Cadet Orso, which I sense is growing thin."

She affirmed this with a curt nod, then lifted her chin at Samar. "Why is your pilot wearing a frock?"

Samar came off the stern bench where he'd taken rest once he'd set their course. "It's not a frock, thank you."

Boreas intervened with a calming hand. "You refer, of course, to the silks hanging from his arms and legs. Think of them more like the folds of skin of the small, gliding paradragons your Master Belen discovered in the Forest of Believing."

Paradragons. *Gliding* paradragons.

Kara pictured Crumpet, her favorite friend in the forest south of the academy, sailing from tree to tree—occasionally missing a branch and tumbling into the brush. "You can't be serious, Councilor."

"Oh, but I am."

"You'll kill him."

Samar crossed his arms, which brough the silk flaps around in a flourish. "I'm not afraid. We need this."

Clearly Boreas had done some convincing. Samar's mind was made up, and Kara saw little chance of changing it. She directed her arguments at the source. Boreas. "What purpose will it serve to make martyrs of your airmen?"

"You know the purpose. I can see you working it out, even as you ask. Our scouts flying in the Celestial Peaks have long reported their frustration at seeing enemies with no way to stop them and no time to call for the sentinel squadrons or watchmen companies. You yourself know what happened to Lieutenant Ilmari because of his zeal in this matter."

Samar cleared his throat as if to speak.

A sharp look from his chief stopped him. "Even now," Boreas said, "our spotters over the White Ridge Mountains must wait for help from below to kill the goblins who burned Val Pera."

"They have their harpoons."

"It's not enough. And goblins are escaping to create more havoc. This . . ." He glanced at Samar, as if still making up his mind as to what to call his strange kit. "This *glide suit* is the solution."

A sandbar took shape out of the calm seas ahead, colored orange by a sun still well above the western Storm Mists. Climbing high, away from the mountains and the haze, out over open water, had reversed the sunset to make the sun rise a few degrees—an odd trick of flight. Could Boreas pull off another trick and give Samar wings?

Kara wasn't ready to believe it. "I made a friend of one of these gliding paradragons you mentioned—Crumpet, so named because Teegan's falcon ate his tail. This has left him . . . unstable in the air. Samar has no tail either."

A snort told her Samar found her phrasing amusing.

Boreas did not. "Don't you think I've considered that? Or have you not heard that I'm the inventor of these ships, or that I began tinkering with flight by making toy craft of paper and silk in many forms for the festivals—gliders too." Without warning, he yanked Samar closer by the suit's leather straps and turned him about. "See? No weight has been wasted. Look at the sheaths of his swords. The air flows between them beneath the pouch on his back and then over the silk between his legs to add stability."

"And what is the pouch for?" Kara asked. "More weapons?"

"More silk." Boreas released Samar, who frowned and brushed his sleeves. Boreas ignored him. "You'll see soon enough, Miss Orso, but without the surprise in the pouch—what I call the *lander*—Samar would not survive."

The pilot's dark gaze widened to one of concern.

Boreas clapped his shoulders. "Don't worry. I've thought of everything." He pulled a vent rope, and the ship descended, slowing as it left the higher winds. "I'll fly the ship for now. You prepare yourself for your glide. We're here."

Here appeared to mean the sandbar Kara had noticed a few moments earlier. The councilor explained he'd chosen this place so they might conduct this test without onlookers. "We must keep this design secret until we're certain it will work."

Or, Kara thought, he wanted to avoid a very public display of gore at his own hands should Samar fall straight to the ground.

Boreas brought the pilot to the rail, checking the straps of his contraption. He showed Samar two rings at his chest—one blue talanium and one copper. "Pull the blue ring to expel your lander. Pull the copper ring once you're down to shed the pouch and free your legs and arms of their silk." He touched them one at a time. "Blue for landing. Red for fighting. Get the order wrong, and you'll fly straight to Elamhavar. Understand?"

"I'm resilient," Samar said. "I might survive a landing with only the silk flaps for gliding."

"You're not a paradragon. Your bones can't handle an impact at that speed. It'd be like leaping from a horse at full gallop." Boreas raised a finger, cutting off a reply from Samar. "And then being trampled by that same horse. At full gallop. Several times over." Boreas stepped back and clapped his hands. "Right. Climb up to the rail, and let's see if this works."

Let's see if this works? Kara wasn't sure she wanted to watch. Why was she needed for this, anyway?

To Samar's credit, despite the ugly picture the councilor painted, he hopped up to stand on the wicker rail, holding a wooden truss with one hand.

"Blue for landing. Red for fighting," Boreas told him. "Aim for the sandbar. Got it?"

Samar nodded and dove into the sky.

23

KARA RUSHED TO THE RAIL. HOW COULD SHE HAVE let it get this far?

Boreas had this way of speaking that made all around him believe—as if he spoke with the authority of the Rescuer. But he was a man, and this man may have sent Samar to his death.

The pilot fell for some time with arms and legs tucked, shouting against the wind in a long, jubilant cry. Then he spread his arms and legs and seemed to stop on the air.

"He's flying!" Kara exclaimed.

"He's gliding," Boreas said, "but still falling fast, if my calculations are correct. Our view is deceptive. Keep praying. The most dangerous part is yet to come."

Samar tracked across the water toward the sandbar, green silk taut and bulging. From what Kara could tell, the silk spinners had sewn long pockets in each flap to catch the air, giving them a shape closer to a bird's wings and tail. Watching him, she thought he might alight on the sandbar like Teegan's falcon alighting on the academy's ramparts. "Are you certain he needs the lander?"

"Oh yes," Boreas said, then drew in a sharp breath. "Oh no!"

Kara stared at him. "What is it?"

"I never told him precisely *when* to expel the lander." He kept his gaze fixed on his man. "Let's hope he chooses sooner than—"

Before he could finish, Samar vanished under a great wedge of gray silk, sewn with the same air pockets as his wings. The wedge flew above him, carrying him with ropes so narrow they looked like puppet strings. Samar slowed down but kept flying, right past the sandbar.

His boots skimmed the water, drawing two lines across the blue, and then he vanished in a tumbling chaos of white foam and gray silk. When the foam perished, only the silk remained.

No Samar.

"We must get down there!" Kara shouted.

Boreas pulled the vent ropes, sending the ship into a fall almost as perilous as Samar's. Kara held on, eyes never leaving the silk wedge that now looked more like a woman's gown floating on the sea.

The councilor brought the ship to an abrupt landing on the sandbar, and both jumped out. Kara, no stranger to swimming, ran to the end and dove into the water. She didn't stop kicking until she'd reached the silk. "Samar!" She treaded water, sputtering. "Samar!"

The lander was not the only part of Boreas's contraption floating there. She found all of it—the harness, sleeves and leggings with the silk wings attached—all joined with straps and piping. "Samar!"

"Over here!"

Turning about, Kara saw Boreas helping the pilot onto the sandbar, both of them grinning like children on Forge morning. Boreas slapped Samar on the back, where his swords were still sheathed, and called to her, "My fool airman left his lander and wings behind. Would you mind hauling them in?"

Far too many minutes later, Samar helped Kara drag the glide suit onto shore. "Apologies, Councilor," he said, wringing out the silk. "When my boots touched water, it jolted me as hard as if it were solid rock, and I tumbled. When I came to rest, I began to sink. I feared the suit might drag me down, so I released it."

"Nonsense, my boy." Boreas beamed at him, as giddy as Kara had ever seen him. "You were brilliant. Brilliant! It is I who must apologize. The lander is too small. Before the next flight, I'll increase its breadth by a third."

The next flight.

Moments ago, Kara thought she'd seen her friend die before their eyes, yet Boreas wanted to pursue this.

The councilor showed Samar how to fold the lander and stuff it into the pouch. "It occurs to me," he said as they worked, "that if the Airguard has both stormwatchers and stormriders, such divisions bear a similarity to the spheres of the Lightraider Order. Although, I prefer to call ours *wings.*" He narrowed his eyes at the pilot. "You, *Lieutenant*, are the first of a new wing. What should we call it?"

Samar did not so much as blink, even at the news of his new rank. The answer seemed to be waiting at the edge of his lips. "*Windfighter*, sir. We shall be the windfighters."

Both men struck Kara as ridiculous. "Aren't you getting ahead of yourselves? Even if they can survive a glide without a sea to catch them, which you've not yet proven, only a few of your pilots are trained to fight."

"That's where you come in," Boreas said. With the lander tucked away, he took the suit from Samar and carried it to the airship, laying it inside. "The lieutenant will train new volunteers in the glide suit. You will teach them combat."

Kara shook her head. "I don't want the job. Samar is blessed with a grace not many possess. Others may not fare as well as he. How many bodies do you expect me to haul from the waves in pursuit of your ambition?"

That, at least, ended the giddiness.

Boreas crossed his arms. "Councilor. You will address me as councilor, Cadet. And you will do as you're told."

No one spoke again until the ship began to rise. Samar set the lamp dials and the rudder while Boreas stood at the rail, fuming.

Finally, he sighed. "We cannot live in fear of what-ifs, Cadet Orso—not in this current age. But, for certain, the concerns you voiced cut to the heart of another problem."

The sun had dimmed to a dull red half orb on the horizon, leaving a chill on the air. Kara sat on the bow bench and hugged her cloak around damp shoulders. "You need a place to perfect this art—to get it right."

"Just so. Lieutenant Ray can't very well train volunteers in the shelter of the harbor—not so near to the rocky shore and the plaza. Do you understand?"

"I do," Kara said, perhaps a little too dryly. Boreas had lost four pilots during the development of the airships, all in full view of Sky Harbor. He'd survived these tragedies with the Airguard and his positions in the Assembly and the guilds intact, but the city might not give him such grace again. "You have the sandbar," she offered.

"But we can't spare the ships to fly there, not for as often as we'll need them. By taking even this one, my own flagship, I'm stretching the line searching for the goblins thin." Boreas turned his gaze forward, toward the crescent ridge guarding the harbor. "I considered asking volunteer gliders to leap from the outer cliffs above the harbor, but the winds do not favor it."

"The cliffs? You mean your fliers may jump from land?"

"If it's high enough. And there are cliffs in our land as high as an airship flies, are there not?"

Kara turned on the bench and saw the councilor looking hard at her. He already had a place in mind. How like him. Always a step ahead, leading his opponent to the conclusion he desired.

She succumbed to his urging and left the pretense that it was her own notion in place. "I know the cliffs you need, and I can smooth your way with the watchmen. We'll train your windfighters at Orvyn's Vow."

24

CONNOR FOUGHT A CONSTANT TURNING IN HIS stomach, looking back north from *The Kingfisher.* For the last tick and more, they'd flown south over the Many Blessings, the chain of islands off the southeasternmost point of Keledev. The bridge town of New Dawn, with a third of its shops and houses on the mainland, a third on the first island, and a third on the bridge itself, now faded to the north, barely more than an imagining on the horizon.

Aethia landed on the wicker rail next to his hand, chattering and chuffing. The falcon seemed to despise the idea of flying while standing still and preferred to trust in her own wings, only stopping for an occasional rest.

He stroked her feathered back. "I'm with you, bird."

Connor never enjoyed traveling in airships, and he liked this voyage even less since Aaron was flying away from the sure portals of the Passage Lakes, not toward them. "Are you certain you know where you're going?"

Aaron made a lazy adjustment to his rudder and answered as if he hadn't heard the question. "These islands have been my favorite view since joining the Airguard. A warm green relief compared to the stark slopes of the peaks. Though, from the matching green in your cheeks, I suppose you disagree."

Connor gave him a half smile and joined Teegan on the bow bench. She called Aethia to her arm and fed her a sliver of meat. "Breathe, Connor. This is where the Rescuer wants us. On that, both the Order and the Assembly agree."

"I wish he'd wanted Kara to join us."

She sighed. "And I'd rather be raiding with Lee right now, but neither is our lot. At least you know where your favored one is."

His favored one. Teegan had made no secret of her care for Lee. And Lee had trouble making a secret of anything at all. Connor and Kara had been more cautious in their burgeoning feelings. Perhaps too cautious. He couldn't recall if they'd even told each other. But the kiss she'd given him on their parting said what words could not.

Connor touched his cheek. She'd returned from her sunset sail a little damp and in a hurry. She was to head north in another ship that night, but she couldn't say why due to a promise made to Boreas. Connor hadn't pressed her and instead had helped her pack for the journey. That was only fair. He'd been forced to keep secrets from Kara, too, and more than just the Rapha Key he now wore on a chain under his tunic.

The last guardian to advise Connor on the night before he'd left Ras Telesar had been Master Jairun himself, who'd called him up to the headmaster's chambers in the ninth-level tower.

You might have asked me about the dagger, Master Jairun had said, *rather than waiting until this critical day to hurl an accusation.*

A cold cavern had opened in Connor's chest. *I didn't mean to . . . I mean, I never thought—*

I know, my boy. I know. This moment found us all unprepared. You did what was necessary.

A quiet had hung between them for some time, one that failed to diminish the empty feeling in Connor's chest, until, finally, Master Jairun had motioned for him to sit. *It's time you heard what your grandfather learned about Lef Amunrel.*

You mean where the dagger is hidden?

That, I cannot say. Not exactly.

That news had hit Connor hard. How were they to claim the dagger if even Master Jairun didn't know where it was? *But Faelin's journal—*

Says that he learned the fate of Lef Amunrel, if I'm not mistaken. I know for certain he didn't know its actual resting place.

He'd been right. Connor had read those pages a hundred times and never noticed the distinction.

And a terrible fate it is, my boy, Master Jairun had told him, *for the dagger, and especially for the raid party that must retrieve it. Faelin believed Lef Amunrel was taken to Heleyor's Vault."*

Heleyor's Vault. According to the headmaster, this storehouse of relics both dear to and feared by the Great Red Dragon lay not in his flaming halls at Ras Pyras, but in King's Cradle, a region that held more dangers for Connor than mere dark creatures.

He was going to the land of his traitorous forebearers—House Leander, the vilest of the traitor-kings. For this reason, along with his caring for her, he wished Kara had been permitted to join their raid party. Her queensblood ancestors of House Arkelon had been joined to House Leander and House Suvor. In both cases, they'd held strong while their sons and husbands bent the knee to Heleyor. Without her, could he stand firm? Could he redeem his bloodline?

One final word from the headmaster had stuck with him after their meeting, never fully leaving his thoughts.

We're not certain of the vault's precise location. We have only legends, some of which contradict each other. But they do all agree on one thing—all those who've sought Heleyor's Vault have died.

The quest to reclaim Lef Amunrel rested squarely in the Rescuer's care. And if he allowed them to achieve it, Teegan and Aaron would have a choice to make. Connor placed his hand upon the Rapha Key under his tunic. He'd already made his choice. The others might think him mad.

Aaron laughed, stirring him, and perhaps attributing the clutching hand at Connor's chest and his farsighted stare to more queasiness. "Stay seated, land lover, and I will describe what you're missing. At present, we're passing over the largest and southernmost inhabited isle—Assurance. She is alive with color. Her coasts are thick green grass, as green as your gills, all the way to the cerulean-blue water that surrounds her, and her fruit trees are lush and full of the sweetest citrus."

Teegan had left the bench to look over the rail with him. "I hear the people of Assurance do well in the diver's folly trade. They say it lies scattered about the seabed like coins from a merchant's purse."

"True." Aaron pulled down on one of his ropes, causing *The Kingfisher* to lean into a slight descent. "The divers sell their harvest to the Apothecarists' Guild, which has deep ties with the Airguard. I've heard one say a wall of fire and steam pours up from the seabed, spitting out diver's folly to constantly replenish their supply. The same wall fuels the Storm Mists all the way to seas bordering the Celestial Peaks."

Connor lifted his eyes to the horizon. "Speaking of . . ."

Aaron gestured for him to go to the bow. "Steel your gut, Connor. A wondrous sight is coming, one you must see for yourself."

Connor obeyed, letting Teegan help him. With the last island behind them, only deep blue water and the gray-white haze stirred up by the Storm Mists lay ahead. He glanced over his shoulder at Aaron. "There's nothing to see."

"Eyes front, Enarian. Just wait."

A shadow formed in the haze towering above the sea, broad and unwavering. Was there a land mass south of Keledev of which Connor had never heard?

"One of the stormwatchers saw it a few weeks ago," Aaron said. "And Boreas sent more ships to get a closer look, in hopes of discerning its purpose. It may have been here all along. Or the Rescuer may have pulled it from the sea for this very moment of need."

Connor listened to his friend, but never took his eyes off the shadow. With every passing beat, it took shape and definition. A stone pillar as broad as a city and as tall as a mountain stood above the waves. From it rose two crescents, curving to form an almost perfect ring and nearly touching at the top. The Storm Mists rolled and tumbled behind it, and a familiar purple lightning flashed between the crescents.

"In truth, we're still a long way off," Aaron said. "This gate is big—bigger than it looks from this distance."

"Big enough to fly ten ships through at once, I'd say." Teegan had recalled her bird and now placed a hood over her head to quiet her and keep her from flying off again. "Would the Airguard dare such a thing?"

"They will, if I'm able to return and report a successful stormride, proving this is, indeed, a portal." He shrugged. "Or if the first stormrider to test it ever returns."

Teegan turned to fix him with her gaze. "The first stormrider? You mean Zel. Did Zel and Lee fly into this thing?"

Aaron nodded, no longer able to take his eyes from the massive structure looming ahead. But he said no more about Lee or Zel. None of them did, for fear of the notion that they had already passed into Elamhavar, or that this very portal had sent them there.

"What do you call it?" Connor asked.

"Stormgate." Aaron made an adjustment to his rudder and vents, vying for the gate's very center. "If the name is apt, I'll be the second stormrider in the Airguard."

"And if not," Connor said, tightening his grip on the rail, "we're about to become the latest casualties in this war."

As Aaron had said, the gate belied its own size. Drawing closer took them longer than Connor expected, and the closer they came, the larger it seemed. He found the councilor's estimation small. The Airguard might fly more than twenty ships through—forty, he thought, if they flew close together and at several heights.

Glittering silver veins spread from the base up along both crescent pillars. A vortex of blue and gray mists bubbled within.

"Is the silver ore shairosite?" Teegan asked.

"So we believe." Aaron's voice had taken on a tremor, and not just because the air had grown rough.

Purple streaks sprang from every junction where the silver veins split, flashing to the swirling core. These streaks held the same proportion to the gate as those Connor had witnessed in the hollow hill portals of Tanelethar so that even the narrowest flash was broader than *The Kingfisher*'s wicker hull.

The bow drifted to port, away from the core.

Connor looked back. "Watch your heading, Aaron. I thought you wanted this."

The pilot stared straight ahead to the south, but his hand pushed the rudder to drive them east. "I'm no longer certain."

"Too late. Have faith."

His admonition had little effect, and the bow kept drifting—not enough to dodge the portal, but enough to send them through broadside, which Connor doubted would be a good thing. Tendrils of mist reached out to mingle with the vapors from the airship's lamps, building a midnight-blue haze between them. "Aaron!"

Teegan added her voice, calling upon the Rescuer with a verse from the Scrolls. "*Sestradov, okeb biyov'anar. Sestradov, ba Rumoshov'anar. Kastregoviana. Bo yadesh thon yeluthmath netvoviana.*"

Do not fear, for I am with you.

I will strengthen you.

I will hold you with my righteous right hand.

The pilot set his jaw and swung the rudder hard over, pulling a vent to aid the correction. *The Kingfisher* banked to run straight again, but lost height, so that it looked to enter below the core. The blue vapors spiraled around the ship.

"Right!" Aaron shouted. He dialed his lamps to full and pulled hard on the vent ropes. "Here we go!"

25

CONNOR
TANELETHAR
THE KINGFISHER

MORE THAN THE TINGLING OF HIS SKIN—MORE THAN
the swirling mist, the squeeze in his ears, and the echoing sense
of an unfathomable void—the floating bothered Connor. Each
time he rode a storm with one of these Airguard pilots, all sense
of the ship vanished. In those long beats of transit, Connor might
have been upside down or sideways for all he knew, with no feel
of the wicker under his boots.

Be calm, son of faith. Take heart.

Under his hand, Connor felt rough strands of fur. Within the
swirling vapors, he saw the ice-blue eyes and white sloped snout of
some great cat. The eyes seemed to speak.

Walk with me.

The strands of fur under his hand became cords of wicker.
The eyes faded. *The Kingfisher* reappeared around him and the
others—a faithful friend that had never left. Connor blinked against
the vision he'd just seen and teetered for a moment, regaining his
balance. The flashing vapors dissipated, leaving them in a cold
cloud that slowly parted like a curtain.

A broad river basin spread below them—a dozen shades of
green checkered with fields of white, yellow, and red. To the west,
gray smoke rose from black peaks. Far to the north, the river

divided—or rather, two branches joined, both fed by waterfalls flowing down a massive natural dam that reached almost the height of their airship.

Teegan, who had pulled Aethia close, eased her embrace on the bird and let out a quiet, "Huh."

"What?" Connor asked.

"Usually, when we pass into Tanelethar, we wind up in goblin-infested hills or dark forests filled with scraggly trees and wraiths. But this . . . this is—"

"Beautiful." Aaron finished the thought for her. He adjusted his lamp dials and vent ropes to hold *The Kingfisher* steady. "I'd spend my festival days here."

"The festivals here are not like ours, Aaron." Connor raised a spyglass to his eye.

"And where is here?"

Connor held his answer until the glass confirmed his suspicion. He let out a breath, though whether out of relief or concern, he wasn't sure. "King's Cradle."

The Rescuer had brought them to the place Master Jairun predicted—a place described in Faelin's journal without reference to Lef Amunrel. Now that Connor knew his patehpa suspected the dagger was here, the maps and descriptions made more sense.

A city crowned the tall peninsula where the two rivers joined, stretching back to the waterfalls. Pillars of colored smoke in yellow, purple, orange, and green rose from the fireclocks in the grand plaza in each district. And through the layers of haze they formed, Connor saw glistening houses and a hundred waterways bustling with skiffs and barges.

He handed Teegan the spyglass. "The great river is the Serpentine, and the chief city is Emen Yan, rumored to be the first human dwelling in all Talania. It's also . . ." He thought better of what he'd meant to say and let his voice trail off.

Teegan passed the spyglass to Aaron. "It's also what, Connor?"

"It's . . . also a danger to our ship. The closer we come, the greater the risk of being spotted. We need to land."

The Kingfisher began a rising turn. Aaron, who was looking south rather than north toward the city, had pushed the rudder over and flared the center lamp. "On that score, I have a thought." He took the glass from Teegan and used it to point off the starboard bow. "Look there."

At the south end of the river basin, the green turned to pale yellow, then reddish brown. Aaron locked their heading on a set of long, snaking landforms—high and narrow tables, perhaps cut by a flood during the making of the world. Connor recognized them from his patehpa's drawings. Faelin had called them Viper Buttes, a name likely taken from their shape.

"See the bowl at the north end of the tallest butte?" Aaron asked with the spyglass at his eye. "It's easily wider than *The Kingfisher* and thrice as long. Plus, the rim rises higher than our silk, and even the birds fly lower. No one on the surface will see the ship there."

Teegan removed Aethia's hood and sent her flying to stretch her wings. "How do you propose we get down from the butte?"

He gave her the spyglass. "Look closer."

She raised it to her eye, then passed it to Connor with a wary glance.

Bones. In the circle of the lens, Connor saw dry snakeskin clinging to a viper's skeleton—a big viper, near as wide as a horse and five times as long. Perhaps Viper Buttes referred to more than the shape of the landforms.

"If that creature found a way to the top"—Aaron pulled his vents to start their descent—"we can find a way down."

Teegan was not convinced. "Dead or not, I don't like the look of that snake. Besides, by all appearances, the creature died up there, meaning it may have been stranded. Connor?"

"Give me a beat to think."

The bones chilled his blood, but the depression where they lay would, indeed, hide the ship. And the red dust collected by the bowl looked soft for a landing. He tucked the spyglass away. "It's worth trying. In the worst case, we can lift off again—find another nest. Take her in."

Aaron showed skill in his approach, mastering the wind so that *The Kingfisher* settled lightly into the dust. The steel runners sank all the way to the wicker hull, but no farther, even after he doused the lamps. The silk deflated, clinging to its trusses and snapping in the wind blowing across the butte. "She's holding fast. We're good."

Good?

From where they rested, near the center of the depression, Connor saw no trail—no way down—only the weathered bones of the giant snake. He lifted his manykit and slipped an arm through the first strap. "That remains to be seen."

They'd brought what provisions the airship could hold. Teegan and Connor wore lightraider manykits, straps with hooks and pouches packed with the usual supplies, plus a purse each of Taneletharian coins and their weapons. Aaron carried a satchel of provisions and a smaller version of the double crossbow gracing *The Kingfisher*'s port rail, with a strap of bolts across his chest. At his side, he wore a sheathed falchion—the long, slightly curved sword favored by the few Sky Harbor pilots who flew armed.

Connor's boots sank deep on his first steps out of the ship, up to his shins in the dust—perhaps a poor trade for the soft landing. "Split up. Let's find the trail down as quick as we can."

The others turned in opposing directions, but all three froze at a sharp rattling.

The dead viper lifted its triangular head and the first third of its body, pouring dust from the skin hanging off its bones. Tiny points of orange light gleamed within the dark sockets that once held its lidless eyes. Distinct words formed under the rattling. "Ssso glad you came, sssailorsss of the sssky. What wisssdom do you sssseek from the viper sssage?"

26

"ARMS!" TEEGAN WHIPPED THE CHAINMAIL NET FROM her waist. "Guard your ears. It uses song sorcery."

Connor drew Revornosh but shook his head. "Not song sorcery. Something else—a form of speech we can all hear."

With a jerk of its head, the viper looked his way. Its jaw creaked open in a reptilian smile.

He ssseesss. He hearsss. He knowsss. Yesss, Prinsss.

"And yet," Connor said, cocking his head, "also song sorcery."

Prince. What did this creature know? Same as all the others, he supposed.

Teegan advanced a step, making a threatening stab with her trident. "Back, creature. Be silent."

The rattling intensified. "Why ssso hossstile? Asssk usss a quessstion. Isss that not why you came?"

Connor tried to rebuke it. "You won't—"

"We seek a weapon of great power," Aaron said, cutting him off.

The cadets turned to glare at him, but he ignored their looks and lowered his crossbow. He stepped between them to the front, whispering through clenched teeth as he went, "The creature thinks we came for its help. A touch of winsomeness here may gain us ground." He raised his voice. "Where might we find such a boon?"

The tiny points of light in the viper's eye sockets canted toward the pilot. "Weapon. Power. Yesss, ssseeeker. I can help."

At the same time, different words formed in Connor's mind. *Why let thisss upsssstart ssspeak over you, Prinsss? Shall I ssstrike him down?*

Not good. Connor pulled Aaron back. "He's . . . um . . . asking for all of us. We desire a treasure my ancestor once carried."

"Wait," Aaron protested. "I have another ques–"

Teegan swatted him with the trident's shaft. "Hush."

The viper held perfectly still for several beats, almost as if the life had gone out of it, leaving the creature as a statue. Connor had to wonder what it thought of these interlopers. It knew his heritage. Did the creature also know they were lightraiders or that the lightraiders existed? By the pits and scoring of its bones, it might have lain here since before the Order first began.

The viper turned its eye sockets north. "It isss well you should asssk usss. For centuriesss we have watched. From on high, we have ssseen all."

The ground began to shift on their left flank.

Aaron had started this conversation. Connor would finish it as quickly as possible. "You know what I seek, then."

The rattling resonated in his mind.

Yesss, Prinsss. We know. You sssseek what isss yoursss—what wasss guarded by your sssacred blood. Any weapon of consssequensss would be kept there.

The viper fixed its eye sockets on him again. The airy voice returned. "Treasssure chamber. A dragon'sss vault. A great risssk. A great reward."

Connor gripped his sword. "Where?"

"Only foolsss ssssteal from dragonsss."

Wisssdom, I offer. Knowledge of the ancientsss. My worth isss greater than weaponsss of war. Turn from thisss quesssst and let me advisssse you a better path, as I did your forefathersss. The triangular head canted toward Aaron. *A sssmall sssacrifice isss all I asssk in return.* The undulations in the dust closed in.

"Connor?" Teegan said. "What are you doing?"

"Trust me." He dropped command into his voice, in the way the guardians had taught them. "Speak, creature. Tell me where to find the vault!"

The viper let out a pained, rattling growl. "The Ssserpentine. Ssseek the sssource!" With that, it arced its bony spine and struck at Aaron.

Connor was ready. While the pilot stood in shock, Connor swung Revornosh up under the reptile's chin and smashed its lower jaw to bits. It convulsed and recoiled.

A second viper burst from the red dust and came at Teegan. She thrust her trident, locking the tines among the bones at the base of the skull, and turned it to jam the creature's head into the dirt.

In flailing, the viper she'd pinned flicked its rattling tail. Three bony spikes sailed Connor's way. He raised his forearm, and his silver shield glowed to life. The spikes shattered.

The first viper reared again.

Aethia soared down and tore the skin from its back, but the creature paid her no mind. It swept Aaron from his feet with a swish of its tail and dove at him.

The pilot rolled over, struggling to bring his crossbow to bear. "Connor!"

Connor jabbed with Revornosh and chipped the bone beneath an eye socket. He did little damage but spoiled the viper's aim.

Aaron pulled his trigger, and his bolt found a target Connor had not yet seen. A decayed text—leather and parchment—hung from a chain within the snake's ribcage. The bolt buried itself in the leather, and the viper writhed in pain. The voice in its rattling became a scream.

"The book," Teegan cried, still pinning the second viper's head in the dust and dancing to avoid its wriggling bones. "Mine has one as well. Get it!"

Bone and chain were not easily cut.

"Aaron, catch!" Connor threw Revornosh to the pilot and drew his crook. He swung it with all his strength to bash the first viper in its bone nostrils, then hooked the creature's spine below the head. Like Teegan, he twisted the creature and shoved its fangs into the dust. "Go for the books, Aaron. Watch for spikes from their tails."

As if to strengthen his warning, bony darts flew at the pilot from two directions. Most went wild, but three disintegrated against the pilot's shield. Aaron gripped Revornosh with both hands and shoved it down through the ribcage of Teegan's viper into the chains holding the book. They snapped. The book dropped free.

"Nooooo!" The viper writhed in fury, then went still. The lights in its eye sockets faded.

Her foe defeated, Teegan added her strength to Connor's, and together, they gained better control of the remaining viper. As before, Aaron drove Revornosh down between its ribs and broke the second book free.

Why, Prinsss. I wasss your family'sss ally!

"Stab it, Aaron! Stab the book!"

Aaron did as Connor commanded, and the last of the rattling quieted, along with the hissing voice in Connor's head.

The three breathed hard, wiping their brows. Connor recovered Revornosh from Aaron and pulled the book from the blade. "I think the dragon sorcery that animates these snakes is tied to some secret or false knowledge they swallowed long ago."

He shook the dust from the book and worked loose the cover's ancient buckle. The writing inside—what little was visible in faded ink on the decaying pages—looked to be a close derivation of the Elder Tongue.

Connor could make out a few words and saw mostly pledges of fealty to the dragons and declarations of the grace of Rumosh. Strange contradictions, to the point of absurdity. But one page near the end stood out. "There's a map."

"A map that looks familiar." Aaron leaned in and touched the page. "That valley looks much like the one we flew over. See? The rivers split around that city."

"Emen Yan." Connor grunted a bit as he nudged the pilot back. "I agree, but I don't recognize the symbols drawn there." With great care, he turned the page, frowned, and turned it back again. "I see no legend."

The second book, freed from Aaron's crossbow bolt, yielded nothing useful—more of the same drivel paying homage to the dragons and some lesser misconception of the Creator at the same time. Connor ripped the map out of the first book, tucked it into his manykit, and headed for the butte's rim. He ripped both books apart and threw the fragile pages into the open sky.

"Why did you do that?" The deep dust slowed Aaron enough that he stood no chance of stopping Connor's destructive work. "You couldn't read all the pages in so short a time. We might have found something useful with a little effort."

"Not likely." Connor paused, about to say more, but let the moment pass. Perhaps Teegan and Aaron wouldn't have cared, or given it a thought, but he'd noticed something in both books he didn't want them to see. Several pages bore noble signatures. The given names varied, but the house name was always the same.

Leander.

Teegan eyed Connor for a beat, then lifted her chin at the pilot. "Connor's right. Whatever lies those vipers swallowed were not likely a help to us. In the future, don't engage dark creatures without our lead, or you'll risk a terrible end. Now, we need to find our way down."

27

A TRUDGING SEARCH THROUGH THE WIDE, CURVING bowl atop the butte yielded little. Connor and the others found no other skeletal vipers, but they also found no trails.

"This is becoming hopeless," Teegan said.

"You may be right." Aaron examined the hull of his ship, as if gauging how hard it might be to lift the skids from the dust. "Perhaps the Rescuer only led us here for the map we found. We may need to fly out while we still can." He scrunched his nose, still staring at the hull. "If we still can."

Teegan frowned at him. "If I recall, it was you who led us here, Aaron."

"*Inspired* by the Rescuer."

"So you say."

"Leave him be, Teegan," Connor said, walking along the rim. "The Rescuer brought us through Stormgate and placed us at the south end of the basin, close to this butte. It yielded the map, yes, but I still believe this bowl is a perfect place to stash *The Kingfisher*. Keep searching. Finding a trail is better than flying out of here."

"Flying." Teegan dropped her forehead into a hand. "Of course."

She whistled, and Aethia, perched on the ship's rail and quietly pecking and shredding her patch of snakeskin, looked up. The falcon flew to Teegan's arm, received a whispered command, then flew over the rim and disappeared.

"Care to explain?" Aaron asked.

"I'm betting more creatures than these vipers have visited this dustbowl. Aethia can find their trails."

In less than a quarter tick, the falcon had narrowed her hover to a small area beyond the rim. Then, with a word from Teegan, she tucked her wings and dove. A beat later, she reappeared, clutching a mouse in her talons.

"Oh good," Aaron said in a dry tone. "You've helped her find a meal."

But Aethia had not harmed the mouse so far as Connor could see. She dropped the little creature at Teegan's feet.

The mouse, unwilling to risk another flight, scurried away.

"Follow it!" Teegan said. "Keep it in sight!"

The task proved formidable. The mouse's fur matched the red coloring of the butte. It skittered across the surface while the cadets tromped after it, sometimes knee deep in the dust. Their efforts clouded the air to worsen their vision.

Connor stopped. "Where's it gone?"

"Here!" Teegan shouted. "I've got it!"

By the time he caught up to her, the mouse was gone, but Teegan showed him a small divot near the rim. "The mouse buried itself."

The three tried digging the creature up and found a long rectangular rock extending from the bowl's rim hidden inches below the dust.

Connor blew the dust from its top, looking for symbols. He saw none. "It's no coincidence the mouse vanished here. Dig around. Look for a lever or a handhold—anything."

They found nothing.

"What about pushing on it?" Aaron asked.

Connor straightened, standing next to Teegan, and crossed his arms. "Go ahead."

Aaron planted his feet and let out a long grunt, pushing from one side of the stone. It didn't budge. He switched to the other side with the same result.

"Well?" Connor asked.

The pilot shot him a frown. "You could help."

"Watching you sweat is more entertaining."

Despite the jest, he and Teegan joined Aaron, and all three pushed. Again, the stone refused to move. Aaron let out a heavy, frustrated sigh and sat on its top.

The rock began to lower beneath him. Stone ground against stone somewhere under the dust. "Ha!" he said, grinning. "I did it!"

"Aaron, quick. Get off—" Connor never got the chance to finish. The ground gave way, not under Aaron, but under the two cadets.

Dust sifted like sand through a timeglass, taking Connor and Teegan with it and swallowing them whole in a choking cloud.

In moments, firm ground found Connor's boots again—firm, but steep. He and Teegan rolled downhill to land in a heap among thorny brush. As they helped each other to their feet and dusted themselves off, Aaron's face and shoulders appeared above, peeking from a crevice below the rim. He touched four fingers to his temple in the Airguard salute. "I think I know where the mouse went."

There wasn't much of a trail, at least that Connor could see. Teegan picked her way, insisting that her Rangers' Sphere skills allowed her to follow the path used by the mouse and other small animals, giving them the best chance at walking, rather than falling, down the butte.

Halfway down, once they'd gained confidence in their footing, she let out a cough. "You know, I can tell you're hiding something."

Connor's stomach went rigid.

"I mean, I saw it in your face during the battle with the vipers and right after we flew through Stormgate."

Which had she guessed? Connor's bloodline? Or that he carried the Rapha Key? Had the headmaster told her any of it after

Connor left the academy with Kara?

The Rapha Key hanging beneath his tunic became an immeasurable weight, as did the knowledge that King's Cradle had once been the seat of his ancestors. Perhaps it was better not to keep both secrets. One, he might share. For now. "Teegan, I—"

"Fine," Aaron said, before Connor could speak another word. "Fine, all right? You've seen through me, as I knew one of you might."

Teegan glanced back. "What?"

At the same time, Connor turned to stare at him. "Say again?"

The pilot nodded, letting his eyes fall. "I have another purpose here, one I should have confessed before we passed through Stormgate."

A sharp look from Teegan said, *I'm not through with you, Connor.*

So she'd been talking to him after all, but she didn't want to pass up Aaron's unfinished confession. Teegan planted her trident in the steep soil for support and squared up to the pilot. "Spill it."

"It wasn't my idea. But I wanted the job—the mission. And I care about her."

For a moment, Connor forgot his worries over the key and House Leander. "Care about who?"

"Zel. The raven from the academy held more than your orders. Your headmaster posted cadets at the Passage Lakes, not only to watch for orcs, but to wait for Zel and Lee to return from their scouting mission. They still haven't."

Connor knew this. So did Teegan. They'd been there when the raven came. "And?"

Aaron puffed up his chest. "Boreas, not Master Jairun, is the head of my order, and he gave me a job to do in Tanelethar. I'm to find his behlna if I can. He told me to find Zel."

28

LEE
TANELETHAR
MINER'S GLORY

LEE WIPED THE LENS OF BALDOMAR'S BIG SHIPGLASS
clean with an already-soggy cloth. "I can't tell a hill from a house
down there, let alone find a cold campfire. Is there any chance
you might keep out of the clouds?"

"Not if we want to hunt in daylight." Zel checked a compass
mounted beneath *The Merlin*'s lamp and adjusted her rudder.
"Even with her coloring, the ship is too exposed in the open sky."

Three nights they'd hunted by moonlight—three fruitless
nights. Near the end of the second watch on the night previous,
Lee had suggested they find a place to land and rest. From then on,
they'd hunt in daylight.

It started well, with the sight of rubbish that could only be
a sign left by a large army. More signs followed, but they'd all
disappeared at Miner's Glory.

"Where could they have gone?" The lens fogged over again,
and Lee sat back onto the bow bench, slapping the wet cloth down
onto the wicker. "We should land and spare ourselves the risk. I've
lost the trail."

The orcs and barkhides had driven their Aladoth army west
out of Sil Shadath to the road called Ambition, which passed along
the northern edge of the inland hills from Fantasia Shieling all

the way to the western edge of Miner's Glory. Such a large army left many signs—trampled grass and bushes, blackened earth from fires, and bones and carcasses from the animals they'd killed.

Those marks had ended at Grindstone, a Cresian town in the hills of Miner's Glory where Ambition intersected the West Midland Road, which ran from the Fulcan Plain to Darkling Shade and onward to points south.

"I've seen nothing for more than two ticks," Lee said. "Naught but two men in wagons. Or perhaps the same man twice. North, south, west. We've searched a league in every direction with no sign of our quarry."

A break in the cold clouds revealed the cobblestone alleys and rows of shops and houses covering the four hills of Grindstone. They'd been running east, and Lee had not felt Zel make the turn back to the west, a curiosity of floating around blind up here that left him disoriented and uneasy. She brought the rudder true again and nodded at the town. "Lots of folks down there. I think it's time we stop and ask for help."

"You can't be serious."

"Oh, but I am." Zel opened a vent to prove her point, beginning a descent. "What can it hurt?"

"A lot. A simple conversation may send us straight into the clutches of a dragon. Every soul we speak to in Tanelethar is a potential betrayer."

"But isn't speaking to Aladoth the ultimate work and calling of a lightraider?"

He couldn't argue. "All right. Find a spot to set her down."

They hid *The Merlin* in a valley at the edge of the Upland Wilds, asking the Rescuer to keep her safe from the eyes and claws of dark creatures, then snuck onto Ambition at a bend in the road where none might see. From there, they plodded toward Grindstone like a pair of travelers who'd been on their feet for leagues on end.

The road Ambition passed east to west through the town in a

tight valley between hills, and in the same way, the West Midland passed north to south. No guards manned the east gate, a blessing that might vanish when night came. Lee and Zel joined a sparse gaggle of travelers and slipped through.

As Zel had hoped, the mining town yielded answers—too many. "Oh yes, I saw the army," one of Grindstone's many bakers told them. He waited until Lee laid down a coin for a loaf before continuing. "Well, *akshually* mah sehna saw them. He saw an army camped in the east hills not two nights back. Says they 'peared like ghosts at dusk. Next mornin' they was gone. Which way'd they go? Haven't the foggiest."

"North," a furrier said as Zel paid for a hooded mantle. "The trappers told me they saw a whole platoon marching north into the Fulcan Plains."

"No, no. Yer trapper's got it wrong." A blacksmith sharpened Lee's sikaria knives, a service that cost him more than the loaf of bread. "South. Saw them with mah own eyes, I did. Two platoons of golmogs and goblins, driven by orcs with strange spiked armor, headed south toward Darkling Shade. But humans? Don't remember seeing any humans with 'em, not even barkhides."

Only moments later, a chandler handed Zel a bundle of small candles in exchange for another coin. "West for certain. Anyone who says different is daft or a liar. I didn't see no army, but a dragon flew over Grindstone, headed that way. Any army as big as you describe is sure to have a dragon watchin' over them. Most folks want nothin' to do with such things. Why so interested?"

Lee laid down an extra coin and took Zel's arm. "No reason. Good day."

"Well," he said as they walked Ambition, heading back to *The Merlin*, "that was costly and useless."

"Not entirely." Zel flipped the hood of her new mantle over her head. "At least now my ears will stay warm in the clouds."

How could she jest while they faced such failure? With an army built to destroy the Keledan missing? With no hope of finding Shan?

She seemed to read the consternation on his face. "Why is an army of Aladoth such a threat when there are far more terrifying dark creatures to worry about?"

"You know we're forbidden from killing Aladoth, right?"

She nodded. "So I've heard. It was always a lightraider problem. But I suppose we must all understand it better now. Why is that forbidden?"

Lee shrugged. "Our purpose is to rescue them, not kill them. To kill an Aladoth is to send them into eternal separation from the High One, without hope of reconciliation."

Zel considered this for a long moment, then peeled the hood back again. "And . . . if the Aladoth army enters Keledev, not only will our reluctance to harm them give them an advantage, but whether they kill us or we kill them, Heleyor gets to revel in the victory. Either he gains Keledev, or he sees more of the High One's children lost forever."

"Now you see the danger." Lee lowered his gaze to the road. "And one of those Aladoth—one who I believe will lead them—is my own brother."

Zel seemed at a loss for words for some time, until finally she asked, "Are we doing what the Rescuer asks?"

"I think so."

"Then that is all we can do. He's greater than our failures or Heleyor's plans, and he's faithful, so let's hold to the hope of his promises."

Lee heard the Sacred Scrolls in her words. *"Let us hold on to the confession of our hope without wavering, since he who promised is faithful,"* he said. "I'm shamed by the truth of your teaching. You speak from the Scrolls with understanding, as one who has studied."

At this, she smiled. "The lightraiders aren't the only Scroll scholars in the land, you know. All Keledan should study the High One's words."

"And yet . . ."

Zel laughed. "Many forget. I know. The truth is my father commands his airmen to seek the High One's wisdom daily. He says that if we're to serve the Rescuer as the Lightraider Order serves him, learning the Sacred Scrolls isn't optional."

Boreas. In Lee's dealings with the councilor, he'd witnessed a lot of disdain for the Lightraider Order, at least on the surface. Yet, more and more, he found an underlying respect. He nodded. "That's good to hear." Then he paused in his plodding and let out a breath. "Should we go back and see if we hear one answer more than the others?"

Zel glanced over her shoulder. "Can't. The sun's setting. The guards may start checking journey writs at the gate."

Lee looked back as well. As she'd said, the sun hung low over the hills of Miner's Glory. Figures, likely the guards she spoke of, milled about the eastern gate.

Yet, as Lee watched, he saw another option. A man pulled a large, covered cart out of the town, heading their way—possibly the same man and cart he'd seen from the sky twice before. "Zel," he said, thrusting his chin toward the cartman, "whatever wares that merchant sells take him all over this region. If anyone here has seen the army we seek, it's him."

The two returned to the same quiet bend where they'd snuck onto the road and waited.

Lee smelled the cartman before he came into sight. He wrinkled his nose. "What's in that cart, I wonder? It carries the stench of carrion."

"Changing your mind?" Zel asked.

"No. I can bear it if you can."

He forced back his revulsion, and a bit of bile, and offered a smile. He lifted half the loaf he'd bought from the baker toward the cartman. "Traveler, rest yourself a moment and speak with us."

Wary, the cartman eased his burden down onto its stilts—short posts descending from the pull shafts. He didn't look like he could afford to turn down a gift of bread. Still, when he took a bite, he paused as if half expecting the sting of poison, then finally chewed and swallowed. "Whadya want? I've no money fer beggars. No wares ta trade fer bread."

No wares? Then what was in the cart?

"We're not seeking coins or wares, only tales." Lee gave the man a waterskin to keep the bread from drying his tongue. "Perchance, have you seen an army pass near Grindstone?"

"Aye." The man took another bite and chased it with a swig from the skin. He gave the skin a frown, as if mere water was an offense.

"A human army," Zel prompted, "not just orcs or goblins."

"Aye. Humans. I saw 'em. Loads of 'em, pressed by barkhides. Ashen-faced an' dead in the eyes, every one."

Hope sprung up in Lee's chest. "My brother is with them. Do you know which way they went?"

"Aye."

Lee and Zel waited. When the man kept silent, Lee gave him the other half of the loaf.

"North. All of 'em."

A breath escaped both cadets. "North," Lee said. "Thank you. How long ago did—"

A loud, gut-twisting chortle interrupted him. The head of some enormous bird with rotting eyes poked out from under the tarp covering. More of the stench came with it, like a blast of air. Suspended on a long, gangly neck, the head bent close to the cartman's ear and chortled again.

"Wait." The cartman shook his half loaf at the cadets. "My memory is failin'. South, I meant. The army went south."

The well of hope in Lee's chest began to dry up. "South. Are you certain this time?"

"Am I certain?" The cartman seemed to ask the bird more than himself.

A second bird's head pushed out from under the tarp. This one eyed the cadets for a beat, pressed its beak close to the man's other ear, and unleashed a quiet cackle.

"West," the cartman said, eyes vacant. "Ya must go west."

Lee watched him, hand inching toward his sikaria. "To seek the army, you mean. We must go west to seek the army, correct?" The first bird leaned past the man to peck at the second then chortled again.

"No." The cartman shook his head, then nodded, then shook his head again. "Aye. South, it is. I must go south." He dropped the bread and the waterskin in the dirt and bent to pick up the cart's poles.

Zel stepped closer to Lee. "This is some dragon sorcery."

Both birds whipped their heads away from their master, rotting eyes fixed on the pilot. They let out a loud chortle and cackle, making the cartman cringe.

"Ya've done it now," he said. "Ya've made 'em angry."

Claws like those of a badger but far larger appeared on either side of the birds, digging into the wood. The tarp ropes snapped away. The two bird heads belonged to a single creature rearing up behind the cartman. Long necks snaked down to shoulders that blended feathers and matted fur. It leapt out of the cart and landed on the road with a badger-like body and limbs, wriggling as if to loosen its muscles for a fight.

The chortling and cackling continued, louder. Lee heard two voices in his mind.

Run, one said.

Fight, the other countered.

Then both found agreement. *Die.*

29

LEE DREW TWO DOUBLE-BLADED SIKARIA FROM HIS leg sheaths.

Zel unfurled her spiked whip.

A beak snapped at them. A warning, not close enough to strike. Both heads kept up their terrible chortling and cackling.

Run.

Fight.

Die.

"What is it?" Zel asked through gritted teeth.

"Nothing I've seen in our texts or training. This is new." Lee raised his voice to the creature. "Be gone and take your stench with you! Trouble this soul no more."

The two voices of the creature's song sorcery kept arguing in his mind.

We leave?

No. They leave.

No. They die.

Yes. Kill them.

He didn't like it when they agreed.

"It wants to kill us," Zel said. "I heard it in my head."

"As did I. Split up. Make it choose which one of us to engage."

The plan worked. He and Zel spread apart, and the creature danced on its badger legs, turning this way and that like a dog unable to choose between bones. The voices never ceased.

The woman first.

The man.

She has a whip. Terrible spikes.

He has blades. Two with two.

Splitting up had turned the bird heads against each other but hadn't spoiled their determination to kill or taken either cadet out of range. In a burst of speed, the creature spun. The heads snapped at Zel while the broad badger tail swung at Lee.

Lee dodged and swiped at it with both blades. The edges met layers of coarse, matted fur, doing little damage.

Zel blocked a pecking beak with her shield and slung her whip. She caught its leg at the ankle, but not well. When she yanked the whip back, the spikes came free.

Chortling and cackling laughter filled Lee's mind and ears.

He ended it quickly. Quinton had taught them that where slicing fails against armor, piercing often succeeds. Lee flung both knives and felt the satisfaction of watching them sink into his foe's badger flank. He ducked a swing of the tail and drew his bow.

The hit he'd scored bought Zel time for another try with her whip. This time, her spikes dug into the creature's leg and held fast. She fought its fury with both hands on the whip, pulling the heads around to Lee. "Kill it!"

He shot arrow after arrow into its chest.

The two serrated beaks snapped at them both.

The woman.

The man.

The whip.

The arrows!

We're dying.

The voices under the song sorcery grew weaker. The pecking heads lost their speed. Lee dropped his bow and rushed in to catch one by the neck. He drew a third sikari and hacked at it until the head came free.

The remaining head let out a weak chortle. Perhaps the mourning noise was still part of its deception, like those of the mudslingers. Zel showed it mercy by drawing her knife and piercing the head above the beak. The whole creature crumpled to the road.

The cartman ran to its pet and buried a hand in its chest where the feathers mixed with the fur. "I . . . I can't hear them anymore."

"I'm sorry," Zel said, wiping black blood from her knife. "We had no choice."

He drew his hand away and looked at her. "Sorry? Why would ya be sorry? I'm free!"

With the cartman's help, Zel and Lee dragged the creature, which Lee had dubbed a *fluster beast*, off the road and into a copse of catclaw scrub. The bushes would hide the carcass but not the smell. "We need to move on, Zel. Quickly."

They helped the cartman, Arlo, with his cart, and headed east, away from Grindstone. "I thought Nagal and Nagil would make me a fortune," he told them as they walked. "For a time, I rode 'em with a saddle from town ta town and folks paid ta hear the wisdom in their songs—always two points of view."

"Wisdom?" Zel asked.

"So I thought. Truth, I used to tell folks, is not found in the words spoken but in the ear of the listener. Soon, though, I couldn't ride 'em anywhere, fer the two heads couldn't agree on a direction. After that, I pulled 'em in my cart." He shook his head, as if fighting off a bad memory. "I'm not sure when it started, but most days, I didn't even make it inta town. I walked the roads between villages, tossed about by the creature's curse."

That explained his emaciated state. The poor man had been imprisoned by indecision, as sure as being locked in a cell. Lee and Zel led Arlo off the road and gave him way rations from their stores. While the Aladoth ate, Lee began to share with him the story of the Great Rescue.

Freed from his roving prison, Arlo seemed excited to make his own choices. And for his first, he chose to believe all that Lee shared. His eyes lit up as he came to understand a new life waited for him—a new life of surety under the Rescuer, guided by real truth. "I want ta be liberated," he told them. "Not just from that double-minded creature, but from the dragons."

Lee knelt in the brush, motioning for Arlo and Zel to do the same. "Then pray with us. Repent and die to your former dragon masters. Rise again as Keledan."

When they'd finished, they embraced their new brother and told him of the new life awaiting him in Keledev. They told him the way to the closest hollow tree Lee knew of—the one in Darkling Shade first shown to the cadets by Ioanu the bear. "I wish we could return to Keledev with you," Lee told him, "but we've a quest to finish."

"Yer quest. Right." The dawn of remembering came to Arlo's face. "Forget everythin' I said before about south or the west. That was the creature. Yer Aladoth army went north fer certain."

"North." Zel let out a breath. "Thank you. That is a great help to our tracking."

"Ya need not track 'em anymore," Arlo said. "I can tell ya the very spot they've gone off ta."

30

"FOR MONTHS WE'VE BEEN HARASSED FROM THE north," Sireth said, shaking his war hammer at Kara, "and now we're being invaded from the south."

Kara looked to Tiran for aid in their argument, but her friend only crossed his arms, clearly siding with his tehpa. She couldn't fault him for that. But she could fault Sireth for his overstatement. "This is not an invasion, Master Yar."

"Isn't it?" Sireth used the hammer to point her toward a window. "Let's have a look, shall we?"

Airships floated on the fjord nearly a league below the lodge cliff, with boats running between them and the docks. Mules carried wool-wrapped bundles on the trails joining the outpost's many lifts. Tents had gone up on every flat ledge accessible by a path or steps, and only a few belonged to the watchmen companies.

Sireth planted his hammer's head on the timber floor. "Why are guildsmen hauling silk and leather and all manner of supplies up my cliffs? This outpost does not belong to Boreas and his Airguard"—he looked from Kara to Tiran—"or the Lightraider Order."

Tiran raised his hands to show he had nothing to do with any of this, which refocused Sireth's scowl on Kara.

"Boreas has a plan," she said. "A good one, which will give us a new advantage."

"And yet I, the outpost watchmaster, am not privy to this plan?" The whole effort had moved too fast. Boreas, as in any of his Assembly maneuvers, had been ready to move forward once he got his way. Kara and Samar had launched with another pilot and two ships the very night of the test, bringing with them other windfighter volunteers. More had followed as soon as enough ships had returned from the goblin hunt, this time bringing guildsmen to fashion the glide suits.

In all their haste, no one had asked Sireth or any other watchmen leader for permission to overrun the post. And even if they had, Kara was not supposed to say why.

"And the worst of it," Sireth said, still fuming, "is that your friend Lieutenant Ray is stealing my volunteers. I've lost twenty to his secret cause already. Do they know what they're getting into? I surely don't!"

"Councilor Boreas wanted to keep this plan secret as long as he might."

"I'd say the sands of that particular timeglass have run thin, wouldn't you?"

Kara held his hard gaze for a moment. Boreas would follow soon to oversee the efforts to create a windfighter training post. The councilor had told her to let him *deal with Sireth*, but she saw an unhelpful rivalry brewing. Sireth was right. Time had run out. "All right. But I can tell only you, for now." Kara glanced at Tiran. "Only the watchmaster."

Tiran's jaw dropped. "You can't mean that. You do realize that you're a lightraider, not a stormwatcher?"

"Tiran, please." Her eyes implored him.

He backed out, never releasing her from his glare. "You've not heard the end of this," he said and shut the door.

With her friend gone, Kara explained the notion of the windfighters, their use and training, and all that Boreas had planned.

The watchmaster stood stunned, hands resting on his upturned hammer. "You've all gone mad, then. I knew it would happen if the war got bad enough."

"I told you. I saw it work." Kara bobbled her head. "Mostly. But with practice from these cliffs, we can perfect the gliding. Imagine fighters descending on the orcs and golmogs from above."

This earned her a dry laugh. "You don't understand. With this new interference, I can barely imagine fighters at all." Sireth left his hammer and walked to a map table, beckoning for Kara to follow. "See here?" He showed two charwood marks near the Vales of the Passage Lakes. "A full sentinel squadron, led by your cadets and manned by my watchmen, must now remain here, and another here, to thwart whatever plans the enemy has laid for the Lakes. And more fighters must act as scouts to the north and south."

Sireth walked along the table pointing to more marks. "And here. And here. And this is the aboveground cave we now call Worm Hollow. I must have watchmen there to stop the creatures from making it a hideout again."

Kara tried to follow his argument, but he had not spoken it plainly. "Why should these postings stop us from training windfighters?"

"Don't you see? We're spread as thin as a morning frost. I've already had to pull men from my towers, and I've no one left to repair the burned way stations." His indignant tone became a frustrated shout. "I can't spare fighters for Boreas and his mad endeavor!"

The door swung open, and Tiran rushed in. At first, Kara thought he'd come running at the sound of his tehpa's shout, but the urgency on his face spoke of another reason.

"Orcs!" he said, pointing northwest. "Spotted by one of the ships. Marching down from the Nine Crags. They're headed this way!"

31

SIRETH RANG A BELL OUTSIDE THE LODGE, CALLING able-bodied fighters to the post's main plaza, a flat expanse of time-worn stone with a timber shelf extending out over the cliff. Samar rode up on a mare, one among only a few who answered. Ever since his glide, he'd worn the twin swords at his back, in their long square sheaths. Every time he drew them, Kara worried he'd slice his own ears off.

"Battle?" he asked, and she nodded. He'd proven himself enough by now that she had no intention of stopping him from joining a fight.

Dag came next, riding his Gladion, with Ioanu keeping pace. Dag's novices, a mix of watchmen and Airguard recruits, came running several paces behind.

Sireth eyed the approaching troop, all armed with blunt steel. "Bring them. We need every fighter we can muster."

"No." Dag sat defiant on the Gladion, who echoed his rider with a mighty snort.

"No?"

"I'll not risk these novices in a skirmish. They're not ready."

Sireth's cheeks and neck burned. "Those are my fighters."

"None are fighters yet," Dag countered. "And only half are

your recruits. The rest belong to Boreas. I belong to neither of you, and I say they stay here."

This brought grumbles of discontent from the volunteers, but a sharp look and a growl from Ioanu stilled their voices. Dag kept his gaze on Sireth. "Would you spend them now, untrained fodder for a pack of orcs, or save them and prepare them for the bigger fight that's coming?"

The older man, one all the cadet scouts viewed as a tehpa, furrowed his brow, then nodded. "Your novices. Your choice. But you and your axes had better make up the difference."

The ride northwest, upslope, took its toll on the horses, and the going was not as fast as any of them hoped. Ioanu snorted hard in her running but kept pace as good as any of the steeds.

"Would that those ships in my fjords could carry us to battle," Sireth said under his breath.

Kara rode close enough to hear him and gave a pointed cough.

He shot her a frown. "Quiet, Cadet, lest you spill your mad secret."

Their company, only nineteen strong, met a sentinel squadron on the march, led by Master Quinton himself. They'd been called by an Airguard herald who rode the opposite direction from the one that came to Tiran.

All told, their combined force boasted thirty-five, and Kara counted this a great blessing when they finally came to a rise and saw their foe. "There might be a hundred or more," she said, riding up between Sireth and Quinton. "I see golmogs among them."

Quinton patted his horse to settle him, the same great breed as Dag's, gazing down into the scree valley below. "An' those ugly black birds. But the orcs are such as I've never seen. Their flesh is gray, almost white, and the ore within it is as blue as a deep sea. We've only encountered iron orcs on this side of the Peaks. What manner are these?"

"Talanium orcs," Dag said. "Or so I'd call them. See the ore's color? The blue fire in their joints? Watch your blades. Talanium is harder than iron. And stronger. And the forging of its steel requires a hotter fire. These things will be tougher to kill than their iron cousins."

He spoke true. Sireth led the charge down into the valley, flanked by Dag, Quinton, and the bear while the archers shifted west and loosed two volleys. A scant few enemies dropped from their arrows. The rest howled in rage, with blue fire in their throats, and ran to meet the riders.

Fat golmogs lumbered out ahead and became the first to fall to Dag's and Quinton's dual axes. The Gladion horses flattened their bulging corpses and trampled the orcs behind them.

Two more golmogs met Ioanu's claws and saw their own gray innards spilled onto the rocks. Kara and Samar, leading the younger cadets and watchmen riders, met the line just after the bear, and from that moment, Kara noticed little beyond the creatures falling to her sword.

Sparks flew from chunks of ore, deflecting Kara's blades. Each strike and thrust demanded precision to sever flesh or tendons. By the sounds of the battle, the other fighters were struggling even more. Cries of anguish told her two, at least, had fallen.

A buzzard flew overhead with a stone clutched in its talons, perhaps to drop it on their rear line. Kara swung away from the orc she was fighting and hurled a whirlknife. It sliced the bird's gangly neck clean through before returning to her hand. The stone fell on an orc's head, and it fell senseless into Ioanu's claws.

"Form up! Rally to me!"

The call came from Sireth. Lifting an eye from her fight, Kara saw the reason. They'd been spread thin, a small version of the greater picture Sireth had shown her on the map. And the danger it brought was obvious. These tougher orcs, once able to isolate a watchman, had no trouble bringing him down. Another rider screamed and fell.

"To me!" Sireth called again.

Quinton and Dag echoed him. "To the watchmaster. Form up!"

Kara fought to obey and noticed Samar to her right, opposite the bear, gold Keledan armor blazing, taking one orc with every two strokes of his blades. Had he been there the whole time?

A sharp, chirping bark caught Kara's ear—a creature she'd never heard before, far more musical than the shrieking and screeching of dragon corruptions.

A paradragon with frost-blue wings and white-and-brown fur as fine as feathers, much like the one she'd seen high in the Clefts of Semajin a year before, flew straight at a pair of buzzards. Kara thought it might strike them with its talons, but the nimble creature rolled to their flank and flew the breadth of their wingspans, spouting a blast of ice.

Both buzzards careened to the rocks and lay there, necks or wings snapped.

The paradragon wheeled and turned its icy breath on the orcs. Thick frost gathered at their joints, melting quickly from the fire inside, but enough to slow them. With hopeful shouts, the fighters took full advantage.

Ioanu caught an orc by the throat and flung it to the rocks. Dag and Quinton spurred their horses and rode in with axes flying. Their efforts drew a swath of escape for those who'd been cut off.

The full force of Keledan formed up and beat back the orcs, aided by their paradragon ally. Archers at the rear shot down the last two buzzards. The enemy troop folded and fled. The Gladion riders ran them down, and none survived.

The cheering was short-lived. Taking stock, Kara saw four Keledan had fallen, with more wounded.

Sireth, grave and angry, organized his riders under Dag's command to carry the dead to Orvyn's Vow. He thanked Quinton and the sentinel squadron and bid them farewell to return to their posting, then came to Kara and Samar. "You two. With me." He turned his horse northward.

Kara sent Samar after him but held back with Ioanu. She had another spot of business to attend to—the paradragon. They found him watching from a high shelf above the valley, wings tucked behind and tail swishing. The creature saw her looking his way and cocked his head, watching her, then leapt from the shelf and flew away.

Kara waved after him. "Thank you!"

When she and Ioanu caught up to Sireth and Samar, the watchmaster sighed. "We must retrace the steps of these orcs—find their origin. And while we ride, we must talk. I may have spoken too harshly of your plan, Miss Orso. Lieutenant Ray, how many windfighters can your ships carry?"

"The largest? Seven, all armed with blades and crossbows, not including the pilot. And we have six of those ships floating now in your fjords. Imagine if—"

Sireth stopped him with a wave. "I've already imagined it. A troop of windfighters, flying ahead of our company, might harry an orc force and reduce their number well before the riders arrive. And if the numbers are as great as you claim, that troop might equal a sentinel squadron in all but the horses."

They searched for some time until the trail went cold, even for Ioanu's powerful nose, and Sireth signaled a turn to the south. As he did, he gave Kara a nod. "All right. I'm in. Boreas can have his windfighters. And he can train them in my outpost."

32

AARON HELD THE SPYGLASS ON EMEN YAN, LIT BY THE sun rising at their backs over the steep slopes of the river valley. "You're right, Connor. The day guards are less careful. They're checking only one in ten travelers for journey writs."

The party had bedded down for the night in a field of tall green stalks laden with many bright orange flowers. The nectar dripping from their bells smelled of honey. Sprite thimble, they were called, known in Keledev as littlebell. The flowers had many uses in trade, and in Tanelethar, their fields sometimes housed swarms of sprites.

With so many fields in the river valley, Connor calculated their risk of running into a sprite swarm in just one of them as small. And he'd wanted to be close to the gate when they woke up—ready to enter. Even so, they'd kept watch in shifts through the night with Aethia flying patrols overhead.

Aaron offered him the spyglass, but Connor declined and let him pass it to Teegan. "Let's wait a bit longer. Better to enter when the crowds are thickest. If we place ourselves well within the throng, sneaking in with our weapons won't be a challenge."

Teegan drew her eye from the glass and cast him a look that said, *You hope.*

The larger cities in Tanelethar's prominent cantons, cities like Emen Yan, required a special imprint on a journey writ for those traveling armed. Swords and crossbows were easily concealed when passing a city gate if there were no close inspections. The crook and trident posed more of a problem, unless a guard saw them as tools.

"The Rescuer will provide the cover we need," Connor said and rolled onto his back. The sun, lighting the orange flower bells from behind, had given him an idea, and he wanted to try it before they set off for the city.

He held the map he'd taken from the viper's book up to the growing light. The sun shone through the frail parchment, so bright it almost washed away the ink. Laying the map on his chest, Connor drew out his patehpa's journal, hesitated a beat, then tore a similar map from its pages.

"What are you doing?" Teegan asked.

"Hang on and I'll show you."

The others sat on either side of him as Connor set his patehpa's map behind the ancient map from the viper's book. He held both up to the sun.

"They're the same," Aaron said.

"Nearly. But not quite." Connor fidgeted with the parchments. "The symbols are different, and the sizes are not matched. I've no reason to think my patehpa knew of the viper's map, but he knew of the vault, and he may have marked its location."

Aaron tapped his shoulder, prompting him to sit up. "What about this vault? Why didn't you speak of it before we met the vipers? How much do you know? What sort of treasures are—"

Connor raised a hand to stop him. "I know very little." He held the maps up to the light. "One thing at a time, Aaron."

By sliding Faelin's map, which was smaller than the other, side to side, Connor could match up various portions of the city. Both parchments had many symbols, but three showed promise. Near the crest of the city, the ancient artist had drawn the shape of a torch within a circle within a square. The placement made it clear this symbol meant the palace.

"The vault may be under the seat of the ruling family," Connor said. "House Fulcor has owned Emen Yan for centuries. And we know they protect their treasures within their households. Fulcan lords like to keep their gold close."

Teegan watched the city through the glass, perhaps eyeing the hilltop dome and the many towers surrounding it. "But Heleyor's Vault may be older, and Emen Yan belonged first to House Leander, before they fell out of favor with the dragons."

House Leander. The way she spoke the name of the most famous traitor-kings struck Connor like a dagger. After the dragons made an example of House Suvor, the Leander king was the first to capitulate—the first to betray the Maker. How would Teegan see him once she knew the same treasonous blood ran in his veins?

"And where," Aaron asked, "if not in the palace, might House Leander keep its treasure?"

Connor glanced toward the city. "I don't know. But the palace is the last place I want to search. There, we'll face Aladoth guards, not dark creatures, and we don't want to put their lives at unnecessary risk."

"Or ours," Aaron said. "Right?"

Connor ignored him and returned his attention to the maps. "This symbol on the eastern side, midway up the city's rising canals, may tell us." He pointed to a diamond within a circle, almost like an eye, on the ancient map. "This diamond looks promising for a treasure hunt. Lee would know for certain. No one adores ancient maps as much as he."

"Would that he were here," Teegan said.

Connor felt the worry in her words. "He'll be all right." He shifted his gaze to Aaron. "And so will Zel. They know their business. We must tend to ours." He matched his patehpa's map against the other. "See here? Faelin drew a symbol in the same place. His looks like three horizontal lines, all wavering."

Teegan rested back with her hands behind her head. "Not very treasure-ish. What are our other options?"

In answer, Connor showed her another symbol on the opposite side of the city, a triangle within a square. Here, Faelin had drawn a long house next to a sword. "This may be of interest. Although, by my patehpa's drawing, I'd say it is a garrison of some kind."

"Or a treasure house," Teegan offered, "with a guarded door."

Aaron pointed her way, waggling his finger. "I like her interpretation."

She reached out to lower his hand. "Easy, boy. Our interpretations don't matter. The vault won't appear simply because we wish it so. We need the truth."

"And treasure is not our goal," Connor added. "Only the dagger. Got it?" He grabbed his crook and rose to his feet among the littlebell stalks. "Let's start with the diamond symbol on the eastern side. Come on. The crowds entering the gate are thickening. Now's our chance."

Aethia returned to her mistress, and Teegan quickly sent her off again, this time to hold watch over the airship. "If more vipers come, or *The Kingfisher* is threatened, come and tell me," she said to the falcon, then lifted her arm and launched her skyward.

Aaron tromped past to walk between her and Connor, flicking a littlebell with his finger. "I still don't believe that bird can understand a word you say."

"That's your folly. Not mine."

33

CONNOR'S TIMING COULD NOT HAVE BEEN WORSE. The crowd moving along the twin valley roads on either side of the river thinned moments before the three stepped from the flowers.

Teegan whispered that they might reverse course and walk the other way for a time, but both Connor and Aaron agreed such actions might draw more attention. "No," Connor said. "Keep pressing forward."

Perhaps he should have considered Teegan's plan more carefully.

"You, there!" A guard pointed a sword Connor's way as their party neared the gatehouse—two white-brick towers joined by a windowed arch that spanned the river. The morning watch were picking individuals out of the crowd on both sides and lining them up in queues for inspection.

With his left hand, Connor acknowledged the guard. With his right, he unclipped Revornosh from his belt and passed it secretly to Aaron. "You two don't know me," he said through gritted teeth. "Move away. Now!"

They separated, with Aaron and Teegan sneaking to another part of the crowd while Connor pushed his way toward the beckoning guard. The young man had a merchant by the sleeve and grabbed Connor's arm the moment he came within reach. "This way. The captain wants to see you." He tightened his grip on Connor. "Especially you, Shepherd."

The guard pushed Connor and the merchant into the farthest queue from the river, next to the gatehouse's eastern tower. A wooden barricade led up to a woman with raven-black hair wearing Emen Yan's green-and-yellow livery, boots propped up on a table. The captain.

A dog sat beside her, with short fur of marbled gray. His majestic head stood higher than his seated mistress, and the set of his gaze upon the travelers implied he held just as much authority. Or thought he did.

When Connor reached her, the captain had just bitten into a boiled egg and handed the rest to the dog. He waited for her to finish, knowing better than to speak without her leave. Should this captain ask for his journey writ, their quest might end within the tick.

"Good morn to you, Shepherd. Do you know why I sent my man to fetch you?"

Connor lowered his eyes to the cobblestones. "Better that you sent him than your hound." He lifted his eyes just enough to glance at her dog. "Is that a Tarlan Duke? I've never seen one up close. I'd no notion they were so large. I expect he could swallow me whole."

She lifted her left hand, covered with a leather glove that stretched to her upper arm—perhaps some trapping of her rank, since her other glove came only to her wrist. "Answer the question, peasant."

Connor winced inside. Guile hadn't worked, distracting her by getting her to talk about the dog. A city guard captain wielded all the power of a town constable and more—far more, in fact. If this woman declared him a threat to the city, she needed no judgment from a canton sheriff or province magistrate. She could have him hanged or run through with a wave of her hand. He tried asking the Rescuer for aid, a tactic he should have chosen first. *Logosaneth Ond krafend ka zabol sikel. Fi torol yadod nim recrethond.*

My words are a sword, hidden in the shadow of his hand.

When he dared lift his full gaze, he saw the captain smiling, chewing on another boiled egg. She shook the rest at Connor before letting the dog wolf it down. "Koteg is his name. My dog. He is indeed a Tarlan Duke, descended from the Tarlan war dogs and deerhounds and named for the duke who first bred them. And I'm still waiting for my answer. Why do you think I sent for you?"

Impatient grumblings rippled through the queue behind him. Shuffling and tapping boots. For these merchants, each beat of delay meant another coin lost. They would blame Connor, not her. He answered with a cordial smile. "My crook, I'd warrant."

"Is it a crook?" The captain eyed the black ram's-horn hook rising from beneath his cloak, wrapped in a spiral of steel down to its sharp point. "I've never seen the like."

"It's an heirloom of sorts."

Her gaze panned down his form to his toes and back up to his eyes again. "As are your fine clothes and that strange leather kit, I presume. For you are certainly better appointed than any shepherd I've ever met, even among the noble cousins of Fulcor who fancy herding as a sport."

"What can I say, ma'am. I'm blessed."

"Blessed enough to have a seal on your writ for that crook? The steel band and spike on the hook make it more than a tool, at least in my town."

He didn't answer, and she didn't press—yet.

The captain sniffed. "You'd be wrong, by the way."

"I'm sorry?"

"As to my reason for calling you here." She scratched her dog behind his flopped ears and lowered her boots to the ground, then drew a sword and used the tip to lift Connor's chin. "Your face is the reason I sent for you. You're familiar to me. Why?"

He hadn't the slightest notion.

Noise erupted from the plaza inside the gate, next to a square pool where canal skiffs collected passengers to take them deeper into the city. A guard broke through the growing crowd and mounted a bridge, waving. "Captain!"

She eyed Connor for another beat, then dropped her sword tip and stood to move the last of the wooden barriers aside. "Go on then, all of you."

Connor did not wait for a second invitation but moved quickly through the barrier.

The captain walked beside him a few paces and caught his wrist. "We're not done, Shepherd. Find me later, and I'll make sure your writ is sound. I'm Thera. Ask any city guard." She let go and split off toward the bridge.

The dog lingered a moment, watching Connor as if trying to work something out.

"Come, Koteg!"

Koteg huffed, blowing out his great jowls, then obeyed.

On the near side of the pool, Connor found his companions. Aaron pressed Revornosh into his hand, using their cloaks as cover. "What was that all about?"

"I don't know." Connor watched the captain join her guards. Two held a struggling captive, having disarmed him of a rusty blade. A merchant stood shouting nearby, bleeding from a wound on his arm. His spices lay strewn about the cobblestones in a dusting of drab colors next to an overturned basket on wheels.

"You want to follow her," Teegan said, as if reading his thoughts.

"The Rescuer allowed her to pull me out of the crowd for a reason."

"*And*"—Teegan moved in front of him to obstruct his view—"he allowed you to escape her grasp. Let's not test him a second time."

"I only want to follow." Connor's interest now lay more in the captain's new prisoner than the captain herself. The struggling man kept shouting for the orcs to let him go, even though there were no orcs about. His ashen face. The sunken eyes, hard and angry. Connor had seen it all before. "We need to talk to that prisoner. He's much like Keir before we rescued him."

"Like Keir?" Aaron walked a pace toward the captain. "As in, like those in the dragons' new Aladoth army?" He nodded to Teegan. "I'm with Connor. We should follow. The vault can wait."

"Because you want to find Zel," she said, "who was pursuing that very army."

The pilot shrugged. "Don't you want to find Lee?"

She ignored him and stepped close to Connor. "What of the vault?"

"Aaron's right. It can wait."

They kept their distance, moving with the crowd or stopping to look at merchants' wares when possible. During one of these stops, as Connor feigned interest in a wool tunic, Teegan nudged him. "She's taken a shine to you, that one."

This earned her a wide-eyed look. "You saw her stick a sword under my chin, right?"

"In the most flirtatious way a woman can."

"Just keep her in sight, will you? And keep clear of the dog. Tarlan Dukes are used to hunt boar and bear, and they can kill with a bite."

After the captain gave orders to the guards, she and Koteg took charge of the prisoner and led him away, over another bridge. Only one other went with them.

Thera forced the prisoner onto a skiff, and it set off under the power of its two punters. They coasted into a lock that would lift the boat to the next level of canals.

"Now what?" Teegan asked.

No other skiff was near, and none was likely to stop for the cadets and Aaron the way they'd stopped for a captain of the city guard. As Connor searched left and right for a solution, Teegan whispered the same prayer Master Jairun had prayed before their battle council.

"Kidef yi kethon do ya kethez panov, ker decton thimiov. Ker kevy, po alerol shurniov."

Your ears will hear this command. This is the way. Walk in it.

"Stairs," Teegan said a beat later, and took the lead.

Not until they had drawn much closer did Connor see the spiral of marble steps materialize out of the shadows. Whether they led to the same canal Thera had chosen, he didn't know, but he'd have to continue on faith.

At the top, they found a sparser crowd divided among half a dozen merchant stalls. A white marble pillar captured Connor's gaze. Fire burned from grates in its sides, and green smoke poured skyward from its top, adding the scent of ritual oils to the air.

Teegan shook his arm. "There they are."

Beyond the pillar was a lock and another canal. The captain and Koteg had gained a sizable lead. The cadets and Aaron hurried after her.

"What is that thing pouring out green smoke?" Aaron asked, holding his cloak to his nose. "It stinks."

"Fireclock," Connor said. "A change in color marks a change in tick. They came into fashion in the northern cities of Tanelethar after the Dragon Scourge—a form of dragon worship. We don't use them."

"But this one tells us something," Teegan said. "Doesn't it, Connor?"

"It does." The sight of the fireclock told him where they were. From the flower field, they'd seen all the big fireclocks sending up their colored and scented smoke from the city's wards. And this one, sending up a cloud of green, marked a ward close to one of the map symbols.

The canals flowed swifter than the three Keledan could safely move without drawing attention. Within a few beats, Thera's skiff turned on to an intersecting canal and traveled out of their sight. It didn't matter. Connor knew her destination. "That fireclock tells us the house-and-sword symbol on Faelin's map is, indeed, a garrison house. And I'd wager that's where they're going."

Faelin's map guided them the rest of the way, up one more level and along yet another canal to a low building with its own reflecting pool. Murals cut into its side danced on the water—horsemen with spears level, chasing off invaders. All the horsemen bore stern expressions, except their leader, who had no face at all. It had been polished away.

"Looks like a barracks," Aaron said as the three walked down a set of steps that bordered the building's plaza, "not a treasure vault. But you can't know for certain your captain brought the prisoner here."

"I can," Connor countered. "Look." He lifted his chin toward the far end of the garrison house.

The building was old, ancient enough to be marked on the map they'd found in the viper's text, which was likely why its plaza and pool sat lower than the surrounding streets. An ancient tradition capped one end—iron cages for city offenders. The threat of sitting there, exposed, where passersby might hurl rotten vegetables or worse, worked well as a deterrent to all but the most dedicated pickpockets and ruffians.

Thera's prisoner sat cross-legged in the corner cell, alone, with no sign of the captain or her dog. The three Keledan watched as a passing boy flung a tomato between the bars. It burst upon the prisoner's head. The child laughed and jeered, but when the prisoner made no response, he moved on.

"Sir," Connor said, leading his party closer. "Will you tell us why you cut that merchant in the plaza?"

"You saw?"

"We did."

"Good." The prisoner kept his eyes level. "Tell General Moach."

"What shall we tell him?" Aaron asked.

"You tell him I can do the job, just like Valshadox wants. You tell him I killed my own. Woulda killed the merchant, too, if them orcs hadn't stopped me."

Valshadox. Lord of Sil Shadath. General Moach, mocktree leader and enchanter of the barkhides. This man had been in the camps with Keir. Connor touched Aaron's back, out of the prisoner's sight, to let him know he had this. "We're a long way from the wanderers' domain, my friend. How did you come to be in Emen Yan?"

For the first time, the prisoner looked up, locking his hard gaze on Connor. "Don't you know?"

"Humor me."

"The orcs dragged us out of formation, threw me an' two others to the roadside."

"Why?"

The prisoner clenched his fists and growled. "Said we was weak."

For the second time that morning, Connor felt a sword pressed up under his chin. He let his eyes shift down the blade to its owner. "Hello, Captain Thera. Hello, Koteg."

The dog gave him a satisfied grunt for remembering his name.

Thera seemed less impressed. "Hello, Shepherd. By what right do you interrogate my prisoner?"

34

LEE AND ZEL CAMPED IN THE HILLS OF MINER'S GLORY
and rose before dawn to fly north, up the West Midland, following
Arlo's directions. The young cartman, pulled to and fro outside
of Grindstone under the torture of his double-minded beast, had
seen much of the Aladoth army. He'd watched them camp in the
hills for two nights, slowly diminishing in number.

You mean they entered the mines, Lee had said.

*Not exactly. No mine 'round here can hold an army that size.
But there's a tunnel, see. Long an' wide, leadin' north.*

The cartman had explained his family had worked the hills of
Miner's Glory for generations. His father had told him of a passage
used for eons by orcs and goblins to transport ore for the dragons.
No Aladoth crews were permitted inside, or even to speak of it, but
goblin miners aren't the most tight-lipped of creatures. *More'n one
spoke of a magic sea cave on the other end, one they call the Sorcerer's
Cave. From there they carry burdens ta the far reaches of Tanelethar.*

Lee held one of *The Merlin*'s trusses, eyes fixed on the gray-
green shoreline north of the Fulcan Plains. "Based on Arlo's tale,
this sea cave holds an unstable hollow hill portal that might spit a
traveler out anywhere. How are we to find the army if they passed
through it?"

"Don't get ahead of yourself." Zel worked her dials and ropes to bring them out into daylight. "Let's find the Sorcerer's Cave first. Then we'll see what we see."

She held a course west along the wide bay known as the Northern Bight—Winter's Bight to folks like Arlo. Both watched the coast, and anytime either saw an overhang or even a large rock, they pressed in for a look. Every one was a disappointment.

"My eyes grow weary," Lee said, after more ticks and leagues than he cared to count. "We could search till sunset and accomplish naught but granting my brother and his terrible army another day's lead."

"Or not." Zel shoved her rudder hard over, swinging Lee's eyes to a peninsula jutting north to form the western boundary of the bight—high, forested ridges of blood-red stone. "Take a look at the big shadow where the westward shore meets the rocks."

Lee had noticed the same land west of them for the last few leagues, coming ever closer, but now he wished they'd flown to it with greater haste. He set the shipglass on the rail and adjusted its lenses. "It's a cave. A big one."

The root of the peninsula, where its ridges made sharp descents into the plain, was broken by a wide fissure as tall as any castle built by men. Where Lee might expect to find sheer walls, washed smooth by the sea and wind, were hexagon pillars—hundreds of columns of varied heights stacked one upon the other, rising on both sides like vast staircases of perfect six-sided steps.

Zel bent her eye to the glass and nodded. "If that's not a sorcerer's cave, I don't know what is. We'd better find cover."

Whatever creatures might guard such a cave were not likely to miss an airship approaching over the frothing sea, no matter the color of her silk. Zel brought *The Merlin* low over the moss and gray gravel of the coastline until Lee spotted a trio of hills. "Put her down there."

Zel eyed the distance to the cave. "Are you sure? We'll have a long march."

"Better a long march than a swarm of goblins."

The march, however, along a gravelly shore that wore on his boots and limbs, took longer than he'd anticipated. The cave was to blame, so big that it skewed his perception of the distance. When they reached the first rock pillar, itself as wide as any cottage in his home fishing village, Lee stopped to rest his hands on his knees, breathing hard. "The nine dragon lords might fly through that opening."

"All together," Zel said. "And they may have." She helped him straighten and pressed him back against the pillar. "We can't walk in along the water line. We've no idea what waits for us."

"True." Lee set his hands low, clasped together, and nodded for Zel to step into them. "I'll give you a lift to the top of this pillar. Let's find out what we're dealing with."

Lifting and hoisting each other, the two climbed from one flat, hexagonal pillar top to the next. They worked their way higher until they came to a small circular landing carved with faded Elder Tongue runes.

Lee studied the wet carvings, almost washed away by time. "This landing was a lookout post."

"Was?" Zel asked.

"According to these, guardianship of this cave belonged to three of the old houses—Fulcor, Arkelon, and Leander—who shared it with the Aropha. Guards likely watched from landings like this on both sides of the entrance."

Zel's gaze wandered over the rocks. "I suppose dragons don't need such watchers. They have other devices."

"I wish we knew what sort." Lee followed the runes around the circle. "Here's a walkway. If dark creatures don't use this landing, they don't use its path either. This is our way in."

The path was broken in some places and worn entirely away in others so that Lee and Zel had to leap across the gaps. The deeper they journeyed, the more the stepped pillars varied in size. Some were as large as towers and others as small as Lee's fingers, all fitting together like a master toy maker's puzzle. Passing through a tunnel made of these pillars, the two got their first look at the cave's true purpose.

"Oh," Zel said. "That's going to be a problem."

The sea flowed in far below them, white and foaming, echoing up among a hundred walkways lit by burning sconces. These walkways joined a chaotic honeycomb of mine entrances below to more than a dozen ancient arches on the levels above, all filled with the liquid black strangeness of a hollow hill portal and each tall enough for a giant.

Keeping her gaze on these portals, Zel knelt and scooped up a handful of gravel.

"What's that for?" Lee asked.

"Just planning ahead."

He was too exhausted to make sense of her cryptic reply. The will and hope that had kept weariness at bay gave out at the sight of this place. His shoulder fell against the rock. "It's worse than I imagined. A collection of portals, and no sign of our quarry. How can we know where they've gone?"

Zel nodded toward walkways far below, near the mine entrances, where packs of goblin workers pushed carts of ore and other supplies. "At least the portals are unguarded. Those goblins are all I see."

Lee wished she hadn't said it.

The rock he'd leaned against began to vibrate. A rhythmic rumble of crunching and grinding sounded within. He jerked away and drew two sikaria. "Zel, get back!"

With a deep *crack*, a creature pulled its rock body from the passage wall and raised itself to twice Lee's height. Collections of the smaller hexagonal pillars formed a thick torso, arms, and legs carved with glowing runes. One by one, what looked like four uneven pits in the central pillar lit up with red pinpoints—eyes that bored into the intruders.

Words formed in Lee's mind, matching the rhythm of the

crunching and grinding emanating from the creature. *Toll, Keledan. You must pay the toll.*

"Rumblefoot," Lee said. "Stone troll, and it knows we're Keledan. Don't listen."

Without giving an answer, Zel let a crossbow bolt fly. It plinked off the rock between the creature's two sets of eyes and flipped back to land at her feet.

The rumble quieted.

Lee shook his head. "That may not have been the best plan."

An instant later, the crunching rumble returned, closer now to a roar.

"Run!" Lee turned Zel toward the portals, but they didn't make it far.

Two more stone trolls crashed onto the path before them. *Toll, Keledan. Pay the toll!*

35

LEE AND ZEL EXCHANGED A GLANCE, THEN SPLIT.
Zel bounded up the rock wall, using the smaller pillars as steps.

Lee had no such option, hemmed in by a sheer drop-off. He let out a shout, lowered his shoulder, and charged the rightmost troll with his Keledan shield.

He slammed into his target in a burst of light and pain—and reeled backward.

The troll, unmoved, let out a deep laugh.

Treat with us. Bargain. Pay the toll.

The thing took one step, then stopped. A spiked leather cord looped around its head from behind. One of the spikes dug into an eye pit.

It was Lee's turn to laugh, grunting against his soreness. "No."

The troll fell back, yanked off its feet by Zel's whip, and crashed down.

Lee ran over the top of it, feeling the rock torso crack under his glowing, armored boots, but he didn't stop to check his work. He and Zel kept running.

"Should . . . we just . . . pay them a few coins?" she asked as they ran. "Is the answer . . . that simple?"

Goblin arrows flew at them from the workers on the ramps. Lee ducked. "It's never . . . that simple."

His training had taught him never to indulge dark creatures, especially trolls. Stone trolls desired wealth, an urge by which the dragons animated them. Many lightraiders had faced the temptation to compromise—to pay them for passage or castle keys or secrets. Such bargains always came with dangerous attachments.

"We can't serve the Rescuer by treating with darkness," Lee said, ducking another arrow.

Zel shot back with her crossbow, dropping a goblin. "Then how do we defeat them?"

"We don't." Lee lifted his eyes toward the giant portals. "We flee and—"

The rumbling behind him grew to a raging frenzy. Glancing back, he saw all three trolls squatting on their thick rock legs. In a ripple of deep *pops*, they launched themselves into the air.

One landed on the path ahead of Lee and Zel. The other two landed on the wall to their left, bodies merging with its varied pillars. The troll on the path swung an arm, and rock shards flew at Lee.

He raised his glowing shield. The missiles burst into red dust. "We need to pass through a portal and escape."

A second troll jumped down from the wall to land within three paces of Zel. She snapped her whip to keep it back. "Which one?"

Lee had given the question some thought. While most of the arches were filled with what looked like smooth black liquid, unmarred by even a ripple, two bubbled with black smoke. Purple arcs—rare but present—flashed across them.

Those two had been recently used.

Lee pointed to the closest, two walkways down and a hundred paces away. "That one. We can reach it if we can get past these things again."

The trolls' song sorcery seemed never-ending—a rhythmic pounding and grinding, always carrying the same thought. *Bargain with us. Pay the toll.* The sound of it throbbed in Lee's chest. He found it an annoyance but feared for Zel. She had no lightraider training.

"Two coins," she said to Lee, cracking the whip at her opponent again. "Perhaps four in exchange for our lives and our quest. What can it hurt?"

The creature caught her whip with a stone hand and pulled her close. With the other it threw a hard punch. Zel brought her shield up in time, but the troll's fist landed hard and sent her flying. She slammed onto her back with a cry.

The creature advanced. The other jumped down from its wall perch and landed beside its comrade.

Bargain with us. Pay the toll. Or die.

"Zel!" Lee bashed his opponent with his shield and slashed with his sikaria. Bits of rock chipped away from the creature's arm. It roared, losing ground.

The space gave him room to reach Zel. He shouted a verse of encouragement, imploring her to hold strong. *"Tav profol halah mi e rath zavol thevenah dar anamod kostrah?"*

Is there profit in gaining the world but losing your soul?

Lee bashed at the trolls with his shield and a glowing fist, one after the other. "Get back! Get away from her!" With each strike, he moved them toward the drop-off, and Zel regained her feet. His limbs burned, strength fading fast. Goblin cackles danced amid the pounding of the trolls' song. They, too, were closing in.

From the corner of his eye, he saw Zel reach into her purse. "Zel, don't!"

She flicked out her hand. Gold and silver sparkled in the torchlight. The trolls reached high with stone fingers, but not high enough.

In that instant, Lee saw her plan. Without a word to each other, they both rammed their foes with their shields. The trolls tumbled over the edge while the coins they desired fell out of reach into the sea.

"Ha!" Zel said, as the creatures smashed into the rocks. One shattered into a hundred pieces. The other two held their forms but landed in awkward shapes, unmoving. "We beat them!"

Lee doubted they were ready to declare victory. "Rumblefeet

are not so easy to destroy. And there are other dangers. We need to move."

They ran for the portal, turning their attention to the goblins. Without breaking stride, Zel loaded new bolts and dispatched two with her crossbow. A third sprang from below the path and landed before them. Lee slashed its neck with a sikari and knocked it away.

"Goblins are hardly a danger," Zel said, taking out another with her whip. "Most of these carry only tools and knives."

The portal, still bubbling, loomed closer, and Lee was grateful for it. "I wasn't talking about the goblins."

A rending of stone like none he'd ever heard tore through the cave, drowning out the sound of the sea. Both slowed and looked back.

One whole section of the cave wall came to life and stood with its feet planted in the water—a massive version of the stone trolls, its tall head set with many red eyes. The two remaining trolls rode upon its chest. The broken troll, it held in its palm.

"Giant!" Lee cried.

As the rock giant took a lumbering step toward the Keledan, it brought the fallen troll to its mouth and crunched it down as a meal.

"Why is it doing that?" Zel asked.

Lee took her arm and spurred her onward. "Go, go, go!"

Terrible sounds followed them—grinding and gurgling. Heat filled the cave.

They had no time to climb down to the base of the portal's arch. Lee pulled Zel beside him and raced for a switchback at full speed. "Jump!"

They leapt, crossing the last several paces to the portal in midair, aiming for its center, well above the ground. The giant opened its mouth and spewed out what had once been its troll companion, now a stream of molten rock. Orange flecks at the forefront of the stream pierced Lee's armor. In the same instant, the portal's black smoke looped out to claim them. He let out a yelp from a sudden burning at his arm, and then they were through. Cold. Blowing snow.

Far too much air between them and the ground.

"Lee!"

Their flight didn't last long. A snowbank cut Zel's call short as the two vanished within it. An impact with frozen earth stole the air from Lee's lungs. A grunt beside him told him Zel had suffered much the same.

His body ached. Pain seared his arm. But he felt no broken bones.

Slowly, Lee poked his head up through the hole he'd made in the snowbank. "Zel? You with me?"

She stared back at him from a matching hole. "Rock giant?"

"Stone trolls occupy caves in threes, and sometimes draw in a giant as their enforcer. In a cave that big, with its valuable contents, I figured there'd be a giant for sure."

"Oh," was all that Zel could manage in reply.

After sitting in the snow a long time, they both turned to look at the portal. Black smoke churned, and jagged purple bolts flashed within a misshapen arch dug into a great snow-dusted mound of earth, rubble, and pyranium scrap.

"Do you think the giant will—" Zel began.

Lee cut her off before she could finish. "No. Its job is to protect the cave. It'll stay there."

I hope.

He added a silent prayer. *Please help us and heal us and give us time to find out where we are.*

An answer came, as clear as his own voice in his head. *You know this place. Look around and see.*

Lee obeyed, and within moments, he recognized the snowy valley. He'd gotten only a short look at it on his last visit before sprites had stung him into unconsciousness, but the impossibly high Celestial Peaks rising to their south were unmistakable.

Among the rubble forming the portal mound were huge plates of black pyranium, pieces of a collapsed dragon stronghold. Lee recognized what was left of the surrounding walls and towers. "Vorax," he said out loud.

"Who?" Zel had dug herself out of the snowbank and seemed to be gathering stones again, slipping them into a pouch with a handful of dirt.

Lee didn't bother asking why. "Vorax the dragon lord. This was his stronghold, where he built the portal that sent goblins and orcs into Keledev and where Connor's grandfather Faelin killed him with the very sword Connor now carries." He shook his head and laughed. "When we first came through the portal, we were only a few leagues west of—"

Pain racked Lee's arm. He drew in a sharp breath.

Zel's eyes narrowed. "What's wrong?"

He drew back his cloak. Small, charred holes marred his tunic. He couldn't get a clear look at the flesh without cutting the sleeve away, not something he wanted to do in this cold. "Burns, I think. From the giant's flaming spit. Nothing deep or dangerous." He brushed snow away from the cloth. "I've already soaked the wounds in ice. What more could I do?"

A grumbling voice reached Lee's ears on the cold air, and he yanked Zel down into the snowbank. "Shh! Orcs."

The two dug through the bank until they found the fallen wall it had formed against. Quietly, they pushed away the snow and peered over. To the south, higher up the valley, a troop of pyranium orcs in black-and-red spiked armor marched down a muddy road into a timber mine entrance. Golmogs trudged behind them. By the slop they'd made of the road, many such troops had passed the same route in recent days.

"Well," Zel whispered. "We've found an army. Is it the one we're seeking?"

36

CONNOR
TANELETHAR
EMEN YAN

"SO, THIS IS GOING WELL," AARON SAID.

"Quite well," Teegan added.

Connor grunted and flicked a bit of rotted squash from his cheek.

Thera had not taken kindly to Connor's appearance at her jail. He'd tried to argue that she'd invited him to find her, but as he spoke, his cloak fell to the side and revealed Revornosh. This led to a demand for a journey writ, which none of them carried. That had been the end of it.

The three now sat in the cage next to the one holding Thera's other prisoner, sharing in the sting of rotted eggs and vegetables cast by children. Thanks to Aaron, they'd learned that challenging or admonishing such ill-behaved children caused them to run away—only to return soon after with friends and more eggs and vegetables.

"Shoo! Enough!" A stern and familiar voice rose over the jeers.

The children scattered.

"Is it enough?" Connor asked as Captain Thera turned from the children to face them. "Have we served our full punishment?"

Koteg sniffed the bits of produce on the bars and scrunched his muzzle. Thera scratched his ears. "Punishment? Nothing of the kind. I simply provided you with a place to stay while you wait for the canton sheriff to return from his wanderings. These are Emen Yan's best accommodations." She gripped a bar, then quickly drew her hand away, having touched green ooze.

The captain pointed at Aaron and snapped her fingers. He rolled his eyes and trudged over. She wiped her hand on his cloak and began to walk away.

Teegan leaned close to Connor. "She still has a fondness for you. It's why she stopped the children."

"What are you saying? I should woo her?"

"No. Just . . . talk to her."

He sighed and stood. "Captain!" Connor approached the bars. "You needn't turn us over to the sheriff."

She seemed to expect this plea. Thera returned, arms crossed, her dog looking unconvinced at her hip. "Give me a reason not to."

Teegan might be right. This captain didn't want to send them into captivity.

"I'm sorry," Connor said. "*We're* sorry. We're sorry we brought weapons into the city without your leave and interrogated your prisoner."

"Also without my leave. You might have asked me first."

To this, he gave a conceding nod. "We didn't think you'd understand our purpose."

"And that is?"

Connor glanced back at the others. Every inch of Aaron's expression warned him to turn from his current course, but Teegan's soft gaze said, *Go on. This is the right way.*

"Don't look at them, Shepherd. Look at me. Why have you come to Emen Yan?"

He swallowed. "We seek a relic, one that belonged to our people. We believe it may stop the dragons from destroying our homeland."

Her lips parted. Koteg looked up at her and let out a short, questioning whine. Thera lowered her voice. "You're Keledan—

from the region south of the impossible mountains."

Connor gave her a half smile. "What other land would the dragons wish to wipe from the face of Talania?"

"And your interest in my prisoner?"

"He was part of an army designed for that purpose—an army of tortured Aladoth, conditioned to kill their fellow man without mercy."

Thera eyed the prisoner, still seated, unmoving at the center of his cage, covered in the filth Aaron's antics had brought upon them all. Her expression changed, as if seeing him in a new light—no longer a beggar or a madman, but a monster. "Why is he here in Emen Yan?"

"Ahem!" Aaron coughed, having inched nearer to their conversation. "We'll tell you, oh benevolent Captain, if you let us go."

Connor shot him a frown, but Thera lifted her chin. "Done. Tell me all you know about this man and those like him, and I'll let you go."

Connor raised a brow. "With our weapons."

"And a journey writ," Aaron said.

Teegan joined them both at the bars, pulling a bit of tomato out of her red hair. "And a washcloth."

Thera stared back at Teegan, eyes darkening, then she and the dog huffed and walked away.

They waited for more than a tick, and still the captain did not return. In that time, Teegan tried to speak with their fellow prisoner. He said little, except that he and two others had failed to execute a soldier who'd fallen ill—too ill to continue the march—and the orcs had cast them out. "I can do the job," he said, as before. "Tell the general you saw. Tell him I killed the other two with my blade, just as he wants. I can do the job." After that he returned to his stillness.

Connor and Teegan attempted to speak to him of the Rescuer, but he made no response.

Aaron passed the time pacing before the bars. "You shouldn't have asked for the washcloth, Teegan. It was too much."

"Yes, Aaron," she said. "After telling her we're Keledan seeking to thwart the plans of the dragons and demanding our weapons be returned, *that* was the final straw."

He shrugged. "Might've been."

It wasn't, as evidenced by the washcloth that landed with a slap against the back of his neck.

Two guards entered the cage, handing over the cadets' and Aaron's arms. With a quiet gesture from their mistress, punctuated by a low bark from Koteg, they made themselves scarce.

Thera held the barred door open wide. "Let's talk while you clean yourselves up."

A nearby gate led into a walled yard behind the garrison house, where numerous city guards talked and sparred together. Thera sat the Keledan down near a trough of water, by which they scrubbed what filth they might from their clothes. More than one of the guards shot wary looks their way.

"Speak quietly," Thera said, wrapping an arm around Koteg, who leaned against her where she sat, "but don't mind their looks, I'm well respected here."

"So I see." Connor accepted the cloth from Aaron and scrubbed his face. "I might even say you're feared."

"I can hold my own. And they know it. Tell me about my prisoner."

Connor held nothing back, despite the occasional alarmed cough from Aaron—for which Thera suggested the pilot see an apothecarist. Connor told her of Sil Shadath and the camps and how they had rescued a brehna there. He told her that her prisoner had suffered, having all kindness and mercy tortured out of him, to the point of making him a murderer, and that his presence in Emen Yan meant the dragons' new army was on the move.

Thera watched a few of her guards sparring in the corner of the yard. "And that means time for your homeland is running out?"

"Just so. What will you do with the prisoner?"

"He stabbed a man at the gates of my city and claims to have killed others. That must be dealt with. I'll hand him over to the sheriff."

"If we may beg another indulgence," Connor said, "hold him in isolation for a time. Treat him well but keep him clear of anyone else until our work here is done. I fear he'll sell us to the dragons to spare his own life."

Without answering his plea, Thera took the rag away from Connor and slung it down on the edge of the trough. "Time for you to go."

She and Koteg led them out of the gate, and then she drew a purse and a small leather-backed scroll from her cloak and handed them to Connor. "You may want these."

Teegan took the scroll from Connor's hand. "A journey writ."

Thera nodded. "One that covers the carrier and any travel companions. I added a seal allowing you to carry weapons."

"If we're caught in our quest," Aaron said, "aren't you worried we'll endanger you?"

"No offense, but my word is better than yours in this town." Her dog nosed the purse she'd given Connor, and Thera rubbed his broad neck. "Right. Almost forgot. The prisoner had those on him. I expect he mined them with the other two after they were cast out and killed them to take the lot. He tried to sell them to the merchant, which started their argument."

Connor opened the purse. Inside were chunks of brimstone metal mixed with a dark orange form of obsidian glass. He remembered Belen's words in the tinker's tower at Ras Telesar.

Brimstone metal, near as soft as clay, mined only from the obsidian under the burning mountains in the Brimstone Heights of Tanelethar.

When he glanced up to thank the captain, Thera was headed for the yard. He called after her, "You've done much for us—far more than we hoped. Why?"

"I told you before. Your face is familiar to me, like an old friend long forgotten." With that, she and Koteg walked through the gate and were gone.

37

FAELIN'S MAP, COMBINED WITH THE MAP FROM THE viper's codex, brought Connor, Teegan, and Aaron to a long, curving row of marble houses overlooking a canal on the city's fourth level.

Connor held the two maps up to the afternoon sun, doing his best to match up the symbols—a diamond within a circle on the ancient map and three wavy lines on Faelin's. "This is the right ward," he said, putting the viper's map away, then showed them a sketch of structures his patehpa had drawn. "This sketch must represent these houses. If that's true, then—"

A pair of locals passed close, and Connor held his tongue for a beat. The two, a man and woman of middle age dressed in fine silks, watched them carefully.

Aaron gave them a nod. "Good afternoon."

They walked on.

Teegan swatted the pilot's midsection with the back of her hand. "Don't draw attention."

"By greeting them?" Aaron gave her a dry chuckle. "We had their attention already, thanks to Connor going rigid at their approach. I was merely covering for him."

They watched the couple take the steps to one of the houses.

The woman looked their way. Connor averted his eyes. "Aaron's right, Teegan. He made the best of my poor showing. But I fear whatever actions we take here will draw suspicion. These homes belong to the city's high-born and high-bred—canton councilors, Fulcor nobles, and their favored friends. Not many outsiders visit this place. We must be quick."

He checked Faelin's map again, then thrust his chin toward the end of the row, where the canal dropped to the third level by way of a lock. "Faelin's symbol puts our next potential vault there."

They found nothing remarkable about the spot.

"Are you certain this is the place your patehpa marked?" Teegan asked.

"It matches both maps. But I see nothing, and we can't linger long in any one place. Thera's journey writ offers us cover. I'd hate to repay her kindness by bringing her trouble."

"Or bringing our necks to the executioner's axe," Aaron added.

The marble houses on the level below held a different shade of white, and the slope of their stone rooftops seemed lower. Otherwise, they looked much the same.

Aaron took the difference as significant. "Remember the garrison house," he said, hands on his hips, looking down at the lock, "how the yard, plaza, and reflecting pool all sat much lower than the surrounding streets?"

Teegan nodded. "So?"

"So from what we saw, I'd say the garrison house is as old as Emen Yan. But the streets around it have grown upward over the centuries."

Connor took his meaning. "You think the place marked on these maps lies under the current streets, buried by time."

The pilot called them to the edge of the lock. "Watch. See how deep it is?"

A supply barge rode the lock down, its poleman looking near asleep on his feet as he waited. As the barge descended, an opening appeared next to a ladder in the lock wall, becoming a temporary falls when the water level dropped below its threshold.

"If a more ancient part of the city lies underneath this street as Aaron claims," Teegan said, "that opening may be our only way in." The lock water flowed out into the lower canal, and the barge moved on. When the doors closed, the level started to rise again.

With a quiet signal for the others to follow, Connor rushed down the ladder and swung into the opening, slipping and nearly falling on a moss-covered floor. "Watch yourselves. The stone is slick."

Aaron came last, and Connor clasped his arm to steady him. "Did anyone see us?"

"None that I noticed, but that will matter little if the water fills this place and drowns us. It's rising fast."

Looking past him, Connor saw the water filling the lock much faster than it'd gone down. The party fled the opening and rushed into darkness. Within a few beats, water lapped at their heels, then their ankles, and soon they were sloshing and sliding along the passage. It occurred to Connor that this might be some overflow channel or other compartment with no outlet. If so, they might be forced to swim out again. He hoped they'd have breath enough for the journey.

More than the fear of a long swim, he worried over the pouch at his hip taken from Thera's prisoner, filled with brimstone metal that might ignite with a violent blast at the first touch of the water.

A flight of stairs appeared in the murky dark, rounded and broad. He and the others took them two at a time, until they reached what felt like a landing, dry and unsullied by moss. They stopped to breathe.

Teegan, always quickest to recover, lit a candle and set it in her travel lantern. The water rippled a few steps below, no longer pursuing them. "It stopped. I'd say the level reached the top of the lock. We're safe."

"Safe may be a premature judgment," Aaron said. "We don't know what's down here."

Teegan raised the lantern high and wandered out in front of him. "A treasure vault, I hope."

To double their light, Connor lit a second lantern. The landing gave way to cobblestone, now flat gray, but perhaps once white like the street above. Tiny flecks in the stones caught his light here and there under the dust. Pillars, unadorned, supported a low ceiling.

Aaron held an arm across his nose and grimaced. "Yet another lovely smell."

"Stagnant water," Teegan said. "Full of decay and who knows what else." She nodded at narrow water channels crisscrossing an old plaza ahead, cut off from the canal. The channel water looked thick and black. "Whatever you do, don't drink or even touch it."

The pilot cocked his head to look her way, arm still across his nose. "Rest assured, neither was in my plans."

"Hush. Both of you." Movement to the left had caught Connor's eye—or perhaps shadows playing between the two lanterns. "Stay alert. We may not be alone."

The crisscrossing channels all came together at a rectangular pool, much like the reflecting pool at the garrison house. Holding their lanterns out over it, Connor and Teegan illuminated a pair of statues on the other side, guarding the pillared entrance to a low marble building. The flat roof had become one with the ceiling of this forgotten realm.

"We found it," Aaron said and set off around the pool.

Connor reached for him and missed. "Wait!"

Aaron ignored his call and outpaced the lanternlight. Without its aid, he stepped into a channel, splashing black water onto the cobblestones. He lifted his knee and shook his boot, dripping with slime. "Ugh. Disgusting."

Before Aaron could set down his boot again, a tentacle with many claws shot out of the channel and wrapped his ankle. He fell, crying out and clawing at the cobblestones as an unseen force pulled him toward the pool.

38

"CONNOR!" AARON SKIPPED LIKE A STONE ALONG THE plaza, one leg in the channel, a ripple of water flying ahead of him. "Help!"

Help came first from Teegan. She timed a throw of her trident to hit the ripple as it reached the pool. The creature screeched and released its prey. The trident, shaft high, roved about the pool like a ladle stirring a pot.

Aaron scooted back along the stones, blood darkening his boot at the ankle.

"Stay there," Connor said, running past him. "Keep clear of the water."

"You think?"

A rock flung from Connor's sling did nothing. He couldn't penetrate the water's surface with any force. He traded the weapon for Revornosh and rushed to the pool's edge on the short side while Teegan took the long. She twirled her chain mail net, ready to sling its spikes. "Watch out, Connor. There may be more than one."

He hadn't thought of that.

He stayed alert, and when the trident came near, he lunged and stabbed. He felt the resistance of flesh.

Another screech.

The trident's shaft canted within reach, and Connor took his chance to grab it. A pink-red body broke the surface. Three tentacles whipped at him, claws flared. He slashed them back with Revornosh.

Before Connor knew it, Teegan was at his side. She dropped her net on the cobblestones and committed both hands to helping him with the trident. Together, they hauled the creature onto the pool's edge, where Connor stabbed it again and again until its screeching stopped.

When the tentacles quit wriggling, the two released their hold and staggered back. Teegan's trident throw, aided by a silent prayer to the Rescuer, had pierced the monster's one large eye. Gray fluid oozed from the wound.

Aaron hobbled over. "What is it?"

"Valpaz," Teegan said. "A water sentry, left by dragons and Taneletharian lords to protect valuables and important roads. Big ones like this are solitary, but the smaller valpaza move in swarms." She glanced down at his ankle. "That looks bad."

"It's not deep."

Connor dropped to a knee beside him. "All the same, we should have a look. Take that boot off."

Aaron had spoken true about the depth of the wound. His Keledan armor and his leather boot had spared him the worst part of the creature's claws. But there were several punctures, eight in all.

"This one." Connor showed his friend one puncture that looked wider than the others. "Does it sting?"

"They all sting."

He sighed. "I'm sure. But can you say if this one is worse than the others? The larger talons contain venom."

After a moment's thought, Aaron nodded. "I suppose so."

Connor patted his manykit pockets until he found a roll of bandages and a small clay jar of balm. Using fresh water from his waterskin, he washed the punctures, making sure to rinse the largest wound as much as possible. Then he applied the balm and wrapped the ankle. "This will hold, and if we change it often enough, you'll heal. But we must also deal with the venom."

"How?" Aaron asked. "With herbs?"

"They'll help." Connor handed him a wool pouch from his gear. "This is coriander, solanum, and goosefoot. Swallow a pinch every few hours for the pain and to settle your stomach. Now, more importantly, we need to deal with the effects on your spirit. Valpaz venom pushes you to lean on your own wits rather than the Maker, and that helps the creature wrap you deeper in its tentacles until there's no escape."

"But I escaped its tentacles."

"No." Connor could already hear the venom setting in. "Your friend, with a weapon steered by the Rescuer's response to her prayer, *saved* you from those tentacles. Remember?"

Aaron scrunched his brow. "Oh. Right. I didn't get away on my own."

Connor made a silent plea for guidance, then spoke a verse that sprang to mind. *"Fi Rumosh, bi koth lavechovu credov, po intelegovu seperov."* Then he spoke the thrust of it in the Common Tongue for the pilot. "Trust the High One. Lean not on your own understanding. Have you heard this wisdom?"

A spark flared behind his friend's eyes, and he smiled against his pain. "I have. I know it and what follows. Councilor Boreas made it part of our daily readings, though I cannot speak it in the Elder Tongue, as a lightraider might. The next verse implores us to acknowledge him in all our ways, and he will make our paths straight."

They prayed aloud together for straight paths under the Rescuer's light, and when they finished, Aaron let out a long breath. Leaning on Connor, he tested the sureness of his leg. He took a step and another. "I think I'll be all right."

They both continued toward the building's entrance, where

Teegan had already gone with her lantern. "I'm glad," Connor said. "I've done my best, but I'm no renewer."

"No, you're not." Teegan held her lantern up to one of the two statues guarding the entrance. "But you're something else, it seems."

The statues had suffered damage. Each was dressed as a lord, armed with a longsword, with a viper almost as tall rearing up beside him. Fire had charred both statues, and one looked to have suffered under an angry hammer, with much of its head beaten away.

The other had fared better, with only two chips missing from its chin and temple. Teegan, on tiptoe, was busy wiping away what soot she might with the hem of her cloak. When she finished, she let her fingers graze the lord's cheek and regarded Connor with curiosity.

"Tell me," she said, holding him with her gaze. "Why does this statue of an ancient lord, ages old and hidden beneath a city far from our home, bear your face? For no sculptor in Keledev could carve a more exact duplication."

39

KARA
KELEDEV
ORVYN'S VOW

KARA MOTIONED A HESITANT VOLUNTEER OUT ONTO the wooden ledge the outpost timbermen had built for their jumps. "Come. This is what you chose. Make the first leap into the fjord, and the rest is easy."

He held his ground and scoffed at her. "How would you know? You've never jumped."

What was she supposed to say? Kara looked toward the lodge. Amid all its bustling activity, she saw no sign of Samar. Where had he gone?

"Please," she said, beckoning again. "Give it a try."

He shook his head and walked away. Two others followed. The last shot her a sad look on his way up the path. "I'd rather die on an orc blade like my friends."

Boreas and Sireth had given him and the others no time to mourn. They had none to spare.

Loss came too frequently, and new attacks too close upon their heels. Orvyn's Vow had fought two more skirmishes with smaller forces since the first battle with the talanium orcs. Kara was not permitted to take part in either.

Training the windfighters took precedence over all else, but that was not going as planned.

Kara watched the clouds move over the water, where fishermen waited to collect windfighter recruits that, thus far, weren't coming.

Much had passed since the battle below the Nine Crags. Boreas had arrived in their absence and tossed all mystery about his purpose into the fjords. He'd gathered his volunteers and told them the full extent of their mission. Not one walked away—not then, at least, under his charismatic voice. Kara wished she had his skill.

In the night, a raven came from Ras Telesar. Attacks against the academy had increased as well. Cadet archers shot buzzards from the sky in every tick and watch. The headmaster himself had led a force of only ten in defeating fifty iron orcs and goblins less than half a league from Anvil Ridge. Not all of the ten returned.

The raven also bore news of a new Keledan who'd appeared at the Passage Lakes. Alone. This man brought a message from Lee and Zel, still deep in their quest. The tortured Aladoth army from Sil Shadath was on the move and missing. They might appear in Keledev at any time and any place.

By morning, Boreas's small army of guildsmen had fashioned ten glide suits. Ten more would be ready on the morrow. Kara had to wonder if they'd keep enough recruits to fill them. She'd lost three in the last tick—not to death, as she'd originally feared, but to fear itself. And no wonder she couldn't convince them to jump. Kara was supposed to train the fighters in combat. Samar was supposed to teach them to glide. But he'd been missing ever since the raven came.

A creaking snapped her eyes from the water to the back of the wooden ledge. Ioanu had taken a step out to join her.

Kara pushed out a palm. "Come no farther. This ledge wasn't made for bears."

Ioanu kept walking, one excruciating step at a time. The planks groaned under her weight. "The timbermen say it will hold."

"The timbermen aren't asked to stand upon it. And what

business have you with them? What have you been up to?"

"Much more than chatting about the strength of wood supports, I can tell you that." Ioanu lifted her snout toward the ridge, directing Kara's gaze.

Samar came over a rise along the trail from the main lodge, burdened with two bundles—one large and one small. He took the branch down to the ledge and stopped where its wood planks met the rocks. "Better come here so I can show you what I've brought. For all three of us to stand on those timbers might be a test of the Maker's grace."

He set to work unwrapping his bundles. The first looked much like a horse's tack, but with a large leather pouch in place of a saddle and with silks joining some of the straps.

Kara walked around to Ioanu's snout and set her hands on her hips. "You didn't."

The bear lolled her great head back and forth, a sign akin to a human shrug. "I did. And with your Councilor Boreas's blessing, thank you. I have my very own glide suit. Help me put it on."

Kara refused, but Samar was happy to lend Ioanu his aid. She watched him work in disbelief. "Why?"

"Why do you think?" Ioanu asked. "I spent my whole life coasting on the mists of the Tagamoor. I have more knowledge of gliding than any in all Keledev." She raised a paw to let Samar slip a harness loop into place. "Is a bear not more suited to flight than these gangly men and women?"

Is a bear not more suited to flight?

The question might have brought a laugh to Kara's lips on another day. "There is no ship that can carry you."

"Not true. But my purpose is not to glide into a fight. Rather, I hope to encourage and teach the volunteers. I hear tell some have said this very morn they won't jump until they see a pig in flight." A grunt escaped Ioanu's throat—a bearish laugh. "I will do them one better and show them a flying bear."

40

SAMAR FINISHED BUCKLING IOANU'S STRAPS. LIKE HIM on the evening of his first glide, she looked a bit like she was wearing a gown.

Kara crossed her arms. "This is not the Tagamoor. There are no mists to catch you."

"But on those mists, I used to soar," Ioanu said. "Don't you see? There I was as sure and graceful as a falcon."

The bear's madness was about more than teaching recruits, it seemed. Kara softened her voice. "You miss it."

"So very much, Queensblood. More than you can know."

Kara allowed herself to take a sharper interest in the guildsmen's work. The leather harness looped all four of Ioanu's legs, with a broad leather piece under her torso. A pair of rings stuck out from under the pouch to rest between her shoulders—a talanium ring to release the silk and a copper one to shed the whole apparatus.

She frowned at the rings. "I see no way for you to reach these."

"Correct, Queensblood." Ioanu ambled around to face her, directing her snout toward the ledge. "I must make the leap with a partner."

As she spoke, Samar lifted a human glide suit from the smaller bundle. He jiggled it at Kara.

She shook her head. "I see your minds, and you're both mistaken. I'm a lightraider, not a windfighter."

Samar held the suit at Kara's shoulder level as if to take her measure. "Why can't you be both?"

"Listen to your friend," Ioanu said. "I remember your flight at my birthplace—when you leapt from the forge window. You took to the air as a dove from a nest while Wartroot fell like a broken leaf." She nudged Kara toward Samar with her great brow. "You were made for this."

Ioanu's push put Kara mere inches from Samar. He smiled, more at ease with this closeness than she. She took the glide suit and backed away.

The bear lowered her head. "Please, Queensblood."

It wouldn't hurt to try it on, at least to make Ioanu happy.

Kara shed her cloak, but when she began to remove her manykit and whirlknives, Samar shook his head. "The tailor made your suit special, with room for your manykit and knives along with the usual swords." He came close again—too close for her comfort—and showed her the spaces meant to make room for the sheaths at the small of her back.

Kara pushed his hand away. "I see it, thank you."

The leather fit well. Had it been Ioanu or Samar who had guessed her measurements? Likely both. Kara cast a glance at the ledge, and the emptiness of the air beyond hit her. What was she thinking? She shook her head. "This is a foolish fancy. I can't. I told you."

Ioanu walked onto the ledge. "And where does that leave me?"

"That is not my problem. And this is not my calling."

Was it? Could a lightraider glide on the air with the windfighters? Could this be what the Rescuer wanted?

Ioanu didn't give Kara time to discern the answer. "Enough talk," the bear said. "I'm ready to fly." She turned to lumber over protesting timbers and leapt from the edge.

A half beat passed while Kara stared in disbelief after her

friend. Ioanu could not release her silk alone. That much had been clear. Samar wore no glide suit.

Either Kara jumped, or the bear died.

Or both.

Clawing for the straps in half panic, Kara tightened her buckles and sprinted for the ledge. *Rescuer, fortify my heart and guide my flight.* She reached the edge at a full run and jumped.

"Ioanu!"

The wind of falling forced a second call back down Kara's throat. She blinked away tears drawn out by the cold. Where was her friend?

There. A blue-gray smudge against blurred water far below. Samar hadn't told her of the difficulty seeing in this type of flight. Kara squinted against the rushing air and flattened her arms against her sides to slice through it better. She had to catch Ioanu.

The bear, for her part, seemed to know her business. As Kara drew closer, she saw Ioanu had spread all four legs out as far as a bear might, with her silks catching the wind. Kara's tucked arms gave her a much faster fall, and a few beats later, she spread her limbs to match the bear's speed.

Aligning herself with Ioanu's back took far more effort, but the skills Kara had learned flying through the Tagamoor and Sil Shadath returned to her. She canted her shoulders and slid sideways against the wind. In no time, she'd come within an arm's reach.

Her voice held no meaning in this strange place between the heavens and the water, but Kara yelled at the bear anyway. "You're mad!" Then she eased out a hand, took hold of the blue talanium ring, and gave it the hardest tug she could manage.

The silk exploding from the bear's pouch knocked Kara into a tumble.

Rescuer, help!

A voice on the wind answered. *I am with you.*

Panic turned to peace. Kara tucked her arms close to her sides to recover the knife-fall she'd used before to catch her friend. It worked. Her tumble ceased, and her body aligned with the air. As it did, the water below came into her blurry view—much closer than she'd expected. She pulled her ring. The silk burst from its pouch and jerked her back.

She had time for only one glance at a landing raft the timbermen had built for the windfighters, a good hundred paces away, steadied by the fishermen. Ioanu stood upon it, watching her. Falling slower now, Kara heard the bear's call. "Feet, Queensblood!"

Feet. Right.

Kara kicked her legs out and tucked her arms across her chest an instant before she hit the fjord. Frigid water closed in over her ears. She pulled the second ring to escape the glide suit and broke the crystal surface to draw a gasping breath. One of the old fishermen was already on his way, a wry grin on his lips.

That bear. Ioanu would have to pay for this. She might've killed them both. While Kara sifted through potential punishments, she heard distant shouting. She looked up to see windfighters and others lining the cliff from the wooden ledge all the way to the outpost lodge, waving and cheering. Two of them leapt from the ledge in quick succession.

The fisherman slowed his boat beside her. "That bear," he said, as if repeating her thought, but with a much different tone than the one in Kara's mind. He offered her a hand. "That bear and you, my dear, will fly forever in song. And your courage will inspire those fighters for the rest of their days."

41

LEE
TANELETHAR
HIGHLAND FOREST

LEE AND ZEL TROMPED THROUGH THE SNOW WITH NO trail or sign to guide them, working their way down the mountain slope in sweeping paths.

Conversation had failed them long ago, driven back by frozen lips and sheer frustration. Lee's only words played in his mind, haunting him.

Dark creatures are corruptions, he'd told Zel, speaking with perhaps more authority than he could claim, *not original creations. They're still bound by the rules of the High One's handiwork."*

Meaning?

Meaning some of them must breathe air, just as we do—not as much, but enough that a deep mine must have airshafts.

They'd both decided crawling down an airshaft to get a look at whatever creatures were gathering in the mine was a better path than sneaking in by the muddy road. In Lee's mind, the task had seemed easy. Simply walk straight upslope to find an airshaft feeding the tunnel.

It hadn't worked.

He and Zel had climbed for at least two ticks before admitting they'd made an error—or that Lee had made an error, as the pilot was quick to point out. Since then, they'd been working their way down, this time moving in long, sweeping paths to the east and west, hoping the search might still prove fruitful.

Without knowing quite why, he looked downslope to the portal in the huge mound of rubble. Like a ghost behind the black void, he thought he saw the giant waiting, runes lit with molten stone, red eyes burning. Such a powerful creature. Long strides to cross the land. The strength to sweep trees aside like snow. Such an ally might aid their search now. If only the Rescuer had created giants of his own for the lightraiders.

"What's wrong?" Zel asked.

Lee set off again, wincing at the pain in his arm. "Nothing. Keep at it."

After another full tick of trudging through snow and climbing over rocks and fallen trees, Zel called him over. A patch of shadow among some stones on a quickly darkening mountainside had caught her attention. An airshaft.

They pulled rocks and earth away to find a square shaft wide enough to squeeze through, slanting downward. Lee wanted to hit himself. Of course, the goblin miners would dig on a slant away from the tunnel. That's why they hadn't found the shaft in their climb due south. Had he expected them to dig straight up?

He took the lead and felt his way until the fear of crawling blind into a goblin's knife overcame the fear of alerting them with a lantern.

"At least in here," Zel said as Lee set a candle in his travel lantern, "we'll only have to fight one creature at a time."

Lee frowned at the thought. The logic worked both ways. Behind him, she'd be no help at all.

As if she'd heard his eyes rolling, Zel patted his boot. "We should change places. You're wounded."

"I'm fine."

"Are you? Your face said otherwise during our search. Those burns are festering."

He pushed on. "We'd have to backtrack up hill to switch. Forget it."

By the Rescuer's grace, the shaft narrowed but a little in a few places—not enough to stop them. In those tight spaces, wet rock grated against Lee's burns. He kept the pain to himself, lest Zel keep fussing.

"Douse the lantern," she whispered. "I see a light."

A yellow glow flickered ahead. How had she seen it before him? Lee refused to admit this. He licked his fingers and snuffed his lantern's candle. "I see it. Tread quietly."

Neither dared to draw an audible breath, placing each crawling knee with care until their shaft broadened to a small shelf overlooking the main passage. Torches lit the underground road, going on for what looked like leagues in a straight line.

Orcs marched below the Keledan watchers, with golmogs and goblins mixed into their formations. Lee had not seen this type before—overlarge black gargoyles with pyranium ore bulging out of their hides, wearing thick armor covered in spikes and red slashes.

One group of these orcs carried four litters, and on them were strapped horrible bird things like the one Lee had fought over Sil Shadath.

Lee thought for a moment that the birds were dead or sleeping, until one rolled its bald head over and the black eyes locked on his. The creature fought its bonds and let out a terrible squawk.

"Back!" Lee whispered, pulling Zel with him. "Get back!"

Orcs below growled and grumbled in their incomprehensible speech, amid the shuffling of clawed feet and the ring of scimitars drawn from their scabbards. After crawling well up into the airshaft, Lee and Zel paused to listen.

The voices and shuffling settled. The ring of weapons ceased. Silence.

Lee, quietly as he could, struck his lantern. He held it back in the small space between the shaft roof and Zel's shoulder.

A dozen eyes reflected the flame. The mandibles of a giant spider spread wide in a hissing shriek.

Zel rolled flat on her back and loosed a bolt from her crossbow.

The missile sank deep into the creature's throat. It shrank back, drawing its hairy legs close about its torso, but the shaft gave it no room to maneuver. She loosed another into its eyes. "Go, Lee!"

The dying spider blocked the tunnel, but Lee doubted they had much time before some goblin pulled it free or cut it to pieces. He scrambled ahead of Zel, banging his head, arms, and the bow slung at his back against every bulging rock and timber support, until the pain radiating from his burns seared his entire form. "Still with me, Zel?"

"Yes! Don't stop!"

In half the time it had taken them to descend the shaft, they climbed out into open air and the cold snow of the mountainside. Lee grabbed the trunk of a fallen pine. "Zel, lend me your hands."

Together, they shoved the pine and two saplings into the opening, then piled rocks around them. Lee brushed off his hands and started down the mountain. "That will slow any creatures at our backs."

"And at our fronts?"

She had a point. Likely orcs or goblins were racing through the main passage that moment to intercept them. Lee unslung his bow and drew an arrow, realizing only then that he had yet to arm himself in the whole time since they'd left the portal. He might have used his sikaria in the shaft. Only by the Rescuer's grace and good sense had Zel been ready with her crossbow. "We must defeat them as they come," he said, "and escape to share what we've seen."

Zel panned her bow's sight across the trees below, watchful. "We finally know how dark creatures are invading our land in such great numbers. They've built a road under the mountains."

"Yes, though I don't understand why they're able to tunnel through the barrier after all these years."

"A hard question," Zel said, setting a faster pace downslope for them both. "But if there's a breach under the mountain, my inkling about dust and stormriding may also explain how Vorax managed to open a portal into our land."

42

LEE ASKED ZEL WHAT SHE MEANT ABOUT HER PORTAL inkling, but she barely got the words *Huckleheim* and *Celestium Codex* out before a short black arrow sailed between them.

From then on, they faced a running battle to reach the portal.

Lee's quiver grew lighter than he'd wish, and the number of crossbow bolts at Zel's waist quickly diminished. "Stop shooting," he told her, pressing her crossbow down when she prepared to take out a goblin in their path. "We'll need all our missiles in the next fight."

They had more stocks in *The Merlin*, but Lee had no plans to return to the ship. Not yet. He and Zel still had to find the Aladoth army before a final flight from the Sorcerer's Cave.

Besides—and this, Lee hoped Zel hadn't noticed—every shot he'd taken at these goblins had missed. The weight of his injury must be throwing off his aim. "Use your whip," he said. "Take them in close combat."

Zel complied without question, fighting with whip and knife while Lee used a double-bladed sikari in one hand and wielded his ash bow as a staff with the other. Even then, his efforts did little damage. His pride took the hard hit of watching Zel make all the headway.

Battling the full patrol took all their strength, especially with Lee's struggles, but the downhill slope offered enough advantage to bring them close enough to the portal for a foot race. When a pair of golmogs lumbered out of the mine, adding to the enemy's numbers, Lee decided it was time. He hooked a goblin's ankle with the curve of his bow and drove the flailing creature into its companion to open an avenue of escape. "Now!"

They raced past, ducking arrows. Out of the corner of his spectacles, Lee saw a golmog swing an enormous sword. He paid it little heed. There were greater concerns.

Zel huffed, pumping her arms in her run. "Do you realize . . . we're fleeing goblins . . . into the arms of a giant?"

The sting of Lee's wounds would not let him forget. "We've no choice!"

Side by side they ran into the void.

One goblin ran in behind them, and Zel, coming to an abrupt stop on the far side of the portal, met it with a knife between the eyes. The crunch of its brittleknit skull was like a dropped stone in the quiet of the cave.

The goblin crumpled, leaving no other sound but the lapping waves.

No trolls and no giant appeared before them. The goblin workers had fled the ramps.

Could it be this easy?

The fire in Lee's arm said otherwise. "Hurry," he said, turning toward the second portal he'd marked during their last visit—the only other portal with purple flashes streaking across its void. The black within seemed more agitated than before. The flashes more intense. But that couldn't be. Perhaps he was remembering wrong. He pointed, glancing back at Zel. "That one. It's been used recently. We need to get through before the giant comes."

Zel glanced away toward the sea and the coming dusk outside. "We're not heading for the ship?"

"We must still find the Aladoth. Or did you see something in that tunnel I missed?"

He gave her no room for reply and set off at a jog. The portal, as tall as a castle, with its arch intricately carved in the flowing manner of the Aropha, beckoned from four levels above their current walkway. They'd have to run up the intersecting paths to reach it. Much could happen in that distance. '

The pounding of Lee's boots on the worn stone path resonated in his burning arm. Part of him hoped the damage done by scraping along the airshaft was the only cause of the pain. Part of him knew it wasn't. And part of him—a part he hated to acknowledge—welcomed the pain.

He chose to ignore that part, and in doing so, he let it take over. Only twenty paces from the second portal, Lee slowed and stopped.

"Come on." Zel caught up and tugged at his good arm. "We're almost there. We can escape the giant."

"I don't want to escape."

Her mouth hung open. "What?"

"Such a powerful creature. We can use him."

A rumbling boomed in the cave in harmony with the waves.

Strength. Respect.

This was an opportunity. A shift in the tide. A revelation had come to Lee. The Rescuer *had* made the giants for lightraiders. So what if he used the dragons in that purpose? Was he not sovereign? And now, after all these years of war, he'd opened Lee's mind to grasp the mystery. "I can turn the giant to our purpose, Zel. I can turn all of them. They want me to. Think how powerful the Keledan will be with these creatures at our command."

The rumbling intensified. Zel's eyes drifted around the cave, seeking their unseen foe.

Strength. Respect.

"Strength!" Lee demanded her focus with the force of his voice. "Respect! Consider a Keledan army, giants marching at the head of their lines. Airships above. Dragons would flee before us."

Strength. Respect.

Lee spoke the next word in time with the rhythm of the creature's song. "Victory."

A massive streak flashed across the portal, shaking the cave with its thundering crack. Roiling smoke bulged out in the shape of a creature as tall as the arch. The giant emerged. It had been on the other side.

Strength. Respect. Victory.

Lee shouldered his bow and sheathed his sikari. "Good creature, you will serve me. What the dragons made for evil, I can use for good."

43

ZEL WATCHED, DUMBFOUNDED, AS HER FRIEND AND lightraider companion stowed his weapons before the giant.

"Good creature," he said, looking up into the giant's many eyes, "you will serve me. What the dragons made for evil, I can use for good."

A deep sound reverberated in the creature—what might have been a satisfied growl.

Zel backed down the stone path. "This is wrong, Lee! Stop it!"

"You don't understand. Perhaps you can't, but I can. I finally grasp what was hidden—what the High One told us. All things, he can use for good. We who are enlightened in his grace can harness the power of what the dragons have made."

"What about the trolls? You told me not to pay them. When I began to compromise, they almost killed me."

"This is different."

"How?"

Lee glared over his shoulder. "It just is!"

As if prompted by his anger, the giant's rumbling song grew louder.

He is strong. Respect him.

The voice pounded in Zel's mind, threatening to split her skull. She grasped her head and let out a cry.

Lee turned back to the giant. "Don't."

The voice ceased, and once again Zel could hear and see. She swallowed hard.

"There," Lee said, a half grin curling one side of his mouth. "Now you understand. I can control him."

The giant knelt, and Lee reached up a hand—a child reaching to pet a village dog.

Zel had seen such dogs bite. Heat surrounded them. The molten rock churning inside the giant turned its stone belly orange, and the glow rose slowly through its chest.

"Lee!"

"Quiet, Zel! Let me do this!"

They were both about to die. Zel's fingers tore at a pocket in her belt until she found a pair of vials her father had given her. She poured one into the other. The learning of an apothecarist—or an apothecarist's daughter—held its benefits. She saw much in the interaction of the Maker's many gifts. Earth and shairosite. Diver's folly and certain vitriols. One might steer an airship. The other could send you flying with far more violence.

While she worked, the giant set its hand down in front of Lee. An invitation he would not ignore. She had little time.

Zel let the empty one of the two vials fall and break, fighting the danger of dropping the other. She sealed the full vial and, with great care, pressed the head of a crossbow bolt deep into its cork.

Lee, unafraid of his new friend, or weapon, or however he saw this creature, stepped onto its hand.

Zel, securing the bolt and its cargo on her bow, thought she heard a laugh and looked up. The molten glow filled the giant's mouth.

"Lee, jump!" she shouted, and let her bolt fly.

The creature's rock hand had only risen to the height of a man when the bolt struck its face, far above. A pink flash lit the cave.

The blast left Zel blind for several beats, ears ringing. When she regained her bearings, she saw the creature reeling back, holding its head. Half its jaw had been blasted away, and molten rock spewed forth, pouring down its chest.

Lee, who had not heeded her call, lay still on the path.

Unwilling to wait for the giant to recover or call its wounded troll friends, Zel stumbled to Lee and dragged him the last twenty paces to the portal. She pulled him through the smoke and flashes.

Cool night air met her on the other side—cool, but not cold like the snowy mountainside where the last portal had taken them. Zel didn't bother taking stock of her surroundings but kept dragging Lee away, calling to him as she did. "Lee! Lee, wake up!"

He made no movement or sound.

His heels left two trails in red dirt almost as dark as the blood-red rock of the Sorcerer's Cave.

"Lee!"

Still nothing.

What if the giant followed? Or the trolls? She couldn't fight them off on her own.

Zel pulled her friend into the cover of some large rocks, then looked back toward the portal's arch. On the snowy mountainside, the portal had opened from a huge pile of rubble. This one was far different—as ancient and ornate as the arch through which they'd come, and just as tall—cut into the side of a red stone butte rising from a steep hill of brush and dirt.

Lightning flashed in the void, and the black smoke boiled. A pounding thrum struck her head.

Give him back.

Zel had two more of her father's vials. They'd come with a warning only to use them in the direst of circumstances.

Was this not the direst of circumstances?

She mixed the compounds and fixed the full vial to another crossbow bolt. This, she aimed at the portal and spoke a prayer her father had taught her. *"Po aleryi serevash sebereglanu, dar men drachel dervalanu."*

Do not bring us into temptation.

Deliver us from evil.

A grinding howl rang in her ears. Her vision blurred, and in it, the unmistakable shape of the wounded giant appeared. Zel loosed her bolt then covered her head, laying her body over her friend. If the blast before had deafened her, this one threatened to tear her apart. The hillside shook. Rocks pelted her back. When the quaking settled and Zel finally gathered the nerve to look up, choking against the dust, the void and the flashes were gone. The arch stood broken, guarding a shallow depression in the rock formation with stones vaguely like the head and torso of a giant pushing out.

"Lee?"

Her friend lay beside her. Zel eased his head up into her lap and tried to rub the dust and black marks away from his face. There were scrapes and cuts, and a great burn from his shoulder to his temple. His spectacles were broken. She pulled them from his head. "Lee, wake up. Please, wake up."

Zel looked up at the stars, glistening in the gossamer haze of her tears. Without a verse to speak, she cried out to the Rescuer. "Help him!"

The stars shifted. A shadow moved within them, spiraling down. Had her anguish called another dark creature? Zel's hand searched for her crossbow. Just as she found it, the shadow let out a quiet cry. She recognized the voice.

A falcon landed on the rocks where Zel had taken shelter and cocked its head, regarding her with clever eyes.

Zel sniffed and wiped her tears with a sleeve, praying this was not a vision. "Aethia?"

PART THREE

THE SHAME OF KINGS

*"For the Scripture says, everyone who believes
on him will not be put to shame."*

Romans 10:11

44

VALSHADOX TIGHTENED THE SPREAD OF HIS WINGS and let the world draw him nearer, that sense of falling he'd long enjoyed in this fleshly dragon form. Black mountains belching smoke and fire grew larger in his penetrating vision—his home for all the future he could see.

He sensed the mud-dweller below, Lord Zonox, head of the earth dragon family—king of bogs and stench—waiting to lord his new authority over him. The half-wit's pride pulsed like an ancient Aropha beacon from the northernmost peak in the range. Did he not see that he was merely a tool of Valshadox's punishment? Heleyor's whip?

How had it come to this?

The lightraiders. And Lord Vorax, that arrogant usurper—undeserving half-breed lord of the firedrake family—who'd built a stronghold in the southern highlands and tried to invade Keledev on his own, only to fall before a Twiceborn dotard and his dog. Fool.

Valshadox had played the good soldier. Never in all the epochs had he reached beyond his station, not after he'd led the destruction of the Suvoroth, not when Vorax had been given the honor and headship owed to Valshadox as a true-blood firedrake. Valshadox had stayed in his dark forest, tending his creatures, cultivating the twisted mockery of eternity his master wanted for the Aladoth. And what had loyalty gained him?

Lord Vorax, in his ambition, had sent his goblins and orcs into Keledev rather than bring his discovery of the breach to the throne. He'd paid for it with the destruction of his ages-old flesh. For that, he should've spent a half century or more in fledgling form. Instead he'd been rewarded with a shaadsuth nurtured in the flame of Ras Pyras, tended by pyranium orcs, the only dark creatures that could reach into the fire's cyclone, destined to rise in the most devastating form any dragon but Heleyor had yet taken.

How did Heleyor not see that he'd granted the most ambitious lieutenant among the Nine Lords the power to challenge him?

Valshadox might have advised him so, but he'd lost the Leander and the queensblood who'd revealed themselves during Lord Vorax's fleshly destruction, and Heleyor would not tolerate that failure. But how could Valshadox have known the Overlord would teach his warriors to fly?

Command of the army Valshadox had built was stripped away. Even the pleasure of entering Keledev—of scorching the Overlord's precious land and roasting his children—had been taken. And now he was subject to this slime-worshiping imbecile.

Such humiliation.

He buried his grievances deep, lest they betray him. Falling lower, he felt the probing thoughts of the half-wit, who'd surely sell him to Heleyor for an acre of swampland.

You are here.

Valshadox spiraled down over the burning mountain. *Yes, mud-dweller, I am here.*

And I am one of the Nine, in case you'd forgotten. You will call me Lord Zonox or Zonox, Lord of Chaos.

Heat welled in Valshadox's chest. *All right, Lord Zonox, I am here.*

He alighted within a gorge cut by magma below the mountain's northeastern slope, on a shelf of crusted black rock streaked with orange obsidian. He made sure to choose a place well below the shelf where the mud-dweller lay. The slime oozing from Zonox's scales had not kept pace with the heat so that the mud he'd brought from his bog had caked in ugly patches all about his form.

Zonox opened a mouth filled with disordered teeth and breathed blue-green fire. "Sorcerers."

A pair of Aladoth answered his call, approaching on a trail on the mountainside—the Scarlet Moon sorceress called Maldora, and Valshadox's own pet, Shan Lee.

Shan, upon seeing Valshadox, dropped to a knee. "My lord. Welcome."

Zonox growled.

Valshadox spat a flare of red flame. "Get up, slave. Lord Zonox is your master now."

Zonox seemed to enjoy this. He chuckled and picked with his cave-formation teeth at his caked mud. "Tell him, Maldora."

"Lord Valshadox," the sorceress said with a slight bow, "the goblin workers have finished. The army marches now to the shore of a lake portal like none the Southern Overlord ever conceived. And preparations to join that lake with Keledev are nearly complete."

"The sorcerers will tear into the fabric." The mud-dweller spoke to Valshadox aloud in its rasping voice, clearly needing the Aladoth to witness his authority. "And you will aid me in ripping it open. Together, we will pry the folds apart so that I may lead the army through."

"And deliver it to its true master," Valshadox said, unable to prevent himself. "Is that not the way of it, Zonox, Lord of Chaos? Are you not meant to deliver this army to the one who waits in the breach?"

Zonox rose, spreading his misshapen wings, and roared, "Aye! That is the way of it. And he and I will fly from there to do what the other dragon lords have only dreamed—to lay waste to the Overlord's Twiceborn—while you remain here on ever-tiring wings to hold the gap open."

"My lords." Maldora took a step forward, head low. This Aladoth had a boldness rarely seen in her kind. "Shall we go and see what your wills have wrought for Heleyor thus far?"

With a grating rumble, Zonox agreed. He dug a talon into the rock of his shelf, and a thin line of molten orange split a jagged path toward the sorceress. "Show him."

The orange line traced a rough circle around the sorcerers. Maldora looked to Shan. "As I taught you."

He nodded, and the two passed their hands, covered in jeweled rings, over the ground at their feet. The mud-dweller added a stream of his blue-green flame, and the air around the Aladoth wavered with heat. The two rose.

Shan let out a tittering laugh. "It works."

"Quiet," Maldora hissed. "Concentrate, lest you fall and disgrace yourself more than usual."

The sorcerers turned on their wave of heat, with the woman steady and Shan wobbling, and set off. Valshadox waited for Zonox to take the air before he spread his wings and followed.

Pride might have filled him as he came around the burning mountain, had this still been his army. Instead, he felt the all-consuming rage of jealousy.

A lake of tar filled the basin of a teardrop canyon, shores glittering with shairosite veins. Upon it rested a fleet of ships. Goblins knocked the last supports of a final vessel away and watched it slide into the boiling black. Two shrieked, burned by the spray. The others cackled and laughed.

To the south, at the canyon's narrow mouth, the army—Valshadox's army—marched in as a long line of platoons, more than a thousand strong.

Maldora turned on her wavering heat. "My lords, your fleet is finished. Your army has arrived. All that remains is the final element, a blood sacrifice joining our land to theirs."

"The sacrifice will come," Valshadox said. "I have seen to it. Through my creatures and the inception of notions in a weak mind, I've given them all they need to find us."

45

BOTH AARON AND TEEGAN—BUT MOSTLY TEEGAN—
cornered Connor beside the statue. Teegan held her lantern
between Connor and the statue that bore his face. "Explain this."

He didn't need to explain. He heard understanding in her
question. "I was going to tell you."

"That the Enarians are Leanders?" Teegan lowered the lantern.
"When were you going to share this? Not when we met on the road
to Ravencrest. Not when we became initiates together, nor when I
first showed you my affections."

Aaron thrust out a hand. "Wait. Affections?"

A hard look from both cadets quelled him.

Teegan laughed. "A Leander king. What a fool I must have
looked—a peasant girl vying for your interest while Faelin held a
queensblood match for you in reserve."

Connor would not allow her to take that road. "I didn't know.
And from my recollection, your interest turned to my best friend,
so what does it matter?"

"It matters. Did Faelin know?"

He lowered his eyes. "Yes."

"And Kara?"

"We learned the truth of my heritage from Ioanu, who smelled
it on my blood."

Teegan remained quiet for some time.

Finally, she stepped a touch closer to Connor, much as she had on a riverbank two years prior during their first trek to Lightraider Academy, and looked up into his eyes. "Why hide this?"

"Can't you see? My forebearers changed our name in their shame—a shame I share. Why would I tell a soul? Our family are shepherds now, the Enarians of Stonyvale."

"Far from the danger of Sky Harbor," Aaron said softly, once again risking an entry into the discussion.

Teegan wrinkled her nose at the mention of danger in Sky Harbor, but Connor nodded. "He's right. I believe the first Enarians kept themselves clear of the Assembly's power and influence—a terrible temptation for those of the old noble lines. But now I must face that temptation for them." He parted them with his lantern and entered the structure, drawing Revornosh as he went.

His light—and Teegan's, which came quickly after—revealed only disappointment. They found a wide chamber of many alcoves, all filled with shelves. These, like the statues outside, were scorched black.

"This is no vault," Aaron said, joining the other two. "It's an archive."

"Was," Teegan said, kicking a burnt scrap of leather and parchment. "It *was* an archive. Now it's an empty shell."

The three explored the chamber, turning over fallen masonry and poking at ash piles with their knives.

"Over here." Connor held his lantern up to a blackened arch over an alcove at the back. "I don't know all the script, but I can tell you this speaks of the glory of dragons." Saying it out loud made his stomach turn—the blasphemous fruit of the Leander Kings.

The ornate decoration over the arch was itself a similar blasphemy. The artist had changed an earlier carving. Connor recognized the flame of the Creator. But the hand and fountain that usually accompanied such an image had been chiseled away, replaced by dragons above and below.

Within the alcove, they found more burned shelves covered in ash and useless scraps. But sculpted into the rear wall was a map of Emen Yan. The artist had molded dragons above the palace, with absurd lines radiating outward, as if the creatures shone with their own light.

Connor flipped open Faelin's journal to a blank page and copied the script chiseled in the spaces around the city. He hoped they might find it useful since they'd gained nothing else for their trouble in coming down here. He didn't want the fight with the valpaz to prove worthless.

Teegan examined the script for herself as he worked. "I recognize some of these words. Power. Trust. Honor bestowed."

Connor stopped writing. "Wait. Now that you say it out loud, it seems familiar." He flipped the journal pages until he came to the torn page where Faelin had drawn the map. On the opposite page, he found a match to the script on the wall. He dropped his head. "My patehpa has already been here. Listen to this."

The two gathered near, and Connor read the translation Faelin had added to the script. "The power of House Leander grows mighty in the trust of the dragon lords. Heleyor himself has bestowed upon us the honor of defending his sacred treasures. The highest token of his faith in mankind now lies in Emen Yan, and we will guard it with our lives."

"But where in Emen Yan?" Aaron asked.

"It doesn't say." Connor closed the journal and tucked it away, wishing he'd understood long ago that this *token* mentioned in the script meant Heleyor's Vault. He picked up a fistful of ash and threw it at the relief. "This gets us nowhere."

Teegan panned her light along the shelves. "If the writing carved into this wall speaks of the vault, then perhaps there were more clues in the texts stored here."

"Which are all gone." Aaron picked up a charred corner of parchment. "Not one jot remains. Who did this?"

Connor had his suspicions. "House Fulcor, I expect. Long

ago, when the Leanders fell out of favor. The new house governing Emen Yan destroyed the remnants of the old." He walked back into the main chamber, holding his lantern wide. "They torched this archive to erase the memory of their rivals."

"The statues," Aaron said, as if to himself. "That's why one had its head hammered off. But the statues are more than just Leander lords." He took Teegan's lantern and hurried out to the plaza, bidding the others follow him. "Each Leander lord has a viper supporter—a corrupted viper as big as a man. Sound familiar?"

Connor answered with a slow and telling nod.

Teegan frowned. "You knew. You knew the nature of those creatures when we fought them. The Leanders walked with lions before their fall. Havarra advisors. And when the lions left—"

"The dragons gave them talking vipers." Connor could not meet her gaze. "Master Jairun told me. He said I might see evidence of the vipers here."

Aaron wasn't finished. "Don't you see? Those were Leander tomes chained in the vipers' gullets—the last remnants of this very archive and perhaps now our only hope of finding the Red Dagger." He held the lantern out toward Connor. "But you, in your great understanding and wisdom, cast that boon away. Why?"

Connor had taken all he could bear of this inquest. He shoved the pilot's lantern aside. "Do you think I wanted to poison my heart or yours with the false faith of the traitor-kings?" Both stared back at him in shock at his outburst, and Connor bowed his head. He let his voice fall to a whisper. "The false faith of my blood."

He walked out across the plaza.

Not long after, Teegan and Aaron followed. Teegan stopped him and wrapped him in a hug. "I'm sorry."

"Not as sorry as I," he said. "Neither of you deserved that."

Aaron laid a hand on both their shoulders. "We'll find another way. We can still try the Fulcor palace at the top of the city."

The Fulcor palace. How were they to get into such a place?

Connor let out a quiet chuckle. "I was hoping it wouldn't come to that."

"It still may not." Teegan gazed back toward the Leander lord, now steeped once again in shadow. "Do you remember what your Captain Thera said, Connor?"

It took him a beat to catch up to her thinking, but he did remember. *Your face is familiar to me, like an old friend long forgotten.* "We need to find her."

46

AARON, WHO'D TAKEN A SUDDEN DISLIKING TO water, suggested they search for an alternate way out of the underground plaza rather than risk a frantic swim to the lock.

Connor relented, and in a short while, a curving passage and the last rose light of sunset led them to a grate in the street above. They passed several drifters sleeping in the passage, along with a few empty bedrolls. On the street, in a refuse-filled alley between the rows of marble homes, Connor wondered aloud whether some who wandered deeper in had become food for the valpaz.

"That would explain how the creature survived," Teegan said, "but we've more pressing concerns. One in particular. What will you tell Thera?"

"The truth. She knows my face because she's seen it before on some statue or other of the Leander Kings. We need her to show us where it is."

Aaron kept pace with them, showing no signs of a limp. "And if she asks why?"

"I'll tell her we need to find Heleyor's Vault and let the Rescuer take it from there."

Darkness fell long before they reached the garrison house. Across the city, the fireclocks still burned in small circles of flickering orange. At night, their smoke lost its color, so all the rising pillars bore different shades of the same gray.

The guard at the yard's gate showed little love for these strangers disturbing his watch. He told them he'd fetch his captain, but only for the entertainment of the tongue-lashing she'd give them before locking them up.

Thera disappointed him. She thanked him for his quick work and set him back at his post, then motioned for Connor and his friends to follow her and Koteg to a quiet corner of the reflecting pool. Koteg seemed less inclined to conversation during the night watches and curled himself at her feet. She knelt to rub his belly. "Why have you come, Keledan? Do you have more to share about my prisoner?"

"I have more to share about you, Captain," Connor said. "I know why you find me familiar."

She looked up with a scowl. "Perhaps I'm finding you too familiar at present."

"Hear me out. We've imposed upon your kindness. Let me impose a little more in exchange for answering a question itching at the back of your mind."

"Fine. How do I know you?"

Connor might play this round of their game several ways. He had no time for any of them but the most direct. "I'm born of House Leander, a descendant of the king's line. You know my face because you've seen it here, in the secret places of your city."

Thera backed away from them, close to the pool's edge, and Aaron, on some instinct, reached for her. In answer, she put her hand on her sword. Koteg leapt to his feet and growled.

Aaron raised both hands, palms out. "Forgive me. I only wished to keep you from falling into the pool."

The captain narrowed her eyes at the pilot, then fixed them on Connor. "You've been to the old archive, perhaps met one of the valpaza."

So there *were* more, as Teegan had surmised. Connor nodded.

"We saw the statue. Are there others?"

"What is your purpose, truly? You said you were Keledan. Now you are a Leander king. Are you seeking to reclaim your city from the Fulcors?" Thera added no threat to the question, though by rights, on that suspicion alone, she might have had them hung. By the duty of her office, she probably should have.

"I–" Connor stopped and corrected himself. "*We* are as we claimed to be. The Keledan have only one king, who is not a Leander. We are here in search of an heirloom of our people, hoping to stop a dragon invasion."

Thera glanced around, as if checking to make sure none of her garrison had come within earshot. The tension eased from her stance, and Koteg sat beside her. He leaned his great head into her side. "This heirloom," Thera said. "You hope to find it in Heleyor's Vault?"

Connor must have worn his surprise like a sign on his face because she laughed at him.

"Did you think I would not know the legends of my own city?" Thera motioned them closer and recounted the rest as if telling children a bedtime story. "The Leanders bragged of their stewardship over the Great Red Dragon's treasures. They named it the token of his faith in men. But once the land was overrun with dark creatures, Heleyor needed no such help. He caused their influence to dwindle, until he gave their northern holdings over to the Fulcors, who never learned the vault's location. The Leanders took that secret with them into oblivion."

"So," Teegan said, "even you, captain of Emen Yan's guard, don't know the vault's location."

"No one knows. And few want to. Heleyor's Vault holds relics of such terrible power even the Great Red Dragon wants them nowhere near him. For centuries, all who've sought the vault have died. The most superstitious fear they'll accidentally step on the vault and bring fiery punishment down on their own heads. Thus, the merchants' curse heard in our marketplaces."

"What curse is that?" Aaron asked.

"They save it for foreigners who haggle for a whole half tick and buy nothing. They'll spit at the offender's back and say, 'May you tread upon a dragon's hoard.'"

Connor had little time for legends and marketplace curses. Heleyor's Vault was real—or so Faelin thought—and it held Lef Amunrel, the answer to all their woes. Thera may not know its location, but she certainly knew places where the likeness of his kin survived. "The statue at the old archive. Have you seen others, perhaps beneath the palace?"

"The palace?" Thera snorted. "You won't find anything there but sewage."

Connor waited, wondering if she only meant the refuse running under the royal citadel or perhaps those who dwelled there, until at length, she rewarded him for his patience.

"But," Thera said, bending to scratch her dog under his chin, "I do know of one other statue. It's not in or under the palace, but nearby, on the north side of the city. Shall I show you?"

They had no chance to answer. A cry drew their eyes skyward, and a silver shape spiraled down, taking the form of a falcon as it passed through the layers of fireclock haze.

"Aethia." Teegan held out her arm with its leather guard, and the falcon landed. She gave her a sliver of meat. "What is it, girl? Why have you come?"

The bird refused to stand still, hopping on the leather perch and lifting one leg as if wounded. But there was no wound. Someone had tied a parchment there. This bought a sour look from her mistress. "Who has lowered you to the rank of messenger raven? Connor, help me." She kept Aethia quiet while he untied the scroll.

"What does it say?" Aaron asked, as Connor took in the message.

"Lee and Zel are southeast of the city, near the place we left *The Kingfisher.*"

"And Zel, is she—"

Connor gave him a grim nod. "Your master, Councilor Boreas, will be pleased with you. Zel is fine." He turned his gaze to Teegan. "But Lee . . ."

Teegan snatched the message from his fingers and read it, drawing a sharp breath. "Lee is wounded—grievously. Zel can't wake him."

47

TEEGAN HELD AETHIA CLOSE, STROKING HER
feathers. "I must go to Lee, Connor. He needs me."

What was Connor to say? This, as Master Jairun had warned
him, was the hardest burden of those in the Navigators' Sphere—
making choices their fellow lightraiders took as hurts. But when
they'd spoken a short prayer for their wounded friend, Connor had
heard not only comfort in the voice of the Helper, but an insistence
he keep Teegan beside him for what lay ahead.

He held his voice even, leaning on the core strength of
gentleness as best he could. "Your duty is here. Aaron can go."

"Aaron is not a lightraider."

"Thus, my decision. Consider our encounters with the viper
and the valpaz. Aaron is . . . less prepared to face dark creatures."
Connor cast the pilot a *No offense intended* glance.

Aaron answered with a *None taken* nod. "I'll help him,
Teegan. None of us are renewers like Lee, but I'll render what aid
I can, using the tools he himself carries."

At this, Thera interrupted. "Our garrison healer can help."

Connor began to protest, but she held up a hand. "He uses
no dragon sorcery in his practices, if that's your worry. And
he's the only healer in Emen Yan who won't. That's why I chose

him. His house is near the garrison, facing the south end of the reflecting pool."

Teegan and Aaron looked to Connor, and though he still saw hope in Teegan's eyes that he might send her to Lee's side, he also saw her willingness to follow his lead. "Aaron," he said, "find them, and bring Lee to Thera's healer. We'll come to you once we've found the vault."

"Better give your friend the journey writ," Thera said to Teegan. "You'll not need it in my company, and he'll not pass the city gate at night without it." Then she turned to Aaron. "My healer's name is Necal. When you knock, show him your writ and tell him Thera sent you. If he balks, tell him to pass my regards to his wife and Miuna. After that, he'll do whatever you want."

Connor narrowed his eyes. "Who is Miuna? His child?"

"His mistress. And few besides me know their secret."

The stiffness the Keledan showed at this news seemed to amuse the captain. Connor found no humor in it. Why must such complications always arise?

Immediately, he heard the answer in his heart. *Because this world is broken.*

With no other options, he gave Aaron leave to seek Necal's services for Lee but took the pilot a pace away from the others and bent his ear. "Take care. Watch Necal and his household. Where a deceitful heart lies, other perils gather." He also gave Aaron the pouch of brimstone metal the prisoner had carried. "Given your new respect for water, you'll do a better job caring for this than I. Don't let it get wet."

Teegan whispered to her falcon and set her to the air to guide him. "Watch the sky," she said, pressing the journey writ and a purse of Aethia's meat into Aaron's hands. "She may fly out of your sight, but she'll always return to make sure you're following."

While Aaron headed south, the rest set a quick pace north to the fourth-level streets and canals around the lower walls of the palace gardens.

Forcing back his concerns over Lee and the healer, Connor prodded Thera about her loyalties. He needed to understand her, now more than ever. "You keep a garrison healer who shuns dragon sorcery. I'm intrigued. You show no love for Heleyor."

The captain kept her eyes on the darkening streets. "Try not to speak so loudly, Shepherd."

"And what of House Fulcor? Are they sewage to you?"

This earned him a sidelong glance, both from the captain and her dog. "I said the sewage was under the palace."

"No. You didn't."

Thera watched a barge pass them on the canal before answering. "My forebearers all served in the garrison or as its leaders, under House Fulcor"—she paused and looked back, as if checking the barge's distance—"and before. Well before."

"That is a long history," Teegan said. "Your family guarded Emen Yan under the Leander Kings?"

"From the days when they walked with the white lions. The many captains in my line have sailed on the winds of change to survive, living at odds with the duty they uphold." She stopped and turned in front of him, lowering herself. "When I saw your face, Shepherd, a living sculpture of my family's first vow, I wanted so much to see my path back to honor—to wipe away centuries of treachery."

Treachery. A return to honor.

How strange to find this Aladoth captain seeking the same road as Connor.

"Huh," Teegan said, poking Connor's back with a subtle finger.

He stilled her with a look, then raised Thera up. "You owe me no loyalty. The Leanders betrayed their vows first. But you and I both owe our hearts to the one they abandoned."

"The Maker," Thera said. "Your Southern Overlord who bears so many names."

"All owe him their service, and all will bow before him in the end." He canted his head and shrugged. "Isn't now a good time to start?"

Thera was not so easily swayed. "Let me think on this." She walked on, leading them to the edge of a manmade river canyon with stepped walls of white marble shored up with pale green vardallium. Shops and gardens lined narrow streets, those reserved for the highest-ranking families of Emen Yan, according to Thera.

She pointed on high to the waterfalls pouring down from Val Glasa, over the great natural dam that held back that icy sea. "The falls feed the two rivers of our valley, which split around the city. Stone ducts fashioned by your forefathers draw part of their waters into the torrent you see below."

The Serpentine. Seek the source. Wasn't that what the death viper had told them? Could this be it?

In the broad channel at the base of the marble canyon, white froth drew ever-changing lines, a hint of the water's speed. The motion threatened to steal Connor's balance. He focused on Thera to steady himself. "Where does this manmade river flow?"

"Into the city's heart, to power the waterwheels of our industries and flush the canals. It also lends its force to the canals used by the nobility, which flow uphill like enchanted streams."

"And the statue you mentioned?" Teegan had moved away from the other two, farther north, as if eager to move on.

Connor followed but tried to offer comfort. "The others won't reach the healer for some time, Teegan."

She shot him a frown. "Those words don't soothe me at all."

"Then perhaps walking faster will," Thera said, heading past them with Koteg at her side.

She led them down a set of staircases Connor had not seen from above—and this, he thought, was the intent of the builders, to lend an air of mystery to this seat of power.

Among these hidden stairs, they came to a landing with a green vardallium door, barely as wide as Thera's shoulders. She slid a key from her belt into the lock. "These passages allow for quick movement from the north end of the city to the south—and east to west—should the need arise. Only the highest lords and a few of my officers know of their existence."

She hurried them inside and took a lantern from the wall, lighting its wick with a flint and steel kept there. Its orange light revealed a curving hallway almost as narrow as the door.

Over the next half tick, Connor counted many forks and steps—mostly leading down—until they came to the upper half of a great waterwheel, turning in a slot carved in the floor. Thera held her light over a square hatch behind it and signaled Connor and Teegan to lift the stone fitted there away by its single iron ring. A rope was attached to the underside, hanging down into the black. Thera raised her voice over the waterwheel's roar. "Down you go."

Connor faltered, exchanging a glance with Teegan.

Thera's eyes darkened. "Don't you trust me?"

Rather than answer, he sat on the hatch's edge, took the rope, and climbed down.

Teegan came next, and Thera followed with the lantern clipped to her belt. Two walls of rough-cut blocks, one a half circle and the other flat, enclosed a small chamber. Char marks spoke of many small fires that had burned there, and items of little consequence were scattered about—a tin plate and spoon, a child's cloak, a rusted knife, and the like.

A solitary statue stood in the crux of the curved wall. It, too, had been scorched and chipped, but someone had taken great care in restoring this lord and the viper that stood at his side.

Koteg barked from above, earning a sharp word from his mistress, while Teegan turned in a slow circle, shaking her head. "Why would you bring us down here? There's nothing to see but the statue."

48

KOTEG LAID DOWN AT THE HATCH SO THAT HIS lolling tongue and flopped ears hung down. He whimpered, and again, Thera hushed him. She glowered at Teegan. "This is not nothing. You asked me for another statue bearing the shepherd's face, and I brought you."

"To an otherwise empty room." Teegan turned to Connor. "She's wasting our time."

Connor had gone to the Leander lord, whose face, even more than the other, mirrored his own. The king wore a stern expression, and held his sword outstretched, the blade level with the marble floor.

"To what are you pointing?" Connor asked.

Thera came near to his shoulder from behind. "For years, I asked the same question."

Those words alone brought the rubbish strewn about the chamber into new light, and Connor saw them for what they were—the old knife, the tin plate, the remnants of old fires—traces of one who'd made this place her sanctum. He bent to pick up the knife, which lay at the statue's feet, and ran his thumb over its blunted tip. "This was yours."

She took it from his hand. "It belonged to a younger me, yes.

I discovered this place as a girl, when my father still commanded the garrison and let me run free in these secret halls. At first, I came here to play. Later, I came to think."

"But not anymore?" Teegan asked.

"No. I can't look upon the lords of my forefathers without shame."

Connor understood that feeling well.

Thera tucked the old knife into her belt and gently moved Connor's cloak away from his scabbard. "May I?"

A glance from Teegan said *Don't*, but Connor relented anyway.

With great care, Thera drew Revornosh and placed it in his hand, then positioned him beside the statue and stretched out his arm to match its pose. She let out a quiet laugh. "How long have I waited to see stone become flesh—for those cold gray eyes to gain the warmth and color of life." She touched his cheek. "Speak, Lord, and tell me where you are sending me."

In haste, Connor sheathed his sword, walking away. "I've no idea, Thera."

"You must know something!" Thera pointed at the statue. "That lord is your kin, your blood! And he is no monument. Look at his face. His sword. He has purpose!" Striding up to Connor, she pressed that pointing finger into his chest. "Tell me what it is. You came to my gate for a reason. If not for the virtue of prudence, I'd have brought you here that very morning. After all these years, do not deny me an answer."

He leaned into her pressing finger, tightening his jaw. "Forget the traitor-kings. Their shame and ours are better left in the deep shadow of secret!"

Thera lowered her hand, crestfallen. "Am I not worthy of sharing that shadow with you?"

"Give us a moment." Teegan took Connor by the arm and led him as far as she might to the corner where the flat wall met the curved. "This debate is not helpful. And while you two prattled on about great lords and dark secrets, I was having a think."

He coughed, casting a glance back at the hurt and angry captain, then returned his attention to Teegan. "Go on."

"Look at the walls compared to the marble floor. Aren't they a later and less opulent construction?"

He agreed and picked at the mortar with a fingernail. "Rough and hasty. Someone built this room to hem in my kin. Why? Why cage a statue?"

Both their gazes returned to the Leander lord. Thera was right, he was no plaza monument. The outstretched sword had meaning. Likewise, the viper rearing up beside him bared its fangs, where the others at the archive had been sculpted with closed mouths.

Teegan spoke what Connor was thinking. "These stones must fall."

Thera, upon hearing this, laughed. "Do you carry a miner's axe under your cloak?" She showed them the blunted knife. "In my youth, I had the same thought. This mortar is strong."

Connor gave no reply but took Teegan's hand. "Together?"

"Together."

The two went to the middle of the flat wall opposite the statue's sword and laid their free hands on the stones. They prayed in unison.

"*Kearma lisolmatenu hal semi kebesar dar hal premav alos Rumosh ma stregar shamel. Shamanu hesifa po koth ga'olon geg keresonol Rumosh hal elevend, po hosalanu koth raya Rumosh obah.*"

Our weapons are not of the flesh.

They are powerful through him to tear down strongholds.

We demolish arguments—every proud thing raised against the knowledge of him.

We take every thought captive.

A sudden heat in the wall prompted Connor to take his hand away. He pulled Teegan and Thera to the center of the room.

Koteg stood and growled and barked at the Leander lord.

Connor had his eyes on the flat wall where they'd placed their hands, expecting some answer there from the Rescuer, perhaps stones falling away to reveal another room or a new portal. Instead, he heard a terrible crack behind him. He and the others turned. Trails of brilliant white raced along the mortar in the curved wall behind the statue. The air grew thick and blasted outward with a resonating *boom* and took every stone block with it.

Blinking and uncovering their heads, the party found themselves on a half circle jutting out into the underground river torrent. The rubble thrown into the water had disturbed luminous plants, prompting them to glow with bright yellows and greens.

Thera stared in disbelief. "You did it. You truly have the hand of a king."

"Teegan and I have the help of a king," Connor said with a laugh, "who lends his hand in ways we often don't expect."

In this case, he'd expected the flat wall to fall, but part of it still stood, separating them from the lower two-thirds of the great waterwheel, powered by a narrow channel drawn from the river.

The curved wall behind the Leander lord had fallen instead. He was guarding a treasure, sword leveled to say *Keep away*, not pointing to some clue.

"Look." Connor knelt at the edge beside the statue. "More of my kinsmen."

Two rows of Leanders with swords held high and without viper supporters descended beneath the rushing water, lit by the glowing plants. Vardallium chains had once joined these lords to form a hallway into the deepest part of the channel, but some chains had broken free, hanging in the current or completely swept away.

The hall of lords led to a domed structure, entirely under water, with a low entrance attended by statues of vipers.

"Heleyor's fabled vault," Thera said, shaking her head. "It does exist."

49

"HOW CAN A VAULT LIE UNDER A RIVER?" CONNOR knelt at the water's edge, feeling the mist of its rapid flow against his skin. "Won't the treasures rust or wear away under the water?"

Thera stood over him, arms crossed. "And who among us can hold their breath long enough to get a look inside?"

"I may," Teegan said. "Though Lee would serve us best here. He grew up diving off ships at Lin Kelan." The thought of him seemed to weigh on her, but she soon recovered and lifted her chin. "Then again, we may find we can all breathe down there."

The other two creased their brows, and Teegan chuckled. "Not in the water itself, but in the vault."

She told them of giant mangroves south of Sil Tymest off Keledev's southern coast. The tight knitting of their roots formed watertight rooms filled with breathable air, even below the waterline. "These roothavens, as we call them, are well known in our region. Tiran and I once swam under the largest tree in the bay and found a breathable space the size of our two bedchambers. When Tehpa found out, he gave us a tongue-lashing like none we'd ever received."

"Why?" Thera asked.

"The air under the trees is not meant for humans. Had we

stayed too long, we'd have fallen asleep, never to wake up." Teegan turned her gaze to the dome under the river. "Plants may feed air into the vault, and we may breathe it for a time, but we can't tarry long."

"Assuming we can reach the entrance," Connor said. "The current is strong, and the way is broken. Without the chains to hold, we may not have the power to get across." He gauged the distance between them, then drew his crook. "I may be able to hook the raised swords and pull myself along."

Thera removed a glove and dipped a hand into the rushing water. "It's a good defense—place the vault deep in the city, under this torrent where many fear to tread, in a chamber that may kill them if they linger."

The problem of getting inside remained. Teegan was the better swimmer, but in the end, Connor decided they should both go, pulling themselves across the spaces without chains using his crook.

He asked Thera to stay and keep watch. "I doubt this river is the vault's only defense. Should you see an enemy, warn us."

She frowned. "And how will you hear my call when you're underwater?"

Teegan handed her a broken stone. "Bang this against the shore, under the water, hard as you can. We'll hear."

Connor and Teegan dove in together and pulled themselves along the chains on the north side of the statue hallway until they came to the first gap with no chain. Connor hooked the ram's-horn head of his crook around the next statue's wrist, below its sword, and discovered the first flaw in his plan.

The moment he let go of the chain, the current took him. His crook held, and he kept his grip on the shaft, but he floated downstream, hanging in line with the flow. Hand over hand, he pulled himself to the statue, and the exertion took much of his breath. He wrapped an arm around the statue and held the crook out to Teegan.

She didn't take it. A banging of stone against stone reached his ears. Thera's blurred form waved at them from the platform and pointed south. At the same time, Teegan stared at something to the west, behind Connor.

A shadow formed at the southern edge of the light from the luminous plants. And looking westward over his shoulder, Connor saw red eyes glowing between the viper statues guarding the vault.

River trolls. Rattlefish. Two of them.

He pointed south, and Teegan took his cue. She braced her body against the chain they'd last used and readied her trident. Her sea-green armor flashed to life to match the glowing plants.

Connor turned to face the creature swimming from the vault and felt his own silver armor blazing. With one arm committed to clinging to a statue, he couldn't draw Revornosh. He had only his crook and the shield glowing on the same arm for defense.

The troll, propelled by the slow swishing of its tail, circled as if the current were nothing. It gave Connor an openmouthed grin, showing a hundred serrated teeth. Its gills quivered. The rattling of its song sorcery surrounded Connor, borne on every drop of the river, far more powerful than his last encounter with a river troll on land.

The prinsss has come for his treasssure, yesss?

Connor glared. He couldn't answer aloud in this creature's domain.

Richesss and wealth. Power and fame. Join usss. Your throne awaitsss.

He jabbed it in the face with his ram's horn.

The troll hit him back with a pulsating screech that tore at his skull and stole the power from his limbs. Connor's hold on the statue slipped.

As he fought to regain his grip, he saw Teegan, also engaged in battle, hips set against a sound vardallium chain for support. Her troll leaked black into the river's flow from many wounds and took yet another. Teegan smashed it across the face with her net weights and stabbed her trident into its gut. The dying rattlefish wrapped its muscled arms about its midsection. The current carried it south into darkness.

Good for her.

Connor's own battle was not going so well. Black claws slashed at his shield over and over, further loosening his grip. He countered with the crook, trying to hook the creature's arm, but the troll fended him off. The blow knocked the crook away, and it floated downstream to catch on a chain in the southern row of statues.

The next blow rang against Connor's glowing helmet. For a full beat, he lost all sense, and in the next beat, he was flying free in the river's rush. He saw his crook sail past, hanging from the chain on the current, and reached for it, but to no avail. The river had him.

The light of the luminous plants dimmed, and with the knowledge that the channel flowed into the city's inner workings, where the little air he had left would not save him, Connor committed himself to the Rescuer's hands. He recalled a verse the guardians had taught them about dying in service and passing on to Elamhavar.

Vykef beathod hal liberah evashem, beathod kostriond. Vykef beathod okebeni kostrem, beathod liberiond.

Whoever wants to save his life will lose it.

Whoever loses his life because of me will save it.

His back smashed against something hard. Spared the worst of the impact by his armor, he opened his eyes and felt with his hands. A large chunk of the wall the Rescuer destroyed had planted itself in the channel, unseen at the edge of the light.

Teegan, having dispatched her foe, turned her attention to Connor's. She swam across the gap to the chain where his crook hung, and with her back against it, dealt the rattlefish two quick blows with her net and trident.

The creature abandoned this more dangerous foe and headed Connor's way. Teegan shouted under the water and loosed the crook from the chain.

Connor got her message. *Catch!*

His skill underwater could not match her intent. Despite his reaching, the crook slipped past his fingers and was gone. He drew Revornosh, praying a sword and the last of his breath would be enough. Then, another shout came to him, this time from the surface.

A form flew over the hall of statues and pierced the water,

surrounded by foam. Thera. The momentum of her dive brought her to the troll, which she wrapped with both arms as if to wrestle it into the silt.

Their fight carried them close to Connor, and with his back braced against the wall, he shoved his dragonslayer deep into the troll's flank. The troll screeched, and as the current carried it from Connor's blade, it went limp and released its hold on Thera.

"Thera!"

Connor's cry was lost in the torrent. The captain and the troll receded from the yellow-green luminescence until the darkness swallowed them both.

Coming to himself, Connor heard the banging of steel against stone. Looking north, he saw Teegan's furious glare. With her hands, she made a clawing motion.

Connor sheathed Revornosh, pressed his boots against the slab and pushed off, digging both hands into the silt. He found cobblestone beneath it and clawed at the joints. Arm over arm, he fought, while his lungs threatened to rupture in his chest.

The light of the plants dimmed.

No. It was Connor's vision. Or was his whole world changing?

His hands dug not into silt, but snow. He pulled himself up a hill into flurries of starlight. A lion waited at the crest of the hill, snowflakes resting on his white mane. His ice-blue eyes bored into Connor.

Rise, son of faith, and walk with me.

How could he rise? He couldn't stand. His chest ached. His legs had gone numb.

I can't!

With my help, you can.

As Connor neared the hillcrest, the lion bent as if to take the scruff of his neck in his powerful jaws.

"Connor!"

Snow became silt. Water and yellow-green light surrounded him, muffling Teegan's call. She had him by the leather strap of his manykit, behind his neck, dragging him into the hall of statues. He grabbed the chain.

Together, they worked their way to the vault's arch, passing between the vipers, where the current was lighter. A host of the same luminescent plants lit up the interior, pouring bubbles upward from their leaves. After a short entry passage, a rippling surface appeared, only inches above their heads.

Connor burst up with a gasp, then pounded the water with his fist and let out an anguished cry. "I let her drown!"

50

KARA
KELEDEV
ORVYN'S VOW

KARA'S EYES POPPED OPEN, BUT SHE REMAINED ON her bed, feigning sleep.

The noise came again, the quiet *crick* of her door opening by degrees. Sireth had offered her a room of her own at the outpost, rather than a bunk in the women's barracks, and she'd accepted. Perhaps she'd made a mistake. This close to the fighting, there was safety in numbers.

Crick.

She snuck an arm to her manykit, hanging from the bedpost, drew one of her whirlknives with its blades closed, and waited.

The noises stopped. Not a good sign. She felt a presence in the room, but where?

Near her. Over her. Within striking range.

Kara snapped her body over and swung the whirlknife.

A force like iron stopped her wrist. "Whoa!"

"Samar?"

The pilot had frozen in his odd position—bent over her, chin raised, wide eyes looking down at her over his nose. He still had Kara's wrist. The tips of her whirlknife's two blades quivered less than a finger width from his throat. He swallowed and let her go. "Don't kill me."

Kara lowered the knife and sat up. "I might. What are you doing?"

"Shh. I came to wake you."

"Ever think of knocking?"

Samar straightened, but did not back away from her bedside, an offense for which she considered taking another stab at him. He glanced toward the open door, keeping his voice low. "I didn't want to wake the watchmaster. He frightens me."

"And you thought, 'Better to enter a woman's bedchamber unannounced,' is that it?"

He shrugged.

Kara pulled her covers to her shoulders. "Go away."

"You didn't ask why I woke you."

"I don't care."

"You will." He walked to her door. "Put on your glide suit and come outside. You'll want to see this."

She didn't have to obey. Nor did she want to. The night watches seemed shorter of late, and rest was fleeting. But, after a few beats of staring at the door, which he'd thoughtlessly left open, curiosity overcame exhaustion. Kara swung her legs out of the bed.

She dressed and donned her manykit and glide suit. She moved to sheathe the whirlknife but chose to keep it in her hand. Perhaps part of her still wanted to use it on Samar. If his reason for waking her wasn't good enough, she might. Nothing grave. Just a little nick under the chin.

The pilot waited in the courtyard outside the lodge and beckoned for her to follow him down the long trail to the jumping ledge, farther inland on the fjord. Several recruits in glide suits waited there. After Kara and Ioanu had made their leap, the mood of their fledgling force had shifted, and some had wanted to train into the night to make better use of the few glide suits. Samar had taken charge of these.

He reached the rise above the ledge ahead of her and bounced on his heels like a child. "Come and see, Kara!"

When she crested the rise beside him and looked down into the fjord, she almost dropped the knife.

A windfighter had jumped a moment before and now sailed with silks rigid and full. But the windfighter was not alone. A creature with pale blue wings, almost silver in the moonlight, rolled and tumbled around the fighter. It dove beneath him from one side to the other, then spread its wings to match his glide.

The creature—the same paradragon that had aided them in battle, as far as Kara could tell—blew frost, and the frost became a line of cloud, showing their great speed.

The recruits on the ridge whooped and cheered.

"He's playing with them," Kara said.

"Not just him." The voice belonged to Ioanu, who sat on her haunches next to the jumping ledge, watching with amusement. "Look farther."

Below the paradragon and his friend, Kara saw another windfighter, close to the moment of expelling his lander. Two more paradragons wheeled around him, puffing frost at each other.

The bear let out a contented huff. "Not since the days of your queensblood ancestors has a lashoroth clan been seen in the open. Our flying has drawn them from the mountain, as if they see the windfighters as kindred spirits under the High One."

"Or they may see us as children to be taught," Kara said with a laugh. "For our flying is no better than Crumpet's, the least of their cousins."

A boom of distant thunder drew their eyes away from the playing paradragons. Kara and Samar hurried up to the rise. Far in the east, a red glow lit the Storm Mists. Lightning split the wall of clouds.

Kara and Samar ran to the lodge and climbed to its highest deck. The red glow remained, flashing with orange and yellow, low on the horizon in the Sea of Vows. "The view here is not much better," Kara said, "not with the Storm Mists so far away."

"It may be better with the right tool." Samar went inside and returned moments later with a spyglass. He held it steady for a moment, hips braced against the railing as if leaning out the extra few inches would help, then frowned. "Hmm. Still a mystery."

Impatient, Kara took the glass away and got a look for herself. She didn't see much. Whatever disturbed the Storm Mists was past the horizon, out of their sight, even with the glass. But when she focused on the brightest spot in the red glow, she could swear she saw a burst of flame.

She brought the spyglass down. "I don't like this, Samar. I don't like it at all."

51

CONNOR
TANELETHAR
EMEN YAN

"CONNOR, STOP!"

Teegan grabbed his wrist, gently but firmly, to still his fit. She dipped it below the surface and wiped away the sticky troll blood still clinging to his hand. "Remember what I said about our time here." With a lift of her chin, she drew his gaze to the luminous plants and the bubbles streaming up from their long leaves. "They bring us air, but our breathing will outpace their gift—much more so if we lose our peace. Grieve later."

How could he hold his peace? How could he fail to grieve?

Connor clenched his teeth, but Teegan refused to let go until he nodded his consent. The two climbed a set of steps into the treasure room. Gleaming gold and silver, unspoiled by the ages, waited for them.

"Aaron will hate that he missed this," Teegan said. "But perhaps it's best he did."

Connor clasped his hands together to keep them from straying. "Let's find Lef Amunrel and be gone as quick as we can."

There were daggers—a great number of them with jeweled pommels and guards formed to lion heads or twisting vipers. Swords lay on silk-covered stands, some too large for even Quinton or Dag to wield, and one with gems of all colors running down the center of the blade. What use were such weapons, except for ceremony—the rituals of the Leander nobles?

The Leanders. His kin. The dead lords to whom Thera had given her loyalty.

His heart fell. "I should have pressed her for the Rescuer."

"Connor, don't . . ." Teegan said.

"I should have stayed our quest at the edge of the city canyon until we swayed her."

"That's not how it works, and you know it." Teegan walked between two stone tables stacked with all manner of chests and boxes. "You planted a seed. We needed time to nurture it and let it grow."

He shot her a hard look. "Time ran out."

"Remember the air, Connor. Control yourself." Teegan stopped between the tables' ends and raised a hand. "Over here."

She showed him a long box of black stone, so dark it drowned the light reflecting off the silver and talanium boxes nearby. "Is this the right shape to hold the Red Dagger?"

He tried the lid, then sighed. "Locked."

Picking locks was part of their training, one of those classes that came with a warning from the headmaster never to use the ability for ill purpose or for breaking into forbidden rooms at the academy. Kara had excelled at it much more than the rest of the cadet scouts.

Connor wished she were with him there—to pick the lock, but also to tell him Thera's loss was not his fault. He might believe Kara over Teegan. Such was his care for her.

Thanks to the favor they shared, Kara had passed some of her lock-picking ability to Connor, refined with happy ticks spent together in practice—perhaps once or twice at the forbidden rooms Master Jairun had spoken of.

He crouched before the table and pulled a pair of tools from a manykit pocket at his chest.

Patience and skill yielded a quiet *click* from the lock. The box cracked open. Teegan waited for Connor to step back, then used her knife to lift the lid.

Both let out sighs of disappointment.

"That is no dagger," Connor said, eyeing a dirty wool sack utterly disproportionate to the box. The lump in the wool spoke of one small item and no dragon-killing weapons.

Teegan pushed the cloth bag open with her knife tip. "But it *does* belong to the Keledan."

She put the knife away and removed a round device of some silver alloy surrounded by six starlots in gold settings. An empty setting spoke of a missing seventh jewel. The glance she gave Connor begged the question, *What is this?*

He shrugged and carefully accepted it when she passed it over. Dried mud marred the jewels and the bag. "I'd say one of the river trolls scooped it into the bag so as not to touch the starlots—else they'd all be darkened by shadow."

The silver device at the center had the look of a clamshell box but much smaller. Connor undid its tiny clasp and pried it open. Inside, a glass shield covered a dial like none he'd ever seen, with odd lines and markings. "What language is this?"

Neither could say, and as Teegan kept reminding him, they were losing good air by the moment. Master Jairun had cautioned Connor not to take anything from Heleyor's Vault except Lef Amunrel, but they both agreed the starlots identified this as a lightraider device, likely made by the Tinkers' Sphere, and decided to carry it home.

"Besides," Teegan said, looking around the chamber as she pressed the device into a manykit pocket, "this isn't Heleyor's Vault, is it?"

The same concern had nagged Connor since they'd first walked up the steps from the water. There were treasures—many treasures with the marks of the Leander Kings—but no powerful relics that Heleyor might both want and fear.

Connor walked among the jeweled weapons and coin chests.

"This is the Leander treasure chamber. A boon for thieves but not us. What if my patehpa was wrong and Lef Amunrel is somewhere else or destroyed? What if Heleyor's Vault was a myth started by my traitorous ancestors to increase their influence?"

He reached the water's edge and turned to face her. "What if it's all just a lie?"

52

NO TROLLS HARRIED THE LIGHTRAIDERS ON THEIR
way out of the vault. The current had taken Connor's crook in the
battle, but Teegan's trident served in its place. When needed, she
locked it under the statues' arms, and the two pulled themselves
across the gaps where the chains had broken.

They climbed the rope from the landing and found Koteg
unmoved by their long absence. He looked up at Connor's dripping
face, brown eyes begging the question, *Where is she?*

Connor scratched his ears. "You're with us now, Koteg. She's
not coming back, and I'm to blame."

Not until they'd found the narrow door to the city canyon,
more with the dog's guidance than by memory or Teegan's ranger
instincts, did Teegan challenge Connor's assertion.

"You are not to blame." Teegan took the lead in climbing the
steps through the garden streets.

"Then who is?"

She remained quiet, as if reluctant to answer, then sighed.
"Thera, for one."

Connor stopped behind her so that Koteg came between
them, looking from one to the other. "How can you say that?"

"Perhaps you're blinded to it, but Thera knew more than she

told us. For years, she visited your stone ancestor in that room. Do you doubt she'd reached the same conclusion about the wall as I did in only moments? Do you think she tried, at least, to pry away a stone or two?"

The blunted knife. Her protest about the mortar.

Connor's gaze drifted to the rushing water. "She'd met the trolls before."

"Or heard their call from the other side of the wall. Either way, she knew of them—looking back, I can see that now. And the guilt of hiding their existence from us, more than faithfulness to you or the Leanders, drove her to leap into the flood."

A poor choice. No Aladoth could outmatch a river troll, not with all the combat training in the world.

Teegan continued upward on the next staircase, with Koteg climbing after her. "All the same, Thera gave herself to save us, and for that I share blame as much as you. I might have thrown my trident."

"That would have been a fool's toss, and you know it, after what happened to my crook. Once she dove in, it was me or Thera, and so it should have been me."

They said nothing more and walked silently, breathing air tainted by the scent of the fireclocks, following the flame of the eastern clock toward the garrison plaza and the healer's house.

More than Thera's death weighed on Connor, and the burden increased with every step—the sense that he'd made a catastrophic error. Perhaps not just him, but the Order and the Assembly too.

He stopped, forcing Teegan to turn.

"Connor?" she asked.

"Is this the end?"

She returned to him, and Koteg stayed at her hip, watching him with quiet whimpers. "I don't follow."

"Our quest has failed. Lee's quest, as well, or he would not lie wounded on the table of an Aladoth healer."

Teegan's gaze, on the edge of tears, warned him not to speak so hopelessly of Lee.

Connor went on, undeterred. "It's not just ours, Teegan. Not just one death—one wounded lightraider. All quests have failed. Keledev is breached. Dark corruptions run amok on the sacred Celestial Peaks. Are we come to the punishment the traitor-kings brought upon us? Is *The Sleeper's Hope* a lie and all the world meant to crumble in blood and dragon fire?"

Teegan stared hard at him, until Connor thought she might slap him. Instead, she wrapped him in a hug. "I can't believe that. I won't. Don't let despair take you, Connor. Pray with me."

She spoke a passage of the Scrolls, declaring the High One's power, and when Connor recognized the verses, he spoke them with her.

"Ke lavechtorol medicethond po mechentu bindond.
Keasteroth talond. Numoth yi koth asteroth gevond.
Hal Ond drior po fi premat rechor. Sebi qez hal intelegon."
He heals the brokenhearted and bandages their wounds.
He counts the number of the stars. He gives names to all of them.
He is great, vast in power. His understanding is infinite.

Connor breathed deep, as if a weight upon his chest was lifted. In the silence, he felt fur under his hand, as he had in the airship when they came through the Stormgate. The lion stood beside him, supporting him with the strength of his back. *Good, son of faith. Keep walking.*

"Connor?"

He opened his eyes. Teegan had released him. Koteg leaned against him so that his hand rested on the dog's smooth coat. Koteg looked up at him with a questioning whine.

"Victory belongs to the Rescuer," Teegan said, "though you and I can't see it with our human eyes. Even Koteg knows this to be true."

He smiled and patted the dog's flank. "Let's go find Lee and get him well."

A lantern burned in the healer Necal's lower window. When they came within sight of it, Koteg abandoned Connor and ran to the door, where he sat, whining and pawing the frame.

The healer opened the door as the lightraiders came walking up, and Koteg shot past, almost taking his knees from under him.

Necal called after the dog, "Why yes, Koteg. Come in. Make yourself at home." His gaze returned to his other visitors, pausing on their wet boots. He scrunched his brow. "Since you bring Koteg, I suppose you're friends of Thera. Seems I'm doomed to a night of unexpected guests and patients."

He led them through a short vestibule to a hearth chamber and kitchen, where two kettles were brewing. He poured himself a cup from the first. "Cider? It's pure brambleberry. None of that goat's milk you'll get in the southern cantons."

Connor tried to hurry him along. "No, thank you. We're quite concerned about our friend."

"As you should be." Necal lifted the second kettle and, with the cup of cider at his lips, led them into the main passage. Tapestries hung between many rooms with gold-and-silver fabric covering the walls behind. Wax dripped from candles in bronze sconces. The whole place reminded Connor more of an inn than a home.

A creaking drew his eyes to the ceiling. Heavy. Slow. Someone walked the floors above. He presumed it was Necal's wife.

"In here," the healer said, gesturing to an open doorway. "I've done what I might for your friend, but I hold little hope."

The breath came out of Teegan as they entered. Connor thrust an arm around her waist to keep her from buckling.

Lee lay on a notched and scarred wooden table, unmoving. Crusted and blackened flesh masked his right side from his shoulder up. His eye looked unhurt, though closed—a testament to the hardiness of his spectacles, now cracked and resting on the healer's stand next to his instruments.

Aaron greeted Connor with an arm clasp. "Glad you're all right." His voice held little joy, even less when he shifted his gaze to Teegan. "We left your falcon to watch the ship. It seemed the best choice. As to Lee . . ." His voice faltered, and he stepped out of the way.

Zel sat on a stool next to the table, holding Lee's pale hand in both of hers. She raised her head as Connor and Teegan drew near. Her lips parted, but no words came. She closed them again and shook her head.

53

"HE'S STILL BREATHING."

The revelation fell with neither sadness nor elation from Necal's lips. "And on occasion there are fits in which he mumbles a name—Azoz, I think. But I can't wake him."

The healer signaled Zel to give him room and used a small bellows to blow steam from the kettle over the burns. The vapors smelled of warm oak but sweeter. "I cleaned his wounds and applied a balm to fight infection. This will keep the flesh limber that we might spare as much as we can from the knife."

Zel gave them her full tale, how they had found the Sorcerer's Cave and fought the creatures there—of Lee's intervention when she began to succumb to the trolls and her own attempt to save him from the giant.

Teegan halted Zel's story at the blast caused by her tehpa's compounds. "So . . . *you* did this to him?"

Zel's bloodshot eyes begged her for forgiveness. "I had to save him from the giant. I knew the blast might hurt him, but I had no choice. The creature invaded his mind."

"I don't believe it," Teegan said, turning her gaze to Lee.

"I do." Connor crouched beside Lee's arm, eyeing a set of holes in his tunic. The scorch marks around them were a lighter shade than those on his cloak and shoulder. He looked to Zel. "Did he take a wound from the giant in your first encounter?"

She nodded.

Without asking, Connor took the knife from Teegan's belt and cut the sleeve away. What he saw made him cringe.

Six misshapen boils, each the size of a gold halfin, had raised the flesh of Lee's upper arm. Red tendrils so dark they were almost black spread like roots around them. The thickest lines stretched up his neck and down from his shoulder to his chest.

"This is why you can't wake him," Connor said, looking up at Necal. "He doesn't want to come out of it."

"Are you questioning my skill in healing, boy?"

"Not your skill. Only the totality of your knowledge." Connor thrust his chin toward the table of instruments. "Much may be accomplished with knives and herbs, but not all."

Lee convulsed, teeth and eyes clenched. The wounded arm reached for empty air. "Azoz. Azoz."

Connor bent to his friend's ear and whispered a verse Master Jairun had taught him after his own encounter with a giant. *"Aya kerath vyk se'wend Ke'Rumosh recertholod krafah, dar fi plenol tresod credend, fi shamar deda recrethond."*

He did not make the High One his refuge.

He trusted in wealth and wickedness.

Lee arched his chest and let out a cry.

Teegan grabbed Connor's arm. "You're hurting him!"

"I'm helping him. Let me work while he can still hear counsel. You gave me aid, now let me do it for him." He shook her off and pressed close to Lee again. *"Hevalesh miyov da'es, ma prematesh aler moremat nakaveth."*

My grace is sufficient.

My power is perfected in weakness.

"You need no giant, my friend. And I need not despair. The Rescuer is sovereign over all."

With a great exhale, Lee's arching back collapsed to the table.

The boils shrank, red tendrils receding and lightening to pink. Quickly, Connor patted his friend's manykit until he found the clay vial he sought. He broke it under Lee's nose, releasing a pungent odor of hartshorn and vinegar.

Lee coughed and groaned. His eyes opened, and he blinked. "I know that shape," he said in a voice weak and rasping, "even without my spectacles. Connor."

Zel shoved Connor out of the way. "Lee! I'm so sorry I hurt you. I had to separate you from that giant. Can you forgive me?"

The scribe tried to raise himself on an elbow, winced, and fell back again. "No forgiveness necessary." He squeezed her hand. "I'm grateful."

As he spoke, the burned flesh lightened, resolving to pink. Cuts remained, and scars like a map of ridges and valleys, but much had been healed.

In all this, Teegan stood patiently behind Connor. Sensing her wishes, he stepped away, and she hurried close to place a kiss on Lee's forehead.

Necal pulled Connor to his instrument table so roughly that Aaron laid a hand on his curved sword.

"Apologies, young man," Necal said. "I mean no threat. I only want to know your friend's secret. The healing sorcery I've seen is always destructive. Those healers remove a limb by fire to stop an infection or draw the very mind from a man to end his madness. But this . . ."

"This"—Connor glanced Lee's way—"isn't sorcery. You tended his wounds with skilled art. I followed your care with counsel and prayer in the words of the patient's Maker."

"His Maker?" Necal asked.

"The Rescuer. We are Keledan."

Necal did not seem to grasp Connor's full meaning. Still, what he'd seen had clearly changed his perceptions. "I know of your Keledan Overlord, though I've never seen his power firsthand. If you carry his favor, perhaps you'd be so kind as to help my other patient."

"Your other patient?" Connor turned to Aaron, who gestured toward the door.

There stood a young woman in a long white frock, raven hair about her shoulders, with a joyful Koteg panting beside her and Connor's own crook in her hand.

A laugh burst from his lips. "Thera?"

54

THERA RETURNED CONNOR'S CROOK, WHICH LOOKED none the worse for its adventure through the city's underworkings.

He couldn't say the same for her. Necal had bandaged a wound on her right forearm, bright red where the blood was seeping through. Deep bruises marked her cheek and chin.

Thera caught him looking at the bruises and chuckled, wincing at the pain it must have caused her. "Without the light of those plants, and with the current carrying me onward, I found it difficult to navigate the channels south of the vault. At times I used my hands to feel the way." She touched the bruise on her chin. "At others, I used my face."

The captain had exchanged her uniform for the frock, perhaps to let it dry, but Connor noted she still wore the long leather glove on her left hand and arm. "And your other arm, how did it fare?"

With those fingers, she'd been scratching Koteg's ears, but now she hid them behind her. "Better."

He didn't press. "I owe you a great debt. You wrestled a troll for me."

"I did what was right. No debt is owed—not by you."

Thera hacked and coughed, and Connor understood what Necal meant when the healer had asked him to help her.

"You breathed in water."

"A great deal."

He moved aside to let her into the room. "My friend, Lee, is training in the healing arts at our academy. He may offer some treatment Necal has not yet thought of. Beyond that, we can offer prayer."

"To your Overlord."

Connor nodded.

"If he heals me, must I bow to him and trade one master for another?"

"That's not how he works," Aaron said. "No one is forced to serve him. We choose it because of his love for us and ours for him."

With her consent, Connor brought Thera to the table with Lee and made the introductions. After the scribe had given her a tincture of herbs and vinegar from his kit, the party gathered around her to pray—and Koteg, too, who might have felt by then that he'd become a veteran at it.

"Better?" Teegan asked, once they'd finished.

Thera gave her a half smile. "I think so. I'll let you know."

"And you?" Connor asked Necal. "What do you think of our great healer, the Rescuer?"

The answer surprised him. "I would serve your Overlord," Necal said, without hesitation. "I would serve him and use my skill to share the news of his power because my life's work is to help and heal. But I know something of your people. I'm not pure enough to walk through your magic tree portals. I'd be burned to a cinder, or so they say."

Zel laughed at the notion.

Aaron snickered.

Connor shot them both a warning look. He sighed. The dragons had woven many webs of lies to hinder a lightraider's work.

Webs. Lies.

The upper floor creaked.

Connor knew what was holding Necal captive. "When you say

you aren't pure, you speak of your mistress."

"Hush, boy. My wife will hear."

"As she must—and will, either now or when the thing in your attic consumes her. Which would you prefer?"

Necal did not answer.

"Your failure is not too great for the Rescuer to overcome. But you must give it to him freely and leave it behind."

"You've heard wrong," Teegan said, joining Connor. "The Keledan are not pure—not on our own. No human can be. It is our master, by his sacrifice, who purifies us."

Light began to dawn in Necal's eyes. He sat in a chair by his instrument table, no longer the healer but the patient. Teegan and Connor offered treatment by showing him the Great Rescue. They shared the story of the Rescuer's sacrifice at Ras Telesar, giving himself as a fountain of water to sap the dragons' fire and then returning to raise the Celestial Peaks and the Storm Mists, ending dragon rule over the Keledan.

One by one, the lightraiders and stormriders spoke the five verses of the Great Rescue and explained their meaning.

Connor spoke *Ke'Aroshkef*. The One and Only. Then he explained, "The High One loves all Aladoth and Keledan so much he sent his son to live and die as one of them."

Teegan spoke *Arosh Nakav*. Not One is Perfect. "All bear the stain of sin, and none are pure enough to wash it away on their own."

Aaron spoke *Zebath Nakav*. Perfect Sacrifice. "The Rescuer is pure enough, and by his sacrifice he made those who accept him pure as well."

Lee spoke *Liberend*. Liberation. "Salvation comes from turning from sin and accepting that gift. Declare the Rescuer as master."

Zel spoke the verse of the *Keledan*, the Twiceborn. "Believe, Necal, and become an heir of the true King."

Necal leapt from the chair and shouted to the sky. "Take my folly! I renounce it and believe!"

A thunderous *crash* sounded from above, shaking dust from the ceiling. A woman screamed.

Connor clapped the healer on the back. "Time to kill the spider in your attic."

55

TEEGAN CLIMBED THE STAIRS BESIDE CONNOR WITH Necal close behind. "We shouldn't bring him," she said. "He's not ready to face a spider."

"He must. Necal has fed this creature too long with his lies and infidelity. We can help, but we can't destroy it for him."

As they reached the top, another scream came from a room at the end of the hall, along with the chaotic pounding of eight heavy legs. Necal stared at the door. "In there. The bedchamber."

Connor grabbed him by the collar, pressing Revornosh into his hand, and heaved him out front. "You must kill this thing to save your wife. Whether she loves you afterward is up to her. When the spider strikes, raise your left arm. The Rescuer will shield you." He glanced down at the sword. "And when you swing that, try not to hit her or either of us. Now, go."

Necal threw the door wide and immediately froze.

The spider filled a full quarter of the healer's overlarge bedchamber. His wife—dressed in her nightgown, hair tied up in ribbons—cried out from the far side of the room, where the creature had her cornered. She looked as angry as she was scared. "Necal, what is this thing?"

His wife had taken a tall standing dressing mirror as a shield, and in the reflection, the spider glared at the intruders. It bared its dripping fangs and let out a screeching hiss.

"I can't do this," Necal said. "I've let the spider grow too big."

"If you don't, it will consume your wife." Connor gave him a shove. "Hurry!"

The healer, stumbling into the battle, made a slash at one of the creature's legs. The spider deftly lifted it out of the way and kicked him. Gray armor flashed. Necal flew back into Connor.

Teegan rolled her eyes. "Oh, please." She pushed past them both and thrust her trident into the bulbous abdomen.

Black blood spurted out. The spider shrieked and thrashed, slamming Necal's wife against the wall. She cried out in pain and slumped down. "Necal, help me!"

The sight of her injury breathed new life into the healer. With Connor's help, he regained his feet and charged. "I'm sorry, my love. So sorry." He slashed again, this time cutting a leg clean through. "This is my doing—my unfaithfulness. I have wronged you so!"

The spider began to turn and shrink itself in that way those foul creatures can, but Teegan corralled it with her trident. Connor came in from the other side and beat it with his crook. Their efforts exposed its center to Necal, putting the head within close reach of his blade. The spider spread its jaws and roared.

This time, Necal did not falter. He shoved his arm so deep down the spider's throat that Connor feared the sword might be lost. Curved fangs as long as daggers clamped down, but the healer's new armor held and glowed bright. The spider's hairy mandibles burned.

The creature pulled in its legs in the throes of death and collapsed.

Necal removed Revornosh, covered in ooze, and dropped it, then ran to his wife.

He raised her from the floor, but she pushed him away, even though her legs refused to hold her. Teegan, instead, gave her aid.

The healer fell to his knees before his wife. "This monster was the fruit of my willful error—my great deceit and the undoing of my vow. I have much to tell you if you'll listen."

The lightraiders placed his wife in a chair and set another near her for Necal. Before they left, Connor pulled the healer close. "We must go tend to our companion"—he glanced over at the dead spider—"and you must clean up this mess. Tell her what you've seen, heard, and believed. Your faithlessness will make it hard for her to listen, but do your best."

As he spoke, a pair of tiny spiders ran out from under the big one. Connor made a face and stomped them under his boot. "There will be many more of those—the offspring of the bigger monster. You must find them and destroy them as you can. Together, if she'll allow it."

He said no more. Necal's wife had begun to shiver, and Connor let the healer go and bring her a blanket. He and Teegan returned to their friends downstairs.

In the infirmary, they found Lee sitting up, chatting with Aaron and Zel and wearing his cracked spectacles. Thera had left with Koteg, perhaps resting in whatever room the healer had given her.

Connor smiled at the scribe. "Looks like you're doing better."

"Much," Lee said, though the frailty of his grin said otherwise. Even so, the word bought him a hug from Teegan. He grunted with alarm. "Yet, still on the mend . . . Still wounded."

"Can you travel?" she asked, releasing him.

"Oh, yes. That I can do. And I look forward to seeing the city. Aaron's been telling me about your map and your progress. He showed me his wound from your battle at the archive." Lee's gaze shifted to Connor. "You did well in dressing it."

"Thanks, but I'm glad you're here now to treat it properly."

Aaron's stories had piqued the scribe's interest, and he asked for a look at Faelin's journal and the maps. These, Connor willingly gave him.

The symbols—the meanings of which Connor and the others

could only guess—seemed to be as good as words in the Common Tongue to Lee. He touched each in turn. "This, as you've learned, is a garrison. And this is an archive. On these old Taneletharian maps, a square represents the martial functions of a city or house while the circle represents anything administrative."

"And the diamond?" Connor asked, pointing to the archive.

"The jewel of wisdom, which the nobility kept using even after the fall. It represents anything to do with knowledge or records. And here, you can see the combination of the square and circle with the torch representing the palace." Lee moved his finger up from the combined symbol over the palace to a small dragon drawn near the falls above. "But this. This is rare."

The dragon had always seemed of little consequence to Connor. "That's a decoration."

"I don't think so." Lee flipped a blue lens down over his right eye and turned the map askew. "Size bears great importance on maps and scrolls of this age. This dragon matches the dimension of the other location symbols. A decoration would be larger— especially one depicting their new masters." He laid the map atop the journal and flipped the lens up again. "No. That's a marker."

A marker next to the waterfall pouring itself into the river. *The Serpentine. Seek the source.*

Connor shook his head at the thought. "If the dragon is a marker, it's too high, well above the city." He opened the journal to Faelin's record of the legend and showed Lee the incomplete copy he'd started of the engraving in the archive. "The old legend says Heleyor's Vault is *in* the city."

Lee turned the pages back and forth from Faelin's writing to Connor's, smiling at the two. "That's amusing."

"Don't poke fun at my Elder Tongue script," Connor said. "It's childish next to my patehpa's and yours."

"On the contrary, your copy is more accurate."

When Connor scrunched his face, Lee chuckled. "I mean, yes, your script is atrocious, as always, but you copied it well enough.

And in your lack of nuance, you avoided the error made by your grandfather."

This brought the others nearer. "Error?" Teegan asked.

Lee showed them a particular word in Faelin's record. "See here? This letter? Faelin, perhaps on instinct, changed it to suit the purer Elder Tongue we've learned from the earliest copies of the Sacred Scrolls." He turned to Connor's entry. "But in your ignorance"—he gave Connor a fleeting half grin—"I mean, in your less studied state, you copied the letter with more accuracy."

Folding the page to show them the words side by side, Lee noted how one letter looked slightly different. "This engraving was carved in the corrupted tongue of the traitor-kings. Your grandfather saw the letter as a Fa, but it's not. This is a Rol." The scribe trilled the letter's sound in a way Connor could never manage, no doubt showing off, a sure sign he was feeling better.

Aaron had been listening with arms crossed, leaning against the instrument table. "I've enjoyed this lesson in the history of our writing." He brought his wrist to his mouth to cover a yawn. "Truly. But it doesn't help us find Lef Amunrel."

"Ah." Lee raised a finger. "That's where you're wrong. Change a letter. Change a legend. Faelin's translation says the vault lies in Emen Yan, but a better translation says the vault lies *above* Emen Yan." He picked up the map again, showing them the dragon symbol. "Likely here, behind these falls."

56

KARA
KELEDEV
ORVYN'S VOW

"THEY LOOK LIKE A BAND OF FESTIVAL PLAYERS,"
Kara said, watching Samar's windfighters train, "all playing the
part of Lee."

It was the spectacles they all wore, which Boreas called *eye
shields*, but Kara saw little difference. The Councilor and Belen
had exchanged ravens regarding sight for the windfighters, some
of whom had red and puffy eyes from too many glides. They'd
solved the problem by having the guildsmen sew lenses into leather
straps, ravaging poor Sireth's lanterns and windows for the glass.

She found the eye shields uncomfortable, giving her a sense
of how Lee must feel every day, but they made a great difference
in her jumps. The view of the fjords on her first glide with them
astounded her.

Kara waited in line with Samar for the ledge. She'd taken
the custom of making one morning jump before joining Ioanu in
teaching combat to the fighters. Their number had grown to thirty,
broken into two squadrons of fifteen, fully stocked with glide suits.
One squadron wore the image of a paradragon as its emblem. The
other wore an image of a bear in flight.

The paradragons still came out to play during the jumps and
seemed to favor those with their picture embroidered on their

suits. Kara was watching a pair of them do somersaults about a gliding fighter, listening to their chirping calls, when a different call reached her ears—stronger and higher pitched.

A lone paradragon, the big one that had first fought the orcs with her, hung on the breeze above the burnt-out way station across the fjord. He puffed out a cloud of white and called again.

Samar took note as well. "Dash sounds upset."

"Dash?"

The pilot gave her a quick grin. "You know, because he dashes about."

Dash flew a tight loop and let out two more urgent barks. He seemed to look straight at them. "Let's see what he wants," Kara said and ran up the trail.

They took the wobbly talanium bridge to the burnt-out way station and found Dash hovering beyond its clearing over the finger's northeastern cliff.

"What's wrong?" Kara asked the creature. "What has you fretting so?"

In answer, the paradragon tucked its wings and dove.

Kara and Samar ran to the cliff's edge. The line of the paradragon's dive drew Kara's gaze to four black forms flying through the narrow fjord. Gall buzzards. Dash seemed intent on fighting them.

"He can't take them alone," Samar said, taking off along the cliff at a run. He sprinted inland, up the cliff trail, always watching the birds, then skidded to a stop and called back to her, "This is the place. If we time it right, we can intercept them."

Kara caught up to him, breathing hard. "You're mad."

"Isn't this our purpose?"

"Our purpose is to glide in and fight foes on land, not tangle with birds on the wing."

"Then let's expand our boundaries, shall we?" He drew the dual blades from his back, twirled them to point the tips down, then ran to the edge and jumped.

Kara set her eye shields in place, snapped open her whirlknives, and followed.

Dash reached the buzzards ahead of them and blew a ribbon of frost across the lot. The birds wobbled in their flight and shouted their strange calls of offense. Aaron was right, to her ear it sounded like *The gall! The gall!* One broke off to fight their attacker. The paradragon's run slowed them, but it hadn't taken any of them down.

Samar's haste had created another problem. This fjord had no landing raft, nor fishermen to row them to the lifts. Kara looked inland to see where they might land and saw a short glade in the opposite cliffside, still a quarter league or more above the water, with a path leading up again. It might work if they played this right.

Movement near the root of the fjord caught her eye. Something large seemed to churn there, grinding upon itself. She had no time to stare. The fight was coming fast.

Samar seemed intent on slashing the leader on his way to the next, a clear play to take two birds in a single pass. He missed his mark, and the second bird saw him coming. It veered in the air and pulled up, showing its talons.

Kara had only a beat to watch her friend go from a smooth glide to a tumbling plummet, wrapped in combat with the bird, before she, too, entered the fray. She focused on the last bird in the pack. The creature matched the posture of the one that had taken Samar, but Kara countered by casting a whirlknife and rolling away.

The blade sliced clean through the buzzard's neck.

Kara spread her limbs to slow her glide and caught the spinning knife on the other side.

A quick search below brought her eyes to Samar, still in flight with Dash gliding at his shoulder. She saw no sign of the buzzard.

Samar wobbled—unlike him, always smooth and steady. Looking closer, Kara saw tears in both wings. She looked ahead to the landing spot she'd chosen. He might still make it.

To reach him, she'd have to ruin her glide for a few beats in the same way his fight with the buzzard had ruined his. She wrapped her arms to her middle, tucking her shoulders, and entered a tumble that dropped her toward the fjord.

One, two, three.

Kara spread her limbs again and searched below. There. She'd brought herself close enough to steer the rest of the way using subtle movements of her arms. She dove underneath her friend and his paradragon escort and rolled on her back to meet his eye.

The damage was worse than she'd hoped. Blood gathered on Samar's suit near his collar and on one hand, which no longer held its sword. There were more tears in the underside of his silks. It looked as if Dash had tried to help by blowing frost over the holes, but the frost was flaking away.

The look the pilot gave her begged the question, *What now?*

He should have thought of that before he jumped. Kara craned her neck back to look toward the landing spot she'd chosen. Samar looked that way as well and gave her a nod.

Kara went first. To make the spot she'd have to spoil her glide a little more, then pull up and throw her lander. The notion that this would be the first windfighter landing on solid dirt and rocks with no room for mistakes was not lost on her. Gauge it wrong, and she might crash into the cliff above or below.

She said a quick prayer for aid, counted the beats as the glade came rushing toward her, made one last correction with a tuck of her arms, and then pulled the blue ring.

A pine tree brushed Kara's boots on the way in. She hadn't noticed it or any of the several trees on the glade. She softened her knees and hit the grass at a run, yanking the copper ring to shed her silks. The moment she came to a stop she turned.

Samar had already thrown his lander and came down hard at a steeper angle than she. He hit the grass and pitched forward into a roll, then lay still. He made no move to shed his silks, and the wind caught his lander. It dragged him back toward the cliff.

57

DASH DUG HIS TALONS INTO SAMAR'S BOOTS AND flapped with all his might, trying to counter the wind's pull. Kara dove for the other boot. Their efforts were not enough.

While the wind dragged all three, Kara clawed her way up Samar's suit to the copper ring and pulled. The silks came loose, but their trek across the grass didn't stop. Samar was lying on the pouch. She wrapped her arms around him and rolled him free.

The silks and straps continued across the grass and over the cliff, out into the fjord. Dash flew out of sight after them, then reappeared and chirped as if to say, *Never mind.*

Samar coughed and breathed. "Kara?" His gaze panned down to her arm, which still lay underneath him. "You finally embraced me, and I missed the whole thing?"

Kara shoved him away and scrambled to her feet. "Don't jest! You might've got us both killed!"

"By jumping? We have the fjord to catch us."

"A fjord I rejected when seeking a place for our training." She swiped the eye shields from her face. "The walls are too sheer at the waterline. We'd have been trapped in frigid water for ticks on end until someone came looking for us. Not to mention the buzzards. I told you we weren't meant to fight in the air."

"Of course we are, and between you and me and Dash, we killed three of four." Samar groaned, stumbling through the grass and laying a hand upon his neck wound. "My fault. None of this is my fault." He bent to recover his one remaining sword, and Kara could swear she heard him mutter *The gall* under his breath.

He straightened, sliding the sword into its sheath, and when he removed his eye shields, the gaze beneath was dark and angry. "If we're casting blame, let's be truthful. This is all *your* fault."

Her jaw fell open. Heat rose under the blue-gray flourishes on her arms and cheeks. "How is this my fault? You're the one who jumped."

"And I only jumped because I must go to such great lengths to impress you. I mean, all of you." Samar threw his hands in the air. "Nothing is ever good enough! For Sireth. For Dag. But especially for you." He stared at her for a beat, some dark intent brewing, then stormed across the grass and caught her shoulders, pressing close as if to kiss her.

Kara stomped on his boot and struck him across the face, sending him two paces back. "How dare you!"

Dash flew between them, drawing a line of ice across the grass. He cast one of his chirping barks at Samar as if to say, *Never again.*

Samar lowered his gaze and touched his chin where she'd hit him. He shook his head. "Why must you always reject me? Why must you hate me?"

Kara's eyes narrowed. None of this sounded like the Samar she knew. She eyed the wound at his neck. Gray and brown mold grew on his skin around the gash. A second wound on his left hand bore the same mold. "Your wound is infected."

"What?"

"Dark creatures carry poison on their weapons and claws. Some breathe it into the air. The bird caught you with its talons or beak. Correct?"

"Both."

"Wonderful. It poisoned you, Samar. I only wish I knew what

type of poison these birds carry."

He let out a scornful laugh. "More reason for you to despise me. More reason I'm not as worthy as your precious shepherd boy."

"Enough, Samar!"

Dash barked another warning.

Samar cast the paradragon a glance. "Are you going to have your pet seal my mouth with ice?"

"I won't stop him if he tries, so keep quiet. Give me a moment to think how we should treat your wounds."

"Don't concern yourself," Samar said. "I may not be as large as Dag, as wise as Sireth, or as noble as Connor, but I'm strong. I'll be fine."

"None of us is strong enough." She had a plan. The guardians had taught them that love was always a good beginning. Kara crossed the line of ice, which caused Dash to hang closer to her shoulder, and drew a cloth and a vial of bluebitter from her manykit pockets. "Hear me. The prayer I speak now is a reminder of the Rescuer's love."

"Only his?"

She frowned. "I told you to keep quiet."

Kara broke the vial over a linen cloth and prayed as she worked. *"Ka keteval nim avahend, ovuneh epo avahendana. Fi avelnesh abidov."*

As the father loved me, so have I loved you. Remain in my love.

She pressed the cloth against the gash.

Samar sucked in a breath. "Easy, now, woman. Are you so bent on hurting me?"

"I'm nothing of the kind."

"Then take care with your cloth. Isn't gentleness one of the nine core strengths touted by your order?" He winced and huffed as she applied the cloth to his hand. "I daresay you'd be more caring with your shepherd. Tell me I'm wrong."

Kara stood back. She could not. But that was none of his concern, nor had it any bearing on his wound.

Or did it?

Had the bird's poison alone called forth such bile? Was it so powerful? Surely not. More was at work here. In the deeper studies of a cadet scout, she'd learned all people are fallen—ever in need of the Rescuer's love—and dark creature maladies feed upon fleshly angers and desires harbored deep within.

The mold fought the healing nature of the bluebitter, still growing. Samar's own bitterness was feeding it. To deal with the infection, Kara would first have to carve out the trouble that had been there before.

Perhaps she should have dealt with it much sooner. She'd seen the signs of his infatuation, but she'd ignored them because of the urgency of the days.

She applied the cloth again. "Samar, we must have something out, and I think you know what it is."

He drew his arm away from her. "Now is not the time."

"Now is the only time. Or this hurt will render you useless to our cause." When he bristled at the word *useless*, Kara pursed her lips. "You know what I mean."

"Do I? Haven't I shown you my skill? My bravery? I've galloped to a cliff's edge to send you flying, leapt into the open sky to show you my worth. Is that not enough to contend with a wool monger raised in the vales?"

The linen had grown too soiled with mold and blood for use. She let it fall at his feet and walked away, trying to gather her thoughts, certain now she had indeed let this go too long. She crossed her arms. "Where do you think you are?"

He contorted his face to imply her question made no sense.

"I mean to say, this is not Tanelethar."

"I'm well aware."

"Are you? Here in Keledev, we let the Rescuer guide us, or so I was told, even—*especially*—in matters of the heart." Kara broke a second vial over another cloth, letting the blue tincture soak in. "This is not Tanelethar, where women are spoils to be won by feats of strength or chests of jewels or . . ." She stumbled, striving to think of a third example. "Or . . . whoever works to smell the best."

Again, Samar made a face.

Kara shrugged. "I suppose that last bit is appreciated in all lands." She pointed at him with the cloth. "But it doesn't determine who a Keledan woman loves. For that, she looks to and prays to the Rescuer, and asks him to steer her path alongside the right man."

"And for you, that man is Connor?"

"Yes," she said, approaching again. "And you and I must agree on that point or part ways. Risks taken to impress me or indiscreet words and glances will only hinder us in our present battle." She slapped the cloth onto the wound.

Samar's eyes went wide. He made a sound like a swallowed cry. "This time, you did it on purpose."

"Yes, I did. To make sure you remember. A touch of bluebitter in answer to your bitter words."

Bitter words. Bitterness. That was the infection of the gall buzzard. Kara smiled. How pleased Master Belen would be that she'd made such a discovery.

She lowered her chin to give Samar a hard look. "Are we clear on where we stand?"

He took the cloth and began to tend his own wounds. "We are. And thank you for your candor. Friends?"

"More than friends. Brehna and shessa, as all in Keledev should be."

They prayed together, and in that prayer, Samar himself spoke a verse from the Scrolls. "*Menov koth morakat, furakat po ragat, gordi po galol elimov, po koth malat.*"

She didn't know it, but she understood the meaning. *No more bitterness. No more malice.*

Two steep trails led from the glade. Kara took the one heading west, toward the fjord's root.

"Shouldn't we go east?" Samar asked, following. "The shorter road will be the way station and then the bridge."

"We will. I want to see something first." The trail took them to a ledge where Kara could look inland along the gentle curve of the fjord.

Samar came up beside her. "What is that?"

Wooden lifts ten times the size of any at Orvyn's Vow moved on the cliff faces where the two sides of the fjord joined. A dock large enough to hold a hundred men covered the water below. And above, on an elevated plain sheltered under a monstrous overhang, an army far larger camped.

"Orcs?" Samar asked. "Aladoth?"

"I don't know. But they sure aren't Keledan."

58

CONNOR
TANELETHAR
EMEN YAN

THE PARTY TARRIED IN EMEN YAN, SHELTERING AT
Necal's home. Connor could not imagine either the healer or his
wife wanting houseguests just then, but she begged them to stay.
The house had plenty of rooms, and she confessed having many
voices in her hallways gave her comfort.

In those short hours, she sought counsel—mostly from Teegan
and Zel—and together they showed her their master's radiance.
Thus, she committed to the Rescuer, and with his aid, the crushing
blow she'd taken was lightened.

Lee wished to move on and continue the quest he and Zel
had started, but all agreed he needed more time to recover from
his injuries and dispel the giant's infection. "Besides," Connor
told him, "I need you a little longer. It was foolish of me to think
Teegan, Aaron, and I might breach Heleyor's Vault on our own.
For this task, we'll need all hands and your sharp mind."

Lee's scars shrank until they seemed hardly noticeable, except
that his ear remained misshapen. Necal took an interest in that
malady and advised them that the blast Zel described had caused
damage beyond the outer flesh. There were gaps in his memory of
the days prior, and when he walked, he often staggered, having to
lean on Teegan or the passage walls. Like the scars, these problems

faded over time, but not entirely.

Thera brought Lee a new tunic in the bright green and yellow of Emen Yan, which were colors he loved, and brought new arrows for his quiver and crossbow bolts for Zel. Apart from that, she spent little time in the house and spent much of the daylight ticks walking the city with Connor and Koteg.

The three walked the walls on the city's north side and used Connor's spyglass to scout the great dam. They had to find a way up to the waterfall—the largest waterfall among dozens pouring down from the icy sea of Val Glasa, known as *Ke'Shafal*—where they hoped to find the vault.

"Over the centuries men have cut many paths and stairways in that dam," Thera told him on their last trip. "So many that some in the city fear we've scored it near to breaking. But no path I know of leads up to Ke'Shafal."

"And we won't find it. Not like this." Connor frowned and put the spyglass away. "The way to such a place will be well hidden. We must come up with a better plan."

"Or a better goal," Thera said, rubbing the arm covered with the long glove, perhaps still sore after her harrowing ride under the city. "Have you considered that the Leander treasure chamber you found is no longer guarded? With my knowledge of Emen Yan and the loyalty of my garrison, that gold might take you far."

Koteg let out a growl, one Connor almost mimicked in his reply. "What are you saying?"

"I'm saying with my help, you could take this city back for the Leanders."

"That's not my quest or my desire, Thera. You know this."

She raised her hand. "Don't set my counsel aside so quickly. You want this Lef Amunrel, a weapon of your people, yes?"

He nodded—slowly.

"To find it may take years, especially working in secret with only your small party. But think how much easier it will be from the palace, with Emen Yan and all its resources at your disposal.

Even if your land is taken, you might raise an army from here that can take it back."

Connor considered the fancy—and the practicality—of her proposal. Was it so far-fetched? There must be more like Thera in this place, loyal to his bloodline. Could the lightraiders gain a seat of power so deep in Tanelethar? Could they enter a new era of war with the dragons on a bolder front?

Another growl from Koteg cut his imaginings short. The dog nuzzled Connor's hand, and Connor obliged him by patting his neck. "If you are as loyal to my bloodline as you claim, Thera, you'll never speak so again."

Despite his stern answer, her words had spawned a new notion for Connor. Thera wasn't wrong in saying the search might take years—even now that they knew where to look—*if* the Keledan had to search on foot.

They didn't.

The dragons and the Leanders had hidden Heleyor's Vault at a time when no man outside House Suvor and the dragon sorcerers ever dreamed of leaping much higher than a horse cart. Now, thanks to the revelations of the Rescuer and the work of Zayn Boreas and the Sky Harbor guilds, the Keledan could fly.

"We've seen several smithies in our walks through the city," he said to Thera. "Tell me, is there one you favor more than the rest?"

59

BOREAS'S FLAGSHIP, *THE BARN OWL*, WITH ITS FIVE black envelopes ornamented in gold, led the Airguard fleet. Kara looked out from its rail across Orvyn's Vow to the ground squadrons on the western end of the fjords, marching toward the hidden shelf and the army she and Samar had found. Watchmen and lightraiders rode and marched together in mixed formations. Not since the Battle of Pellion's Flow had more than fifty Keledan gathered for a fight. These numbered in the hundreds.

The Windhold and Ravencrest were emptied. Thousand Falls spread their company east to fill the gaps with some still on the move on their way to reinforce Orvyn's Vow. A scant few cadets under Belen and Silvana guarded Ras Telesar. All others rode or marched now with the formations, heading to what Kara hoped was the last battle.

So many fighters. Too many to hide for long.

Did the enemy know they were coming?

The airships hung back. Boreas would lead them up the narrow fjord and descend upon the enemy from the east, while the main force drove down the mountain slope from the west. But this plan wouldn't hold if the dark creature platoons shifted west first to meet the Keledan.

Dark creatures. Not Aladoth.

Kara couldn't say whether she'd felt relief or angst once the scouts brought back reports of the hidden army. A bit of one and a large helping of the other, she supposed.

Hundreds of dark creatures had gathered on the level ground under the giant overhang. Ore creatures of three varieties formed the main force—iron, talanium, and copper. Among their tents scurried cave and forest goblins, and the scouts reported armored golmogs, which Dag suspected would form their vanguard. There were trolls too—mocktrees and rumblefeet—but no iceblades or rattlefish, and that was a blessing.

Boreas had sent two ships up with flags to read the winds, and the ravens they sent him landed on the bow in quick succession. He opened their scrolls, wearing an inscrutable frown.

Kara waited as long as she could. "Well, Councilor?"

"The Rescuer is with us. The low air will carry us into the fight, so we may remain hidden as long as possible." Boreas looked out toward the steep terrain beyond the fjords, the sheer slopes of the Impossible Peaks. "But once we rise, the windfighters must move fast. The mid winds will play havoc with our silk, and the upper will carry us away again." He shot a glance at the stern. "Would that we had a consistent way to propel ourselves against it."

Two big cylinders were lashed to the hull between the skids. Kara had seen them when her unit boarded, and she'd seen a similar device in action before. "You have those flaming nightmares strapped under our wicker. Won't they propel us?"

His eyes seemed to chuckle at her choice of words, but he shook his head and began scribbling notes on his two tiny scrolls. "Dangerous. And good for only one use." Boreas tied his notes to the ravens and sent them off. "We need something more reliable, but that is a question for another day. For now, our time has come. Prepare yourselves."

Kara and her fighters kneeled. Boreas sounded his ship's

horn, powered by the vapors in his center envelope, and kneeled with them. His signal had called the fleet to prayer.

Each ship prayed the same, using the Common Tongue so that all might seek the High One in unison.

I will say concerning he who is my refuge and my fortress, the one in whom I trust . . .

Verse by verse they called to him for aid and strength.

His faithfulness will be a protective shield. You will not fear the terror of the night, the arrow that flies by day . . .

Kara had worried she might not remember what to say, but the voices around her gave her confidence, and her voice gave confidence to them. The last verse she loved most of all.

Because you have made him—my refuge, the Most High—your dwelling place, no harm will come to you.

No matter what blades or arrows she might face this day, these creatures could not harm her spirit—could not subject her to the second death. Elamhavar and victory waited.

The fighters and Boreas stood, and the councilor himself took the vents and the rudder. "Onward, windfighters. To battle!"

The fleet descended—myriad colors, falling slowly over blue water. Deft pilots formed into lines of three behind the flagship, silks almost touching, to fit within the fjord.

Looking up, Kara saw the talanium bridge hanging between the charred way stations. The scouts had figured the reason the goblins had burned them. The orc camp lay hidden from all the outpost's watchtowers, thanks to the curve of the fjord and the great overhang above their tents. But from the upper floor of the western way station, a sharp observer might have spotted their camp. Only from the air midway between the cliffs had Kara seen it. Samar's leap to fight the buzzards may have been foolhardy, but it had given the Keledan a chance to end this.

The winds moved fast in the lower reaches of the fjord. In moments the talanium bridge disappeared above *The Barn Owl*'s silks. The water passed so close under their hull, Kara thought the skids might touch it and send up spray. Boreas knew his work. She saw why his pilots loved him.

"Here it comes!" he shouted to the fighters. "Be ready on the starboard side!"

The ship took the curve in the fjord as smooth as any boat, keeping to the center between the cliffs. The huge dock and the lifts appeared before the bow. No one yet understood their purpose. The dark creatures had no ships in Keledev.

With the docks in sight, Boreas flared his lamps, and the ship began to rise. The camp came into view—a mass of empty tents.

The councilor pounded his rails. "They saw us coming! They're on the move!"

60

ORC PLATOONS, FLANKED BY RUMBLING STONE trolls and wood trolls ambling on their roots, marched up the western slope of their hidden valley. Armored golmogs lumbered at the front, ready to take the brunt of the first assault.

If they made it to the rim before the Keledan reached them, all advantage would be spent. A fight on level ground might cost the watchmen and the lightraiders dearly.

"Surprise is gone," Boreas said, working his rudder and vent ropes to steer the ship west toward the dark creatures. "Let's get their attention." He sounded two quick blasts on his horn.

Answering blasts echoed in the fjord. The creatures shrieked and howled. Their march slowed to a halt.

One of Kara's fighters shouted, "It worked!"

"Don't get too excited," Boreas answered. "There's a reason we didn't want this."

Black arrows came flying. Two lodged in their wicker. Two more sank into their silks. The councilor dumped a vial of fuel into his lamps to keep the ship on the rise and turned her full broadside. "Go!"

Kara leapt first over the rail, watching more arrows pass to her left and right. Even the wind in her ears could not hide a scream that came from behind. Already, one had fallen.

You will not fear the terror of the night, the arrow that flies by day.

The councilor's broadside turn had carried them toward the marching army. Kara dipped an arm to bank west. Only a few more arrows came her way in the glide. Perhaps the creatures' soulless eyes were drawn to the giant silks of the ships.

She picked a spot for her landing on the army's southern flank and started her count.

One, two, three . . .

In two quick motions, Kara pulled her blue ring and drew her whirlknives. When the silk snapped taut behind her, she sent her blades flying.

The knives spun into a pair of goblins. Kara touched down in a run, pulled her copper ring to shed her silk, and caught the knives in their return. In the next beat, both blades were cutting deep into a golmog's neck. Another golmog came at her from her flank. She couldn't pull her knives from the first in time to stop its charge. She braced for a jarring blow, armor glowing, but the blow never came.

A harpoon from above went straight through the golmog's breastplate and knocked it from its feet. The creature fell and burst its ugly gut on the rocky slope.

So much for its armor.

Harpoons kept the trolls and golmogs busy while the ships rolled in, sending off their fighters. But that help wouldn't last. Looking up, Kara saw one ship crash into another, cracking their trusses. The mid winds, as Boreas had warned, played havoc with their silks. Both damaged ships rose fast into the higher breeze that carried them away.

More windfighters had landed beside her. Kara's squadron wore the emblem of the bear. She tried to count their number while the battle raged. Twelve that she could see—out of fifteen. Had more than one fallen? Or had some not made it out of the ships?

Samar's fighters were there as well, wearing their paradragon badge. They were still landing, blue-and-gray silk wedges wide behind them. Some of the silks flew into the creatures when released, covering their heads and causing howls of rage. The fighters with crossbows loosed volleys into them.

More paradragons than Kara had yet seen—with scales and fur in blue, gray, green, and gold—flew in from the north, catching the dark creatures unaware. Their icy blasts slowed the orcs and goblins, giving the fighters a chance to gain a foothold.

Keledan armor glowed on every side of Kara. Shields flashed, bashing opponents back or burning arrows to dust.

A rootlike tentacle whipped over her head. A mocktree. She heard its evil song and knew what came next. Spores on the air. "Cover!"

The fighters were ready for the call. Every one of them pulled a cloth over nose and mouth. This would hinder their breathing for certain, but they were better off suffering that challenge than taking in the poison of the enemy.

Kara moved toward its hollow, thumping song.

A queeen I seee. This queeen can ruuule. Ruuule with her love. Powerrr. Controlll. An end to warrr.

She sliced away one of its curling tentacles. "Still your rotted tongue, corruption." Kara sent a whirlknife straight into one of the creature's three eyes and followed it with a declaration of the High One's power, not her own.

"Mod ke'Premor pressend vesomav romum koth premoroth po prematoth, premavat po presegat, po koth regol gevenend. Se okef fi ke'epokol narav, dar fi ke'epokol sossav."

He is far above every ruler, every power and dominion, every title given.

Not only in this age but the next.

The mocktree's roots began to wither, and it shrank in stature. Two of Kara's fighters moved in with their dual swords and severed its branches, knocking its axe and spikes away. Kara ran up the middle, drawing her own sword, and stabbed it in the throat. The spores ceased flying.

Orc creatures moved against them before the tree had fully fallen. Copper orcs with red and green ore growing from their necks and backs howled from gargoyle jaws. They swung curved scimitars of black pyranium, and the strength of their onslaught pushed the windfighters back against a steep slope.

How long could they keep this up?

"Well met, Queensblood!" Ioanu's bearish growl broke through the battle's din. Her claws sparked against a copper orc's scimitar.

Kara smashed a goblin skull with her sword hilt and brushed the creature aside to stab Ioanu's orc in its flank. "Where did you come from?"

The bear slashed another orc's throat in a double sweep of paws armored in glowing deep blue. "Need you ask?"

Horns blew from above—not Airguard horns, but the horns carried on the hips of the sentinel squadron commanders. The creatures faltered and turned, seeing this new threat descending the slope.

Boreas had timed his winds well so that the ships came in only moments before the riders at the head of the watchmen and lightraider companies.

The copper orcs backed up, uncertain which way to turn, and the windfighters pressed a new attack.

Dag and Quinton rode down the slope at the head of the ground force, riding their Gladion stallions. Their axes hewed orc and mocktree alike. Goblins fell under galloping hooves.

Master Jairun rode at their flank, wielding a staff like none Kara had ever seen him carry. The knot at its head was a blue talanium mace, serrated on every side. Instead of a foot, its base was a giant spearhead as long as Kara's sword. He shouted to the heavens, and a few of the words met Kara's ear.

Premat po stregat. Yadovu. Se'arosh gegov pav qumov.

Power and might. Your hand. None can stand against you.

At a sweep of the headmaster's mace, a dozen orcs disintegrated into scattered piles of ore, destroyed by the Rescuer's hand.

The rest of the horsemen followed with Sireth at their center, and with the slope still in the Keledan's favor, golmogs, orcs, and goblins fell against the wave. A stone troll cast a hard strike at the watchmaster's horse, but Sireth would have none of it. He smashed the creature's fist with his hammer and removed its head with the backswing of the same blow.

Pedrig the wolf leapt over the troll's tottering remains and dove through a mass of goblins with his forest-green Havarra armor ablaze. The creatures unraveled before him, and he pounded to a stop against another stone troll. Rocks flew from the impact.

In moments, the riders had driven a wedge deep into the enemy formation, striking creatures down on every side. The orc flanks, driven by more tree trolls, tried to close behind them only to fall when arrows struck them from behind.

Archers loosed their missiles from the ridgetop. Marchers followed the riders down. Kara's windfighters closed from the southern flank while Samar's squadron moved to the eastern. Soon the enemy was caught in an ever-tightening ring. The last shrieks and cries of the dark creatures faded into the fjord.

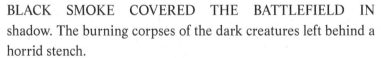

BLACK SMOKE COVERED THE BATTLEFIELD IN shadow. The burning corpses of the dark creatures left behind a horrid stench.

Kara and Samar met Master Jairun and Sireth at the top of the giant lifts the creatures had built, looking southeast along the fjord. Three of Sireth's watchmen hauled the remains of a stone troll past them to cast it over the cliff.

"Take care," Sireth said, waving his hammer to gain their attention. "Don't damage the dock below. And keep the corpse fires back, lest an ember set the whole thing ablaze."

As he spoke, a pair of lightraider cadets sent a cart filled with flaming tent canvas over the cliff behind him. The bundles bounced on the dock, spreading fire all about. The timbers quickly caught.

The watchmaster turned on the cadets. "What have you done?"

"Blame me, Sireth, not them," Master Jairun said, stepping between them. "They acted on my orders, passed through their swordmaster. Had you wanted to preserve the dock and lifts, you might have said so a bit sooner."

The seething watchmaster and his hammer stood toe to toe with the much taller headmaster and his bladed war staff.

Samar nudged Kara and whispered, "This will be good."

She shot him a frown to say *Don't be crass*. Yet she couldn't take her eyes off the argument.

"That was not your decision," Sireth said through gritted teeth. "This fjord is part of my outpost."

"The outpost belongs to the Keledan," Master Jairun countered. "And those docks and lifts were wrought by the hands of the enemy for our destruction. Do you really want to leave them and learn Heleyor's plan as it plays out in our blood?"

Sireth gestured with his hammer, arms wide. "The battle is over. Look around you."

"The battle. Not the war. And to preserve the enemy's foothold thinking we may use it for our own purpose is a dangerous path." Master Jairun sat on a boulder, resting his staff against it. He patted the rock, bidding Sireth sit next to him.

The watchmaster hesitated, then rolled his eyes and obeyed.

"Have you forgotten the Aladoth army?" Master Jairun asked.

"Not in the least. But have I seen such an army or any sign of one? Perhaps the dragons had some other purpose for the camps your cadets saw."

Kara bristled. Her brehna had been tortured in that camp. And her older brehna had died trying to prevent his capture. Lee's brehna was a victim as well. The lightraiders' report of its purpose was sound. She took a step and opened her mouth to speak, but Samar caught her arm and shook his head, no longer jesting. "I think your headmaster has this well in hand."

More lightraiders dropped burning timbers onto the lifts. Master Jairun gave them a grateful nod. "Sireth, we've won a great victory. But a harder battle may yet come. We cannot fight the Aladoth the way we fight dark creatures. To destroy those we're meant to save would be doing the enemy's work for him."

"So," Sireth said, gesturing out toward the empty fjord, "where is this army?"

"I don't know, but by Arlo's report—the man sent by Mister Lee and Captain Boreas—it numbers a thousand or more." He glanced toward the depths of the overhang, whose shadows hid a giant tunnel mouth discovered after the fighting. "They may come from under the barrier, but I'd say this dock tells us they're coming by sea."

By sea.

Kara raised a hand, hurrying to the two masters before Samar could stop her. "The Storm Mists. They glowed red east of the Sea of Vows the night before we fought the birds."

Master Jairun rose from his rock, taking up his staff. "What birds?"

Had no one told him? "The buzzards Samar and I fought in the air. If not for that skirmish, we'd have never seen this camp. A paradragon showed us four birds flying up the fjord, heading out to sea."

The headmaster narrowed his eyes. "Did any of these four escape?"

PART FOUR

THE FAITHFULNESS OF LIONS

"Let anyone who has ears to hear listen to what the Spirit says to the churches. The one who conquers will never be harmed by the second death."

Revelation 2:11

WHY ME? WHY AM I HATED?

The gall.

The buzzard's wings beat in cadence with its song.

I am rejected. Despised.

There is no justice.

How long it had flown, it neither knew nor considered. The creature had but one purpose—one aim fixed in its being.

The Storm Mists, the hated barrier, had grown monstrous in its sight, ever larger in the night and then the morning. The gray, unsettled clouds rose from the waves to the highest reaches of the sky.

Shield of rejection.

Why do you hate me?

The gall.

Blue water became red, a boiling cauldron—a ring of fire under the waves, feeding the hated barrier with its mist. An answering fire burned in the buzzard's gut. It adjusted course and gave one last beat of its wings. The ring came beneath it, and the buzzard dove, shrieking its final song.

Why me?

The gall.

61

THE PARTY LEFT EMEN YAN UNDER THE COVER OF darkness. They left Koteg in Necal's care—a promise that Thera, at least, would return.

The captain led them out through a secret tunnel under the eastern river. "House Fulcor built this passage." She passed a lantern over a carving of a falcon flying above a troop of soldiers. "They began it years before the dragons gave them the city and used it to bring their men inside unseen. Fulcor has always been a family of plotters and deceivers."

A dark patch on her cloak caught Connor's eye—one shadow moving against the rest. An instant later, the patch was gone, perhaps a trick of her lantern, so he let it be. "Not all the Fulcors of the past were bad," he said, turning his gaze to Zel. "Isn't that right?"

The airship captain smiled, clearly remembering the same moment as he, when they'd discovered the underground Elder Folk sanctuary in the Fading Mountains. "Connor speaks of the *Lay of Luco and Kaia*," she said to Thera, "and their companion, the winter fox. They were among the Rescuer's first followers—the beginnings of our people. Luco was a Fulcor noble and Kaia a thrall of Advor. Both found freedom under the High One."

Lee, who walked with one hand on the tunnel wall to keep his balance, snapped his fingers. "The coins. Zel, you threw the coins to defeat the stone trolls in the Sorcerer's Cave. I remember now. Well done!"

The whole party paused and went quiet. None had spoken a word about trolls or the Sorcerer's Cave that whole day.

Zel gave him a half smile. "That's right, Lee. I did. After you charged them to save me."

Teegan moved to his side and placed an arm under his.

"What are you doing?" he asked.

She gave a gentle shake of her head. "Nothing. I'm glad your memory's coming back."

Outside the city, beyond sight of the guard towers, they split up. Connor had tasked Lee, Zel, and Aaron with crewing *The Kingfisher*, which they'd have to recover after a long march to the butte.

Now that they were out of the city, Teegan argued against Lee's part in that mission, but she relented when Lee himself would not be dissuaded.

"It's a scouting mission," Lee said. "I'll be fine. And I prefer to fly. Climbing the dam seems much harder just now."

The pilots and Lee carried special harpoons for *The Kingfisher*'s big crossbow, made by the blacksmith Thera and Connor had chosen.

Connor, Teegan, and Thera took a trail to the dam wall. Connor had picked out a route that climbed the paths and staircases to a landing. From below, the landing looked wide enough for the airship, and the red stone of the region would mask *The Kingfisher*'s silk.

To reach the landing by sunset was no easy feat. They kept a strong pace so that by the time they stepped off the last narrow stair in the cliffside and onto the flat stone of the landing, all were breathing hard.

It was then that Connor saw the dark patch moving on Thera's cloak again—this time exposed in sharp relief by the sinking sun. He called it to Teegan's attention, and together, they approached the captain.

"Thera," Connor said. "You can't go with us to the vault." The hurt in her eyes wounded him, but he held firm. "I do this out of love. For all you've seen and heard, you still haven't believed the one we serve. Without him, you won't survive."

Her brow compressed in anger. "How can you say that? I fought the troll to save you!"

The patch appeared at her shoulder—a spider of the form they'd seen in Necal's house but the size of Connor's hand.

"To save him?" Teegan asked, sweeping the thing from her shoulder with a flick of her net. "Or to ensure we removed the trolls from your path?" The spider tried to crawl away, but Teegan cast her net and pinned it down.

Connor gestured with his crook. "Do you see this spider? It clung to you after we killed its forebearer in Necal's house. Since then, it has grown, feeding off your deception."

"I have no deception. I—"

The spider wriggled and grew, threatening to overpower the net.

Connor ended Thera's protest with a pointed look at her gloved hand and arm. "You've met one of those trolls before. The creature spoke to you—struck you with a spine or a claw, did it not?"

"You bear the mark of its poison," Teegan added. "Expose that mark to the light." Her voice deepened with command. "Now, Thera."

Wincing, the captain ripped off the glove, exposing an arm black and blue with the troll's poison. The wound darkened the nearer it came to her hand so that her fingers had turned entirely black.

As if suddenly repulsed by the sight of the wriggling spider, Thera crushed it under her heel. The creature died with a sickening *crunch* and a burst of gray-green ooze.

"I met the troll as a young woman," she said, looking to the lightraiders. "I chipped away the mortar, certain of the secret that lay beyond that wall around the statue, and when I removed a pair of stones, the troll came to me. With its rattling song, it told me of the treasure and lured me to reach through the hole I'd made. When I did, it bit me—one small cut on my finger."

Connor took her arm to examine the wound. "You're strong. Many would have torn those stones away and become food for the troll. You put them back."

"I did, conflicted in my sense of duty to both houses. But the desire for the Leanders' gold has consumed me ever since. I'm sorry I didn't tell you of the creatures. I've heard stories of the judgment and hatred the Keledan carry, and I thought if you killed the trolls, you'd rid me of their curse without me ever having to show you my shame."

The judgment and hatred the Keledan carry.

Another lie. One of the best conceived by the dragons because its rumors cast mud upon the Helper's gifts of discernment and faithfulness. And the Keledan, predictable in their human failings, fueled its fire each time they killed an Aladoth or abandoned their lord and homeland and took the ships to bring distortions of the Scrolls to Tanelethar.

Thera sat on the ground beside the net and the dead spider. "I'm utterly fallen—a betrayer like my ancestors. My shame almost caused your death. Will you ever forgive me?"

"You have our forgiveness," Connor said, bolstered by a nod from Teegan. "But much more, you need the forgiveness of the High One. His son, our Rescuer, made that forgiveness possible with his sacrifice. You've heard us tell the story to Necal and his wife."

Thera lifted her eyes. "I want that forgiveness. I want it so."

Teegan took Thera's blackened hand and lifted her up, rubbing a balm from her manykit into Thera's wound. "Let go of your desire for the troll's gold and all its deceptive hopes. If you believe and love the Rescuer, you'll turn from that greed right now."

Thera, eyes closed, breathed a great exhale, and the mark on her hand and arm faded away.

62

"THERE MUST BE SOME SIGN OF THE PATH NEAR THESE falls." Lee adjusted his spectacles to keep the cracked lens from spoiling his sight. "And we must find it ere the moons reach their apex."

Zel kept *The Kingfisher* near the dam, so close that the waterfall's spray wet their silk. Aaron had relinquished command of the airship without much argument. Zel was the better and more experienced pilot, better suited to fight the strange winds in the shadow of the cliff face. Admitting this, however, did not stop him from nagging.

"Watch the falls, Captain," he said, giving a sliver of meat to Aethia, whom they'd found patiently waiting at *The Kingfisher*. "They're thrice the breadth of our full ship. Once we're in them, there'll be no getting out. We'll plunge straight to the valley floor."

"Thank you, Lieutenant." Zel simultaneously pulled a vent rope for one envelope and sent a blast of flame into another. "I'm well aware."

Lee agreed with Connor's plan, but the timing had not helped matters. Connor had bid them launch before the rising of the moons so their passing near the city would go unnoticed. That meant a near run to the ship, negating his hope of a lighter path when he chose not to climb to the landing. With his current struggles to stay on his feet, that run had been a real trial—one he'd failed, slowing the mission down.

The two brighter moons, Phanos and Tsapha, already stood several degrees above the eastern horizon. Once they reached their apex, they'd overcome the shadow under the dam and expose *The Kingfisher*. The sparing light the time in between offered the pilots and Lee was their only hope.

"I see a gap. Hold her steady!" Lee leaned over the side and immediately regretted it. His world tilted, as if the whole airship had turned upside down.

Aaron pulled him back by the neck strap of his manykit. "Perhaps you should guide our eyes instead."

Once Lee talked their gazes to the spot, Zel had no trouble bringing the ship closer.

Empty spaces opened in the red cliff face like natural windows to a grotto. Following their line eastward from the falls, Zel found more, slowly descending. "I'd say we're looking at a staircase," she said, "one heading straight for the falls. This is the path we need."

Connor's plan hinged upon what he'd called a reverse shortcut. They might spend weeks in a fruitless search of the trails and staircases all over the dam. Yet, by using the airship, Lee and the pilots had found a path high up, near the marker on the old map. They could follow it down and show the others the way.

Lee loaded one of the blacksmith's special harpoons into the crossbow and spoke a quiet prayer before shooting it into the red rocks. It held fast, and Zel lashed the rope that trailed from its end to a cleat on the bow rail. A second harpoon and line held the stern.

"Are you sure about this?" Aaron asked before Lee crawled over the rail.

He nodded. "I can do it. As long as I hold tight and don't look down."

The second part proved harder than he thought with the combined movement of the ship and the rope. In the end, Lee closed his eyes and pulled himself hand over hand until his head bumped against the dam.

From there, he hauled himself through the opening.

Aaron followed and quickly cut both lines. "We'll see you below."

Zel saluted them, and *The Kingfisher* drifted away.

Lee hit the lieutenant with a frown. "Perhaps you might have waited to see if this is really the path we seek before sending our only other means of escape off into the night."

"Oh." Aaron let out a quiet laugh and shrugged. "Too late now."

A light seemed a risk, especially if a city guard spied it from below, but Lee saw no other option. The stairwell had been hewn too deep into the cliff face, too deep into the darkness. He lit a candle for his lantern, and the two set off in a slow climb. The steps angled northward into the cliff, and the waterfall grew louder with every step, until at last, they came to a place where the torrent fell as a thick wall between the rocks.

A coldness struck Lee. He raised his light high and saw ice marred by red dirt and gravel above. Had they climbed up under Val Glasa itself?

A *crack* split his ears, backed by a tremendous roar.

Aaron barreled into him from the side. "Look out!"

CONNOR
THE LANDING, PARTWAY UP THE DAM

CONNOR WATCHED THE NORTHERN TRAILHEADS AT the landing. There were four, and he expected Lee and Aaron to come plodding down one of them at any moment, assuming they'd found the path to the vault.

Zel was confident they had, but she'd left without finding out, and that frustrated him. He had half a mind to send her back in the ship, but the moons were too high.

When Zel had brought the ship, she'd found Thera crying and worried for her until Connor and Teegan explained she'd joined the

Keledan. From then on, the pilot had not left her side, telling her of all the wonderful places she'd see.

"What of Koteg?" Thera was asking just then. "How will he join me if I can't explain the Rescuer's love to him?"

"He knows the Rescuer's love," Zel answered, "the love of his Creator. It speaks from every fiber of his being and inspires the unbreakable love he shows you every day. Koteg will walk through the hollow tree beside you and revel in your joy."

Connor smiled at Zel's answer, seeing in her the same gift of speech her tehpa held.

Teegan also sat with Thera, allowing her to stroke Aethia's head, and told her of the Keledan armor. She explained the peace and courage brought by the Rescuer's promise. Connor might have told her to leave such weighty lessons for the guardians to teach, but now that Thera was Keledan, she insisted on joining them in this fight, and he couldn't dissuade her.

Another tick went by, and still Lee and Aaron made no appearance. What had happened to his friends?

Connor went to the northernmost path, the one he thought most likely to connect with the waterfall passage. "I'm going up. We need to look for them."

All agreed, and in short order, they were all beside him with weapons girded to begin the climb.

"Where are you all going?"

The question came from *The Kingfisher*, which they'd deflated and pressed back against the dam to hide its silks—a voice with no master, until Aaron squeezed out from behind the wicker hull.

The pilot rested a hip against the ship's rail and crossed his arms. "Nice work, blocking our exit. I take it you didn't even see the trail back there." He laughed. "Understandable, it's hidden behind a stone hatch."

Connor held his elation at seeing Aaron in check. One friend was still missing. "Where's Lee?"

"Here," Lee said, stepping out from behind the airship,

"thanks to Aaron and the Rescuer. It turns out lanterns and ice don't mix well. Aaron saved me from a cave-in up there."

"Ice," Teegan said. "You mean . . ."

Lee nodded. "We found stairs up to the falls and the underside of Val Glasa itself. I fear I almost brought the whole frozen sea down on my own head."

"He did more than that." Aaron clapped him on the back, almost knocking him over, earning frowns from both Lee and Teegan. He ignored their looks. "Wait till you see it. The cave-in uncovered a wondrous door."

63

THE PATH UP TO THE FALLS BRANCHED IN SEVERAL
places, and Lee explained he and Aaron had retraced their steps
more than once on the way down. He'd dripped wax from his
lantern's candle to mark the way, so the journey upward took far
less time.

Zel climbed the steps beside Connor. "Why doesn't Heleyor
keep his treasures near him, within the fortress of Ras Pyras?"

"The vault at Emen Yan holds neither gold nor jewels,"
Connor told her. "That's what Master Jairun says. In this world
exist relics of mystery perched on a line between our realm and the
realm of spirit—like the dragons and the Aropha, and perhaps the
lashoroth. Heleyor fears such objects."

Zel looked up toward their destination. "And he collects them
and keeps them here to maintain control?"

"Just so." They reached a small landing, and Connor tapped
Aaron on the shoulder to signal a rest. He didn't want his party
to enter battle exhausted. "Master Jairun believes Heleyor uses
his dark creatures to find and hoard these things, thus shielding
himself while keeping control of any he may use as weapons."

"Weapons?" Teegan, who'd left her bird to guard the ship
again, handed Lee a waterskin and pressed him to drink. "Are

giants and dragon fire not enough for his war against us?"

"The weapons in the vault are not meant for us," Connor said. "Heleyor presumes his own dragon lords will one day turn on him the way he turned on the Maker."

The last flight of steps took no time at all, and when they reached the wall of water and the fallen chunks of ice, they all took care to keep their lanterns low.

"Here," Lee said, guiding them along a path revealed by the collapse—one that took them behind the falls. He brought them to a door of silver metal, almost a mirror, still partially covered in ancient ice at the top and bottom. No threshold was visible, nor hinges or even a split where it might part. "Could this be the vault we seek?"

Thera stepped up between Connor and Lee, carrying one of the lanterns. Despite a warning cringe and a groan from Lee, she held the light close to the door's odd face. "And what is this?"

Circles of green metal seemed to be part of the door, set at the center. Four concentric rings. On each were engraved four matching symbols. One of these, Connor knew for sure—the Aropha symbol for light. "A lock?" he said, meeting Thera's gaze, then tilted his head toward Lee and grinned. "It's for puzzles like this that we bring him along."

Lee pursed his lips. "You bring me for more than that, I hope. I like to think I'm of some use in combat." Despite his comment, his eyes never left the symbols. "The earth, the air, the sea, the light. If I'm right, this was once an Aropha sanctuary. In the Elder Tongue, these words would be *kefar, keveer, kevala, kelas*."

The rings turned, as if responding to his voice, aligning each symbol he mentioned in order from top to bottom. When the motion ceased, there was silence, long enough for Lee and Connor to share a glance—then the symbols glowed bright with orange fire.

The ice above them groaned. The passage quaked, and cold dust fell from above. Connor heard a distant *crunch*. The fire in the symbols dimmed to nothing.

Aaron hissed at Lee, "Are you trying to bring the roof down again?"

"I'm sorry. How could I know the door would respond to my voice?"

"Or that the wrong combination might kill us?" Connor touched his friend's arm. "Is there a way to be sure of the order?"

The scribe brushed the dust from his shoulders and stepped forward again. "Of course . . . I think. These are the first elements brought into being by the Maker at the dawn of creation. The key must be the correct order, and every Keledan knows it."

"Light, air, earth, sea," Teegan said.

"Correct." Lee gave her a nod, and then his lips parted, as if to speak the same words in the Elder Tongue.

Aaron raised a hand. "Wait!"

The ice groaned again.

Aaron crouched and lowered his voice to a whisper. "Wait. Isn't this Heleyor's Vault? What if he twisted the order? Isn't that what he does? Corrupt, twist, and destroy?"

All eyes in the party looked to Connor, as if he should know. He swallowed. But something about the question sounded familiar. What had the guardians taught them about false teachings in Tanelethar?

There will be times in your quests when it seems you must regurgitate the lies of Heleyor to survive—when you fear you must affirm a lie or be destroyed. Do not fall into this trap. Speak the truth.

Connor set his jaw and gave Lee a nod. "Speak the truth. All else is a waste of breath."

The scribe raised his voice, showing no fear of the mass of ice hanging over them. "Kelas, keveer, kefar, kevala."

The light, the air, the earth, the seas.

The rings turned, lining up the symbols, followed by a pause as before. Connor, with confidence, stepped to the center. "Form up behind. Draw your weapons. Temper your armor."

As the others followed his command, armor blazing to life, the four symbols glowed green, one after the other, each ringing with a quiet tone. A divide appeared down the center of the mirrored silver. The last of the ice fell away, and the door split open.

Hot mist billowed out. A long silver spike, thin as a needle at its tip, shot out and pierced Connor's shield, almost to his eye. With a shout, he wrenched his shield sideways and broke the strange weapon.

The shards dropped at his feet, becoming beads of liquid metal, and rolled back into the mist. Something within the vault let out a terrifying shriek.

64

CONNOR ADVANCED INTO THE VAULT, PARTING THE warm mist with his ghostly shield. "Watch your step," he called to the others. "The floor is lava."

Metal paths, cool under his boots, passed between gently curving streams of molten rock. The walls and ceiling, visible in the spaces between the clouds of vapor, gleamed with the same metal.

"Where is the creature we heard?" Teegan asked.

Connor squinted into the vault. "No sign of it."

A pair of molten streams curving through channels in the floor divided the party so that Connor struggled to see them all through the mist. Sweat beaded on their brows. Lee wiped steam from his spectacles. "Sure is hot in here."

Zel cast him a sideways glance. "Should we expect anything less from Heleyor's Vault?"

Teegan had stretched ahead of Connor on the right flank, too far away for him to clearly see her. He leapt over a bend in a stream of lava, feeling the threat of its scorching heat, trying to catch up. "Teegan, stay close."

She turned, concern in her gaze. "Connor, look."

She'd found a silver statue made of the same gleaming metal as the floor.

"Oh good," Connor said, coming up beside her. "Another likeness of my cursed kin."

"Not just a likeness."

The hush of her tone worried him. Connor eyed the Leander lord with more care. The statue wore his clothes—carried the same shepherd's crook. The nearer he came, the more his own features aligned to become a pure reflection in the silver metal. "What is this?"

"There's another over here," Thera said. "A woman."

The vapor had grown too thick for Connor to see her. "Is she a queensblood?" he asked, remembering his family's history with the Arkelian queens of Kara's bloodline.

"No." Thera's voice had grown quiet like Teegan's. "She looks like me."

The vapors parted, and Connor saw the silver statue mirrored Thera in every way, down to the fall and folds of her cloak. A lesson came to him from his earliest lightraider training.

The mirror masters.

"Thera!"

The statue slashed at her with its sword, connecting with her shield in a burst of sparks.

Connor's reflection in his statue contorted into a gargoyle sneer, sprouting fangs and curling horns. He jumped back, teetering on the edge of a lava stream, and stabbed with his crook.

The creature parried his blow with its copy, but the silver crook coiled around his. Liquid metal coated the shaft and rolled up toward his hand.

A sweep of Teegan's trident severed the mirror crook. It fell into beads and rolled back to its host.

"Watch out!" Connor called. "Quicksilvers!"

How many times had the guardians warned them?

Quicksilvers are the most dangerous of ore creatures—able to shift form at will and near impossible to destroy.

Great.

"There's another!" Lee cried, loosing an arrow from his string. His target parted in the middle as if cleaved in two by an axe, and the arrow passed right through.

Three gargoyle ore creatures of shining silver closed on the party's tightening formation.

"Shields!" Connor shouted. "Watch the fire at your feet."

The quicksilvers spread their grotesque jaws and shot long spiked tongues at their foes. The Keledan shields held, forming a single arced wall glowing in many colors, but the impact knocked Aaron back. His cloak dipped into a stream of lava and took flame.

"Aaron!" Thera lowered her shield to pat out the fire and exposed their flank. A quicksilver sprang for the gap.

Aaron and Lee pressed their shields together, and the creature smashed against them, long claws gripping the tops, sizzling and sparking. A forked tail came up underneath and drove straight into Aaron's leg in the same place the valpaz had wounded him. He let out a cry and stumbled.

With the fire put out, Thera leapt and brought her sword down hard into the creature's head. The orc collapsed to liquid, only to arc like a fountain over the stream of lava and once again rise in its gargoyle form.

On their side, Connor, Teegan, and Zel faced the other two. He wielded Revornosh only. The constant onslaught from the orcs prevented him from swinging his crook with his shield hand. Zel snapped her spiked whip around one's neck, and Teegan stabbed her trident into the other's eyes. The results were the same. Each hit scored seemed more a danger than a victory as the creatures' strange metal flesh coated their weapons.

Near impossible to destroy.

What had Master Jairun added to that warning? A verse from the Scrolls—a question from the first Keledan and the answer from the Rescuer himself.

Vyk, edai, pav liberend?
Who then, can be saved?

Bi rath, ker hal semethal, dar ba Rumosh, koth methal.
With him, all things are possible.

Aaron took a knee. Blood pooled beneath his foot and spilled into a stream of lava. Black smoke billowed up.

As if exhilarated by the smell, the orc on that side roared and sprang to land on Lee's and Thera's shields. It clawed at them, slashing deep into Thera's cheek. Its tongue shot out and pierced Lee's shoulder.

The creature on their left flank pressed Zel and Teegan back until they could retreat no more, thanks to the lava licking at their heels. Stinging sweat poured into Connor's eyes, blurring the forms of all his companions. Was he not their navigator? What had he led them into?

Lee's strained cry reached his ears. "Hold them! We must hold them!"

With him, all things are possible.

In what remained of his vision, Connor saw Master Jairun standing by the pools in the lower ward, teaching his lesson.

There are times in a lightraider's journey when the light fades and all turns to darkness and gloom—when the onslaught of evil and loss is so great, we feel we must drown in its black flood. At those times, remember the first battle prayer taught in every village of our land.

Silver talons came at him. A warped gargoyle face bared its fangs. Connor shouted at the breaking point of his lungs. "The first battle prayer! From the Scroll of Songs! Call out to him now!"

Connor had spoken the same prayer defending Mount Challenge Lake. Would the others remember?

Every voice but Thera's rang against the metal walls and floor, even the pilots'.

"*Yi rusa kazelatesh elevana. Men taya veni zoweresh? Men ke'Premor, bi keshema po kezavol ke'Krafor.*"

I lift my eyes to the mountains.
Whence comes my help?

From the King, the Maker of the heavens and the world.

"Rescuer," Connor prayed. "Help us."

A still, small voice answered, *I am with you. Always and forever.*

A bright flash filled the room.

The orcs flew back into the mist, tossed like sacks by an unseen hand.

Connor's eyes cleared. Cool breath dried the sweat from his brow. He surveyed his party. Aaron stood, testing his leg, and laughed. Thera touched her cheek, and Connor watched the bleeding slash close on its own. Lee rolled his shoulder and grinned.

A cold struck Connor's fingers, and he looked to his weapons. Frost spiraled down the steel of his crook and up Revornosh's blade.

The rest of the party's weapons bore the same frost.

Thera turned her frozen sword in her hand. "What's happening?"

"Help has come," Lee said. "From the mountains."

The party advanced, shields ready, until they came to a broad space where only one wide stream of lava crossed the floor, spanned by a metal bridge. Here the mist was thick.

"Watch how the vapors move," Teegan said. "The mist will betray these monsters before our eyes perceive them."

The mist in front of Connor swirled. He thrust into the heart of the vortex with his crook's frozen spike, and a creature screamed. Drawing the shaft back, he found a writhing quicksilver orc impaled upon it. The creature seemed unable to melt away as before. The frost spread through its body until every movement ceased. With a heave, Connor drove it down onto the floor, and the orc smashed into a hundred pieces.

The other creatures appeared at the flanks, more wary. Aaron lunged to stab one in the chest. The creature howled until spreading frost cut off its voice. The last turned to flee, but Lee shot it in the neck. The orc clawed at the arrow, but the frost moved too quickly. The creature tripped and fell into its frozen companion, and both toppled over and shattered.

Connor looked up into the mists gathered in the vault's high ceiling. *"Onoriov, Rumosh."*

"Connor." Teegan gestured at the remains of the first fallen orc with her trident. The frost had melted. The shards of the orc wriggled in place. "It's not over."

The smallest pieces turned liquid once again and gathered into a pool.

Zel uncoiled her whip and shook her head. "This isn't over. The heat is too much. This lava makes everything a trial."

65

A FROZEN WALL BARRED THE PASSAGE UNDER THE mountain. Kara smashed her sword's pommel into it, causing hardly a dent. "This ice makes everything a trial."

Master Jairun waved her back to the place where they'd halted the horses. They'd encountered more and more ice the deeper their party rode into the mountain, heading west and north, to the best Kara could tell. Patches of it clung to the roof, dropping sharp chunks on their heads or making the floor slick for the horses. But they'd seen nothing like this. It filled the tunnel from floor to ceiling, as tall as the barbican gate at Ras Telesar.

In council together after the battle at the fjord, Master Jairun, Sireth, and Boreas had decided to split their forces. They'd sent most back to their posts. All three men feared the enemy might have drawn the bulk of the Keledan fighters to one place so they might more freely attack other places on the mountain. Sireth took charge of the effort, working from his lodge at Orvyn's Vow.

Boreas, the council decided, would repair and resupply his airships, and he'd sent a pair of scout ships east into the Sea of Vows to look into some suspicion of Master Jairun's. Samar was leading that mission.

The headmaster himself had chosen a small force of mounted

lightraiders to scout the tunnel they'd found under the overhang, including Kara. He'd allowed Pedrig and Ioanu to come with them, noting that he likely couldn't stop them if he tried. Now, he stood staring at the wall of ice, arms crossed about his war staff, and grunted. "There's something in this passage they don't want us to see. The iceblades or frost goblins that did this might have joined the fighting. Instead, they fled and walled themselves in."

Quinton walked up beside him. "Ya mind if I give her a go?"

The swordmaster spat on his hands and drew one of his axes, then paused and glanced over his shoulder. "All o' ya might wanna ease back a bit more. If I don' get this jus' right, the ice'll come down in some right monstrous chunks."

Dag chuckled, but when Quinton raised his eyebrows, he nodded and spread his arms, ushering the whole party—horses and all—several paces back along the passage.

With that done, Quinton returned his attention to the ice wall. He laid a hand on it, sniffed it, and then placed an ear against it.

Ioanu grew impatient. "What are you doing, Swordmaster?"

"Shh! I'm listenin' fer the crackle o' weakness. Pick the right spot, an' the whole mess'll shatter into snow."

Pedrig lay down and rested his head upon his paws, saying something in his wolfish grumble that sounded like, "Here we go."

Quinton laid his ear to another spot, then grunted and nodded. "I've got it. Watch this."

With his eyes locked on the place he'd chosen, the swordmaster stepped four paces back, and then ran at the wall and hit it with a mighty swing.

Something clinked onto the tunnel floor—not a piece of ice, but a shard of steel from the axe. Quinton groaned. "I s'ppose that's it, then. We've no chance o' breakin' through."

While this drama had played out, Master Jairun had taken a seat at the side of the passage, head bowed, lips moving. After the swordmaster's failed attempt to break the ice, he stood and looked down the tunnel in the direction from which they'd come. His eyes brightened. "Oh, look. Miss Orso's new friends have come to join us."

Kara saw nothing—at least, not for several more beats. Then frost-blue wings appeared, and their visitor let out a chirping bark.

"Dash!"

More barks answered, and the whole squadron of paradragons flew in behind him. They landed on the horses, whose ears shifted back, less than happy about these uninvited riders, but they made no move to buck the paradragons off.

Master Jairun caught Kara's attention and gave a slight tilt of his head toward the ice.

She blinked, then caught his meaning and waved at Dash. "Come here. We need your help." What help a paradragon might give, other than adding to the ice, she didn't know. But Master Jairun seemed confident enough.

She walked to the wall with Dash, who darted about its surface, poking at it with his snout and talons. Occasionally, he let out a bark at the ice or gave it a light puff of frost. After a time, he returned to his family, and the squadron took to the air. They flew to the wall and began puffing frost in earnest at one spot near the center.

The paradragons spiraled around one another in an ever-growing white cloud, until all the Keledan raised their arms and garments against the cold.

When the onslaught ceased, Kara lowered her cloak and drew a breath. The paradragons had made a spiraled horn of ice extending out from the wall.

"That's quite pretty," Quinton said. "I'm glad they came. Now what?"

Dash flew down to hover in front of Kara. He clawed for a moment at her whirlknives, then flew up to the ice horn and blew a puff at the tip. With this done, he flew back to join his family, now seated once again on the horses.

Kara squinted at the paradragon.

Dash extended his head, canting it to one side.

She touched one of her knives. "This?"

Dash bobbed his head.

"All right. I'll try." She cast a questioning glance at Ioanu, whose tight bear lips seemed to say, *I have no notion what it wants, and I'm growing bored.* Kara appreciated that the bear didn't say it out loud.

She needed more room than Quinton's four paces for what she was about to try. And she'd need perfect aim. Kara walked well behind the horses, spoke a quick prayer, and with a running start, she let her whirlknife fly.

The knife spun in a curving path and stuck in the very tip of the spiraled horn.

Nothing happened. Not at first.

A light *crick* sounded from the ice horn. Then cracks and fissures shot along its length to the wall. They spread and branched like lightning until the horn and wall had gone white. In one reverberating *pop*, the whole thing burst over the party in a cloud of white dust.

The paradragons reveled in it, turning flips over the horses.

Quinton spat the ice dust out of his beard and brushed off his manykit. "Snow. Told ya."

"Arms!" Master Jairun called. "Defend yourselves!"

The white cloud settled. From behind charged a host of frost goblins.

Kara ran ahead of the party to recover her fallen whirlknife.

"No, Kara!" Master Jairun caught her shoulder as her hand closed around the hilt between the blades. He yanked her back. "Get out of this tunnel. Flee!"

Why would he want her to flee?

Swords made of murky ice came at her. Kara fended them off with shield and blade. Goblins drove themselves between her and the headmaster. Master Jairun knocked one senseless with the mace on his staff and pointed toward the horses. "Flee, I said!

Run, Kara! This is the breach. Don't you understand?"

He almost never used her given name. And Kara had never seen fear or doubt on his wizened face. Now, she saw both. Yet, how could she obey when her friends faced such danger?

Baldomar, Tiran, Quinton, Dag. They all fought the flood, as lightraiders should. Kara couldn't turn and run.

She threw herself into the fight. Amid the cloud of thought and awareness brought on by battle, she sensed Ioanu not far away, desperately clawing at the flood of goblins. The bear seemed unable to reach her usual place at Kara's side.

Two north trolls, called iceblades in Tanelethar, appeared above the smaller creatures. Dag and Quinton cut a line to one and set upon it with their axes. The other almost vanished in a mist of frost made by the paradragons. When the frost cleared, the creature stood unmoving, stuck in place by a mound of ice at its feet.

The iceblade drew the mound into its body and used it to transform its own arm into a huge, faceted lance. This, it leveled and stepped as if to drive it into Quinton, but Dash flew in and nipped the end. The lance and the troll shattered into snow in the same manner as the ice wall.

Kara held her sword high. "Well done, Da—"

What she saw beyond the shattered troll ended her cheer. Pyranium orcs marched her way, and the goblins parted before them. The creatures' spiked armor, marked with red slashes, seemed an unnecessary addition to their near-impenetrable hides. By this, and by the resolve of their march, Kara guessed they'd been sent for some terrible and singular purpose.

She tried to press back toward the horses, but the wave of goblins swept her forward, no matter how many she killed. They burned themselves upon her shield to keep her moving.

"Queensblood!" Ioanu called to her, storming through goblins, but she soon became mired in fighting them off.

Pedrig, too, raced toward Kara. He planted his paws and let

out a resonating bark that sent a green sphere over the creatures, melting them to dripping piles of lichen. But when he tried to race through the path he'd blazed, more goblins filled in the gap.

Pyranium hands took Kara by the shoulders. She struck at her attackers with sword and knife, and both broke against the creatures' armor.

"Kara!" Several voices called for her.

An orc hand closed over her mouth. She fought to breathe.

With fading consciousness, Kara heard the headmaster's remorseful shout. "I should never have brought you here! This passage leads to Tanelethar!"

66

CONNOR
TANELETHAR
HELEYOR'S VAULT

"WHY DIDN'T HE..." CONNOR STARED AT REVORNOSH, still coated with frost. The Rescuer had healed his friends and cast off the orcs. He'd altered their weapons so they could fight the creatures. But the orcs were not yet destroyed.

Silver puddles gathered in the heat. Aaron stabbed one with a sword, and it froze, but soon it began to melt again. He looked to Connor. "What does it mean? Should we flee?"

That didn't sound right. Connor remembered passages from the Scrolls that spoke of fleeing evil, but always in the context of turning to do what was right.

Do.

The word shook in his chest. A sacred verse followed. *Logos hal paloroth po se okef thimor.*

Be doers of the word and not hearers only.

The Rescuer had saved them, but he still wanted them to fight.

The silver puddles flowed together, all as one. The creature grew, forming from the clawed feet upward into an armored orc with a scimitar as big as Connor himself.

Aaron stabbed its thigh so that the frost spread from his blade, but the creature bashed him away, and the frost receded.

"All together!" Teegan shouted, and the party converged.

Those with close weapons harried the creature at its knees while Zel and Lee shot bolts and arrows at its head. The Rescuer's frost took hold at the legs and neck, yet always, the creature found a way to fight them.

When an arm froze, another grew from its belly and swatted them away. When the head froze, a second head grew from its shoulder.

Thera severed a claw from the creature's oversize foot. When the claw began to thaw, becoming an inching worm, she let out a cry and kicked it into the lava. Molten rock and flame spouted up, threatening to burn her. The giant orc reared its second head and roared.

Connor saw no silver flowing out of the lava stream to rejoin its monstrous host. That piece had been destroyed.

Ice was not enough. They'd needed ice and fire.

"Chop it down!" he shouted. "Drive the pieces into the stream. The Rescuer gave us the weapons we need!"

Dodging the swings of the monster's scimitar, the party jabbed their weapons into the legs, freezing them solid. Before the creature could shift form, they hacked them away in frozen chunks. Every piece that fell, they kicked or swept into the fire, until the legs began to crumble under the creature's own bulk.

The arms flailed. The body came tumbling down. "Teegan!" Connor called, and together they used crook and trident to press the falling mass into the molten flow. A great fountain of lava shot to the ceiling, sending out fiery spray.

Orange droplets fell against the party's shields and turned to red rock that clinked and skittered on the metal floor. In the stream, three small flaming masses, no larger than apples, rose to the surface and blackened, spouting green flame.

"What are those?" Thera asked.

The green flames died, and the blackened objects turned to cinder. Connor watched them float out of sight into the vapors. "The quicksilvers' corrupted hearts, perhaps. Whatever they were,

I think their destruction means our enemies are no more."

The party took stock of their wounds and weapons. Their steel warmed, banishing the frost. Their bodies bore no permanent hurts from the battle. Aaron's leg was as whole as it had been when they left Keledev. Thera's cheek and Lee's shoulder were just as healthy, though the scribe still bore his earlier scars.

None, for a time, made any move toward the bridge, the most obvious path forward. Connor didn't begrudge them this reluctance. He felt it as well. Lef Amunrel, perhaps, lay close to his grasp, but after the quicksilvers, did he really want to face what lay on the other side of that stream?

Aaron finally gestured with his sword. "So what are we waiting for?"

If only Connor could have conceived of a good answer. He strode past the others. "Nothing. We're waiting for nothing. Let's go."

He regretted this action immediately, feeling the blast of heat as he crossed the bridge. Out of the mists, two more figures loomed, one on either side at the far end. Soon, he saw them, metal figures twice his height. "Not again."

But these figures didn't move, even when Teegan poked one with her trident. Coming closer, Connor saw their faces had been bashed away, as had part of a wing on the statue to his right and half of a bowl once carried by the statue on his left. "I know these figures. Their faces have been destroyed, but I can still see them."

Lee crossed the bridge and wiped the mist from his spectacles. "You know them because we see them every time we return to the academy. They are the Lisropha warrior and the Rapha servant. Before this was Heleyor's Vault, this was an Elder Folk sanctuary. For all their boasting, I doubt the Leanders ever set foot in it."

"Thus, the quicksilvers," Connor said. "The Leanders guarded the valley below yet never had their supposed honor of looking upon Heleyor's treasures—a perfect solution to keep human hands off any relics that might threaten his rule."

The Elder Folk statues may have posed no threat, but Connor kept his guard up. He formed up the party on the far side of the bridge and bid them advance as a wedge. Moving this way, they came upon the source of the mist. A cone of pure crystalline ice hung down from the ceiling and trickled water into a bubbling circle of lava that fed the streams. This was no natural occurrence but some work of Elder Folk design—likely part of their forever worship of the High One as the Fountain and the Flame.

"Val Glasa is above us," Lee said, looking up. "The Icy Sea. If lava flows through this dam, that explains why its many waterfalls keep pouring on the valley of Emen Yan while ice crusts at Val Glasa's other shores and around the Frost Isles."

Connor was less interested in ice and water than what he saw beyond the circle of lava.

In raised alcoves carved from silver-veined walls rested a strange array of objects from ages past. The first to catch his eye were three jewels that gleamed with their own white light, shining from a thousand perfect facets. Each looked no larger than a walnut in its shell, yet Connor sensed a great weight in them.

In an alcove close by was a red polygon, slowly rotating, with no pedestal to support it. In another, a long relic of black stone rested on a silk pillow. From the white alloy grip, Connor guessed it might be a spear.

"What do you suppose this is for?" Aaron asked, having walked with Zel to an alcove about waist level that held a wooden box. The lid was raised. Joining them for a look, Connor saw an unknown depth of many-colored dust inside. Aaron lifted a hand as if to touch it, but Zel slapped his wrist. "Don't. We know nothing of the dangers these objects pose."

"We came here for just one, did we not?" Teegan asked, looking hard at Connor.

He nodded, glancing around. Through the rolling vapors, he saw a black blade glittering with stars. "And there it is."

The party followed him to the dagger. Those who'd forged Lef Amunrel—working in secret in an ancient Aropha forge north of the barrier—had made it near as large as a short sword, with a ruby enamel hilt wrapped in supple yellow leather and a red starlot in the pommel. Each end of the cross guard formed the roaring head of a leopard.

"The Faith Walker," Lee said. "The constellation in the celestium blade matches the leopard we see in the sky at night—he who walks with confidence in his Maker." He looked to Connor. "There's no doubt, my friend. This is the dagger your grandfather lost all those years ago. This is the last human weapon capable of destroying Heleyor."

Again, Aaron stretched out a hand, and again, Zel slapped it, this time shaking her head. "No."

He frowned.

Connor barely noticed them. Unlike Aaron's, his own hand refused to move. It was Thera who prompted him. She gently took his elbow and forearm and pressed them outward. "This is what you came for. Finish your quest."

He obeyed. Wrapping his fingers around the smooth enamel and feeling the suppleness of the leather, Connor lifted the dagger from the silk.

But his quest was not finished—not even close.

Teegan met his gaze as he turned to face the party, and Connor saw understanding. She knew his second secret. Her eyes narrowed. "We're not going home, are we?"

"You are. I'm not."

Connor raised a hand to quell the rising grumbles around him, then reached into his tunic and withdrew the Rapha Key. "I didn't come all this way just to recover the Red Dagger. I came to end the war."

"That's not your choice!" Teegan stormed away from him, only to turn and stamp the metal floor with her trident. "We *must* leave that decision with the Order and the Assembly."

"You weren't there," he said, shaking his head. "You didn't see them when Kara and I brought our quest to the Sky Chamber. Endless debate. Fruitless arguing—even after Val Pera burned.

They'll be locked in their quarrel for ages, while orcs or worse overrun the land."

Teegan looked to Zel. "Tell him he's wrong. Tell him your tehpa will help."

"My father will help, but Connor's not wrong. The Assembly blunts every lofty goal with the stone of compromise. And you're talking about an attack against the Great Red Dragon himself. They'll never allow such an extreme."

"I've come so far, Teegs." Connor pointed north with Lef Amunrel. "Ras Pyras lies there, near the center of Val Glasa's northernmost isle, closer to us now than Sky Harbor is to Pleasanton." He held up the dagger and the Rapha Key together. "And we have all we need to enter the fortress and destroy its master."

"You mean *you* have all *you* need to right the wrongs of your family's past."

He lowered his head. "That's not what this is about."

"Isn't it?"

Lee, who'd been wiping his spectacles, waved his cloth at the two of them. "Let's take a moment and think, shall we?"

Teegan gave him a nod, as if he'd taken her side, but Lee hadn't. "Connor's right," he said. "I know Sky Harbor. If we return Lef Amunrel to Keledev, it'll wind up on a rock shelf under the Second Hall, never to be seen again."

"Thank you," Connor said.

Lee hit him with a hard look. "Don't thank me. I see your intent. You want us to carry on the fight here and in Keledev while you go to Ras Pyras alone."

"I must, Lee. Remember what happened to Talin the First?"

The scribe's spectacles had fogged over yet again. He removed them, frowning. "Talin charged a firedrake with the first celestium blade. The flames split around him, and he plunged the sword into the dragon." His voice slowed. "Both vanished in a white flash."

"Both," Connor said. "This quest has no return. I can't ask that of the rest of you."

Teegan had gone ashen despite the heat. "You're planning to die?"

"I'm at peace with it."

"Well, I'm not!"

Zel stepped close to Teegan and pulled Aaron in beside her. "We're not either. We're not letting you run off to your death alone. We fight as one, right, Aaron?"

"I . . ."

"Aaron!" She hit him with a glare.

"Whatever she says."

"That settles it," Zel said, returning her gaze to Connor. "Besides, even if Ras Pyras is as close as you say, it's still leagues away—days of travel over a half-frozen sea and the Frost Isles. Without a ship, you'll never make it."

Whatever scabbard had once been made for Lef Amunrel had long since been lost. Connor tucked the naked blade into his belt beside Revornosh so that their two starlot pommels—one ruby, one amethyst—rested close together at his hip. "I don't need the Airguard."

Again, Connor held up the Rapha Key, this time laying his palm on its carved face. "I have this, the lost key to the Bread Gate of Ras Pyras. If Master Belen is right, the bread gate is a channel in the fabric of creation—a portal. And to use it, I need only leap from the right starting point, which he believes is any Aropha sanctuary."

"But Connor," Teegan said, approaching within an outstretched arm. "Lee said this vault was once an—"

She vanished.

The whole vault, with its metal walls and molten rivers, blurred and disappeared, along with Connor's friends, replaced with a cloud of swirling snow and the bared fangs of a roaring lion.

67

TEEGAN STOOD DUMBFOUNDED, ARM STILL outstretched as if to take the key from Connor's hands. She dropped her arm and looked to the others. "He's gone."

"We can see that," Aaron said. "But gone where?"

She hated to say it, lest by giving voice to her thought, she'd make it so, but holding silent could not change what had happened. Teegan felt the truth like a ball of ice deep in her core. "Connor used the Rapha Key—perhaps not as he intended, but he used it. He's gone alone into Ras Pyras, into the fortress of the Great Red Dragon."

Teegan stood in the place her friend had been only moments before, trying to fully grasp the dreadfulness of the moment. Connor had gone to Ras Pyras to face Heleyor. And by his own admission, he'd gone there planning to die.

Thera, who'd been closest to him when he vanished, coughed, stirring her. "Can you get him back?"

"How do you propose I do that?"

The captain's concerned expression flattened. "I've only known you for a few days, but I've seen more wonders in that time than in all my years in Emen Yan. How am I to know what other powers you lightraiders can muster?"

"We have no powers," Lee said, sparing Thera the sharp answer on Teegan's lips. "We depend on the Rescuer."

"Then ask him to bring Connor back."

The group exchanged glances, and though Teegan hated to admit the new girl had come to a better conclusion, she nodded. "All right."

Teegan led them in prayer, first thanking the Rescuer for their deliverance from the quicksilvers, then asking him to bring Connor safely back to them.

Thera opened her eyes and blinked, looking around. "So . . . will he just reappear, then?"

Aaron left them and walked along the wall of relics. "Perhaps he wants us to use one of these. Heleyor views all of them as threats, right? Perhaps we should try them, one by one."

The rest of the party answered in unison. "No!"

To steer Aaron from temptation, Teegan ushered them out to the path in the dam wall, taking care as they traversed the passage behind the falls.

"Connor's part in this is up to him and the Rescuer," Lee said on their way down the staircase. "And we have our own parts to play. Zel and I must find the Aladoth army."

Teegan breathed deep, feeling the cooling spray coming in through the natural windows and trying to think. Was she to part with Lee, too, after finding him nearly killed the last time? "Aaron and I will go with you."

"You can't," Zel said, descending behind them. "You and Aaron must take *The Merlin* to Keledev and report all that's happened."

"Um." Lee glanced up at her, eyes narrowed behind his spectacles. "My memory has not been perfect of late, but I believe *The Merlin* is beyond our reach. Didn't you tell me you'd destroyed the portal to the Sorcerer's Cave?"

"We don't need the Sorcerer's Cave. We can take them there in *The Kingfisher*."

"That will take two days, at least," Lee countered.

"No, it won't." Zel gave him a satisfied grin. "I figured out how to control the stormrides."

When they arrived at *The Kingfisher*, Zel showed them a handful of blood-red pebbles. "These are from the Sorcerer's Cave. And I have more that I scooped up with purpose from the hill above the airshaft we found in the south."

"You collect rocks," Aaron said, taking turns with Teegan in giving Aethia her meat slivers. "That's wonderful."

"Keep scoffing, Lieutenant. This is how our order and theirs will travel in the days to come."

Teegan left the feeding to Aaron and came closer. "How so?"

"The Sorcerer's Cave was a confirmation of what I'd already begun to suspect. I saw all those hollow hill portals grouped together, then the shairosite veins visible on both sides of the two we used, as if rooted in the soil at each place, and I knew." Zel lifted a pebble from her hand. "By mixing the earth of one location into the shairosite we pour in our lamps, we'll tell the storm the story of where we want to go."

Lee crossed his arms. "Shouldn't we let the Rescuer direct the storm?"

"But stormriding is a tool he's given us," Zel said, "like sailing ships. I think he expects us to learn how to use one just as we've learned how to use the other, always endeavoring to direct them in the way that best serves his purpose. Remember when you commandeered my ship?"

He gave a tentative nod and turned, as if defending himself from an incoming punch.

Zel laughed. "Did I not tell you I had an inkling there was more to stormriding than dumping shairosite into a lamp? That I thought the Rescuer wanted us to take the reins of this steed?"

She had much more to say on the subject, continuing as she used a toolkit from the ship to pound a few pebbles into dust. She believed the tunnel they'd seen from the airshaft ran to a breach under the Celestial Peaks, caused by too much mining in search of more celestium. That breach, combined with earth stolen from the Keledev side, had enabled Vorax to open the first portal the lightraider cadets had closed.

When she had a small pile of red dust, Zel carefully collected it in a pouch. "We can use this to get us to *The Merlin*. From there, Lee and I will use powder I'll make from the obsidian Thera confiscated from her prisoner and fly to the place he was cast from the Aladoth army. By the Rescuer's grace, they'll be close by. The rest of you will fly *The Kingfisher* home."

Thera lifted a hand. "Not me. Until this war is over, I think Necal and I will serve the Rescuer best as the guard captain of Emen Yan and her healer, even though I long to see our new home in Keledev."

Keledev. Teegan longed to see it as well, but part of her was afraid of what they'd find upon their return. When she'd left with Aaron and Connor, Val Pera still smoldered. Goblin marauders ran wild in the White Ridge Mountains. In the long days since, what might have become of their homeland? She fought a hope that she might see it soon, but that hope found root as they began to take action.

Within a tick of Zel's claim to have learned the secret of stormriding, she'd been proven right, and she and Lee sailed away from Teegan and Aaron in the smaller ship, leaving them with *The Kingfisher*.

A roof of gray clouds blocked the moons above the Sorcerer's Cave. Teegan watched *The Merlin* climb until its hull and silks became impossible to discern. Zel's technique had worked, but to Teegan the stormride had felt off—an oppression of light and heat. Aethia agreed. Once *The Kingfisher* had settled in this new place, she'd flown up to the high trusses where she still remained, chuffing and ruffling her feathers.

Lightning flashed above, tinted blue by the shairosite vapors. "They're gone," Aaron said. "On their way to find the Aladoth"—

he let out a wry chuckle—"guided by powdered obsidian."

Teegan pulled her cloak about her. "And what powder shall we use to tell the storm we want to go home? Did you happen to bring a pouch of dirt from Sky Harbor?"

The pilot answered with a blank look.

"Wonderful."

When stuck for an answer to some puzzle or difficulty, the guardians had taught the cadets to stop and pray. Teegan took Aaron's hand and bowed her head. She considered her words for a moment, listening for the Helper's voice in making her request.

The peace of home.

A smile touched her lips, and she prayed, *"Qezid berna po sherna, selebov . . . casecherov, shalomov, po biov Premor avel po shalom hali."*

Rejoice. Be of the same mind. Be at peace.

And the lord of love and peace will be with you.

The image of Aethia soaring over the Forest of Believing south of the academy came to her—blue spruce below, white clouds above. Teegan's hand went to her manykit. "I have it."

She crumpled herbs collected in that very forest in her hand, herbs carried by every member of the Rangers' Sphere. Aaron flared the lamps to ascend into the clouds, then spread a pouch of shairosite across them. Teegan cast her crumpled herbs in after.

The gray ceiling dipped down, and the lamp vapors mixed with the clouds to color them deep blue. Purple flashes arced about them. The hull seemed to disappear and reappear like an apparition. Teegan's heart quickened.

The strange heat and light were back.

The wicker rail slammed into her side. The ship quaked, spars groaning. Teegan fell to the aft bench and looked up into the swirling blue storm. "What's happening, Aaron?"

"I don't know! It's not like before!"

She hardly heard his answer over a growing whine that soon became a scream in her ears. A white aura glowed about her. A patch of night sky appeared within their storm off the bow, revealing a section of a pale moon. Teegan didn't recognize its scars. Aethia flapped among the trusses in distress like a cathedral dove caught in the rafters.

Aaron stared down at Teegan, clinging to a spar for dear life, eyes locked on her waist.

She looked down and found the source of the white aura, blazing from her side. Brilliant colors flowed from the manykit pocket where she'd placed the starlot object she'd found in the Leander treasure chamber. Hesitant, she pulled it out, finding it almost too hot to hold, and the spinning colors threatened to blind her.

Within the flat plane of the starlots' many-colored beam, the storm clouds parted. The section of moon became a full sphere—alone among the stars and unlike any of the three moons she'd known her whole life. More than that, across its glow flew the source of the terrible whine. Birds? No. Their wings were stiff and unnatural. Their song was as the turning of a thousand gears. Ocean waves the size of mountains rolled beneath them.

"Aaron, do something!"

The pilot, still clinging to the spar, threw another handful of shairosite across the lamps. *The Kingfisher* shook with such violence that Aaron's spar cracked. He fell into Teegan, knocking the artifact from her fingers. It skipped off the rail and disappeared over the side.

The quaking stopped. The deep blue storm gathered around them once more, and the hull vanished. A few beats later, the ship reappeared about them and sailed out from a curtain of gray. Teegan looked down to see the pines of the Forest of Believing. Aethia shot out from under the hull to make for the familiar ramparts of Ras Telesar.

They were home.

68

CONNOR
TANELETHAR
THE FROST ISLES

CONNOR BRACED AGAINST THE SUDDEN COLD OF frozen wind blowing through a massive black colonnade. A fortress of interwoven black crystals loomed above him and spread below, down from a high hill into an icy plain. The Rapha Key had done its job.

"Ras Pyras," he said out loud.

All the stories of the sanctuary the academy had once been returned to him. Ras Telesar, the Hill of the Fountain—sister to Ras Pyras, the Hill of the Flame. The key had brought him to an open colonnade in the third ring-wall of Ras Pyras. Four of these crystal lattice ramparts, each higher than the other, rose from a charred hill on the northernmost of the Frost Isles, as if born from the magma under the islands rather than built.

A dark jewel crowned the hilltop fortress. What once might have been a chapel had now become a monstrous faceted keep, many times the size of Ras Telesar's chapel, Nevethav, with spires like fangs jutting up into the sky. A column of fire blazed up from within to paint the clouds red. Streams of lava poured from its base, mirrors to the streams falling from Nevethav's colored windows. This liquid fire flowed in channels throughout the fortress to cast orange light across pyranium-paved wards and archways.

Movement drew Connor's gaze to his right. An orc of the same black pyranium as the pavers rushed him, jaw wide and throat aglow with flaming rage. In a single move, Connor unsheathed Revornosh and sliced into the creature's neck between its helm and its spiked armor. Molten blood spurted forth. The orc clawed at the wound. Connor ended its misery with a second stroke and sent its head rolling.

He broke into a run.

He'd envisioned leaping straight to the enemy's feet. Now, racing along this open porch, Connor wondered at his own folly. According to the lore in his patehpa's journal, the Rapha Key opened the lost Bread Gate of Ras Pyras. Connor should have known it would bring him someplace closer to the kitchen than the throne room.

The rising of the Rescuer's Celestial Peaks had jumbled the halls and ramparts of the twin fortress at Ras Telesar. Yet, having lived there for the last three years, Connor felt he recognized this place. All seemed familiar, though woven from black crystals and far larger.

He took a sloping ramp down, knowing with full certainty he'd find a courtyard, and across it, another ramp and an inner stair leading up into the fourth and innermost ring-wall. From there, broad steps and a bridge he'd spotted from the colonnade would bring him to the keep.

In barely more than a beat of his heart, Connor reached the base of the downward ramp. He stopped, reeling. Had he run that distance in three strides?

The Rapha Key vibrated at his chest, singing with a low tone. The last time it had done that, Valshadox had been bearing down on his party to the south of the Forest of Horrors. If the key sang now, Heleyor might already know of his breach.

His eyes confirmed it. Creatures poured into the courtyard—pyranium orcs and clacking metallic scorpions, pincers snapping the air. Red eyes burned in the arachnids' chittering skulls.

Connor sought the Rescuer's aid. *"Ke'Rumosh recretholenu po stregenu, zowor fi lama drachel vyk kazend kolal."*

He is our refuge and strength, a helper who is always found in times of trouble.

A silver sphere shone about him. *"Onoriov, Rumosh."* Connor picked the nearest orc and charged.

In one stride he was there. Revornosh plunged through spiked pyranium into the orc's chest. The key sang even stronger than before. Was this some property it carried in its own home, enabling him to flash about like a Lisropha warrior?

Connor charged again and again. Each time, he met his foes in a single stride, and Revornosh melted through their armor. The scorpions, too, posed little danger. Every pincer fell with one sweep of his blade. A stinger stabbed at him, but Connor knocked it away with his crook, spun the shaft, and drove the spike into the creature's head.

A voice came to him. *Well done. Your skill is great indeed.*

An echo under its whisper seemed to say, *This is your Maker.* But that was a lie.

The dragon.

Connor brought *The Sleeper's Hope* to mind and let its words and melody flow in his consciousness as the guardians had taught them. Layered above the song, he continued the prayer for aid he'd started moments before.

"Sestradianu, liteh kepamar qashod po kerusa aleryi maqoth keval rostogetu."

We will not be afraid, though the earth trembles,
Though the mountains topple into the seas.

He reached the ramp up into the fourth ring-wall. Each lightning stride sent him ten or twenty paces and blasted orcs and scorpions aside. Each creature he challenged fell to his blade and crook.

Flying reptiles with black iridescent wings descended from above, each one as big as a man. Their talons scraped against the sphere of protection the Rescuer had built around him. Connor stabbed up with Revornosh, and one reptile veered away to crash into a lava river. His crook sent another thrashing and screeching into a pair of orcs. Connor rushed past them.

"Sestradianu, liteh eona keval rogonel po chamagonel, po kerusa bi framordomel qashetu."

We will not be afraid, though the water roars and foams,
Though the mountains quake with its turmoil.

He came to an archway, and then a spiral stair, that dwarfed mortal men. Their size didn't matter. Connor left them behind in three strides and laid waste to the creatures descending them. In the next instant, he stood upon the high bridge to the keep.

Heat blasted up from a river of lava flowing below. Black, shining gates towered above him, spires piercing the sky.

Bursts of flame broke the river's surface on both sides of the bridge. Skulls of crusted rock emerged, each glaring up at him with four orange eyes in uneven hollows. Shoulders and arms and fists dripping with molten lava followed. Magma giants. Rumors come to life.

One giant punched the bridge from beneath and sent lava flying up around him.

Air devoid of all moisture threatened to steal Connor's voice, but he kept speaking his prayer. *"Onevoroth gagetu, rostogetu premonev. Missonel kezavol kid kowlod elevond."*

Nations rage, kingdoms topple.
The earth melts when he lifts his voice.

A fist came pounding down. His shield and the gray sphere held under the blow, but Connor dropped to a knee. With a spin of the shaft, he sheathed his crook at his back and drew Lef Amunrel. The stars within its blade shined bright.

"Hal ke'Premor Lisar bi'anu. Hal Ond stregarenu."

The Lord of Armies is with us.
He is our stronghold.

The giant drove its fist down for another blow, but Connor

rose to meet it, slashing with the dagger. The giant's fist exploded in a shower of rock and flame.

It howled deep, but another voice quickly drowned out its cry.

"*Stop!*"

The roar shook the fortress.

The magma giants lowered their arms and backed away. The gates, each a mass of woven black crystals, opened in utter silence.

"Enter, warrior king."

The Rapha Key buzzed at his chest. In one lightning stride, Connor stood within the keep before the Master of All Enemies.

69

CONNOR BRACED AGAINST A ROARING WIND OF PURE heat. His armor glowed silver white around him, near as solid as steel. Without it, he knew, the blaze would melt his flesh.

Within the gates, the woven crystal bridge became a jagged platform extending out over the inner keep. The cyclone of flame shot up from below, and before its fire, ruby wings spread wide. The Great Red Dragon rose.

Two rows of three eyes each gazed down at Connor. The Chief of Traitors bent low his horned chin and grinned, showing countless pearl-white teeth. "Welcome, Lightraider. What brings you to my abode?"

The wind never ceased, and in its blast, Connor feared Lef Amunrel might fly from his hand and be lost forever. To toss the weapon against such force seemed a doomed hope. He'd have to stab it into the dragon's heart. But how?

Connor thrust Lef Amunrel out, and the light of its stars split the hot wind like a ship's bow, giving him a reprieve. "I've come to kill you, Lord of Lies. But I'm sure you know that."

"Oh, but that isn't entirely true, now, is it? You've come seeking redemption. What a glory that you came to me instead of your master."

The heat hit him again. Connor staggered back a step, then redoubled his effort and pressed forward on the uneven crystal floor. "Save your trickery. I've come to end this war."

"I have good news for you, young king. The war is over."

The waves of song in Connor's mind—the last of *The Sleeper's Hope*—broke against a dark and rocky shore. A vision smashed through. White slopes—the north side of the Celestial Peaks, perhaps. An open tunnel heading deep into the mountain. His mind flew into the tunnel, passing orcs, goblins, and spiders.

The flight slowed and alighted in a monstrous chamber at the root of the mountains, not far from a huge hexagonal crate made of pure pyranium. Frost goblins cast its lid aside, and underneath, nestled in black sand, a red egg pulsed. Fire split the leathery shell. Scarlet wings studded with black jewels pressed forth.

The vision flashed to a battle. Frost goblins swarmed the guardians and Pedrig. An iceblade troll thrust an arm like a lance into Quinton's chest. Agony contorted his face. Kara reached for him while pyranium orcs dragged her away.

"No!"

"Oh yes, mighty friend of the fallen. It is true."

Connor was on the ridge east of the academy now, called the Hammer and Tongs. A ball of fire sailed over him and obliterated the westernmost tower. The giant Lisropha warrior at the barbican gate, with its fireglass crown, toppled and crashed onto a rising airship, sending out a cloud of smoke and flame.

When the smoke cleared, the vision had returned to the cavern. The egg and crate lay smashed. In their place stood a dragon like none Connor had seen or studied before. A row of angular pyranium horns stretched from its red snout down its spine. The spiked tail was like a mace. Its talons, like black diamonds, cut into the stone at its feet, and dark fire spewed forth from its jaws. Connor knew the dragon's name. Vorax the Returned. Pedrig and Ioanu fell before a sweep of its tail. Master Jairun vanished behind a curtain of black fire. Orcs carried Kara through the breach, leaving no sign of her in the vision but her screams.

Tears poured down Connor's face, dried in the heat before they reached his chin. "Monster!"

"Victor, I think you mean. I will say it again, young king. The war is over. Now you must choose. I offer my mercy and a path forward for you and your people. Won't you take it?"

The vision faded. In its place, within the bulwark formed by Lef Amunrel's light, Kara stood.

Connor swallowed, desperate to wet his voice. "It can't be you."

"It is." Kara stretched out her hand, pale and clean with a silk sleeve that came to her knuckles to cover her queensblood flourishes. In place of her cloak and manykit, she'd donned a blue-and-silver gown—the gown of a queen, with sparkling embroidery that matched a circlet of dark gems on her brow.

Her tears matched his, falling to stain her dress. "I'm here, and I've no more stomach for battles. We've lost so much. To keep fighting will only cost us more. This is the way forward, Connor—the way of peace. Won't you choose it?" She took a step, coming close enough that her fingers grazed his cheek. "Won't you choose me?"

Kara's sweet fingers moved to Connor's wrist and traced up to wrap the hand holding Lef Amunrel. She pressed ever so gently, as if to lower the weapon.

She was perfect. Kara had always seemed so perfect in his eyes.

Yet something about her nagged at him. Her tears. Why weren't they drying in the terrible heat like Connor's?

The song came back to his mind full force.

Banish dark with light divine.

Let fire dim. Let starlight shine.

Let thunder fade. Let storm clouds break.

His shield glowed to life about his right arm, and with it, he shoved Kara back.

She laughed and changed. Indigo eyes turned green. Platinum hair turned raven black. Thera gave him a sultry smile. "Have your tastes changed, my lord? Would you prefer me instead, a captain of an ancient bloodline? He can work with that."

"Get out of my head!"

Let Watchman rest.

Let the Sleeper wake.

The false woman screamed and disintegrated into swirling ash.

Connor let out a roar and raised both dagger and sword against the dragon. "Die, Traitor!"

Fire rained down in a blistering wave. Connor tried to rush into the open void between him and Heleyor using the lightning stride the key had given him. But against the rushing wind, he could not prevail. Under its gale, he heard a rumbling. The stones at his feet shook.

Oh, no.

He turned in time to raise his shield against some blend of sword and spear made of crusted magma. It flashed against the gray sphere around him, and the giant raised it for another strike.

Even as the spear came down, a second magma skull appeared at the side of the platform, inside the keep. The creature roared. Hot stones pelted Connor's shield. In desperation, he struck against the onslaught with Revornosh and managed to split two of the flaming missiles.

The lava blade crashed against the sphere again, and Connor buckled.

Deep laughter filled the keep.

Pain screamed in Connor's flesh as he fought to stand. He struck out with Lef Amunrel and landed the blow, obliterating the giant's hand and wrist up to the forearm. But the move had turned his full back to Heleyor—a grave mistake, and Connor knew it.

Ruby scales. Rippling red tendons. Gleaming talons. So much fire.

The impact seemed to smash his bones to dust. Connor flew from the bridge and saw only the flaming cyclone. He heard a single, final word.

"Fool."

70

LEE
TANELETHAR
BRIMSTONE HEIGHTS

THE MERLIN HIT WITH A PRONOUNCED *THUMP*, HARD enough to cost Lee his footing. He dragged himself up by the rail. "Did we crash?"

The clearing of the storm cloud gave him his answer. Sky, not earth, flowed under the skids–a good bit of it between them and a black mountain peak, and the ship was still rising, vents whistling as white vapor rushed out.

Zel gave him a withering frown. "*I* did not crash. The storm brought us much higher than before, and the air we brought with us is too thick. What you felt was a sharp rise." As she spoke, their ascent slowed, and she closed the vents. "We're stable now, and our silk is sound." Zel looked down past the rudder. "But where?"

"The Brimstone Heights, I expect, based upon the brimstone metal clinging to the obsidian taken from Thera's prisoner. But these mountains cover a vast range of the northwest coast. We may have days of searching still ahead of us." Lee brought a lens down over one side of his spectacles, a green one that sharpened the edges of every rock and crevice on the mountains below. "Or not," he said and pointed. "Look there. The prisoner's fellow outcasts."

The two, just as the prisoner had said, lay dead beside the road–murdered by their companion to prove himself to orcs that had already abandoned him and moved on. They lay not far from tall boulders of the same orange glass Lee had pulverized to mix with *The Merlin*'s shairosite. "The Aladoth army came through here."

After the long delay to help Connor find Lef Amunrel, Lee's hunt for the army of Sil Shadath and his brother Shan was on again. Looking back with the aid of *The Merlin's* shipglass, he saw the distant waterfalls of Emen Yan. The stormride had brought them far, but not as far as he'd hoped.

With a sigh, he turned his attention to the road beyond the bodies. "The army's path took them deeper into the Heights—a hard slog. Let us hope they marched at a slug's pace." He pressed his lips together, glaring at the dark path. "Assuming, like a slug, they left a trail we can follow."

"Or"—Zel pushed the rudder, turning them away from the westward road that climbed into the black range—"we might make a reasoned guess and make up the time."

An orange haze flickered to their north. Smoke and flame poured up from a tall peak. Lee snorted. "The whole region shakes from the veins of lava flowing under its black rock. There are many such mountains."

"But none with so great a fire." Zel kept her heading. "Trust your pilot and her gut, Cadet. I'm telling you, whatever power Valshadox wishes to use to send his army into Keledev lies there."

Leaving the army's trail behind was a risk, but Lee saw no other option if they wanted to make up time. He sat on the bow bench and watched the mountain's fury. "All right. Let's see what we find."

The ticks brought the fiery menace closer, until a shadow took form, circling within the haze. Lee stood from his bench. "A dragon, Zel. Take us lower."

"I'll try."

She pulled her vents, dropping *The Merlin* into a black, razor-sharp maze of valleys and ridges. Within a few beats, the stench of sulfur hit them, and the ship began to buck and tremble. Lee gripped the rail. "What is that?"

"Heat and vapors." Zel worked her rudder and vents to keep them clear of the steep slopes. "The Celestial Peaks have their winds and pockets of cold that steal the air from under the hull. These mountains have their own dangers." She dropped even lower, and *The Merlin* jerked from side to side.

"I said low, but not this low!"

"Do you want to fly?"

He turned to glare at her. "Do you? This feels more like an endless crash."

She gritted her teeth against a heavy buck and pulled her vent ropes. "We've no choice. The northward air is lowest. Any higher and we'll stagnate."

"Are you sure you can manage it?"

"Am I not already?"

The heat in her answer told Lee he ought not question her flying again. He set his eyes ahead and held tight to the rail, trying and failing to suppress small grunts and gasps as obsidian shards passed within inches of their silk.

"Oh, stop it," Zel said. "I've got this."

The mountain's peak flew in and out of sight as *The Merlin* sped through deep valleys. Until, at last, the haze resolved into a column of smoke pouring upward, flickering like a lantern's flame.

"We're close." Zel brought *The Merlin* a little higher into slower and smoother air. She turned the ship to steer clear of a ridge, and they came into a descending gorge that widened into a vast teardrop canyon. A tar sea sat within the canyon's lowest pit, and on its shore camped the army Lee and Zel had been seeking.

Lee scrunched his brow and lowered a lens into place. "Are those . . . ships?"

"A whole fleet of them," Zel said. "Enough to carry a thousand or more."

Lee gave a slow nod, shifting his gaze to the soot-covered tents on the shore. "More, I'd say." Aladoth, driven by barkhides and iron orcs moved in and out of the tent village, carrying crates along timber docks to the ships. Others milled about, eating or sparring. "What are they waiting for?"

"I assume they're waiting for those sorcerers to open a portal."

Sorcerers?

Lee shot a glance back at Zel, then followed her gaze to three burning peaks that bordered the canyon on the far side. At the foot of the largest and centermost mountain, two pairs of obsidian giants rested, leaning on their massive forearms as if asleep. Between each pair was a red silk tent with a burning altar. Robed figures stood before them.

Lee turned the shipglass to get a closer look. "I see him."

Zel set her vents and rudder and came to stand next to him, letting the airship drift closer. "I'm sorry, Lee. I know you hoped to find your brother here, but a great foreboding in me hoped otherwise."

He regarded her for a moment, trying to discern what she meant, but after searching all this time, Lee could not keep his gaze from his brother Shan for long. He found him again with the shipglass, dressed in black-and-scarlet robes, eyes closed and hands passing over the burning altar.

"Oh, Shan, what have you become?" Lee shuddered to think what might have died there. "But who's the other sorcerer?" he asked, looking to the second altar and finding a woman there in robes like Shan's. "Do Heleyor's efforts to corrupt the Maker's creation here require two?"

"Not just two sorcerers, Lee." Zel patted his arm and steered the glass upward. The blur of clouds and smoke resolved into focus. Not one, but two shadows circled above the canyon.

A long breath escaped his lips as he straightened and regarded his friend. "Two dragons, Zel. Four giants. An army a thousand strong. How are we to stop such a foe?"

71

ZEL BROUGHT *THE MERLIN* HIGHER IN THE VALLEY and set the bow into a turn. "We must run to Keledev and warn them."

"What good will that do?" Lee changed rails as the ship turned, pointing at the shore of the tar lake. "See the silver veins? That's shairosite. The lake under that fleet is the portal. Valshadox plans to send those ships into our seas. His army might land on any shore in Keledev. We must stop them here."

"What are you saying? Fight the whole lot?" Zel kept turning. "We'll arrive in Elamhavar with our cloaks smelling of smoke and the laughter of two dragons ringing in our ears."

Lee snapped his fingers. "The dragons. There may be another way. How close do you think you can bring us to that mountain?"

"You mean the middle one, with the great column of smoke and fire, about which the dragons are circling?"

He nodded. "We must bring one of them down into the lake— destroy the portal before it opens fully. It worked with Vorax two years ago."

"What if one dragon isn't enough?"

"We have to try."

The snaking gorges of Brimstone Heights proved useful in their endeavor, cut by lava from many spouts. Thanks to Zel's skillful flying, one red path brought *The Merlin* around the canyon's outer rim to a saddle between two of the three mountains.

A molten cataract flowed from the center mountain, and Zel flew so close Lee thought their wicker might burst into flame. She set the ship down on a rock shelf and released the vapors from the silks to keep her from rising again. "I daren't take us closer. Those dragons may be flying in a thick haze, but their eyes are not like ours."

"Agreed." Lee shed his cloak and hopped the rail. The instant he landed, heat pushed up through his boots. He slid his bow from his shoulder. "We climb from here. Not the whole way. I need only get close enough for a few clean shots, so long as we stay out of sight."

The constant thunder of rocks bursting and new earth spouting forth rumbled in their ears, so much so that the higher they climbed, the less Lee heard when Zel spoke to him. Both were loath to shout so close to a pair of wyrms.

Without warning, she yanked him down by his quiver, forcing him to plant a gloved hand on burning rock. He shook the cinders from the leather and hit her with a questioning glare. Zel thrust a hand west.

A pair of iron orcs lumbered there, armed with pyranium scimitars.

Lee crouched lower. What a fool's hope it had been to think the peak below the dragons would be unguarded.

Once the orcs passed, he gave Zel a nod, and the two moved on with greater care.

Mountains were tricky things. Lee had learned that well enough in the Celestial Peaks. The high ground was never as near as a climber thinks, with many surprises between. One such surprise stopped them cold. Their chosen route brought them over a rise to a ledge above a river of lava, with no hope of crossing and climbing higher.

Lee gauged the distance to the dragons. *It might be enough.* *With a little help.* He motioned for Zel to keep watch, then drew his bow. With the feathers at his ear, he spoke a prayer that only he and the High One could hear under the mountain's roar.

"*Ka kelas kelam hal vy yeluthoroth. Someh bari po someh bari lutked sevetlam brilond. Dar vy kepachor ka kemorol morsom. Tav forthletu trepah sehowdetu.*"

The path of the righteous is the light of dawn,
Brightening unto the midday.
But the way of the wicked is the darkest gloom.
They don't know what makes them stumble.

"Let her fly true, Rumosh. Please."

He loosed the string, and the arrow pierced the haze. Though the smoke whipped around it, the arrow flew true, and it seemed to Lee a dome of light grew bright about its tip.

Until a ball of flame knocked it from the sky.

Aladoth soldiers rushed in upon Lee and Zel from both sides. Two each held them fast with dirty, blackened fingers. A fifth put a pocked and nicked blade to Zel's throat.

"Don't!" Lee shouted and found he could hear his own voice.

A hush had come over them, as if some force had blocked all other sound. A second voice, much like his own, gave support to Lee's plea. "Do as my brother says. Hold fast."

Shan rose from below the ledge, dressed in black armor marked with a scarlet that also tinged his eyes. The air wavered beneath him. He alighted in front of Lee and set the tip of Lee's own sikari knife against his throat—the knife he'd thrown at the buzzard over Sil Shadath several days before. "Hello, brother. I'm so glad you've come."

72

COLD. SEARING PAIN.

Connor felt every fiber of his body and none of them at the same time.

Rise, son of faith, and walk with me.

A white crystalline haze blurred Connor's sight. Snowflakes trapped in his eyelashes? He wiped them away and found the effort accomplished little beyond intensifying the pain. Not in his arm so much as his right leg.

His hand came to his chest. The Rapha Key remained, still hanging from the chain Belen had made for it. Slowly, he reached to his belt.

Lef Amunrel. Gone.

Lying there, still fighting the haze and the pain pulsing up his leg, Connor felt around in the snow.

Nothing.

He'd dropped the dagger in Ras Pyras—a worse failure than Faelin's. His patehpa had lost Lef Amunrel. Connor had laid it at the feet of the Chief of Enemies.

"I have to get it back."

The broken husk of his former voice startled him, but he ignored the worry it brought and tried to stand. He had the key.

He could get back into Ras Pyras. He'd recover the dagger or die in the attempt. Heleyor had called him a fool, but the dragon had been a fool to let him live.

Connor rolled to a knee and planted a foot to stand. With every muscle quaking, he pressed himself high enough to plant his other foot.

He screamed and fell to the snow, grabbing for his right leg, but the offense of his own hands only caused him more pain. Spending more breaths than he could count, he lay there, waiting for relief that never came, until finally, Connor sat up.

The tears of his suffering soothed his eyes, and his sight cleared. In the next instant, he wished it hadn't. Connor stared down with horror at his leg, burned and blackened below the knee. Of his boot and foot, there were no sign. Like Lef Amunrel, they were gone.

Connor fell back into the snow and wept.

He didn't know how long he lay there, sometimes staring up at the wheeling stars, sometimes sinking into a terrible darkness—never sleeping, but losing time.

After a long while, he became aware of warmth flowing over him—a slow rhythm of balmy air like the forest breeze of Teegan's Sil Tymest. He let it go on, mildly conscious of a half-remembered story Master Belen had once told of giant ice bears with a taste for man-flesh.

What would it matter? Let them feast.

The slow rhythm of air continued. Cold. Warm. Cold. Warm. Then it ceased, and Connor wondered if perhaps he'd been consumed and hardly noticed. The stars passed over and beneath him. He felt nothing. Was this the way to Elamhavar?

White fur, dusted with snow, hung over him. Ice-blue eyes gazed down over a sloped snout and large black nose. "This is not the way."

A lion, not a bear. Was it speaking to him? It couldn't. The white Havarra lions of the north were all hunted and killed long ago, betrayed by Connor's own kin. The guardians had said so.

The blue eyes turned stern. "Rise, son of faith, and walk with me."

Connor answered, mocking this imagined being and his own delirium, "I can't walk, lion. Look at what my failed quest has cost me. I'm lame and defeated. My homeland is overrun, and all the promises are broken. If you're not here to kill me, then leave and let me die."

"Promises broken? What a faithless notion after all you've endured—after the great blessings you've been given." Rounded ears peeking out of the lion's mane flattened. Black lips peeled back to reveal white teeth. "You fought Heleyor himself and lived. And now, for the lack of one paw out of four, you wish to die?" The lion growled low, as if to himself. "Perhaps I misjudged your blood and your heart."

The lion fell silent, waiting, and the rhythm of his warm breath began again.

"I saw you," Connor said, when it seemed clear his imagined lion would not leave. "When the key brought me to Ras Telesar, I saw your face."

"I saw you first."

What did that mean? Connor frowned and struggled to sit up against the terrible pain. He expected the beast to vanish in that moment, but the lion pressed his broad skull against Connor's back to aid him and then lay beside him in the snow.

Perhaps he was real after all. "Explain, please," Connor said. "Do you mean you saw me when I used the key before I saw you?"

A huff escaped the lion, perhaps a laugh. "No, son of faith. I saw you when the storm first brought you to King's Cradle, the birthplace of your bloodline."

The lion in the storm. "Yes. I remember now. I felt your presence when we passed through the Stormgate."

"Mmm," the lion said. "A good sign, but I saw and felt much more. You and I are joined. This is how we were created."

The blue eyes bored into him, and before Connor could say that he didn't fully understand, the lion nodded. "You Leanders forsook and forgot our bond generations ago."

Connor's gaze fell away, brought low once again by the shame of his Leander blood.

The lion growled. "Look at me. Know me. Though the sin of the traitor-kings condemned many, you are no longer bound by it."

"How do you know what's in my heart? Is my pain so clearly written on my face?"

Another huff. "It is clearly written there, but as you've guessed, I can also see your mind. In time, if you want, you'll learn to see mine."

For a moment, the shadow of Connor's loss lessened under the light of his wonder. "You can see my thoughts?"

"Your thoughts. Your strongest memories. That is how some from my line escaped before the traitors sold every one of us to the dragons. The strongest of us saw your forefathers' purpose, even though they tried to conceal it deep in their hearts because they knew of our ability." The lion shut his eyes for a moment, as if pushing the shared memory of Connor's ancestors away.

When his eyes opened again, their feline serenity had returned. "In a way, son of faith, all cats can see the minds of your kind, although those that cannot speak have limited understanding. But the white lions of the Havarra and the lords of House Leander bear a deeper bond. We are both children of faith, and for us, faith is sight. As I said, we were created that way."

"To what purpose?"

"To serve the Maker, of course. To see him and see each other. The white lions were meant to advise you, and your house was meant to lead mankind with House Arkelon at your side."

It was Connor's turn to laugh. "I am no leader for mankind."

"Fear not. Your forefathers spurned that calling, and it will not come to your line again. That was part of the deception Heleyor planned. But you and I may still serve the Maker's will"—the lion laid his head on his great paws and lifted his brow to look up at

Connor—"if you wish."

"I do," Connor said and meant it, despite his misery. "What can we do, though, now Heleyor has won?"

This time, Connor felt the lion probing his thoughts, bringing forth the same vision the dragon had shown him. He saw again the murder of his friends and the destruction of the academy. "Why are you showing me this?"

"So that you may see the lie. Look, son of faith. Heleyor's deceptions are masterful, but they are flawed, as he is."

Connor watched the vision in the cavern. He saw Kara, yet he did not recognize her cloak or her manykit. When he saw the academy, as the fireball flew over him, he focused on the cadets manning the ramparts. Connor knew every cadet at the academy, yet these were unfamiliar. One, as if found out, met Connor's eye with a glare of malice, and the vision dissolved. "It was a lie," he said, blinking as the night and the snow returned. "Keledev remains. The academy still stands."

"Not for long if we do nothing." The lion turned his white mass around and pressed his head under Connor's arm so that Connor's hand lay buried in his mane. "I'll say it once again. Rise, son of faith, and walk with me."

73

THE LION'S HELP LESSENED THE ANGUISH OF STANDING, though not by much. Connor leaned on his new companion and used his crook as a crutch under the other arm. "You haven't told me your name," he started to say but stopped as the name came into his mind. "Meh . . . ham . . . mo . . . noo . . . thasyr."

"Good. You're learning, though your mouth is not made to speak our words. You may call me Thasyr. In your Common Tongue, it is akin to *envoy* or *ambassador*. In mine, it has deeper meaning."

"Thasyr, then," Connor said. "Where shall we walk in this frozen waste?"

The lion had begun to turn Connor about, and even before he did, Connor had a sense of what he would see, thanks to their growing bond. They stood on a high plateau above the snowy plain. Far in the distance, Ras Pyras still painted the sky red. Nearer, only a few paces away, was a pale blue arch crusted with snow.

A shared thought from Thasyr told Connor the arch was how he'd arrived on the plateau. Behind it, the sculpture of a fountain poured out in all directions to form trees, animals, and winged Dynapha. This place must have been a waypoint used by the Elder Folk as they strode across Talania. When the dragon struck Connor, the Rapha Key had borne him out of the fortress in much the same way it had borne him in.

"The key saved me," he said aloud.

"The key is a tool. The Maker saved you. Without the Maker's will and purpose, Heleyor would surely have killed you." Thasyr lifted his whiskered chin to the north. "Even now, the dragon's giants come forth to seek you and finish his work."

Connor did not have the lion's vision. Squinting, he saw orange distortions wavering before the black hill of Ras Pyras. Then, suddenly, the distortions grew sharp. The magma giants he'd faced at the keep lumbered their way. "Am I seeing with your eyes?"

"You're seeing with my help. There's a difference."

"Either way, those things won't take long to reach us. We'd better go."

"An excellent notion," the lion said, yet he didn't walk straight for the arch. He turned Connor aside a few paces. "Before we leave, oughtn't you reclaim the weapon you came to Tanelethar to find in the first place?"

The snow was deep and fresh on the plateau, deep enough that Connor could imagine his foot still present, hidden where his leg met the powder. He tore his mind away from that thought and focused on what the lion wanted him to see—an elongated depression, new but already filling with snow.

Supported by Thasyr and his crook, Connor bent to reach into the cold white and wrapped his fingers about a soft leather hilt. "Lef Amunrel."

"The dagger came with you. By the Maker's grace, you held it fast until you'd flown through the portal, else it might lie even now in Heleyor's keep. He would not touch the celestium, I dare say, but neither would he allow it to fall once again into Keledan possession."

"I am blessed," Connor said.

"As I told you. Now, let us go."

Thasyr brought Connor to the arch. "You must learn how the

Aropha walked the land. Their strides were great and covered many leagues. These portals and keys like the one you carry aided them."

"I learned some of this in Ras Pyras," Connor said. "Within the fortress, I moved ten paces at a time, and the force of my running was like a great ram against my enemies."

"True. The Lisropha ran this way in battle. For a human, though, I think the key will only grant this ability in an Aropha sanctuary. Likewise, the key needs whatever elements are part of Aropha construction when leaping across Tanelethar, and it also needs your direction. Before we can go anywhere, you must give it a command."

Connor didn't need to ask how. With the key pressed against his skin under his tunic, he need only think with intent about the portal to which he wanted to travel. Perhaps that was how he'd leapt from Heleyor's Vault to Ras Pyras.

"Will you fight beside me, Thasyr?"

A growl rolled in the lion's throat. "I thought you'd never ask."

Connor slid Lef Amunrel into his belt and wrapped his arm once more over the lion's neck. "Heleyor, in his deception, showed me his ending. At the same time, he exposed his soft middle. A breach under the Celestial Peaks makes his assault possible, and a new and horrific form of dragon guards it."

"You saw Vorax," the lion said, speaking what was on Connor's mind. "His spirit traveled to an egg—a shaadsuth—once his flesh was destroyed. I believe the egg was incubated in Ras Pyras, rather than the desert sands, to create a terrible foe for this invasion. This dragon, both new and ancient, is a grave danger. I will help you and your friends in fighting it." Thasyr crouched low. "Climb on my back. I will be your legs, and you will be my sword."

With no small amount of effort and pain, Connor slipped his ruined leg over the lion's back.

Thasyr approached the portal. "Where is this breach, son of faith?"

"Zel and Lee found a tunnel under the Celestial Peaks in the Highland Forest, near the first portal Vorax corrupted."

Thasyr let out a grumbling huff. "Ha. I see your goal. Keep it at the forefront of your mind, and the key will aid us. When you're ready, hold tight to my mane."

Connor tucked his crook away and buried his hands in the lion's thick fur. The moment he secured his grip, Thasyr unleashed a mighty roar. The portal became a roiling black storm. The night flashed and spun, and the lion leapt into flight.

74

KARA
KELEDEV
UNDER THE CELESTIAL PEAKS

THE *DRIP, DRIP* OF ICY WATER ON KARA'S FOREHEAD
returned her to awareness. Hair like a white feathered goat's
beard hung over her, along with a blade made of grimy ice.

Kara's eyes flew wide, and she tried to pull back, but a wooden
barrier prevented it. She struggled against rope lashings. The
creatures had tied her to a litter and left her on the floor.

Gray-green lips spread into a grin, exposing yellowed fangs.
"Hello, pretty icecap. Pretty thing. Pretty thing." The frost goblin
set its knife against her cheek. "I long to see you cry. To cry
your tears."

Another tittered beside the first. "Tears, he says. Cry. Cry,
pretty thing. Pretty thing." It set its knife against her gut. "I'll take
the middle. The middle I'll take, and you'll take the top."

Heat and dark fire blew over Kara's form, making her shut her
eyes and scream. When she opened them again, her ropes were
singed. Nothing remained of the two goblins but sizzling lichen
and brittleknit bones.

More goblins quaked near her feet. A voice spoke to them,
and she heard it in her head and in her ears. "The queensblood
is not to be harmed. Our master has a use for her. Understand?"

The goblins skulked away.

Fear gripped Kara, but she rolled her head over, unable to stop herself.

A dragon held her with its gaze—a dragon like none she'd ever imagined, with broad scarlet scales and edged horns of pyranium. Black jewels studded its wings.

To the best she could see, Kara was still under the mountains, in a cavern of white stone and ice, lit by sparking torches. The dragon, though huge and terrifyingly strange, felt familiar. It canted its head, as if listening, and the name entered her mind.

Vorax the Returned.

The dragon lord of the Highland Forest was back. She saw a leathery egg, burned open, in a destroyed pyranium crate not far away. Vorax, a ruined Aropha spirit, had survived to take a new fleshly form as such creatures had done in the past. Yet this version of Vorax could not be a fledgling—not at such a height. How long had this terrible creature been down here?

Vorax grinned and spoke in her mind. *Good. Fear me. I am eternal. No mortal may destroy me.*

It could hear her thoughts. She sang *The Sleeper's Hope* in her mind to force it out.

Vorax laughed, belching smoke. "Foolish girl. Betrayer who graced my fortress and then brought it crashing down about my creatures. Murderer. I offered you much, and you sold me to my enemies. Now your favored shepherd is dead, and you will pay." The dragon bent its neck low so that a red eye like a faceted ruby came near to hers. Dark fire spouted from its nostrils. "Go ahead and sing your song, Queensblood. You're mine."

At the shouting of his orcs, Vorax pulled away. "What is it?"

The creatures grumbled in their coarse corruption of the Elder Tongue.

Vorax growled, "Then stop them. Kill them. Do the task you were made for."

The dragon moved off, talons like shadowed diamond scimitars crunching into the stone floor. Kara put away her fears over the dragon's words and set her mind on her bonds. She fought against the ropes and found them loose enough she might inch one hand to her back.

Her whirlknife.

Kara's sword and her other knife had broken against the pyranium orcs' armor, but the creatures had failed to notice the second knife sheathed at her back and hidden by her cloak.

She rolled her body back and forth and twisted her hips. With each motion, the ropes loosened, and in a few beats, she had enough room to pull her knife from the sheath. Quietly, she worked the blades open and set one against the closest rope. In two difficult strokes, the rope snapped.

Her hips were free. Kara arched her back and set the blade to work again, this time with more force. Another rope snapped, and then another.

A goblin looked her way and shrieked. More came running.

Kara rolled on her side and cut the last ropes holding her down. They broke as the first goblin reached her. She dodged its stabbing knife and removed its arm, then ended its shrieking with a slash across the neck.

This was no flood of goblins like she'd faced before—more of a trickle. She held her own.

But orcs with the same, red-marked armor as those who'd taken her before were on their way.

Behind them, battle raged at the chamber's mouth. Vorax blew fire. Dark creatures roared and squealed. Kara heard Master Jairun shouting commands and sacred verses. By the look of things, they'd reach her too late.

The orcs, in their spiked armor, came trundling toward her, a deep red fire burning to bring the runes carved into their arms and faces to life. One pointed a scimitar and bellowed in the Common Tongue. "Back onto the board, Keledan. Lay down, or I'll—"

The creature fell on its face with an axe lodged in its back.

Dag, encased in a deep blue sphere of light, came soaring

through a curtain of dragon smoke—not on his own feet or on the Gladion but riding on Ioanu's back. The bear leapt from shelf to shelf along the chamber wall and landed on a pair of goblins, snapping their brittleknit spines.

Dag dismounted and met an orc with a ringing blow against its helm. While the creature reeled, he drew his other axe from its companion's back and set to work on the rest. He bashed an orc toward Ioanu with his shield.

The bear slashed at its face, knocking its helm free. "Queensblood, can you fight?"

In answer, Kara lifted the pyranium scimitar from the first orc's dead fingers and jammed it through the neck of Ioanu's foe. "What of the others?"

"Your swordmaster is grievously wounded. The paradragons retreated at Master Jairun's bidding, having spent their frost against the dragon's strange fire." Ioanu hit another orc with a double slash of her claws while Kara brought the scimitar down to sever the hand gripping its halberd. "This is a hard match."

The dragon backed into the chamber, surrounded by armored orcs. Arrows flew at its chest and wings, but it gave them no heed.

Kara spied Master Jairun and Baldomar, locked in battle with an iceblade. The rest of their party, a few lightraider cadets and Pedrig, fought the jabbering mass of goblins. Were they enough?

As if in answer, a narrow stream of black fire from Vorax broke through a cadet's shield. He fell and disappeared under the goblins.

Ioanu rammed her glowing blue armor into an orc hacking at Kara's scimitar with its halberd and knocked it from its feet. The bear was breathing hard. "Our time in this world may be over."

———◆———

FAR EAST OF ORVYN'S VOW, TEEGAN AND AARON RODE with Boreas in *The Barn Owl* on their way to the Storm Mists. Ravens from Samar and his scouts had bid the councilor and his fleet come as quickly as they could.

"My lieutenant thinks he's found a portal from Tanelethar," Boreas said. "And by your headmaster's concern over the buzzard that escaped Cadet Orso, I fear he's right."

Teegan was not so sure. To enter here, through the Storm Mists in the Sea of Vows, the Aladoth would need ships, and she and Aaron knew from Thera's prisoner that the Aladoth army had gone into Brimstone Heights. There were better roads to the sea.

As they drew nearer to the scout airships, though, all doubt in the councilor's conclusion faded.

The ships held low over the waves near a crusted stone arch that made them seem as small as festival toys. The vapors of the Storm Mist gathered thick within it, and underneath—just below the water's surface—some natural cauldron boiled.

"Fire under the sea," Aaron said, watching from the rail next to her. "That's what the divers say feeds the Storm Mists. Here, it's come to the surface."

Boreas brought *The Barn Owl* to a hover and scratched his chin. "I see the veins of shairosite in the arch. Yet, this portal looks tamer than the Stormgate." He shook his head. "Whatever sorcery the dragons are working here has not yet been completed."

75

LEE
TANELETHAR
BRIMSTONE HEIGHTS

BARKHIDES HAULED LEE AND ZEL TO THE SHAIROSITE shore between the two red tents. Two others held their weapons, admiring the blades and bolts as if they meant to keep them.

Shan hovered before them on waves of heat. The woman Lee had seen before rose from the eastern tent to join him, wearing scarlet armor decorated with black, both a match and an opposite to his. Looking close, Lee saw a crescent brand under her right eye.

He turned his gaze to Shan. "A Scarlet Moon sorceress. You keep venerable company."

"More than you know, Brother. This is Maldora, and we are one."

The woman gave Lee a nod, as if they'd been introduced at a family feast. "Shan and I were meant to advise your friends in their rule, but I'm told we'll now rule in their place. A once future king has fallen."

Shan seemed to see the horror overcoming Lee. "Yes. Your friend, the shepherd. He might have ruled Keledev, but when he came before the Great Red Throne, he was found . . . unworthy."

Lee bucked against his captors. "What did you do to Connor?"

"I?" Shan laid an armored hand over his heart. "Nothing. That honor belonged to Heleyor. But Maldora and I will reap the benefits. When next we see our parents, Brother, they and all those who banished me into exile will bow at my feet."

"*Our* feet, Husband," Maldora said, earning an apologetic glance and a hasty nod from Shan.

Zel snorted. "No one in Keledev will bow to either of you, not in a thousand years and more."

"Well." Shan slowly spun on his wave of heat and lifted his gaze skyward. "Perhaps *you* won't."

The shadows circling above slowed and descended, wings spread wide. From the haze, the first dragon took full form, black, with wings and snout tipped in red. It landed on the center mountainside. Valshadox. Lord of Sil Shadath.

The second dragon landed above and east of the first, far uglier, as dragons go. Putrid ooze dripped from the cracks between its brown scales. With a misshapen head and chaotic teeth, it snapped at Valshadox, who snapped back before glaring down at the two Keledan.

Always at war—with the Rescuer, with each other. Lee wondered if, like Vorax in his stronghold two years before, these dragons had their will bent upon the portal, which left them subject to their contentious instincts.

The eyes of Maldora and Shan glowed scarlet. When next they spoke, they spoke as one, with the echoing, dissonant voices of both dragons.

"Welcome, Keledan," the dual voices said. "Your coming was foreseen. You are the last piece of the incantation which will join this land to yours."

"Last piece," Zel said. "I don't understand."

Through the sorcerers, the dragons answered. "The breach your own people dug under your Overlord's peaks allowed Maldora to sense an ancient and sunken hollow hill. That hill has risen, and our bird has gifted it with shairosite from this canyon. All that remains to form the link is the body of one born in Keledev, nourished from its springs and fed from the fruit of its vines."

The red in Shan's eyes dimmed. His voice returned to him, and he smirked at Lee. "Your friend is food for the lake, Brother. Her death will open this end of the gate for our army." He lifted his chin to the barkhides holding Zel. "Now."

They tried to pull her away, but Lee shoved one of his captors and locked his arm in Zel's. "Don't do this, Brother. Please! This is not the path you were made for."

A cackle escaped Shan, deepened by a shadow of the dragon's voice. "None of us were made for any purpose. I'm making my own path—my own destiny. Aid me, Trang, or die."

"Never!" Lee shouted.

His brother sighed. "So be it."

Shan balled his fists, and one of the obsidian giants behind him stalked forward to tower over Lee.

"See the power you might have wielded?" Shan raised his arm and held it there. The giant mimicked his pose. "Serve me. Kill your friend and open the gate or die with her and accomplish the same."

Obsidian. Glass. How easily the rocks from this region had shattered when Zel made the powder for their lamp.

Lee held silent.

Shan shook his head, mimicked by the giant, then drove his fist downward.

The giant's massive fist and forearm—all one jagged block— came rushing down over Lee and Zel. The barkhides released them and ran.

"Shields, Zel!" Lee shouted and threw up his arm.

She raised her own arm, and they grabbed each other's wrists, crouching under the impending blow. Their glowing shields joined and broadened.

The giant's fist crashed into them with a blinding flash. The fleeing barkhides fell, impaled by black shards. The creature wailed and reeled back, its arm obliterated. It stumbled into the mountainside and cracked the slope. Orange lava seeped out.

Zel released Lee and pushed him. "Run!"

The barkhides holding their weapons had dropped them in their flight.

Zel grabbed her crossbow and its strap of bolts, while Lee swept up a triple sheath of sikaria.

A change in the air, like the change that goes before an ocean wave, warned Lee of what was coming. He saw a big rock to their left and pulled Zel behind it. The giant's other fist slammed down, and bits of obsidian flew over them.

"You can't run, Brother! There's nowhere to hide!"

The giant's fist slammed down again, and the rock split. Zel pulled back and shot a bolt into one of its five red eyes. Lee, seeing his chance, grabbed the creature's arm and let it carry him upward as it reached to claw at the wound.

Master, he heard the giant say under its inner rumblings. *Command me.*

"Not this time," Lee said and heaved with both arms to launch himself at the creature's head. He jammed a sikari deep into its center eye, then pushed away and rolled across the rocky ground.

Wailing with a voice to shake the canyon, the giant fell back into its companion, and both crashed into the cracked slope. Their impact set the lava free.

A fountain of burning orange burst forth, heading straight for Shan's sorceress companion. Shan flew as if to aid her. "Maldora!"

What Lee saw in her eyes when she looked at his brother was neither gratefulness for the warning nor fear of the lava. He saw only ill intent. The Scarlet Moon sorceress thrust her forearms together, and the giants at her command closed before her as a shield.

The stream of lava deflected off them and slammed full force into Shan, carrying him into the tar lake.

"Shan! No!"

Zel wrapped her arms around Lee, keeping him from running to the shore. "There's nothing you can do!"

His brother burned from within his black armor, jaw open wide in a silent plea. The fire engulfed him, and he sank beneath the tar, leaving behind a small red flame.

The dragons—in their dual voice—laughed and launched themselves into their previous circling path.

Where the red fire burned, curling smoke rose, split by purple lightning. The hole spread slowly, the size of a wagon wheel and growing. The portal. The gate to Keledev was opened.

How? Lee wondered. With his grief, came the answer. Shan, his brother, was also born in Keledev. Maldora had made him the sacrifice to complete the dragon's wicked incantation.

The sorceress floated their way, followed by her giants. Aladoth soldiers and barkhides ran along the shore. Lee pulled off his spectacles to wipe away his tears. "We have to go, Zel," he said in a choked voice, reaching for her. But he found her ripping her own sleeve. "What are you doing?"

"Hang on!" She tore away a long strip of her sleeve ending in her stormrider emblem and tied something within it. Then she tied the whole thing to a bolt on her crossbow and offered the weapon to Lee. "Shoot this into the portal. You have the better aim."

"What? Why?"

"Just do it."

He donned his spectacles again and took the crossbow, feeling the sorceress and her giants coming. Dropping to a knee, Lee blinked another tear away and let the bolt fly. It arced toward the boiling smoke and dropped through.

76

THE SMALL CIRCLE OF BLACK GREW NEAR THE CENTER of the arch.

"The portal's changing," Teegan said. "Something's coming."

Boreas acknowledged her with a nod and blasted his airship's horn, bidding his pilots to form a stacked broadside line with harpoons ready.

She watched him bark orders at their own harpooner, telling him to watch his aim, and frowned. "You can't shoot their ships. They'll sink. Few Aladoth know how to swim."

"That is not my problem."

"They'll drown!"

"What would you have me do, Cadet? Let them reach our shores? Draw your trident. I expect a dragon to come with them, or should we spare its life as well?"

She couldn't let him send so many Aladoth to watery deaths. These were the very people she had sworn to rescue. Her lips parted, about to make that argument, when an object sailed through the spreading black smoke. Small. Almost imperceptible from the airship's height. She might have thought it nothing, except sparks and fire shot up from the water where it landed.

Without asking, Teegan pulled the spyglass from the councilor's cloak and set her eye upon the spot before the sparks ceased. She drew in a breath. "Councilor Boreas. You need to see this."

She held the glass steady while Boreas, after giving her a dark look for taking it in the first place, pressed his eye to the end. "It can't be," he said, taking hold of the glass.

"Do you know that emblem, sir?"

"I do. And only one person in all Talania wears it. My daughter, Zelacia."

77

THE SMOKE WITHIN THE TAR LAKE HAD SPREAD, NOW much larger than a village fishpond and growing. A part of Lee wished Shan might suddenly reappear within it, gasping. But he knew this to be a false hope. He'd seen his brother burn. Shan had loved the desires of the Dragon Lands too much, and it had cost him his soul.

Fighting his grief, he ran with Zel upslope toward the teardrop canyon's northwestern rim. Maldora leaned into her flight and cast balls of red flame at their heels. The giants at her flanks hurled spears of obsidian that shattered around them and sparked against their Keledan armor.

A trail in the rim slope offered hope—a retreat with many large rocks for cover. The sudden turns as they ran up its crooked path spoiled the aim of the giants.

"There is no escape!" Maldora shouted at their backs.

Cued by her call, Lee turned in time to raise his shield against a pair of fireballs.

"End this indignity," she yelled. "Let me send you to your brother!"

The canyon rim seemed so close. If they could reach it and cross over, they might find a hiding place on the other side or a way to return to *The Merlin*. But even now, Lee could see the final climb was too sheer and steep.

They were trapped.

The giants closed at their backs. Orcs from the Aladoth camp drew near from the west.

Down on the tar lake, Aladoth ran across the docks to board the ships. In a short while the portal would send them all into Keledev.

Lee and Zel jumped into a shallow cave in the sheer rim—deep enough the giants might not reach them. Zel pressed her back against the rear wall beside him. "I'm sorry, Lee. Sorry about your brother. Sorry it's come to this."

"Don't be. I grieve for Shan, but you and I have fought and endured as good soldiers. The victory belongs to the Rescuer."

"Truth," Zel said amid a nervous laugh. "But this is still going to hurt."

Both crouched down, shields raised together in a final effort to deflect the coming blows. Zel returned the strength to her voice. "The Rescuer is with us!"

Lee answered as he'd been taught and as he believed. "Always and forever!"

Grinning with deadly malice, Maldora appeared at the mouth of their shallow cave, flanked by her giants. She raised a hand high, and the red flames within it became a spear.

A clap of thunder turned her head.

Lightning sprang up from the tar lake to strike the sky. The air in the canyon coalesced into a ring of deep blue storm clouds, flashing from within. Maldora rushed away with her giants in tow, and Lee and Zel came to the cave mouth to look.

Out of the storm, straight across the lake from them, sailed a vessel with black-and-gold silks.

Zel let out a jubilant shout. "My father's ship!"

A horn blew, resonating in the canyon, and from within the ring of blue clouds flew a fleet of airships.

Seeing the sorceress distracted, Lee grabbed Zel's crossbow and loosed a bolt. It took Maldora in the shoulder, and she screamed.

The giants turned to glare at Lee, but harpoons rained down from above. The creatures jerked with the impacts and clawed at their backs, bodies breaking into shards.

The voice of Zayn Boreas rang out from above. "To the north! See to the dragons. Bring them down!"

Near half the ships followed at his command. The others descended over the Aladoth army on both sides of the lake, hemming them in. Harpoons broke through the ships' timber hulls, and several listed. Aladoth fled down the docks.

The portal slowed its growth. The dragons ceased their circling and dove to meet the attacking ships. Harpoons flew across the hazy sky. Fire answered. Two of the airships caught flame and fell.

To Lee's shock, their crewmen dove over the rails, as if preferring to fall free instead of crashing. Yet, their falling seemed more like gliding. Billowing silk snapped open behind each fighter, and they hit the ground in a run with dual swords drawn. Their ships forgotten, these brave souls charged into a clash with orcs.

Three more such fighters battled the orcs coming after Lee and Zel. The two left their hiding place to lend aid, Zel shooting her bolts and Lee bashing the creatures with his shield, and the orcs in their small skirmish were quickly vanquished.

One of the gliding fighters paused for a breather amid the battle and slapped Lee on the back. "Well done, Lightraider. I see you hardly needed saving."

Lee just stared at the emblem on his arm. "Is that a flying bear?"

High above, three more ships burned. But many that had launched their harpoons held fast to their quarry. Valshadox, lord of Sil Shadath, thrashed and spit flame, tethered by a dozen ropes. Cued by another blast of the councilor's horn, fire shot out from devices on the airships' hulls. With this force, they dragged the dragon down over the center mountain's fire.

"No!" Lee yelled. "Drag him into the portal. Into the portal!"

None stood any chance of hearing. A final harpoon pierced the dragon's chest. The ropes burned free, and the creature fell roaring into the flames.

The explosion that followed shook the whole of creation—so it seemed to Lee—canyon, lake, and sky. Fire and molten rock exploded from the mountainside. A wave of smoke and power ran before it and leveled all in its path. Brimstone metal. The mountain carried it in its veins. Connor had warned them of its dangers when Aaron had passed them the prisoner's pouch.

Lee and Zel and their Airguard companions ducked down behind the sheltering rocks. The barkhides, orcs, and Aladoth soldiers running to fight them were not so fortunate. The wave passed over them, and they lay where they fell, unmoving.

The other dragon, seeing its companion defeated, turned and fled, and the ships did not have the speed to catch it.

When his ears stopped ringing, Lee looked around, and found no enemies to fight. That didn't mean more wouldn't come from the other side of the lake—or nearer. "Where is Maldora?" he asked Zel. "Where are her giants?"

Zel thrust her chin toward a pile of black dust and obsidian shards. "Her creatures became her tomb. She's buried under their remains, and I doubt we'll see her rise again."

As quiet returned, they heard shouts from the far side of the lake.

The barkhides cracked their whips, driving their Aladoth up the docks toward the remaining ships. The Airguard had spent its harpoons, and the Keledan fighters below seemed unwilling to strike at the Aladoth—just as Heleyor had planned.

Orcs and goblins harried them, preventing them from subduing the more dangerous foe.

Though the other dragon had fled, it must have kept its will still fixed upon the portal. The opening continued to spread, crawling toward the last ships. Without some action, fast and sure, hundreds of these tortured fighters would still enter Keledan.

"How do we stop them?" Zel asked, running to a ledge overlooking the lake.

Lee walked up beside her, shaking his head. "I've no idea."

78

IN HIS TRAVELS AS A CADET OF THE LIGHTRAIDER Order, Connor had traversed many portals. He'd grown accustomed to cold descents into the Passage Lakes and the welcoming warmth of a hollow tree, the churning mist and lightning of a stormride, and the squeeze in his ears as he jumped from one corner of the Maker's creation to another.

But this was altogether new.

Billows of blue-and-gold dust rose about the galloping lion, lit by silver sparks from the impact of his paws. Long paths like the one upon which Thasyr ran trailed off like mountain roads into clouds of deep purple ether. Some ended in night sky or green hills. One, near to their path, ended at a wall of red rock and the broken form of a giant.

"Where are we, Thasyr?"

"Within the threads of the Maker's tapestry."

This answered a part but not all of Connor's question. "How, then, are we here?"

"By his grace. These are the paths of the Aropha, and we may run here thanks to the key he allowed you to receive and the bond between our blood he has now renewed."

A snow-white mountainside materialized from the purple

clouds ahead. Thasyr lowered his form and tore into their blue-gold path. "Draw your sword! The Lightbringer's Prayer, do you know it?"

"I do."

"Speak it now, son of faith. Shout it that the world may hear!"

Connor needed no delay to remember the words. The prayer sprung to his mind from the depths of his soul. Long ago called the Lightbringer's Prayer, the Order had taken it as the Lightraider's Prayer, and all cadets knew it. Connor shouted it to the ether and to all the places revealed in its clouds, and he felt the deep reverberations of Thasyr shouting with him. *"Keqez kelel veneronel, po ner hal kelam. Thin zanavelanu deda amord po shalar kelas imbrakov."*

The night is nearly over,
And the day is near.
So let us discard the deeds of darkness
And put on the armor of light!

The blue-gold path became a blur, and the snow-laden mountainside rushed to meet them. Light shone from Connor and the lion—the Rescuer's light shining through them. His armor became as solid as white steel, as did Thasyr's, ornamented with gold flourishes.

The mountainside passed around them and became the tunnel Lee and Zel had described. In the light from the lion and his rider, the enemy's torches lost their color. All seemed gray.

Orcs, goblins, and spiders crumbled before them. Each sweep of Revornosh felled ten or more, aided by the lion's roar. Thasyr lowered his head and smashed through a platoon of iron orcs. He caught the last in his teeth, then spat it out as a boulder tossed against a pair of screeching goblins.

In this, Connor saw the ending of their charge. Thasyr's speed waned. They fought on, but the lion ceased his direct attack and bounded off shelves and outcroppings in the tunnel's rough walls.

Connor slashed at the orcs until a spider came at them from

the roof, as large as the one he'd fought in the healer's home. He stabbed Revornosh through its eyes and nearly lost his seat, falling back against the lion's hips to shed the creature from his blade. Without his right foot, he should not have had the strength to hold on, yet he did. He didn't have time to wonder why.

As Connor sat up again, Thasyr slowed and circled at a wide station with stockpiles of tools and crates where the tunnel began a sharp descent. Together they cleared a space to stand among their enemies. "What became of our speed?" Connor asked, parrying an orc's halberd. He removed the creature's head. "Why are we stopping?"

"The Maker's ether was to us as a bowstring is to an arrow." Thasyr bit into a goblin and cast its limp body aside. "The arrow's flight is spent. It carried us far, but we must fight on. You must dismount."

How could he dismount? Connor grit his teeth and thrust Revornosh into the last orc in sight. He lowered the blade and took a breath. "I can't stand, Thasyr."

"You can, and you will." The lion shook, breaking Connor's grasp of his mane, then dipped his flank.

Connor slid free. His instinct to catch his own fall took over, and he planted both boots on the rocky floor.

Both boots.

He stared down at his armor, still as solid as it had been in the ether. Two boots of silver-white steel. He laughed.

The lion chuckled at his joy. "Walk in faith, young Leander. *Fight* in faith."

Thasyr raised his muzzle toward a mine cart. "That is your new steed. I'll give you a push and then act as your rear guard."

"You're not coming with—" Connor caught himself and nodded, climbing into the cart. "I see. I must do this alone."

This earned him a half snarl, showing one of Thasyr's fangs. "Did you learn nothing from your failure at Ras Pyras? Never face a dragon alone. I'm not going with you now because lions don't fit in mine carts."

The coarse bellowing of orcs and shrieking of goblins came to them from the tunnel behind. Thasyr growled, bending his head to the cart, and gave it a mighty heave. In the next moment, the wheels found the edge of the steep descent, and the downhill run took over. The lion's roaring voice called after it, "I'll follow as soon as I may!"

Small groups of goblins and orcs sailed by. Connor ignored them. By the time one called to the next, he'd already flown past. One unfortunate frost goblin stood on the tracks, yellow eyes going wide at the approaching spectacle—a knight in blazing silver-white armor riding a speeding mine cart. Lichen flesh and brittleknit bone did nothing to slow Connor down. The creature offered little more than a jolt and a sickening *crunch*.

Too few, Connor said to himself as the cart's track flattened. *Far too few.* The low number of dark creatures in the tunnel meant most had marched through into Keledev.

Ahead, the walls made a stark change from dark gray to glittering white, and the tunnel opened into a great chamber. In this mouth, lay a huge black hexagonal crate with the lid thrown aside. The leathery egg inside was burned down the middle. Heleyor's new dragon had hatched, but how long ago?

Connor heard cries and shouting voices. One, he knew for certain. He leapt from the slowing cart and ran. "Kara!"

79

SPRINTING INTO THE WHITE CHAMBER, CONNOR found a battle raging.

The dragon he'd seen in his vision towered over the fight, spitting black fire with abandon, though it melted the monster's own goblins. This was no fledgling, but looked to Connor like the largest full-grown wyrm, neck bent where its edged pyranium spines scraped the chamber ceiling.

Master Jairun held fast against the dragon's flames under a silver-blue shield, raising a bladed war staff with a mace head and crying out declarations from the Scrolls. Each one seemed to hit the monster like a blow.

Tiran, Baldomar, and Pedrig fought at his flanks, with more cadets behind, mired by frost goblins and north trolls. A cluster of orcs with goblin supporters pressed Kara, Ioanu, and Dag against the wall to Connor's right. He ran to their aid, swinging his crook and Revornosh.

He buried his blade in an orc's neck from behind, and when the creature fell, a pyranium scimitar followed it, swinging for Connor's face. He raised his shield, but the scimitar stopped short.

"Connor?" Kara lowered the weapon, then turned it to skewer a goblin. "Vorax said you were dead!"

"Dragons lie."

They had no space for other pleasantries. Though harried, the lightraiders with Master Jairun had pressed the battle full into the chamber. Not one inch of the floor could be seen—only goblins, orcs, and trolls. Smoke hovered at the roof, alive like a nest of serpents. One of these surging tendrils snaked down to coil about a cadet. Eyes locked on Vorax, she dropped her weapons. The goblins moved in.

Their numbers were failing.

Thasyr, Connor thought, hoping the lion would hear. *Where are you?*

On my way, son of faith. Don't give up. Victory belongs to the Rescuer. He supplied all you need.

Lef Amunrel. But the last celestium weapon was meant for Heleyor.

The eyes of Vorax fell upon him. Connor avoided the dragon's crippling gaze, knowing its danger from his last encounter with Vorax. But he couldn't avoid its voice.

"You cannot kill me, boy, as you could not kill my master. You are the child of the traitor-kings. As your forebearers sold their people, so will you sell yours. It is in your blood. Kneel now. Accept who you are and beg my mercy."

The orcs harrying Ioanu and Kara turned and pressed toward Connor. He fended one off with his crook. Was Vorax right? Was the Leander bloodline cursed and unable to wield celestium? Was that why he'd lost at Ras Pyras?

Dragons lie.

Connor's own words hit him. In his training he'd learned to fight back with truth.

He punched the pressing orc in its exposed chin with his glowing white steel glove. "I'm free of the Leander sins, Vorax! And I'm free of mine. *Id pacholothanu sovehanu, hal Ond amunav po yelav yi'anu pacholothenu sololah po men koth seyelolat anu nakah.*"

If we confess our sins, he is faithful to forgive.

Vorax let out an angry cry and blasted fire. Connor and Kara bashed orcs away and knelt to raise their shields against it. The creatures howled and screamed. Connor winced and groaned against the heat, and when they stood again, he stumbled into Kara.

"What's wrong?"

Glancing down, he saw his armored boots still holding. He shook his head, bearing up against the pain in his leg. "I'm all right. Keep fighting!"

His battle with Vorax made room for the other lightraiders to advance. Tiran cut through a trio of goblins like a harvester through wheat. Master Jairun and Baldomar smashed a north troll and shortened the distance between them and Connor's group. "Lef Amunrel!" the headmaster shouted, eyes on Connor's belt. "Wield the dagger!"

Vorax swatted one of his own goblins through the tunnel mouth beside the egg. "The old man wants to save himself. Will you die for him? An escape lies open, boy. Take your love and your weapon and run. Live to fight again."

Kara fought close at his shoulder, defended on her other flank by Dag and Ioanu. "Don't listen," she said. "We can do this. All of us together."

Kara struck at the orcs bearing down on him with her scimitar, and Connor did as Master Jairun commanded. He drew Lef Amunrel.

The orcs staggered back, shielding their eyes against the light of the blade's celestium stars.

"We are faithful together!" Connor shouted at the dragon. "Just as the Rescuer is faithful! *Men soqafel do ga'ol pal sehnol, dar bi tevremat kuran kashah someh precor ka'ov!*" He drove his shout into the monster's lie as if it were a blade, sinking it all the way to the hilt, with all the understanding of the passage of the Scrolls surrounding it.

Do nothing out of selfish ambition, but consider others more important.

Just as the Rescuer never exploited his divinity, but gave himself to the point of death.

"I am a faithful friend, as he is a faithful friend!"

Again, the dragon cried out, and this time, his answering fire broke upon the light from the dagger. As the fire ceased, something fluttered within the shelter of this light—frost-blue wings and fur as fine as feathers. The creature landed at their feet, a match to the Aropha sculptures of ancient lashoroth Connor had seen in the Fading Mountains.

"Dash!" Kara said, kneeling close as if she knew the creature well. "You came back!"

The paradragon bowed low and covered its head with its wings. Kara glanced up at Connor. "Down!"

A watchmen horn blew in the tunnel behind the lightraiders. The creature had brought reinforcements.

Connor and the others knelt with Kara as arrows flew overhead. Many goblins fell. Orcs howled in offense. The lightraiders advanced, with Connor and the dagger at their head.

"Wait for your moment!" Master Jairun called, driving his bladed staff through two goblins at once. "Strike when the dragon is weakest!"

More arrows passed over them, not flying at the dark creatures but at Vorax himself. Some plinked harmlessly off the dragon's broad scarlet scales, but those that passed through the light from the dagger sank deep.

Vorax screamed. "Faithless, I name you! Will you squander the last hope of your people? Vanquish me to save your skin, and you'll never defeat Heleyor!"

The last hope of his people. How long had the Keledan hoarded the last remnant of their celestium? What had their fear of losing it cost? If Zel was right, the Huckleheim miners had caused this breach in their relentless search for more.

Dag's twin axes sparked off pyranium armor well to Connor's left. "Don't listen! The Assembly and my forefathers put their hope in the Maker's gift instead of in the Maker himself!"

Faithless the Keledan had been in hoarding the Rescuer's provision, in failing to use his gift. Connor lifted his voice to Elamhavar. "Is this what you want? Is this my time?"

Trust me now. Use what I've given you. See what happens next.

With the answer came a verse from the Scrolls. Connor shouted it at the dragon. "*Sho'ema'ovu Premornesh ge'avond gelalim tresolothod onormath fi ke'Rumosh.*"

He will provide all your needs according to his riches in glory in his son.

"Whatever he has in store"—Kara kicked a frost goblin away and slashed at an iceblade with her scimitar—"whether death or peace, or the ending of this world, we're with you, and the Rescuer is with us all!"

"I trust him!" Connor shouted, not to her but at the dragon, as if the words were a spear. "My hope is in the Rescuer alone!"

Vorax convulsed and cried out. Black flames leaked from the dragon's wounds, welling up inside its body. Lashoroth wheeled about the dragon's head on gleaming blue, white, and gold wings and spat streams of frost mixed with gray ether.

Pedrig and Ioanu leapt against the monster. The wolf, forest-green armor as solid as Connor's, latched on to its wing. The bear, in blue armor, dug her teeth and claws into its leg.

Thasyr galloped in from the mine cart tunnel, silver-white armor gleaming with its gold flourishes, and bounded off the side of the chamber to tear into the dragon's neck. His voice came to Connor's mind. *Now, son of faith. Use the Rescuer's gift.*

All others who'd spent the celestium had died in its use. If that was the Rescuer's will for Connor, so be it.

Connor set his jaw and charged, struck an orc down with his crook, and hurled Lef Amunrel at their enemy.

The dagger sank into the dragon's chest until nothing but the ruby starlot in its hilt showed, a match to the surrounding scales.

Vorax shook, red eyes glowing. Within the reptile flesh,

a ghostly form took shape—akin to a Lisropha but with broken wings and twisted limbs bound by the white-and-gray frost of the lashoroth. The face, in agony, bore the gargoyle likeness of the orcs.

Pedrig, Ioanu, and Thasyr released the monster and retreated. The lion roared, "Get back!"

Before the Havarra reached the paradragons and lightraiders, the dragon became a flash of blinding pink. A wind stronger than the wind he'd faced in Ras Pyras rushed over Connor, knocking him and his friends to the floor.

An instant later, the wind and the flash were gone. Connor's ears rang. Darkness had closed utterly around him.

"Kara?"

"I'm here."

He heard steel on flint, and three lanterns glowed to life. Master Jairun, Baldomar, and Tiran held their lights high.

Vorax had vanished. So had his dark creatures, both living and dead. None but the Keledan, the Havarra, and the fluttering lashoroth remained.

Baldomar held his lantern close to the wall. "Look what he's done." The tunnel leading into Tanelethar was closed, filled with the glistening white core of the mountains. The rest of the chamber walls and ceiling seemed like a midnight sky full of twinkling stars. Baldomar laughed. "Celestium. Look at all the Rescuer has provided."

Kara struck her own lantern and immediately gasped in horror. She clapped a hand to her mouth. Tears sprang to her eyes. "Connor! Your leg!"

He sat up and stilled her fright with a calming hand. "I know. It's all right." Thasyr bent near him, and with the lion and Kara's help, he stood. "I'm alive. What more can I be than grateful and content? Whatever the Rescuer has in store, I'll walk in faith."

80

THE AIRGUARD FLEET CLOSED OVER THE ALADOTH army. "We can't kill them," Teegan said to Boreas. "That's not our calling."

"Then tell me how to close this portal."

With a great and thunderous *clap*, lightning shot up from the black smoke circle to touch the sky. A ring of matching light spread across the tar lake, and in its wake, it left black rock, as smooth as polished granite.

The ships cracked, split by this rock where their hulls met the surface. The wooden docks broke and collapsed. Aladoth fled to the shore.

In the place the lightning struck, a tree sprang up, made of the same black stone. Jeweled orange and yellow leaves sprouted from its spreading branches. A hollow opened in its broad trunk, and from within, Teegan saw a warm and welcoming light.

"What does it mean?" Boreas asked.

Teegan smiled. "I'd say it means we won."

Below their ship, the windfighters killed the last of the orcs and goblins while many of the Aladoth and barkhides fled into the mountains. Many more Aladoth stayed and dropped to their knees. Hundreds lifted their heads and fixed their eyes on the flagship.

Teegan inched away from the councilor, whispering, "This is what you were meant for. This is why he gave you your voice."

Boreas nodded, drew a breath, and began. Verse by verse, meaning by meaning, he shared with them the Great Rescue.

Even after the power they'd witnessed, some refused to believe, and they wandered away grumbling and arguing among themselves. But many did believe and cried out for forgiveness to the Rescuer, and the windfighters guided them to the new hollow tree at the center of the black lake.

EPILOGUE

MASTER JAIRUN STOOD AT THE FOURTH-LEVEL ramparts, with Connor and his class behind him and the waterfalls of the chapel Nevethav flowing above. "What an auspicious and hope-filled day this is—the first graduation day at Lightraider Academy after the Order's long dormancy."

Connor squirmed a bit, trying not to show it. They'd been standing up there a while, and he still hadn't grown used to the talanium foot Baldomar and Belen had fashioned for him. Lee gave him weekly treatments of balm, but the stump still itched.

Stop fidgeting, Faith Walker, he heard in his mind and glanced at Thasyr, who stood at his side. The lion lifted his nose—a motion for Connor to keep his eyes forward.

Thasyr was not the only one to call him Faith Walker. Lef Amunrel was gone. To the one who'd spent it, standing on faith alone, many in Keledev had given its name.

Among the crowd watching from the third-level ramparts were several more of Lee's and Master Jairun's patients who'd also lost limbs, all wearing Baldomar and Belen's inventions where a hand, arm, foot, or leg had been. Some were watchmen. Most were cadets— two of whom had fallen under the goblin flood in the breach tunnel and yet survived. Not all who'd fallen to that flood had fared so well.

Much had passed since the Rescuer had closed the breach under his mountains. With the consent of Connor's class, the headmaster had delayed their graduation until the first day of summer, thus giving Keledev time to mourn the fallen and celebrate their passing to Elamhavar.

They also celebrated the coming of hundreds of new Keledan. These had sprung like fields of morning glories all at once from the Passage Lakes, much to the fright—and then joy—of the cadets manning the fireglass tower there. Only by the word of the escorting windfighters did they know that the battle was won and these newcomers were not invaders.

On both sides of the cadet class stood the guardians. This also was a reason for the delay. Master Quinton needed many weeks to heal before he could stand again. He'd taken an iceblade's lance to the chest, almost as Connor saw in the dragon's vision, but not quite. The lance had struck nearer to the swordmaster's shoulder than his heart. His arm still hung in a sling wrapped about his middle. But Master Jairun and Lee both said he'd regain full use one day—just not any day soon. For Connor and his friends, it was enough that their beloved swordmaster could stand with them that day.

Dag stood nearest to Quinton, as a member of his sphere and the apprentice who would ease the burden of the swordmaster's work. According to Master Jairun, Dag's dedication to new recruits had shown his true calling.

Dag's family had ridden up from Huckleheim. They watched from the level below with Baldomar's relatives. In the ticks before the ceremony, Connor had heard them grumbling about the celestium. The Rescuer had restored this incredible ore to the Celestial Peaks, and the miners had found dozens of veins. But the Assembly forbade them from digging it up.

Many councilors, Stradok included, laid the fault for the breach on the Huckleheim miners' shoulders, forgetting that it was the Assembly who'd hoarded the last weapon and sent them looking for more celestium ore in the first place. After all they'd suffered—after years of battle inside Keledev brought on by their refusal to trust in the Rescuer's provision—the Assembly was still the Assembly. The celestium remained locked in the mountains, waiting on endless debates.

Would they never learn?

Connor hoped he had learned. One lesson was given to him by Master Jairun in the moments after Vorax was destroyed. The headmaster had looked down on his wounded leg with great pity and known without asking what Connor had tried to do.

Speaking before the academy and the families of the guardians and cadets, Master Jairun repeated that lesson now. "If these hard years have taught us anything, I hope it has reinforced our faithfulness to the Rescuer's commission. We know our mission without question, and that mission is not to storm Heleyor's gates. Let the Rescuer himself choose the timing of the Great Red Dragon's destruction."

Connor was grateful the guardian didn't fix him with a stare as he said this.

"Let us instead storm the Dragon Lands," Master Jairun said, "and rescue the lost. Again, the Rescuer showed us this path. By his grace, in the final battle at Brimstone Heights, he turned the tragedy of the breach into the victory of hundreds saved."

As if in answer, Connor heard a sharp bark from among the onlookers. Koteg stood with his muzzle held high at Sireth Yar's side. His mistress remained in Tanelethar, unable to leave her post for long without raising suspicion. But, with Teegan's help, Thera had trained Koteg as a go-between to carry messages. Thera's risk brought them vital news from the important city of Emen Yan, such as the rumors drifting among the Fulcor nobles that a new stronghold was being built near the center of Val Glasa—an isolated crag of rock and ice governed by a bitter dragon lord oozing slime from its scales.

A smile crossed Connor's lips, and he resisted the urge to

glance at Pedrig, standing a pace behind the headmaster. The wolf's own work bringing messages across the barrier seemed so long ago. Yet, the sight of it had served as a quickening at the start of Connor's lightraider journey.

Master Jairun turned halfway and stepped back beside Pedrig to gesture with his wooden staff at the cadet scouts. "These six, the first class of the restored Lightraider Academy, played more than an integral part in that victory at Brimstone Heights." He laid his staff across his arm and clapped his hands.

As their families applauded, Connor stole a glance down the row at his friends.

Kara's blue-gray flourishes brightened, on full display with no coverings at her hands and her hair tied back. Ioanu's bearish lips seemed to smile beside her.

Tiran and Teegan, with Aethia on her arm, remained stolid, acting as good soldiers should. Lee tried to do the same, but he puffed his chest, much like he had on the day he and Connor had first met.

A tear rolled down Dag's cheek. He sniffed.

The applause settled, and Master Jairun raised his staff, addressing the cadets. "You have one last task in your studies. A recitation. Speak it together, and for once, I'll let you speak it in the Common Tongue. Say for me and for these gathered here the Lightraider's Prayer."

With smiles, the cadets joined their voices together. The guardians and Ioanu, Pedrig, and Thasyr spoke it with them.

"The night is nearly over, and the day is near. So let us discard the deeds of darkness and put on the armor of light!"

A gift of light from the Rescuer shone over them, falling from the chapel Nevethav's many-colored windows. The itch in Connor's stump left him, and glancing down, he saw a silver-white boot. Every cadet's armor glowed, as sure and solid as the armor in the painting of Connor's patehpa over his tehpa's hearth in Stonyvale—Connor in silver white, Kara in indigo,

Teegan and Tiran in sea green, Lee in red, and Dag in bronze. Pedrig's, Ioanu's, and Thasyr's armor glowed to life as well. All were decorated with gold and silver scrollwork, remembrances of their battles and rescues.

Master Jairun tamped his staff loudly on the stones, unable to quell the onlookers' cheers. He shouted over their praise, "Well done, all. You are now scout reliants, the first rank in the Order. Congratulations on your graduation from Lightraider Academy!"

END

NAMES

INDIVIDUALS AND FAMILIES

Advor (ĂD-vohr)
Advoran (ĂD-vohr-ən)
Aethia (Ā-thē-ə)
Arkelon (AHRK-ĕ-lahn)
Arkelian (ahr-KĔ-lē-ən)
Baldomar (BAHL-dō-mahr)
Belen (BĀ-lĕn)
Berothan (BEH-rŏth-ən)
Berothor (BEH-rŏth-ohr)
Bordu (BOHR-dū)
Boreas (BOHR-ē-əs)
Cresian (CREH-sē-ən)
Creson (CREH-sahn)
Enarian (En-ĀR-ē-ən)
Fulcor (FULL-kohr)
Fulcan (FULL-kən)
Ilmari (Il-MAHR-ē)
Ingaru (Ēn-GAHR-ū)
Ioanu (Eye-Ō-ə-nū)
Jairun (JEYE-rūn)
Kaivos (KEYE-vahs)
Keir (KEYR)
Leander (Lē-AN-dĕr)
Orso (OHR-sō)
Quinton (KWIN-tən)
Ralian (RĂ-lē-ən)
Ralon (RĂ-lahn)
Rumosh (RŪ-mŏsh) [Exalted One]
Samar (Sə-MAHR)

Silvana (Sil-VAH-nə)
Suvan (SŪ-vən)
Suvor (SŪ-vohr)
Tarlan (TAHR-lən)
Tarlor (TAHR-lohr)
Teegan (TĒ-gən)
Tiran (TĒ-rən)
Yar (Yahr)
Zayan (ZEYE-yən)
Zayor (ZEYE-yohr)

LOCATIONS

KELEDEV (KĔ-LĔ-DĔV)

The Anamturas (Ăn-əm-TOOR-əs) – The primary river of Keledev, meaning the Soul's Journey. It descends from the Celestial Peaks and empties into Val Ratavel at Sky Harbor.

The Celestial Peaks – A barrier formed by a massive mountain range. Three days after a horde of dragons spent all their fire to vanquish him, the Rescuer returned, raising these impossibly high peaks. Together with the Storm Mists, the Celestial Peaks protect the peninsula of Keledev, the Liberated Land, so that the Rescuer's followers will never be subject to the dragon's wrath again.

The Central Plain – South of the Dayspring Highlands and the five vales. North of the White Ridge Mountains. These are the main grasslands and the agricultural center of Keledev. Much to the frustration of the Sky Harbor Cartographers' Guild, the towns on the northern fringe prefer to divide the region further into the Central Plain and the Northern Plains. Maps from these towns often make no mention of the Central Plain.

The Clefts of Semajin – A network of clefts northeast of the academy. The colossal main fissure of these clefts on the upper slopes of the Celestial Peaks looks narrow because of its great height, but its base is far wider than the whole of Lightraider Academy. The interior shadow of this fissure hides a network of smaller clefts and caves. It is in the highest of these caves, in windswept caverns open to the interior of the clefts, that pale blue snowflowers grow—a powerful medicinal gift from the Rescuer. Some say that ancient ice-breathing *lashoroth* (paradragons) guard these flowers.

Dayspring Highlands – High terrain meeting the foothills at the southern base of the Celestial Peaks. The highlands descend to the south into the rolling hills and dells on the northern border of the Central Plain. Dayspring Forest covers much of the Dayspring Highlands with pines, chestnuts, oaks, and elms.

The Eastern Hills - Stepped hills covered in grain fields at the southeast extent of the Central Plain.

"The five vales" - A colloquial term for the valley towns in the southern portion of the Dayspring Highlands. Spread among the grassy hills at the northern edge of what some call the Northern Plains, the five vales are shepherding and farming villages. Pleasanton, in Pleasant Vale, is the most populous town in the vales and the region's center of trade, but it is by no means the largest in terms of land.

The Gathering - A small river whose source is the hot spring within the chapel Nevethav at Lightraider Academy. It joins the Anamturas north of Ravencrest.

The Gulf of Stars - A gulf on the western edge of Keledev, separating the Keledan coast from the Westlings. The Storm Mists hang in this gulf as a barrier between Keledev and Tanelethar.

The Gulf of Vows - A gulf on the west side of Keledev, separating the Keledan coast from the Desert of Sin and the Eastlings in Tanelethar. The Storm Mists hang in this gulf as a barrier.

Lin Kelan (Lin KĔ-lən) - A coastal town on the northwest coast of Keledev. Resting at the mouth of the Ruames River, Lin Kelan is the primary coastal Keledan town on the Gulf of Stars. The fishing folk of Lin Kelan are known to rub red paste in their hair to keep the water from soaking their heads when swimming or diving in their daily work. In the Elder Tongue, Lin Kelan means Candle Sound. The town draws its name from sea candles—saltwater plants that shine with their own light. The Gulf of Stars is filled with huge sea candles, but the smaller plants dotting the protected sound of Lin Kelan glow brighter.

The Many Blessings - An island chain extending from the eastern corner of Keledev, joined to the mainland by the bridge town of New Dawn. The warm southern waters are rich with fish and diver's folly. The Many Blessings supply much of the fruit sold in Keledev's markets.

Orvyn's Vow (OHR-vin) – The easternmost outpost in Keledev's northern foothills. Orvyn's Vow and its fjord towers guard the eastern slopes of the Celestial Peaks where the mountain runoff enters the Gulf of Vows. The outpost is a series of structures on the fjords joined by wood, stone, steel, and talanium roads, bridges, lifts, and ferries—Orvyn's Vow is by far the largest of the highland outposts.

Pellion's Flow – Broad "rivers" of solid ice broken by small ridges and rock islands on the upper slopes of the Celestial Peaks. The flow sits well north of the academy, but not so far north as the Clefts of Semajin.

Ras Telesar (Rahss Tĕl-ĕ-SAHR) – The former Aropha worship and administration center that is now the jumbled fortress of Lightraider Academy. The Hill of the Fountain. This ancient structure was much transformed by the rising of the Celestial Peaks. Once it was a hilltop temple with four concentric walls, many towers, and a fountain chapel as its central jewel. During the rising of the peaks, those walls and towers shifted and jumbled to become the stepped, labyrinthian ramparts and passages of Lightraider Academy. Only the Rescuer could have taken them apart and put them back together again in this way as a new creation with new purpose. The original fountain chapel Nevethav still stands on an outcropping that forms the fifth level of the academy fortress.

Ravencrest – The second outpost from the east in Keledev's northern foothills. Here, the Black Feather inn bridges a waterfall that pours down into Dayspring Forest. Thanks to its position as the closest outpost to Ras Telesar, Ravencrest serves as an important link between the academy and the rest of Keledev.

Rosland Cape – A small peninsula at the southwesternmost extent of Keledev, ending in cliffs that overlook the sea. It is partially forested with willows and magnolia.

The Second Hall of the Assembly – The seat of government in Keledev's capital of Sky Harbor. This circular building with its great blue dome and high stained glass windows graces Sky Harbor's waterfront plaza. It is interesting to note that the first government hall built in the early days of Keledev, much smaller and made of timber and wattle, was also called the Second Hall.

Sil Tymest (Sil TEYE-měst) – Also called Cloud Forest. Northeast of Rosland Cape, this is a wetland forest of large willows, beech, and magnolia where white mists hang in the tree branches. Tymesthav, the largest town, is mostly composed of treehouses.

Sky Harbor – The capital of Keledev, named for the natural harbor where it rests. The Keledan built Sky Harbor at the mouth of the Anamturas where the river empties into Val Ratavel, the Sea of Goodness. The tranquil but busy harbor is sheltered by Crescent Ridge, which extends into the sea from the White Ridge Mountains.

Skynest – An Airguard community built around the first cloudloft, situated on Crescent Ridge. What was once an empty ridge has become a small town of its own surrounding the Airguard's main launching platform and command lodge.

The Southern Hills – Low, sparsely forested hills descending from Rosland Cape to the Central Plain.

Stonyvale – One of the five vales. Stonyvale is a small shepherding town of the same name on the southern edge of Dayspring Forest between Pleasanton and Harbor Joy.

Thousand Falls – The westernmost outpost in Keledev's northern foothills. Perched on the sheer western cliffs of the Celestial Peaks, Thousand Falls houses its company of watchmen in long timber barracks. These are joined by wooden walkways with a central platform overlooking the Gulf of Stars. New recruits often think the outpost's name comes from the many cliff waterfalls visible from the platform, all pouring into the wind to feed the Storm Mists. They are wrong.

The Vales of the Passage Lakes - Long mountain valleys of portal lakes. There are seven Passage Lakes in all, divided between the Eastern Vale and the Western Vale. These are the primary means by which the Rescuer chooses to send his lightraiders on missions through the barrier and into Tanelethar. The Vales of the Passage Lakes should not be confused with the five vales.

Val Pera (Văl PEHR-ah) - The largest farming town in Keledev. Val Pera means Sea of Bread, an apt name for this sprawling farming town positioned on the Anamturas River at the intersection of the Central Plain, the White Ridge Mountains, and the Eastern Hills. The farmers of Val Pera like to claim that without their fields, the Liberated Land would starve.

Val Ratavel (Văl RAHT-ah-věl) - The Sea of Goodness. This is the great sea south of Keledev, shrouded by the southern Storm Mists.

The White Ridge Mountains - Rugged mountains running along much of Keledev's southern coast. The slopes have some ash, beech, and pine, but they are mainly covered in white applethorn scrub. At the eastern edge, they descend into a small plain of cane fields that points southeast toward the Many Blessings.

The Windhold - The second outpost from the west in Keledev's northern foothills. The Windhold outpost houses its watchmen in a series of caves above a crystal-clear lake. The Windhold is a natural water catch that snatches moisture from the wind blowing over the steep domed rim. Air blowing upward across the southern wall carved the honeycomb of caves that became the barracks for the company of watchmen. Most in Windhold Company describe the low tones of the wind blowing through the caves as the Rescuer's own music.

TANELETHAR (TĂ-NĔL-Ĕ-THAHR)

Ander's Rampart – A high, jagged wall of ice that acts as a dam for the southeastern corner of Val Glasa. The rampart is leagues long, and in a constant state of breaking and reforming, yet it never fails. Should that happen, Val Glasa would empty itself upon the northern lands of Talania, and many would perish. This landmark is named for Ander, the first king of House Leander.

Brimstone Heights – Active volcanic mountains north of the Pyrons and the Mirror Peaks. Green pines and blue spruce grow on the lowest slopes on the inland side. To the south and west above Fell Bay, these mountains are mostly black and barren. Miners willing to brave this precarious land with its sudden bursts of scalding, poison air have been known to find orange obsidian, volatile brimstone metal, and diamonds.

Copper Bluffs – Bluffs south of Miner's Glory and Darkling Shade that hold few minerals besides copper. To the west their sheer southern cliffs border the Malvan Wastes. To the east, they descend into Darkling Shade and the Upland Wilds.

Darkling Shade – A narrow forest west of Sil Shadath and the Upland Wilds. Darkling Shade was once part of Sil Shadath but shrank and became separated due to heavy logging in the early days of dragon rule.

The Desert of Sin – This cursed place is named for the famous Zayan Scarlet Moon sorcerer Peshar Sin (Pĕ-SHAHR SĒN). It is a vast expanse of sunbaked desert where sand and rocks form otherworldly shapes. The dragons use the dunes here to incubate dragon and granog eggs.

The Fading Mountains – A mountain range on the east coast of Tanelethar, also known as the Muddled Mountains. This range seems to be constantly fading due to a clinging fog created by the vapors seeping from the Tagamoor.

Fantasia Shieling – A lake region called a "shieling" because it is sheltered from the cold northeastern winds by Storm Heights. Lakes and low green hills dotted with maple, ash, and white pine define this region. The largest central lake (Misty Wood Lake) is big enough to contain four islands of its own.

The Fulcan Plains – Arid plains that were once the southernmost holdings of House Fulcor and still bear the name. Many of the villages here farm wheat and barley or keep orchards of goat-nut shrubs.

The Frost Isles – A series of large islands to the north of the main continent. They hold in the high, half-frozen sea of Val Glasa. The Frost Isles sit a thousand or more feet below the ice continent of Arkelia but still rest well above King's Cradle and the Snake Hills. To the north, they are joined to Arkelia by thick sea ice. The Frost Isles top a highly volcanic region.

Highland Forest – A Taneletharian forest region north of the Celestial Peaks in the province of Berothor, bounded on either side by small mountain ranges known as the Eastlings and the Westlings.

The Ice Adder – A long island far below and a little east of Ander's Rampart. Minerals from the water color its icy shores indigo, giving the appearance of a monstrous iridescent snake to sailors in the Northern Bight.

The Iron Mountains – These mountains, with slopes covered in spruce and lodgepole pines, are the primary source of iron in Tanelethar.

King's Cradle – A deep valley on the northeast extremity of the Talanian continent. High cliffs extend from the northern reaches of Brimstone Heights all along the north rim of King's Cradle to the western edge of Ander's Rampart. Near the north center of the Cradle, mineral-rich waterfalls pour down from Val Glasa into the canyon valley, feeding the headwaters of the Serpentine (the river running south toward Miner's Glory). The volcanic activity beneath the soil heats the river and the land, and the Viper Buttes to the southeast help hold in moist air so that King's Cradle is more temperate and lush than the nearest lands to the south and east.

The Lion's Teeth - Frozen rocks sitting at the base of the steep islands on the eastern extremity of the Frost Isles. A fisherman can make a fortune dragging nets between the Lion's Teeth, but a good many have died trying, with their ships smashed among the rocks.

Miner's Folly - High hills in the northeast of Tanelethar, stretching from the Iron Mountains in the east to the Upland Wilds near the north center of the continent. In the early days, the mines of these hills yielded riches like their sister hills to the west, but those mines soon ran dry. Even today, fortune seekers dig into Miner's Folly, seeking veins of gold and finding only empty caverns.

Miner's Glory - High hills in the northwest of Tanelethar, stretching from the Mirror Peaks in the west to the Upland Wilds in the north center of the continent. The mines in these hills yield copper, talanium, vardallium, and other workable ores, but their primary riches are gold and silver.

The Northern Bight - A broad curve in the land forms this gulf-like feature. Thanks to the cold waters, sailors often call it "Winter's Bight." The sheltering landform creates calmer seas than those found off Storm Heights or Fell Bay, making the coastline here the largest fishing region of Tanelethar.

Ras Pyras (Rahss PEYE-rəss) - The former Aropha worship and administration center that became the seat of Heleyor's power. The Hill of the Flame. This ancient Aropha temple still stands, but it no longer glorifies the Creator. The hill of Ras Pyras is crowned by four concentric black walls supported by many towers. A pillar of fire sprouting from the volcanic underbelly of the northern Frost Isles burns constantly in what was once the central chapel. Heleyor, the Great Red Dragon, made that chapel his throne room.

The Serpentine - A river fed by waterfalls pouring down from Val Glasa and heated by volcanic activity in the ground beneath. Its mineral-rich waters give abundant life to the deep valley of King's Cradle. Past Viper Buttes, the land is more arid and not as lush.

Sil Shadath (Sil SHǍ-dǎth) – A dark forest in eastern Tanelethar. In the Common Tongue, its name means the Black Forest. Sil Shadath is the home of Valshadox, a lesser dragon lord. Ever since the ancient battle between House Suvor and the dragons, its shaggy black pines have held a heavy gray-green mist. Terrible creatures both large and small make their home there, and strange lights wander and flash in the mists. The Aladoth call it the Forest of Horrors.

The Snake Hills – A peninsula of rocky, crimson hills topped with deep green pines. Before the Dragon Scourge, these hills were the center of House Advor's power, where they walked in peace and fellowship with the Aropha.

Storm Heights – The highest and northernmost peaks of the Iron Mountains, sheer on the north and east sides. Sailors leaving the Northern Bight know better than to sail too close to Storm Heights. Those who push too close will be smashed against the cliffs by the strong winds. There are some who say a giant valpaz lives on the southeast side of Storm Heights.

The Tagamoor – A moor canyon in eastern Tanelethar. This canyon moor was the ancient home of House Suvor who were said to fly in battle. Ioanu's clan of Havarra bears still survive there, able to leap great distances on the mists. On the Tagamoor, Ioanu first taught Kara to fly.

Trader's Knoll – A hilltop village in the Highland Forest. Trader's Knoll became the adopted home of Faelin Enarian during his long, self-imposed exile in Tanelethar. We are not yet certain why, but we believe it has something to do with Kara Orso.

The Upland Wilds – To the north and south between Darkling Shade and Sil Shadath are the high Upland Wilds. Taller and larger than the hills of Miner's Glory and Miner's Folly, these hills and ridges hide wolf packs and bears. The shadows between make them hard to traverse without getting lost, except along the passes of the east–west road called Ambition or the north–south West Midland Road. The four-hill mining town Grindstone lies at the intersection of these roads.

Val Glasa – A half-frozen sea sitting high above King's Cradle. Its waters are kept partially melted by the volcanic activity below, and they are held in by the surrounding isles and walls of ice. The longest ice wall, Ander's Rampart, joins the eastern edge of King's Cradle to the larger eastern island.

Viper Buttes – Tall land formations of red stone and dirt rising to the south of King's Cradle. The tops of the buttes include bowl-like depressions, some of which are thought to have once been used as Leander watchtowers. On a clear day, when viewed from the high hills of Miner's Glory, the buttes look like red snakes. This may be the source of their name. Or the source may be something else.

TERMS

Aropha – Also known as the Elder Folk. The Aropha walked Talania before the Dragon Scourge, serving the High One by caring for and protecting his creations and acting as arbiters between the great houses. In those days, no one in Talania starved or thirsted. The peoples of the Aropha are the Rapha servants, the Lisropha warriors and arbiters, and the tiny Dynapha worshipers. Their artistry is visible in the smooth walls of Ras Telesar, the stairways of Sil Elamar, and in the jeweled trees at the southern gate of Vy Asterlas.

The Aropha and the Dragon Scourge – Heleyor, chief among the Lisropha, betrayed the High One and took many followers of his own kind with him, stealing and corrupting the form of the *lashoroth* into monstrous dragons. He took Ras Pyras as his throne—a fiery crown at the northern tip of the continent. Over time, most of the great human houses fell to Heleyor's deceptions, increasing the size of his armies. Although the High One's victory against Heleyor was never in question, a war between Ras Pyras and the remaining Aropha would surely have destroyed Talania. For the sake of humankind, the Aropha withdrew and have not been seen since.

The Assembly – The government of Keledev. Councilors from all over Keledev meet and debate at the Second Hall in Sky Harbor to decide the laws of the land. The Assembly is overseen by members of the Prime Council who prayerfully seek the will of the High One.

Celestium – A black ore as deep as a night sky and filled with points of light like stars. Celestium was only found in veins within the Celestial Peaks, but the mines ran dry. Like shairosite, celestium is an ore that touches our realm and the spiritual realm. It was a gift from the Rescuer, and weapons formed of it were known to utterly destroy a dragon, preventing its fallen Aropha spirit from fleeing to a new egg.

Cloudloft - An airship station much like the watchmen outposts. A cloudloft includes a landing/launching platform for airships, a command lodge, a silkhouse, and other buildings unique to the Airguard's expanding mission. In the safety of Keledev, small towns like Barleynest, Silknest, and Elamnest quickly grew around the cloudlofts so that most are now known by the town name.

Colloquial family terms - Talanians in much of Keledev and Tanelethar use these terms, though not as much in the cities or wealthier households.

- **Behlna** - Daughter
- **Brehna** - Brother
- **Mamehma** - Grandmother
- **Mehma** - Mother
- **Patehpa** - Grandfather
- **Sehna** - Son
- **Shessa** - Sister
- **Tehpa** - Father

Councilor - A member of the Assembly. Councilors serve their cities and villages by representing their hopes and concerns at the seat of government in Sky Harbor.

Dark Creatures - Monsters cobbled together from corrupted natural elements and animated by the dragons. Some dark creatures use "song sorcery," a form of rhythmic music from within their bodies, to charm their victims. Messages unique to the victim are often heard in the undertones. Many dark creatures employ poisons or infections.

- **Apparition/Ghost** - A dragon corruption formed from rot and mist, designed to deceive mankind into believing they are the risen dead.
- **Giant** - A huge dark creature formed using elements from its environment. Sand giants are blocky creatures of sandstone and desert foliage. Forest giants appear as

beings of twisted roots, vines, and clay. Giants may be eight times the height of a man or more and are known to employ song sorcery. Once a giant links itself to a human or group of humans, it demands more and more of them and can be extremely difficult to get rid of. A common jest among lightraiders states that "Giants make terrible houseguests."

- **Goblin** – Goblins come in many forms and sizes. Frost goblins are formed of northern lichen. Cave goblins appear to have flesh formed from cave fungus. Spore goblins are terrifyingly small and toothy and known to inhabit Taneletharian deserts. All goblins are vindictive and delight in torturing humans and animals in many ways.
- **Golmog** – A foul-smelling dark creature a little taller and much heavier than a grown man. Fat and lumbering, golmogs serve the dragons most in manual labor but can be terrible foes in battle.
- **Granog** – A winged dark creature that looks like it shares dragon and human heritage, a littler larger than a grown man. The appearance of granogs is a dragon deception and likely a poor attempt at making creatures that look like the ancient Lisropha warriors. Granogs serve as dragon administrators in Tanelethar.
- **Mudslinger/Muk** – A slimy mud creature found in Taneletharian swamps and wetlands. Muks are known to moan at their victims, luring them into a sense of despair. Spines may grow from their bodies and fling poisonous slime that burns through clothing.
- **Orcs** – "Ore creatures" formed from various minerals. Iron orcs and coal orcs are the most common. Quicksilver orcs are considered the most dangerous, able to shift form at will. The dragons filled their orcs with burning rage, often exhibited by fire blazing behind their eyes, within their joints, and from the runes carved into their hides.

- **Rime Runner** - A long black worm found in ice tunnels where frost goblins live. Rime runners attack in great numbers and attempt to burrow into their victims' flesh.
- **Spider** - Giant arachnids used to terrorize and deceive mankind. They are known to share the influence of the same dragons that control giants. Where giants are found, the caves and burrows are usually infested with spiders.
- **Sprite** - A creature formed to mimic the ancient Dynapha, which many remember today as faeries. They are masters of illusion, hiding their roach-like features and ugly intent. Sprites employ stings that inject their poisons. As with goblins, there are several forms.
- **Troll** - Four forms of troll are currently known in Tanelethar—wood troll (mocktree), water or river troll (rattlefish), stone troll (rumblefoot), and north troll (iceblade). Trolls are known to employ both song sorcery and infections/poisons.
- **Wanderer** - A wan and withering humanlike thing designed, like ghosts, to deceive mankind into believing it is a form of lingering dead. Wanderers carry lanterns and are known to roam Sil Shadath and Gloamwood.
- **Wraith** - Although this term may be used throughout Talania to describe different and often imagined creatures, an actual wraith is a specific form of orc made in the ancient days from Suvoroth ore by the dragon Valshadox. They may be found in Sil Shadath, where they float on the mists flowing from the Tagamoor.

The Five Quests - Cadet missions that serve as the tests required for promotion from cadet stalwart to cadet scout. Most cadets endure these quests as a class, working together like a lightraider raid party. Each of the Five Quests is named for and overseen by one of the five lightraider spheres.

Fjord - A strange word referring to a finger of a sea reaching inland between high, sheer ridges. The cliffs above the fjords of Orvyn's Vow, descending from the Celestial Peaks, are thought to be the highest in all creation, some reaching nearly a league above the water. According to legend, the word fjord is a Fulcan amalgamation of the Elder Tongue phrase *fi v'yort*, meaning to pass through (literally "in then out"). The name implies "a pass," which a fjord is not. Thus, using it at all is likely a mistake.

Havarra - The Havarra are the shepherds of the beasts. They are animals capable of speech, tending to be larger than the creatures they shepherd. The Havarra were nearly wiped out during the Dragon Scourge, and the survivors went into hiding. We are not certain of the number that remain, but talking falcons, bears, wolves, stags, and horses are known to the Lightraider Order. Some choose to become companions to lightraider knights, following them into adventure in the service of the High One.

Lightraider Academy (Ras Telesar) - The seat of the Lightraider Order and the fortress where they live and train, including training new recruits.

Lightraider Order - A knightly order in Keledev, commissioned for service by the Rescuer himself when he appeared to his people after he raised the Celestial Peaks and the Storm Mists.

Lightraider Spheres - The primary divisions of the Lightraider Order. The five spheres include the Navigators' Sphere, the Tinkers' Sphere, the Rangers' Sphere, the Comforters' Sphere, and the Vanguard. Members of each sphere may choose additional specialties such as becoming a knight of his creatures, a renewer, or even a lightraider bard. Some specialties are unique to certain spheres, but not all.

Manykit - A leather harness with many pouches, buckles, and sheaths for carrying kit and weapons. Lightraiders prefer to wear manykit in place of carrying packs. Manykit harnesses come in a number of forms, with broad and narrow bands of pouches and sheaths that may strap to the chest, waist, arms, legs, or any combination thereof. Large lightraiders like Dagram Kaivos may wear manykit with spikes on the shoulders. These look imposing in battle, but they are designed as hooks from which to hang additional satchels filled with supplies for the party.

Queensblood – A Taneletharian term for a member of the matriarchal Arkelian bloodline. House Arkelon never bowed to the dragons and was decimated. A queensblood will often have identifying traits like hair so silver it appears blue and blue freckles that form flourishes on her arms, feet, wrists, or face. The granogs fueled hatred of queensbloods in Tanelethar with the rumor that their ancestors invaded from Arkelia, a separate continent, to become one of the prominent houses of Talania.

Starlot – A jewel formed from crystalized dragon fire. Starlots are the tokens of the Lightraider Order, symbolizing a lightraider's willingness to venture north of the barrier on missions to rescue the Aladoth. Starlots formed when the dragons blasted their fire against freezing winds at the start of the Great Rescue, amid the rising of the Celestial Peaks.

Vanquish – A game of skill and strategy using a table with pockets and leather rails played in many corners of Talania, including at Lightraider Academy.

AUTHOR'S NOTE

PRAISE THE LORD! GOD IS GREAT AND HAS BLESSED me greatly with the opportunity to write this series and continue the game Dick Wulf started so many years ago.

The cast of heroes to thank grows larger with each book. My wife tops the list as always, providing every kind of support on top of reading and editing each chapter in multiple iterations as it comes off the printer. Steve Laube and Harvey Klinger are also up there. Without either of them or their graciousness, we would not have this series in such a beautiful form.

The dedication mentions several people who work behind the scenes on different facets of Lightraiders, from books to tabletop games and beyond. They are all amazing in their professionalism and Christian love. I'll say it again. I am so blessed.

The dedication also mentions the Lightraiders teens. These are teens in Houston and Florida who have dedicated their time to supporting the launch of Lightraiders in several ways, especially in helping us create videos for our social media. They are truly awesome. I'd like to give a special mention to Gavin, Tristan, Aiden, Sophie, and Gabe. These five are the teens I've worked with the most and whose laughter, smiles, and insight have given me and our adult team so much joy. All the Lightraiders teens together are an exceptional group of volunteers with bright futures as leaders in the Kingdom.

This is the last installment in the Lightraider Academy trilogy, but it is not the last adventure in the Lightraiders Realm. This grand quest to change hearts and disciple youth is just getting started. Our swords are drawn and our charge into the mist has begun. Won't you join us?

You can learn more about us at www.lightraiders.com

ABOUT THE AUTHOR

AS A FORMER FIGHTER PILOT, STEALTH PILOT, AND tactical deception officer, James R. Hannibal is no stranger to secrets and adventure. He is the award-winning author of thrillers, mysteries, and fantasies for adults and children, and he is the developer of Lightraider Academy games. As a pastor's kid in Colorado Springs, he guinea-pigged every youth discipleship program of the 1980s, but the one that engaged him and shaped him most as a Christ-follower and Kingdom warrior was *DragonRaid*, by Dick Wulf—the genesis of the Lightraider world.

IF YOU ENJOY

LIGHTRAIDER ACADEMY

YOU MIGHT LIKE THESE OTHER FANTASY SERIES:

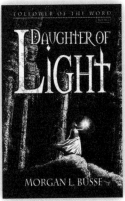